THE SEX LIFE OF A COMEDIAN

A Novel About Show Business

by

Dave Thompson

Dedicated to comedians on the road.

Copyright: Dave Thompson 2011

All rights reserved. No reproduction, copy or transmission of this publication may be made without written permission. Copyright theft is stealing. No paragraph or picture of this publication may be reproduced, copied or transmitted save with written permission from the author or in accordance with the provisions of the Copyright, Design and Patents Act 1988, or under the terms of any license permitting limited copying issued by the Copyright Licensing Agency, 90 Tottenham Court Rd, London, W1P 9HE, England.

Any person who does any unauthorised act in relation to this publication may be liable to criminal prosecution and civil claims for damages. The author has asserted his right to be identified as the author of this work in accordance with the Copyright, Design and Patents Act 1988.

Disclaimer:

This story is a fantasy from and for the imagination. It's not an instruction manual on how to behave. Any resemblance to persons living or dead is coincidental.

First Published July 2011 using Print On Demand from Lulu

ISBN: 978 – 1 - 4476 – 9515 – 8

Acknowledgements:

I've worked with many comedians in lots of countries. I'd like to thank them for the laughter and happy times. Some have given encouragement by paying me to write, perform, or both. I'm particularly grateful to these comedians:

Ben Elton, Harry Hill, Al Murray, Jim Tavare, Boothby Graffoe, Sean Meo, Dominic Frisby, Stewart Lee, Geoff Whiting, Phil Nichol, John Moloney, Charmian Hughes, Bob Slayer and Paul Zenon.

THE SEX LIFE OF A COMEDIAN

A joker in the spotlight, a lover in the shadows

PART ONE

The Nineteen Nineties

Chapter One

I love squeezing Mummy's knife, because after a while it feels like her warmth is flowing from the knife into my hand. It's a German pruning knife, and the blade is folded into the brass-lined groove in the wooden handle.
My left hand cradles it, nestling in the front pocket of my jeans, as I walk to the plane.

My earliest memory is of sitting in Mummy's lap, looking out of an aeroplane window. There were fluffy white clouds, and I felt I was in heaven. My tummy churns with excitement now, because I'm about to fly, and I'm performing tonight. My love of flying and doing stand-up comedy makes me want to skip like a spring lamb, as I emerge from the shadow of the terminal building. The sunlight hits my eyes. It's a short walk to the plane, and I let go of the knife in my pocket to put my sunglasses on. I can see the pilot through the cockpit window, preparing for the flight to Jersey. The sky is bright blue. It's perfect flying weather. Savouring the spring smells of the Sussex countryside mixed with aviation fuel, I climb the steps into the plane.

Wow! The flight attendant is young and blonde and fresh. The red airline dress hugs her lush figure. My friend Neil Gosling would consider her fat, but he hates women. To me she's cuddly and fertile. Our fingertips caress as she checks the stub of my boarding card. I hope I don't look pretentious in my sunglasses. Otherwise, I feel confident about my appearance. Trainers, blue jeans, and a black long sleeved T-shirt. My hair is brown and short. I'm 6'3" tall. That's 1.91 metres. I'm used to writing my measurements down on casting forms when I go to auditions.

"Seat 1D. First row on the left," she beams.
My leather business class window seat looks wide and inviting. I've chosen the starboard side of the plane because it affords the best views during the flight. I remove my notebook, a pen, and a novel from the

flight bag, and deposit them in the pocket in front of the seat. This is my standard procedure when flying.

After stowing my black leather flight bag in the overhead locker, I settle down with 'High Wire'. I'm sure they won't be able to start new airlines soon, because they're running out of names for the in flight magazines. Glimpsing through 'High Wire' to kill time before the tug pushes the plane back, I silently swear. Arnold Shanks smiles from the glossy page. I don't know what it is about flying that makes people's fingers get very greasy, but when I hold an airline magazine I have a nagging urge to wash my hands. The slick, shiny glamour they try to project is undermined by the sordid, greasy edges of the pages. This well-thumbed, travel-worn quality is in perfect accord with the face of Arnold Shanks, who, the magazine informs me, is the "Maverick owner of London's most exciting comedy club". I recognise the "Why not me?" emotion that all comics feel when we see one of our peers in the media. But Arnold isn't a comic. He tried to do stand-up, and died painfully during all four attempts.

After that, he realised promoting comedy is a lot easier than doing it, and got into running gigs. Three years later, he's made enough money to buy the lease on a derelict warehouse, and convert it into a comedy venue. Now he's using it as a hook for his own self-promotion. Remembering to think positively, I tell myself that Arnold getting interviewed in a small airline's magazine is good. The fact that I know him means that I'm closer to the success I crave. Better to know the subject of a magazine article than not. I'll read it later.

Outside my window the baggage handlers are still loading the luggage into the hold. I can hear the thud of the heavier cases as they're thrown in. I flip to the next article. It's about how nice The Isle of Man is. Unsurprisingly, the airline flies there. My eyes open wider as I see Kev Knight, a stand-up on the comedy circuit, wrote the article. That's amazing. Then I remember that Kev was a freelance journalist before moving into stand-up comedy. Even though Arnold Shanks books him to play his club, and the other venues he books for, Kev is still keeping his hand in with the journalism. Hence this article in 'High Wire'. Arnold's venue is handy for Heathrow, which explains why the airline features it in their magazine. I bet Kev introduced the editor to Arnold. The media is a cosy little club. It's getting in that's difficult.

A man outside with a talkback plugged into the plane guides the pilot as the tug pushes us back from the parking place. A Boeing 747 looms over us as it sidles past the terminal building, on its way to another gate. I wonder if anyone famous is on board. The man with headphones disconnects his wire from the side of the plane, and waves the pilot goodbye. The engines get louder, and we move forward towards the runway.

I can't understand why my friends complain about how much flying they do. For me, the novelty has never worn off. I love flying, especially on sunny days like today, with a beautiful girl demonstrating the emergency procedures about three feet away from me. I watch the demonstration for the first time since I last fancied the flight attendant like mad. I remember the flight, even though it was a month ago. KLM to Amsterdam. Her name was Sylvie, and she had a clear complexion but for one pimple on her forehead. I felt for her. Aircrew work long hours. It's a lifestyle that invites pimples on faces that don't deserve it. The in flight magazine has fallen open on my lap. Arnold Shanks smiles up at me. Now *there's* a face that deserves pimples. If that face showed Arnold's inner beauty, it would be an open sore, oozing puss.

We lurch along the runway, and Gatwick airport drops behind as we head west. Shortly afterwards, we turn south, and I recognise the waters of Southampton as my reverie is interrupted by the delicious young flight attendant as she offers me refreshments. I take a small bottle of champagne, and smoked salmon sandwiches. The Isle of Wight is entirely visible as we climb to our cruising altitude of 24,000 feet. It occurs to me that I'm having a champagne breakfast. I look at my watch. It's half past twelve in the afternoon. I was up until three, and didn't feel hungry when I got up this morning. What a fantastic evening I had with Sunita. I love her smooth Asian skin, and brown doe eyes. And that perfect figure – smallish hips, but generous sized tits. She really is the best girlfriend I've had. I adore making love with her, but after coming, I also love falling asleep in her arms. And, more importantly, I love waking up beside her in the morning. This

11

relationship could be the big one. We've been with each other a year, and I've never been unfaithful to her.

"More coffee, Sir?" My God this flight attendant's beautiful.
"Mm yes please." She smiles as she pours coffee into my Business class china cup. There's something about the energy of this girl. She pulsates with vitality.
"How many flights have you done today?"
"This is the fourth. We started in Antwerp this morning. We've done Antwerp to London City. London City to Antwerp. And Antwerp to Gatwick. When we get to Jersey the aircraft will change crew and go to Zurich."
"Wow. It must be very complicated, working out the timetable."
"It's beyond human capability. Only a computer can do it. It's so complex a computer programme had to write the programme that writes the schedules."
"I thought the same planes just shuttled back and forth between their home airports and their destinations."
"They do where they can. But often the plane might fly to several destinations in one day. And spend the night in a European airport."
"So you're staying in Jersey tonight, then?"
"At the Hotel Bristol."
"I am too. I might see you there."
She smiles shyly and moves on to offer coffee to a fat, ugly businessman two rows behind. I'll swear she made her tits wobble slightly before leaving me.

Chapter Two

The top of the Normandy peninsula basks in sunshine as I make out the breakwater outside Cherbourg. One ferry is just leaving, and another is steaming towards the port, probably on its way from Portsmouth. The Captain announces we're starting our descent into Jersey, and I move back to my original seat on the right hand side of the plane. That's the beauty of business class – it's usually not full, so one can switch to whatever side of the plane has the best view. Alderney is already disappearing behind us, as we slowly lose height and pass Sark and Guernsey. Jersey nestles amidst the silvery blue sea, a green paradise for those with money. I love doing gigs in The Channel Islands. It's so much better than going to Manchester or Birmingham. Even better is the fact that I'm doing a corporate gig for a thousand pounds, in the same hotel where they're putting me up. No stress getting from the accommodation to the gig. The only negative thing is that I have to wear a suit on stage, instead of the usual jeans and T-shirt.

My face is glued to the window as I watch Jersey's magical landscape rise to greet the plane. Stone farm buildings, big houses with swimming pools, roadside pubs, and lots of hilly fields. No wonder it's got more millionaires per square mile than anywhere else apart from Guernsey, Beverley Hills, and Stuttgart. And Monte Carlo and Catalina Island off the California coast. And all those other places they tell you have the biggest concentration of millionaires per square mile.

Gradually we get lower, until we touch down at Jersey airport. It's very small, and within a couple of minutes the plane's at a standstill with the door open ready for us to exit. The bubbly blonde flight attendant and I smile flirtatiously at each other as I leave with a copy of 'High Wire', the airline magazine, in my bag. Whenever I get off a plane that hasn't docked with one of those tunnel things that actually cover the door – I think they call them jetways - I have a perverse desire to kiss the tarmac as if I was the Pope. I've never done it, but before I die, I'm going to. Maybe when I've had quite a few drinks on the plane, and I'm with friends.

Some cotton wool white clouds float high above us as I walk towards the little terminal building. The air has the salty tang of sea in it. Our luggage is already being manhandled out of the hold. I hope the people I'm working for have a car waiting to collect me...

Chapter Three

I check my face in the mirrored wall of The Hotel Bristol's lift. Unfortunately that stubble will have to come off before the gig. When I'm doing a comedy club, I go on stage with one or even two day's beard. It suits my weirdo persona. But when the BBK Bank of The Channel Islands pays a thousand pounds, plus hotel and business class flights, Doug Tucker gets his razor out.

As I walk along the yellow carpet of the corridor, I play the usual guessing game with myself. Left or right? Will my en suite bathroom be on the left of the door, or the right of the door? As someone who sleeps half of my nights in hotels, I know what the layout of the room will be. I'll go through the door, and there'll be a bathroom on the left or the right. There will be a space for hanging clothes, possibly with a safe, opposite the bathroom. Beyond will be a double bed on the same side of the room as the bathroom. Opposite the bed will be a colour TV and mini bar. The window will be straight ahead. Depending on the quality of the room, I'll have anything from a small chair and occasional table up to a three-piece suite. I guess the bathroom will be on the left of the door, and stop at room 331.

I like the blue colour scheme. The bathroom's on the right. What's this! The window offers a view of the rear car park, and when I open it I can hear the hum of the air conditioning machinery. When I asked the receptionist for a room with a nice view, I wasn't thinking of an assortment of cars, and a vile 1960s office building. I phone reception, and politely insist that I be given a better room. Before I leave room 331, I relieve it of all coffee and sugar sachets, little plastic milk cartons, and miniature shower/bath gel bottles. You can never have too many of them, and it saves having to ring down and request them later. No matter how expensive the hotel, it'll probably take half an hour for them to send an underpaid, reluctant, no hoper with bad skin up to the room.

Room 462 has the bathroom on the left. It was a good ploy to remind the receptionist that the BBK Bank of The Channel Islands is paying a lot of money for me to stay here, because the sea view is great from the full-length window. And it's even better from the private balcony. I relax in the white plastic chair, and admire a yacht anchored in the bay. Balmy southern air wafts into my face as a seagull cries overhead. I'm about to check the huge TV works, and what satellite channels are available, when the phone rings. It's Melissa, my agent, in London.

"Good news, Doug. You've got a recall next Friday. Apparently it's down to three of you."

This *is* good news! Like every stand-up on the comedy circuit, I'm aware that nobody's going to give me a gold watch when I'm sixty-five. I want to get rich and famous on telly, or (even better) the cinema screen. Performing stand-up in the clubs is good for a while, but it's a plateau. Everyone's trying to be funny on the screen. When you get famous, if you still want to do stand-up, you can do it on your own terms. In theatres, to audiences who've paid a lot of money, because they love your comedy.

The alternative to becoming a star is to tramp round and round the circuit as a hack nobody's heard of. You perform to groups of drunken office and stag parties who are spending a fortune on entrance, food, and drink. Especially drink. Club owners like Arnold Shanks become millionaires in the comfort of a swivel chair; whilst creative people like me stand out there in the firing line. Half the time it isn't even about being funny – it's about controlling the crowd until the show's over and the dancing starts. Live comedy is a tough business, but compared to television comedy it's a womb. Television is all about getting high ratings, so as many people as possible see the adverts. Live comedy is about selling beer. Television comedy is about selling beer and cars. I'd rather be selling beer and cars.

Two weeks ago I auditioned for the part of Cedric in a new sitcom, called 'Bare in Mind'. It's not the main part, but big enough to be in every episode. If I get the part, and the show is a success, it could be the break I've been waiting for. They auditioned a hundred actors and comedians, and Melissa is telling me I've made it to the last three. If I was a TV star, I could charge ten thousand pounds for doing a corporate gig like the one tonight.

"More good news, Doug. Your mate Arnold Shanks phoned. He's programming the comedy at The Ming Club in Birmingham. He gave you four weekends as the headliner. £250 a night, plus hotel. Hanging out with him in the Groucho Club must have paid off."

"Were you really with Arnold Shanks in the Groucho Club?" I ask, impressed that Melissa's getting off her backside and schmoozing on behalf of her acts.
"Not me, Doug. I thought you were."
"I don't know Arnold Shanks that well. And I've never seen him at the Groucho Club. I've only been there four times."
"My sister thought she saw Sunita sitting at Arnold's table there on Saturday, and assumed you were there too. No matter, it must have been someone else. Anyway, wonderful news about the recall, Doug. I'd better go, the other phone's ringing."

I put the phone down and return to my balcony. Melissa's a lovely person, but sometimes it bothers me that the ideal agent isn't necessarily an ideal person. How can she think I was at the Groucho Club on Saturday night, when she knows full well I was working in Newcastle? I laugh at the idea of Sunita socialising with Arnold Shanks. She's an educated sophisticate who wouldn't give the time of day to a philistine like him. If she finds most of my comedian friends too crude, a lot of whom are graduates, she's not going to hang out with an ex-convict like Arnold Shanks.

Gazing at a white sailing yacht slipping her moorings and sliding effortlessly towards the open sea, I drift into a reverie in which I get the part of Cedric in 'Bare in Mind'. How delicious life would be. But now I've got to go down and meet my contact from the bank so he can brief me for tonight's gig. When I leave my balcony and go back into my room, I turn the telly on just to make sure it works. I've been caught out too many times by rooms that seem luxurious, only to get back after the show and find the telly doesn't work properly. Typical! Every channel is fuzzier than if the arial was a safety pin. I ring reception and they tell me a maintenance man will be up soon. I go into the bathroom for a shit and a shave, aware that he'll probably knock on the door when I'm on the toilet.

Luckily, he doesn't. Showered and shaved, I look for my notebook to take down to the Brunel Suite to meet Mr Laroux, my contact from the bank. I can't find it in my flight bag, and I realise I left my notebook, novel, and a pen in the seat pocket on the plane. Damn. I feel naked without my notebook. I can't believe I've been so forgetful. I always keep a notebook, pen, and novel with me when I'm on a plane. Some of my best jokes come to me whilst gazing out of aeroplane windows. Cursing myself, I get some Hotel Bristol stationary from the desk, and go down to be briefed by Mr Laroux.

He's older than I am, and probably earns more than me. Nice guy, though. He offers me a drink, and I take a coffee. The Brunel Suite is the hotel's biggest conference room, and has a high vaulted ceiling. That isn't good for comedy, which needs a low ceiling. The exception is if it's in a theatre, in which case the building will be designed to have good acoustics. Unless it was built for a council in Britain during the nineteen sixties, in which case the whole building will be crap.

Mr Laroux, who is Swiss, explains to me that most of the audience will be employees of the bank. A few will be from Jersey and Guernsey. The rest will be from Stuttgart in Germany, and Zurich in Switzerland. Senior management will be there with their wives, so please keep it clean and tasteful. I know that islanders from Jersey and Guernsey don't get on. If that isn't bad enough, I've got people from the country that occupied them during the Second World War, and who are renowned for their lack of humour. In fact, the only country with a reputation for having less of a sense of humour than the Germans is the Swiss. In addition to that, I've got to work clean.

It gets even worse when Mr Laroux shows me the 'stage'. There isn't one. I've got a corner of the room next to the doors the waiting staff use for entering and leaving the kitchens. I ask about stage lighting. There isn't any of that either. The PA system looks like it was designed for use in a cloakroom.
"Oh, I forgot to mention. There will also be twenty of our Japanese clients from Tokyo. They don't speak English".

Now I'm angry with Melissa for putting me in this situation. It couldn't be better set up for a spectacular death if they'd hired a feng shui expert.

"How long do you want me to do?" I've read the contract and it says half an hour, but I always ask the client how long, in case they say a shorter time. Mr Laroux ponders the question.

"About forty minutes?"

"The contract says thirty minutes."

"Well in that case, thirty minutes. Whatever you feel comfortable with."

No stage, no lighting, and an audience who doesn't speak English. I'd feel comfortable staying in my room watching telly. Assuming they repair it.

"I'll see how it goes. Can I sound check the PA?"

As I suspect, the length of the microphone lead is more appropriate for that of a dog's lead. If I were any taller, I'd have to stoop to hold the mike. And I'll have to hold the mike, because there's no microphone stand.

"Will there be a sound man?"

"A Deejay, yes."

"If you could get me a radio mike, it would help. I think the situation will require me to walk around, work the room."

"I'll see what I can do. By the way, this table is where the bank's President will be sitting. Please don't refer to him or even look at him. His wife died yesterday."

So I'm here to make a man whose wife has just died, laugh. I go back to my room for some serious editing of my comedy material. When I put my dress shirt on, I discover my cufflinks are still at home in my flat in Lambeth Walk, London.

Chapter Four

As I stand near the 'in' and 'out' doors of the kitchen, I hear the anticipatory hubbub of two hundred employees and clients of the BBK Bank of The Channel Islands, in the conference room beyond. The enamelled cuff links I'm wearing glint beneath the fluorescent striplights. They are hideous little effigies of footballs, which a waiter lent me at the behest of the duty manager, who hadn't offered to lend me his own gold ones. I rang reception when I realised I'd forgotten to pack my cufflinks, hoping to borrow a pair. The receptionist had told me the hotel kept several pairs of cufflinks to lend to guests who'd forgotten their own. Unfortunately they lent out more pairs than they got back, and their stock had dwindled to nought. There was a selection of cufflinks for sale in the jewellery display cases in the foyer, but the cheapest pair was £85. I would have been happy to buy them, but I didn't like the look of any of the cufflinks on sale. They were all too modern and chunky. In the end, one of the waiters had substituted bent paper clips for his own cufflinks, which the duty manager had sent up to my room.

I'm cross with myself for forgetting my cufflinks. Like many comics, I'm a bit superstitious. I've got a lucky pair of silver cufflinks that I always wear if I'm doing a gig that requires a suit. I bought them in an antique shop in St Albans, when I got my first proper acting job in a touring company. It was a production of 'Earth Spirit' by Frank Wedekind, set in nineteenth century Germany. I wanted to wear authentic cufflinks that were old enough to have existed at the time my character would have lived. Every stage performance since then that's required me to wear cufflinks, I've worn those antique silver ones.

The clatter of plates and metal food containers surrounds me, and whenever I try to move out of the way of the overworked waiting staff, the leather soles of my shoes stick to the floor. I'm wearing my best dinner jacket with a Harrods dress shirt and silk bow tie. I'm nervous, but not so nervous that I don't notice several of the waitresses are so

gorgeous I'd kill a dragon to taste their delicious bodies. A lot of the Channel Islands' manual work force is from the Atlantic island of Madeira, and their descendents. I fancy four of the waitresses who are so busy clearing the desert course and supplying the audience with their coffee, they're practically running in and out of the kitchen doors. Three are dark complexioned, with shiny black hair. That passionate Portuguese look. The fourth is blonde. She has a pout that makes me want to ravish her. There's something about a waitress uniform that I find incredibly sexy. The white blouse and black skirt. There's one particular waitress who can be no older than eighteen. I want to grab her at the end of her shift, rip her blouse off, and lick the nectar from her armpits. The fresh sweat would rouse me to a rigorous …
"Guten Abend Dammen und Herren. Good evening ladies and gentlemen. Please welcome, top London comic Douglas Tucker".

I can't believe it! The stupid wanker is putting me on stage without checking I'm ready. It's ten minutes before he told me I'm on, and I need a poo. The waiting staff are still clearing the desert plates and serving coffee, and I've wandered twenty feet away from the doors. In a panic I dash towards the conference room, and nearly try to go out through the 'in' door. As I walk the short distance across the polished wooden floor to the stage area, I look down at my watch and start the stopwatch function. The next thing I know, I've stepped on a greasy patch where one of the overworked waiting staff has spilled something very slippery, and I go arse over tit. As my skull hits the floor my overwhelming concern is that my expensive dinner suit might be irrevocably stained. I wasn't impressed with what I saw coming out of those saucepans. And the kitchen smells of something rotten. I've already wondered whether I should breakfast elsewhere in the morning.

My reverie is interrupted by a crushing sensation, followed by a scalding pain, and sounds consistent with those of a metal coffee pot and crockery clattering to a parquet floor. A fusion of beer and tobacco breath penetrates my disorientation, and I look into the retreating face of a waiter as he removes himself from my chest.
The strongest Liverpudlian accent I've ever heard whispers
"Sorry mate. I never had time to stop."

As I get to my hands and knees I realise that the Scouse waiter didn't whisper. He spoke very loudly. It just sounded like a whisper, because the room is full of two hundred people helpless with laughter.
"That's okay man," I say privately to the Scouser. He's got a shaved head and bright blue eyes. He looks more like a prison inmate than a waiter in a five star hotel. He gathers his silver tray and coffee stuff, and retreats into the kitchen from which he so recently emerged.

When I stand up the audience sees the extent to which my attire has been splashed by coffee. The piping hot liquid makes contact with more of my skin, and involuntarily I wince with pain. The laughter doubles in volume. Even the waitresses are pissing themselves. Several tables of Japanese men are having convulsions. One of the Germans has fallen off his chair, and remains on the floor, tears of laughter streaming down his cheeks. I grab the radio mike from the top of the loudspeaker, and look at the room. The hilarity still has the momentum of a large wave before it starts to break. I look down at my previously white dress shirt, and exaggerate the pain with my facial expression.

Surreptitiously I glance at my stopwatch. One and a half minutes. The audience is still in hysterics, and I haven't said a word. I notice the president's table. A silver haired older man is chuckling and smiling at me. My comedic instinct takes over, and as the laughter shows the first sign that it's beginning to subside, I take a few steps and fake another slip. Just enough to lose balance for an instant. They laugh louder. Whilst my back is turned I discreetly twist my bow tie so it's skew whiff. If I'm going to look stupid, I might as well go the whole way.

I tap the mike slightly to check it's switched on. I look towards the kitchen doors with mock anger.
"I said I wanted my coffee white!"
Huge laugh. I look to the audience and smile. Then look down at my black coffee soaked shirt.
"I'm not going to milk it". Another huge laugh. The Japanese, Germans and Swiss haven't even understood the play on the word 'milk', but they're so keen to be involved they pretend they understood.

"It's great to be here in Jersey." I look down at the disaster that was a smart dinner jacket. They laugh again. They don't even know what they're laughing at; they just want to keep laughing.

There's only one terminal at Jersey airport, and it's tiny.
"I flew into Jersey airport this afternoon. I think we came in at terminal one".
Big laugh. That's my first joke, and I've already been on for three minutes. I casually walk towards one of the tables, cheating another slip as I approach. The whole room loves me. I just have to talk to them, and they'll eat out of my hand. I can do no wrong.

Half an hour later, I've taken the piss out of the Japanese clients to the delight of everyone else. I've offended one of the Germans, but I think he's forgiven me. And out of the corner of my eye I've monitored the bank's president, whose wife died yesterday. He's rocked with laughter, and applauded several gags. Maybe he didn't love his wife that much. I thank the audience and exit to the kitchen, with one table giving a standing ovation. Shouts of "More" come through the doors, and that's what I'm going to leave them wanting. I'm quitting that party whilst it's still swinging. I feel stupid in my horrifically stained suit, but for a thousand pounds I don't mind looking stupid. I was lucky to have slipped over on that greasy spot. It broke the ice at what promised to be a very tough gig. There's a distinct aroma of marijuana smoke in the kitchen. Mm, interesting.

The really young Latino waitress smiles shyly from near the cutlery trays. The blonde one walks past me and pouts. Little minx! I'd like to do some very rude things to her. The Liverpudlian waiter I had the collision with comes over and shakes my hand with a firm grip.
"Spot on, mate. I really enjoyed dat."
"Thanks. We had a successful double act, there."
I like his easy Liverpudlian manner, but we're interrupted by Mr Laroux holding a pint of lager.
"Thank you, Doug. Your performance couldn't have been a bigger success. Mr Yelland is delighted with how it went. The clients loved it too. Is Stella Artois all right? Or I can get you something else..."
I accept the pint of Stella from him and take a slurp. It's delicious.
"This is fine. Thank you. Is Mr Yelland the president?"

"Yes. For a while there, he forgot that his wife has just died."
"Thirty-seven minutes, actually." I always time how long I do. I don't mention the forty-three seconds.
"Look, we'd be flattered if you'd join us for a drink. A lot of people would love to meet you. And by the way – a young woman called Alison was asking for you. She says she's got some things of yours. You left them on the plane?"
"Oh yes. That must be the flight attendant."
"She asked me to tell you she's in the Clifton bar. Very good looking, if I may say so."
"Thanks. I'd better go upstairs and get out of this suit. I'll be down later. I have to make a phone call."

One drawback to doing corporate gigs is that they want a piece of you afterwards. It can be fun, but more often it's as boring as talking to a herd of be-suited wage slaves who've sold their souls to the money devil. I'm sure they're all very nice people, but I've got more interesting things to do than answer the same old questions people like that always ask. Like having the shit I was going to have before this plonker put me on stage without any warning. Mr Laroux shakes my hand.
"Thanks once again, Douglas. I'll see you down here later. And by the way: Mr Yelland insists that the bank pays for your suit to be cleaned."
I follow him out of the smelly kitchen, and drink the pint of Stella quickly. I make my way out of the nearest door into the corridor. I have no intention of going back into the Brunel Suite. I've earned my thousand pounds and now my time is mine. I don't want to go into the Clifton bar with my clothes in this state, so I'll go upstairs and change quickly and then pop down to get my notebook, pen, and novel from the flight attendant. I've already made up my mind to talk to her briefly, and then retire to my room. I'm going to phone Sunita, and watch telly before going to sleep. I fancy the flight attendant like mad, but I love Sunita and am faithful to her.

In my room I feel the results of knocking a pint of Stella back quickly. I give myself a large gin and tonic from the mini bar, and immediately the phone rings. It's my darling Sunita. There's a phone in the bathroom as well as the one in the bedroom, and I multitask by having that poo I wanted whilst talking to her. We have a cosy lover's chat for ten minutes. She's got to be up early in the morning, so can't talk for too long. I love her so much.

I remove the suit and have a quick shower to get rid of the stickiness of the coffee. I must have taken a good litre of it, and am amazed I wasn't seriously scalded. Back in jeans and long-sleeved T-shirt, I feel a lot more comfortable. I finish the gin and tonic, remove Mummy's knife from my jeans pocket, and go down to the Clifton Bar. I'm going to have one drink, and then come up to my room and watch TV.

The pretty blond flight attendant is sitting at a table with a man and the other flight attendant, who is also pretty. It's just that the blonde one is so pretty she eclipses the other one. She stands and greets me.
"Hi, I'm Alison. Did you get the message?"
"Yes thanks. My name's Doug."
"We know that. We watched your show. We sneaked in the back. You're brilliant. We were debating if you were supposed to slip over and have that waiter trip over you, or if it really was an accident."
"Thanks. I can assure you it was an accident."
"This is Chris, by the way. He flew us here today. And this is Jackie, who you probably recognise."
I shake hands with them. I'm always happy to meet a pilot. It's one of my ambitions to learn to fly. When I'm rich and famous.
"What flight are you getting back tomorrow?" Asks Chris. He's a typical pilot. I can't say why, but something about his short brown hair and medium build screams out that flying planes is how he makes his living. I can also tell that he's ex military. I guess that he either flew transports for the RAF, or helicopters for the Royal Navy. I've met quite a few of both whilst performing to the troops in The Falklands and Northern Ireland.
"I'm getting the four-thirty afternoon flight to Gatwick. I don't like getting up too early in the morning. I thought I'd do a bit of sight seeing before I go. I love the beaches here."
"I'm out of here on the seven-thirty, I'm afraid." Replies Chris. I notice his glass holds what looks like a soft drink. He must be observing the 'twelve hours from bottle to throttle' rule that pilots are supposed to abide by.
"The girls are off to Manchester on the ten o'clock."

An involuntary jolt in my being takes delight in the fact that Alison doesn't have to go to bed so early, and therefore might be material for rumpty tumpty. I fight down the urge to try to sleep with her. I'm in a monogamous relationship with Sunita.

Whilst Jackie gets a round of drinks, I make polite talk with Alison and Chris. There's definitely a spark between Alison and me. She gives me a lot of eye contact, and my notebook and pen.
"You left these in the seat pocket."
"Thanks. Did you find a book as well?"
"Oh I'm so sorry. I left it in the crew room at the airport. It's 'Nana' by Emile Zola, isn't it?"
"That's right. Have you read it?"
"No, but it looks interesting. I'm afraid I was reading the bit about the author, and forgot to put it with these." She indicates my notebook and pen. I wonder if she's read anything in my notebook. One of the first rules of comedy is that you always carry a notebook. Every vaguely funny idea, you write down. Brilliant jokes emerge from stupid, insignificant little thoughts. The thoughts you think you'll remember, but forget if you don't write down. I'm on notebook number 73. I've been keeping them ever since I was doing A level drama, before I knew I'd be a comedian. In those days I wanted to be a playwright.

Alison seems embarrassed, and I wonder if it's because it looks like she forgot to bring my novel from the airport so we'll have an excuse to meet again. I decide not. She seems too genuine to contrive anything like that.
"I'll leave your book at the ticket desk. You can collect it tomorrow."
I thank her and ask Chris how he started flying, and sure enough, he used to be a helicopter pilot for the Royal Navy. I enjoy a second pint of Stella Artois with Alison, Chris, and Jackie. Some of the BBK Bank staff trickle into the bar. The free booze is over in The Brunel Suite, and they're carrying on the drinking in here. I make my excuses, and bid Alison, Jackie, and Chris good night.

As I walk to the lift, a pang of remorse churns my viscera. I'm trying to be good and monogamous, but a huge part of me wants to know if

Alison would let me go to bed with her. An even bigger part of me is desperate to explore her body with my tongue. Now!

I flop down on the bed and turn the telly on. I don't believe it! The picture is still so fuzzy it's unwatchable. I crossly ring reception and ask why the maintenance man hasn't sorted it out.

"We're sorry, Sir. The maintenance department has been very busy this evening."

"Can they send someone up to make it work now?"

"Sorry, Mr Tucker. They went off duty at ten."

"So I'm stuck with a television that doesn't work?"

"I'll leave a note for the manager. He might be able to get a reduction off your room."

"The BBK Bank is paying for the room. So I can watch a decent telly."

"All I can do, Sir, is apologise on behalf of The Hotel Bristol."

Fantastic! I put the phone down. I've got a TV that doesn't work, and my novel is locked up in Jersey Airport. The only reading material I've got is the in flight magazine. I start to read the article about Arnold Shanks, but can't finish it because it disillusions me. Firstly, because almost everything it says is untrue. Secondly, because I feel jealous that *he's* being interviewed in a magazine and not me. I feel bad about myself for feeling jealous. It shouldn't matter. It's only a stupid little airline magazine. But he isn't a comedian. He's just a bloke who exploits comedians to pay for his drug habit.

I throw the magazine aside and resign myself to going to bed, even though it's only eleven o'clock. I'll get up early tomorrow, and go for a walk along the beach. Then wander around the marina and admire the yachts. I return from the bathroom after cleaning my teeth, and see the novelty football cufflinks on the dressing table. It was nice of the hotel to arrange for me to borrow them. I want to make sure the waiter who was pressured into lending them to me gets them back. They might be important to him. For all I know, they could have been a present from someone he loved, and is now dead. A lot of my colleagues on the comedy circuit wouldn't bother, but to me it's clear that the moral thing to do is to return them to their owner before I go to bed. At the very least, I'll deliver them to the reception desk.

Chapter Five

The staff that was on earlier has retired for the evening, and the girl at the reception desk can hardly speak English. When I say the cufflinks belong to one of the waiters, but I don't know which one, she points towards the kitchens.
"The waiters is in kitchens."
I wander back through The Brunel Suite, hoping not to bump into Mr Laroux or any of the BBK Bank employees. As I assumed would happen, the DJ has given up and gone home. Bank employees want to drink in the hotel bar, not dance in the same function room they had to sit through dull presentations in. It's empty but for one member of the bar staff, who's clearing dirty glasses from tables. He directs me to the kitchen. If the kitchen reeked of dope smoke earlier, it's so thick with it now I need extra muscular effort to walk as far as the cluster of waiters and a waitress, who are sharing a perky looking joint. I didn't bring anything with me, because airports and marijuana don't go together well. I'd kill for a smoke right now. They jump when they see me, as though I'm an authority figure who's just caught them red-handed. Except for the Scouse waiter I had the collision with. He's cool and calm, his bright blue eyes radiating mischievousness. As I approach, he offers me the joint.
"Is there tobacco in it?"
"Some, but not much."
"I'm okay, thanks. I don't smoke tobacco. Smells good, though."
"It's the only skunk weed on the island."
"Have you got any to sell?"
"Not tonight, but you're welcome to a smoke. Have you got a pipe?"
I shrug my shoulders
"I flew in. Not good to have pipes in your luggage."
He nods in assent.
"I've got a pipe at home. The name's Mick, by the way."
The same firm handshake he gave me earlier, before Mr Laroux interrupted us. As he turns to introduce the others, I notice a recent scar going down the back of his shaved head. A shaved head that

hasn't been shaved for a day, the stubble of which lends that 'recently out of prison' look.

I shake hands with the others, and instantly forget their names. When I produce the football cufflinks from my pocket, the other waiter, who's Portuguese, smiles and nods. He shows me his cuffs, which are fastened with bent paperclips. I thank him and give them back.

Mick the Liverpudlian chimes in
"Do you want an E?" As he says this, his hand reaches unthreateningly towards my mouth, a small tablet nestling between his fingertips. The decision is made before I have time to consider it. I say
"Alright" and don't close my mouth. Mick's tobacco-flavoured fingers pop the ecstasy tablet into my mouth, and I swallow it. Almost with the same movement he swoops a glass of lager into my hand, so I can help it down. The other waiting staff all smile their approval.
"I've got a place a little ways away. We've just dropped our E's a few minutes ago. Come back with us for a smoke and dat."
Mick's one of those charismatic people I can't help feeling comfortable with. I don't know him or any of the people I'm going back with, or whether I can get back to the hotel from there. But I'm a bit pissed, and I feel like an adventure.
"Okay."
"We're just waiting for Maria and then we'll be in the motor, like. Talk of the devil…"

The gorgeous young Latino waitress I fancied earlier wanders in. She's still in her uniform, and carries a bag on her shoulder.
"Doug, meet Maria. Maria, this is Doug." We smile and shake hands. We say goodbye to the guy whose cufflinks I borrowed. Apparently he lives in the hotel's staff accommodation. Mick, Maria, the other waitress whose name is Susan, another bloke, and I all make our way out of the back door and emerge in the car park. As we walk past an array of Mercedes, Porsches, and a couple of Rolls Royces, I ask my new friends why they haven't changed out of their waiting uniforms before leaving work. It's because they want to get away quickly, before their boss asks them to help out in the Clifton bar, which is short staffed.

We pile into Mick's old Ford Fiesta, and a few minutes later we're on an unlit country road with lots of hills and bends. Mick's girlfriend is called Susan, and she's in the front. I'm sharing the back seat with Maria and another member of hotel staff who's cadging a lift for some of the way. Mick's cornering is vigorous, and the three of us squeezed in the back, are thrown hard against each other in the darkness. I'm next to Maria, and as soon as our hips touch, I feel heat radiate from her body.

There's no conversation, as Mick's put some very loud dance music on. I've no idea what it is, but I want to buy it. Right now, it's the best music I've ever heard. I realise I'm already going up on the ecstasy, and can't understand why as it was only a few minutes ago that I swallowed it. Of course! I haven't eaten since before the gig. I'm not hungry now, though, as the MDMA swirls around my being. I'm riding the crest of a wave of excitement. A few minutes ago I was about to get undressed and get into bed for a sensible early night. Now I'm in a car full of the hotel's catering staff, tearing along dark country lanes at sixty miles an hour.

We drop the other person off outside a house, and afterwards there's more room on the back seat and Maria and I don't have to sit quite so close to each other. I really miss the sensation of her leg against mine. I grind my teeth as rush upon rush of ecstasy floods into my bloodstream.

Chapter Six

We stop in a lane with no street lighting in a little village I've no idea where, and pile out into a clear, moonlit night. All of us are gazing up at the stars and laughing. Mick's girlfriend – what's her name? Oh yes that's it – Susan, shushes us. It's after eleven at night, and most of the villagers have gone to bed.

Mick has a bit of trouble getting his key in the front door of a large Victorian house. As we troop up the stairs Susan explains that the owner of the house is away. Mick rents a room on the top floor. It's a tiny room with a sloping ceiling and a gable window. All there's room for is the double mattress on the floor, a large old telly, a chest of drawers with a stereo on top, and a wardrobe. There's nowhere to sit, except on the mattress, which has a duvet on it. The only light comes from a lamp next to the telly, fitted with an orange tinted bulb. Susan lights a joss stick and a large candle, which she puts in front of a mirror that leans against the wall next to the mattress.
"We need that mirror," says Mick as he holds his hand out for Susan to give it to him. She slides it out from behind the candle, and Mick puts it flat down on the mattress in the middle of all of us. As she diligently wipes it clean with a sheet of blue paper towel that was obviously liberated from the Hotel Bristol's cleaning stores, I marvel at her face. The pout is so alluring. She's quite friendly, yet has an air of reluctance about her that gives her an unavailable quality. I desire her, yet feel like she's always about to reject me. Her blonde shoulder length hair hangs down as she bends over the mirror, and she absent-mindedly flicks it out of the way. My gaze wanders along her body, until it gets to Mick's hand stroking her rump. My eyes meet his, and they're even more sparkling than before. He smiles at me, and nods towards Susan.
"I've fucked that. She's beautiful, isn't she. Eighteen years old, aren't ya pet?"
"Nineteen in two weeks," replies Susan. She's obviously used to this sort of talk. Having finished wiping the mirror, she screws the blue paper towel up and tosses it towards a small waste paper basket that's

overflowing with other squares of the same crumpled paper towelling. It doesn't take much imagination to guess what the others were used to wipe up.

Maria is putting a tape of 'Generations of Love' in the stereo, Susan hands me a bottle of water. I didn't realise how thirsty I am.

"Knock it back, mate. We've got lots more." Mick urges, as he feels for something underneath a corner of the mattress. A white envelope appears in his hand.

"How much do I owe you for the E?"

"Absolutely nowt for the E. But if you want to buy any Bolivian marching powder…"

He holds the envelope upside down over the mirror, and several little zip lock polythene bags of white powder tumble onto the glass. I score a gram off him. It's the least I can do. He only charges me £60, and it looks a generous deal.

A lot of the comics are doing coke. I do it rarely, and buy it even less. If I'm offered a line at a party, the chances are I'll say yes. Otherwise, my only vice is smoking marijuana without tobacco. I don't even do that regularly. I've tried lots of drugs, and see them as being created for our enjoyment. It's our responsibility to keep them just that – a source of enjoyment. For me that means taking them occasionally, whilst celebrating an achievement. From what I've seen, drugs become a problem when they get too important in your life. Comedy is the most important thing in my life. Drugs will never be more than something to have fun with.

I leave my little bag of coke on the mirror and invite someone to chop some lines out. Mick puts his coke stash away, and has four lines chopped out of my bag so fast I'm slightly shocked.

Mick and Susan are sitting cross-legged at the top end of the mattress, and leaning against the wall. Maria and I, being at the bottom end, don't have a wall to lean against. We're sitting cross-legged, and sweating from the E. We're rocking slightly to the music, and catch each other's eye. As we smile at each other, I remember how much I fancied her earlier when I was standing in the kitchen waiting to go on. If she looked beautiful then, she looks even lovelier now.

"Are you from Jersey?" I enquire.

"Yeah I was born here. But I'm going to college in Southampton next month."
"What are you going to study?"
"Media Studies."
"Nice." I feel that now I've asked a couple of questions, I can ask the one I've been wanting to ask from the beginning.
"How old are you?"
"Same as Sue. Eighteen. Nineteen soon."
I'm completely spellbound by her.

"Coke's up." drawls Mick in that broad Scouse accent. It's so clean I don't feel it go up my nostrils.
"Right", says Mick. "You came back here for a pipe."

We all share a few bowls of skunk from a long kif pipe Mick brought back from Morocco. It's a bit of a waste, really, because the ecstasy is so powerful it eclipses the effect of the dope.
"You've got to hand it to The Hotel Bristol. Their staff certainly give the guests a good time."
"You gave us a good time. You were dead funny, like."
The girls nod in agreement, and I discreetly change the subject by complimenting them on the music. One reason I'm so relaxed with these people, is they don't talk about comedy to me.

I chop out another line, and as Susan stands up to go out of the room, she steadies herself by putting her hand on my shoulder. There's no mistaking the fact that she caresses the skin of my neck. I watch her go out of the door, and catch Mick's eye. He gives me a conspiratorial wink.

After Susan returns from the loo, I go there myself. It's just across the landing, and I stare at my face in the mirror. My hair is stuck to my forehead with perspiration. The bathroom is small, and the blue bath and washbasin are desperate for a clean. In my cocaine and ecstasy inspired state, it's the best bathroom I've ever been in. I'm grinding my teeth, and when I take my cock out to have a piss, it gets hard. I laugh to myself at the ridiculousness of my situation. I really want to piss, but my cock is pointing at the ceiling. I stand further away from the toilet and angle it down. At last it streams out, and some of it hits

33

the rim of the toilet under the seat hinge. Anywhere else I'd be concerned, but Mick doesn't strike me as the house-proud sort.
When I go back in the room, the mirror we've snorted the coke off has been moved on top of the telly, where it sits flat awaiting the next line. Mick and Susan's holiday snaps are being handed round. Maria's moved to where I was sitting, so I sit next to her at the end of the mattress, opposite Susan, and diagonally opposite Mick. Despite the room's only being lit by an orange light bulb and a candle, I join in the photograph appreciation. Soon I'm entranced by Mick and Sue's recent holiday in Egypt. The pyramids and the Valley of the Kings start us all marvelling at the thousands of years they've lasted, and the conversation turns mystical. There are lots of shots of Susan wearing a bikini on a sandy beach, with blue sea and palm trees in the background. That peeved schoolgirl look is present in every close-up of her face.

Mick takes great relish in showing me the pictures of Susan in a skimpy bikini, repeating in his croaky Scouse brogue
"I've fucked her, you know." Susan smiles with resignation. She's so used to Mick's raunchy manner, she isn't embarrassed any more. I keep looking between Susan and Maria. The coke and ecstasy have made me feel so horny, I'm worried I'm going to disgrace myself. Right now, I'd fuck anybody. I'm not gay or bisexual, but my groin is like a coiled spring, and it's got to go off on or in another human being.
"This is the best coke I've ever had." I exclaim, smiling at Mick.
"Let's have some more."
Everybody laughs, and I stand up to get the mirror down from on top of the telly, and feel someone's hands hold my legs in a gesture of support. The mirror looks like it fell off a wardrobe door. It's irregular in shape, and has no frame. I handle it carefully as the broken edge looks sharp.

We do the line, and look at each other's faces in the mirror as it occupies the middle of the mattress. We decide we're all beautiful, and Susan stands up to change the tape in the stereo. As she steps across the mirror, the other three of us get a wonderful view up her little black waitress skirt. Mick whistles, and Susan makes no attempt to avoid it happening again when she returns to her place.

Earlier on I got the story of how he came to have that scar down the back of his head. He'd been in a nightclub a week ago, and had an altercation with a couple of Irish blokes. One of them had glassed him. When he'd told the story, he'd smiled and said
"But you should have seen what I did to them."
He's not the sort of bloke I'd want to get into an argument with, but at the same time he seems to show no territorial claim on his luscious eighteen-year-old girlfriend.
"I know, how about Maria puts the mirror back on the telly? Only she has to stand over it first, like Susan just did."
Maria smiles, and I quickly come in with
"If you do, I'll put another line on the mirror before you do it."
"Done" she replies.
Whilst Mick chops the line, I can see that Maria's enjoying the prospect. When she does it, she doesn't stand over it for long, but I see a white knicker gusset and some very inviting buttocks. She bends down to pick the mirror up, and I see down the top of her white waitress blouse, towards her smallish bosoms. Mmm.

When she's put the mirror on top of the telly and sat back down next to me, Mick's holding a pack of playing cards.
"Right. What do yous want to play, then?"
I hear myself say the words, but can scarcely believe I'm saying them.
"What about Strip Poker?"
There's a pause, and we all laugh. Mick's right in there with me. Thank heaven for Mick.
"I'm for it. What about you girls?"
The girls nod and giggle.
"Let me put my shoes back on, then." Says the gorgeous Maria.
"No shoes on the duvet. Susan doesn't allow it."
"That isn't fair." Says Susan.
"You boys have got socks on, and we're not wearing tights or stockings."
Mick removes his socks. I follow suit.
"Happy now? Right, I deal. To make it more interesting, when you lose a hand you don't take an item of clothing off yourself. The person to your right takes it off for you. So I take it off Maria. Maria takes it

35

off Doug. Doug takes it off Susan, and Susan takes it off me. And before anybody tries it – watches and jewellery don't count."
He says all this whilst he deals three cards each. There's a lot of confusion about which cards are dealt face up, how many we get, and who shows their hand first. I let the others argue the details; I'm just looking at the girls and relishing the prospect of seeing those waitress uniforms come off. And more to the point, undressing Susan.

I lose the first hand. Maria takes my T-shirt off. The reality of what we're getting into impacts on all of us with the sight of my naked torso. Mick loses the next hand, and Susan removes his white waiter's shirt. His body is tanned from that holiday in Egypt, and from his muscles I guess he's no stranger to the gym. I've got what feels like the biggest erection I've had in my life. With the girls both still fully clothed, I start to wonder what's going to happen if I end up being the first to be naked. Maria loses the next hand, and Mick unbuttons her white blouse, and takes it off. I realise what he's up to. He's in a relationship with Susan, and fancies Maria. This is his legitimate way of fulfilling that desire. Susan looks quite relaxed. Maybe this is what people in Jersey do, and I'm just joining the party.

I catch a whiff of Maria's armpits as she sits next to me. The scent turns me on. Susan requests a break to go to the toilet, and whilst she's there Mick fixes her cards so she'll lose the next hand. I know she's Mick's girlfriend and the last thing I want is a drug-ravaged Scouser on my back, and yet he suggested that I take her clothes off. As I slowly unbutton her blouse she subtly presses her bosoms against my fingers. We've all lost one item of clothing. I've got jeans and boxer shorts. Mick's got black trousers and presumably underpants. The girls both have skirts, bras, and knickers on. We know that because we saw them when they stood over the mirror for us.

Maria loses the next hand. She stands up for Mick to undo her skirt, and pull it down over silky legs. As she steps out of it, she puts each of her hands on my and Mick's head to steady herself. She openly runs her fingertips over our scalps, which causes ecstasy-enhanced tingling down my spine. From the way Mick moans in contentment, he's enjoying it too.

Mick passes the cards for Maria to take over the dealing, but she's too out of it to shuffle, and we vote Mick to remain Dealer. He loses the next hand. When Susan takes his trousers off, it's obvious she's used to it. He lies down and lets her pull them off. His bright red briefs can hardly contain his huge erection. We laugh, and Maria gestures towards his crotch with her naked foot. For a moment I think she's going to stroke the bulge with her toes. The tension mounts, especially for me as I'm the next to lose. Maria kneels close to me.

"On your feet."

I stand up and she looks into my eyes as she undoes my belt, the zip of my Levis, and begins a series of little pulls to get them down. My penis springs out through the flies of my boxer shorts. Mick and Susan collapse with laughter, but being the players in this scene, Maria and I keep our posture. When she pulls my jeans off she remains on her knees, her nose close to my cock. Without breaking eye contact with me, she tosses my jeans behind her, and licks her lips. I sit down and put my cock back in my boxer shorts.

My eyes drink in the sight of Susan's shoulders, armpits, and bra. Her tits look bigger than Maria's. More melon-shaped, and I can't wait for her to lose a hand so I can spring them from that bra.

I have to wait, though. Maria loses the next hand, and Mick takes her bra off. We all cheer. Those pert little Portuguese breasts deserve hymns to be written about them.

Mick's next to lose, and as Susan takes his red underpants off, his huge, uncircumcised knob lurches out. It's bigger than mine. He's so aroused he can hardly contain himself. At last Susan loses another hand, and I take her bra off. Her breasts really are magnificent, and my penis pokes out of my boxer shorts again. I'm desperate to suck her nipples and lick her armpits.

Susan loses the next hand as well, and I pull her knickers down. I can smell her partially shaved fanny. Every cell of my being yearns to get my tongue in that crack. I feel Maria tug at my boxer shorts.

"Come on, you might as well get these off. Your donger's sticking out anyway."

"No cheating." complains Mick. He might be a wild one, but he's got respect for the rules. Maria abandons my boxer shorts around my knees.

"We've got to keep playing properly until everyone's nude. If someone who's already nude loses a hand, they get their bottom spanked by the person to their left."

Susan and Mick are naked, Maria and I still have our pants on.
"You've played this game before, Mick."
I say in a mock accusing manner. Susan joins in
"In a cell in Strangeways Prison, I expect."
"Watch it." He replies. Then he loses the hand. I take great delight in watching Maria spank his hairy arse. I lose next, and Maria finally gets my boxers off. Now she's the only one wearing pants. Susan loses next, and I smack her bottom nice and hard.

I lose the following hand, and Maria sneaks in a bit of gentle stroking of my buttocks before smacking me hard. At last she loses a hand, and Mick's got her knickers off in a flash. Susan asks the question we're all thinking.
"What now?"
We all look at Mick for an answer. I might earn more in one night than he earns in a month (not counting his drug dealing profits), but in this context I happily acknowledge him as the leader.
"Doug goes down on Susan for a minute. Susan goes down on Doug for a minute. I go down on Maria for a minute. She goes down on me for a minute. Then we decide again. Doug – your stop watch please."
As I hand him my wristwatch with the stopwatch function, I'm beginning to wonder if Mick is a re-incarnation of Aleister Crowley. Susan smiles at me, but even so that tantalising expression of reluctance is still there. She lays back with her head on the pillow, and opens her legs. I caress her thigh with my tongue as my face moves towards her muff. A thought of Sunita flickers through my mind, but only for an instant. What must be done, must be done. I'm like a dog who loves his master, but out in the forest my wolf soul has taken over. I've gone rogue.

Susan's quim is wet and tastes exquisite. It's got just enough natural saltiness to heighten my arousal, without being too pungent. She moans as my tongue strafes the area around her clitoris. I could do this for hours.
"Time's up. Now I do Maria."

Mick hands Susan the watch. Maria's looking a bit shy, and he throws her backwards and goes to work on her vag. She's quite hairy down there, and I like that. Susan forgets to keep an eye on the stopwatch, and Maria gets a minute and a half of licking before I urge Susan to check the time.

Now it's time for Susan to suck my cock. I'm not circumcised and I'm glad I had a shower after my gig. I'd feel embarrassed if I thought she found under my foreskin unpleasant. I lay back, and she gives me that pout again, as she moves her hair aside and takes me in her mouth. Her tongue swishes around my German helmet a few times, and then she takes me deep into her mouth. Her fingernails caress my balls.
"Time!"
Maria's voice brings me back to reality, and as Susan removes her mouth from my member, she sucks hard, causing an audible slurp.

I take my watch back and time Maria as she licks and sucks Mick's cock. He's very loud in his appreciation. I leave it an extra twenty seconds before calling time. I do love watching a cock being sucked. Is that normal?
"Now free improvisation" announces Susan, and moves towards me. A few minutes later, we're all in the missionary position. I'm on top of Susan, and Mick's on top of Maria. Susan's stroking Maria's breasts, and Maria's caressing my lower back. I look into her eyes, and even though I'm enjoying fucking Susan, it feels like I'm having Maria too, because of the sustained eye contact.

Ordinarily I'd have come by now, due to the excruciating period of anticipation before we got down to the actual bonking. But we're all crazed with ecstasy, and nobody's going to come for a while yet. By unspoken mutual consent, we all change to doggy fashion. Mick and I catch each other's eye again, and he winks at me in an almost matter of fact way. Like he was a bus driver who's just let me off ten pence of the fare.

Susan asks for a piss break, and whilst she's in the loo, Maria sucks my cock whilst Mick fucks her from behind. Then Mick pulls out, and kneels the other side of her, and she alternates between sucking his cock and my cock, wanking whichever one isn't in her mouth. Susan bounds back onto the mattress, and kneels in front of Maria. She also grabs a cock in each hand, so Mick and I have one of each girl's hands holding our cocks. They alternate between each of our cocks. I look down at the top of the girl's heads. At one time Maria has just the tip of my member between her lips, and she's flicking it with her tongue. At the same time, Susan's hand is jerking the shaft. The sensation is exquisite, and they're so good to look at too. I haven't enjoyed myself this much in my whole life.

A few minutes later, Maria sucks Mick's cock so vigorously, her tits are bouncing up and down. I haven't sucked them yet, and move to do so. I lick each one in turn, three fingers of my left hand rhythmically jerking inside Susan's fanny. Then I'm fucking Maria from behind, whilst she goes down on Susan, who's sucking Mick's cock. Mick and I aren't in physical contact, but all four of us are moving to the same rhythm.

The orgy continues and Susan comes loudly. I watch her face as she gasps. Maria comes more quietly. Maria's giving me a hand job, whilst Susan wanks Mick off on Maria's tits, and the sight causes me to accidentally spurt all over Susan's face. I apologise profusely, and Mick hands her some of the blue paper towelling nicked from the Hotel Bristol's cleaning stores. We all collapse in a panting heap. Mick reaches out and produces a litre bottle of sweet cider, and the four of us empty it straight away. Ever the perfect host, he conjures up another one, and we glug it down.

We lay there in contentment. I've got my head on Maria's tummy, one of her lovely little bosoms nestling near my nose. Susan says she's feeling cold, and we all get under the duvet. One by one, each of us gets up for a piss. I'm the last, and when I return, Susan's sitting on top of Mick, who's lying on his back with his hands behind his head. He grins at me, and I get in beside him. Maria gets on top of me, and her wet pussy slips onto my erection. She grinds her hips in a circular movement, and places my hand on one of Susan's boobs. I usually need half an hour after an orgasm before I'm ready to do it again. But I haven't usually taken an ecstasy tablet and several lines of cocaine. I look from Maria's face to Susan's. Daylight is showing through the curtain, and they both look so pretty in the morning light. I look at

Susan's face, framed by her butter-blonde hair and remember how I ejaculated on it. This time, I want to come in someone's mouth. Will it be Susan's or Maria's? I look at each of them in turn. Maria's black hair and brown eyes compliment Susan's fair skin and blue eyes. They're like colours in a rainbow. Each one is more beautiful when seen next to the other one.

I think Susan and Mick are consolidating their relationship, because this time we stick to the same partners. Maria comes whilst she's on top of me, and I go down on her for a few minutes and she comes again. Mick and Susan are still going at it hammer and tongs, and I turn over onto my back, with my head hanging off the bottom of the mattress.

Maria sucks me whilst simultaneously wanking me so fast her bracelets jangle. I close my eyes in a delirium of pleasure. I'm fast approaching orgasm, and so are Susan and Mick by the sound of their yelling. I get there first, bursting into Maria's mouth. She carries on sucking and swallowing, and my fingertips stroke her scalp. Susan screams with the intensity of her orgasm, and suddenly there's an almighty crash next to my throat.
"Don't move!" Shouts Mick. When Susan came, her foot kicked the chest of drawers, which wobbled the television on top. The mirror we've been using to snort coke off has fallen five and a half feet from the top of the telly, and landed edge down on the floor next to my throat. If it had fallen a few more inches to the left, it would have severed my windpipe.

The others draw the curtains and switch the ceiling light on. I keep my eyes closed until they've thoroughly checked my eyelids for shards of glass. I get up, and we all avoid the area where the mirror shattered.
"Seven years bad luck." Says Susan.
"Not necessarily," Mick replies.
"It was good luck we finished Doug's gram off, and no coke was wasted."

We abandon Mick's attic room, and repair to the luxury of the landing below.

"I'm not allowed to use the rest of the house. But the geyser who owns it lives abroad, and these are extenuating circumstances."

Mick leads us into a huge bathroom with a large corner bath. The walls are painted burgundy, and the sash windows have clear glass in them. As water cascades into the bath, I admire the kidney-shaped swimming pool in the garden, beyond which green meadows stretch towards what must be cliffs. The sea is bright blue, and the blue of the sky is even brighter. A plane rumbles over us, and heads out to sea. That'll be me in a few hours time.

Mick's voice breaks into my reverie.

"The rest of the house is well fancy, like. I'd show you round, but if the Guvnor found out, he'd beat the shite out of me."

I look at the Bourgeois style of the spotlessly clean bathroom, and in my minds eye I see a tweed jacketed, middle-aged gentleman owner. The idea of a young ruffian like Mick being afraid of him makes me chuckle.

"I thought you said he's abroad. Anyway, I'd put my money on you if it came to a rumble. I mean, from the décor, I'd say this place belongs to someone much older."

Mick's eyes flash with fear, which for a moment darts into my stomach. It must be the effects of the coke and ecstasy, because the terror during that instant is unbearable, and I'd rather die than face it.

"This is just one of his houses. He's got them all over the shop. When he comes, his ...people jump on ahead, like. To see the place is right."

He's said more about his absentee landlord than he meant to. The cavalier manner has gone, and the greater his anxiety, the more curious I become about the house's owner.

"I suppose he's in banking?"

Mick looks around as if we were in a public street, and he's checking to see that nobody's watching us.

"You're safe, aren't you? I'll show you something, but keep it to yourself, like."

The girls are busy running the bath, and debating whether its gold fittings are solid or plated. Mick leads me along the landing, past a grand pair of panelled doors. He points to a large framed black and white photograph on the wall just past them.

"It depends what you mean by banking. That's him on the right. With one of his friends, like."

The photo was taken on a film set. I don't even look at our mysterious host, because my attention is drawn to his 'friend'. It's ____, Britain's prettiest film actress. She starred in a popular television show, which got her a leading role in a British film. It was a runaway success in America, and she moved to Hollywood, where she's risen to even greater stardom. Now she appears opposite Hollywood's biggest names, and is an 'A list' celebrity herself. She's a brilliant actress, but she could be a superstar model just on her looks.

Two film cameras point towards a drawing room set consisting of an occasional table in front of a chaise langue, and a marble fireplace. Tripods support generic film industry lights, with their barn doors trimmed to illuminate the set. I recognise it as being from one of her less successful films, made before the move to Hollywood. If I remember rightly, it was shot in France. It didn't do that well at the box office, but I saw a matinee when I had an afternoon to kill whilst working in Leicester. I thought it was an excellent film.

What looks like a huge wolf, but must be a male Alsatian dog, is standing on his hind legs, his front paws leaning against ____. His right paw is on her left shoulder, and his left paw is pressing into her right breast. She's being pushed backwards by the weight, and she's in the act of averting her face from the very long tongue that lolls from its jaws. The dog is taller than she is, and wears a collar that's encrusted with what appear to be diamonds. A dog leash hangs loosely between this collar and the right hand of a thin man in his late thirties or early forties. Funnily enough, he's wearing a tweed jacket, but he doesn't look English. There's so little flesh on his head as to show the outline of his skull. ____'s face is creased, either with laughter or fear. The man in the tweed jacket looks calmly at the camera, apparently unaware that his dog is dominating a film star. The dynamic nature of the shot prompts two questions. Firstly, is ____ being knocked backwards onto the chaise langue, or will the man holding the lead pull his dog off her? Secondly, why is he looking into the camera apparently oblivious of what his dog is up to?

"What's his name?" I ask.
"I'd rather not say. Considering what we've done in his house. I've got to be dead discreet, with the coke and that."
"So he's in the film business, then?"
Mick laughs.
"Not hands on. He's in the money side of things. Don't get me wrong, but it's a small world. I mean you work in show business, like. I'd be grateful if you'd keep your mouth shut about tonight. I'm not supposed to have visitors."
I'm about to mention that pub comedians don't tend to hang out with film executives, when Susan's sweet voice floats from the bathroom.
"What sort of bubble bath does everyone want? Camomile and clover, or ylang ylang?"

Chapter Seven

My forehead leaves a greasy mark as I rest it against the plane's window. I'm so tired I've hardly got the strength to support the weight of my head. I watch Jersey drift downwards as we gain height. Stone farm buildings, neat hedges, fields and copses slide beneath. As we near the coast, I look out for the little village where Mick lives. There it is! I recognise the house from the kidney shaped swimming pool. The car parked outside is probably Mick's. Sunlight flares off the house's windows, and it's as if it's winking at me in acknowledgement of what we did within those granite walls. The cliffs pass beneath us, and we're over the sea. Phew, what an adventure that was!

I'm feeling delicate from lack of sleep, but at the same time elated by that raucous night. If you'd told me a day ago that I'd be unfaithful to my girlfriend, I wouldn't have believed you. If you'd told me I'd have unprotected sex with two girls, who were both having unprotected sex with a Liverpudlian drug-dealer *at the same time*... Well, I'd have laughed at the idea.

What am I going to tell Sunita? I can't tell her what I've done. But it would be wrong to have sex with her before I've been checked out for diseases. And it takes over three months to be completely sure you haven't got HIV. I can't believe I did that. But the guilt and the exhaustion can barely match the thrill I feel after that night. I had such a fantastic time!

The plane turns north towards London Gatwick. Alison got re-routed from the Manchester flight to this one. She looks even brighter than she did yesterday as she asks me what I want to drink. I choose champagne. I'm feeling vulnerable, and my knob's sore. I want to cuddle her, and be mothered. She hands me 'Nana' by Emile Zola, with my champagne. It's good to have the novel back. I've really been enjoying it. I'm too knackered to read it now, though.

I watch her as she moves up and down the aisle handing out drinks. She's got a Florence Nightingale quality to her. Her red uniform dress shows her slim waist and ample bosom off really well. If I'd tried last night, would I have got to play with her breasts? They're bigger than Maria's or Susan's. God knows what she must think of the way I look. The last time she saw me I was going up to bed for an early night.

I look out of the window. As we've got nearer to Britain, a sheet of cloud has slipped in between the sea and us. I resort to the in flight magazine. It falls naturally open on the photograph of Arnold Shanks standing in front of his comedy club. A neon sign proclaims its name: 'The Clap Clinic.' Arnold's face is beneath it, making what he imagines is a funny expression, but in truth is a grimace. I look into the eyes of someone who's in comedy for the money, status, and power. I bet *he* doesn't participate in orgies. But then again, he's a notorious skirt chaser. Perhaps he does.

My reverie is interrupted by a woman passing forwards along the aisle. I'm on the right side of the plane, in the third row. The Club Class cabin is nearly full, and the only empty seats are 3C, the one beside me, and 3B, its opposite number across the aisle. The woman's only in my peripheral vision, but it's enough to make me glance up as she passes on her way to the toilet. Her long blonde hair is in ringlets, and I'm fascinated to see if her face is as alluring as the back of her head. I finish my second glass of champagne, which, instead of lifting my spirits, has made me feel melancholy. I start to feel sad about having been unfaithful to Sunita. The sadness turns to fear of herpes or worse, and I realise I'm having one hell of a comedown from last night's drugs. I try to get up to go for a wee, but don't have the strength to stand. After a moment of panic, I realise my seatbelt is still fastened! When I finally make it to my feet, I nearly lose my balance.

Standing outside the toilet door, my fingers absent-mindedly fondling Mummy's knife in my pocket, I notice Alison having a break in the galley. We only have time to exchange smiles before the sound of the toilet lock turns my head towards the door. I want to see the ringlet-haired woman's face when she emerges from the toilet. When she does, I step back in horror. She's looking benignly down at a young boy, who I guess is about four years old. I don't even register the woman's face, I'm so desperate to escape from the child. It's not his fault, it's just that I'm afraid of children. I can't control it, which is why being a stand-up comedian is the perfect job for me – I don't meet anyone below pub age in comedy venues. I suppose I didn't see the kid walk along the aisle because he's too short to have been in my peripheral vision.

I stagger backwards towards Alison in the galley, and the mother and child are met in the aisle by another flight attendant.
Alison has stood up to see if I'm alright, and I assure her I am as I dash into the toilet and quickly lock the door behind me. I break into a cold sweat, and after I've urinated, I lean against the bulkhead and take slow deep breaths to calm myself down. I hadn't noticed that kid or his mother in the Club Class cabin, and guess they were allowed to come forward from economy so they could use the toilet, possibly due to some emergency. Come to think of it, she was walking quite fast when she passed me. I stay in the toilet for as long as I deem appropriate. I don't want Alison and her colleagues to start wondering if I'm alright, but I want to give the intruders plenty of time to return to economy. My face freshly splashed with cold water, I venture back towards my seat, when panic grips me for the second time. The kid is in my window seat, and his mother is sitting next to him!

Alison's colleague, who turns out to be the senior flight attendant, has been anticipating my arrival, and comes towards me with a glossy smile.
"These passengers have been upgraded, Sir. We hope you don't mind moving across the aisle, but as you can see, these are the only free seats in the cabin."

The obvious solution is to let me keep my window seat, put the woman next to me, and her kid in the seat on the other side of the aisle. I'll still be freaked by his presence, but if I look out of the window, I'll survive. I've got nothing against children, I just go wobbly if they come near me.

"Surely they can have the two empty seats, and I can keep my seat by the window." My God I hope they're not going to put the kid next to me!

"Our policy is to keep families together, wherever possible. These are the only seats next to each other." She's lost the smile now, and her voice has taken on a slightly stern timbre. The little boy has stopped looking at me, and returned to gazing out of my window.

"I don't believe this is happening. You're moving a passenger who's paid Club Class fare, and favouring someone who's paid economy fare. You didn't even ask me. You just took my seat whilst I was in the toilet!"

The senior flight attendant winces when I say "toilet", as if I've sworn in front of the child. I'm secretly proud of myself, as my indignation at being deprived of my window seat is making a considerable dent in my out-and-out fear of the child. Normally I'd be begging them to downgrade me to economy, just to get away from him.

The other passengers are watching our drama with interest, whilst the woman with the ringlet-hair is burying her face in my copy of 'High Wire', pretending everything's normal. She's not that pretty. Her features are hard, probably from the stress of looking after a young child. I'm stealing myself for another verbal assault on the senior flight attendant, when my shoulder relaxes to a soft touch from behind. I turn to see Alison standing in the aisle behind me, and smell her delicious perfume at the same moment.
"Excuse me Sir. I could ask the Captain if he'll let you sit on the flight deck. Then you'll be able to see out of both sides of the aircraft." She looks inquisitively at the senior flight attendant's face, which nods approval for her plan.

I've sat with the Captain and pilot on the flight deck many times before. I used to ask to almost every flight I did. But to be honest, the view isn't always that great from the flight deck. You can see straight ahead very well, of course. But sometimes the sideways view from the jockey seat behind the flight crew isn't as good as from the windows in the passenger cabin. However, I don't hesitate to accept Alison's offer, as the chance of meeting a kid in there is nil. I ask the frumpy senior flight attendant to pass me my stuff from the seat pocket, and follow Alison back to the galley, opposite the front toilet. She leaves me perched on a fold down seat whilst she phones through to the Captain to ask if I can join them in the cockpit. All the time, I'm feeling angry because I'm being deprived of my view out of the window.

Alison completes her call, and tells me the Captain and his First Officer are busy at the moment. Please bare with them, and they'll be happy for me to join them in a minute. There's a moment's awkward silence as we look into each others eyes, and I start shivering uncontrollably. Her response is that of a woman to a man, rather than of a flight attendant to a passenger, and she hugs me. I'm still in the fold-down seat, and she's standing in front of me. I press my face into her tummy, her soft breasts resting on top of my head. The warmth from her vagina ripples through my chest, and calmness descends. Instinctively I try to bury my face in her cleavage. She holds me to her tummy, the fingers of one hand caressing my hair. I want to disappear into her body, and stay in that paradise forever.

"I'd be sacked if they caught us like this." She says quietly into my ear, pulling the curtain across to afford us what little bit of privacy the crew are allowed during their off-duty periods. I don't answer, because if I tried to speak I'd burst out crying. They gave my window seat to that little boy!

Chapter Eight

I walk along the Kennington road from Lambeth North tube station to Lambeth Walk. I live in flat 123, Wormwood House, which I bought two years ago. I love living in Lambeth Walk, because Charlie Chaplin grew up around here. I like to think that by living in the street he spent his childhood in, some of his success will pass to me. I walk wearily past The Three Stags, the pub he last saw his father alive in. Having only had three hours sleep is telling on me now. The weight of my suitcase and flight bag drag me down, but nothing like as much as the guilt. Every step I take gets me nearer to the love nest I share with Sunita, and the moment I have to either confess, or deceive. What if I've got HIV, or herpes? If I make love with her, I'll be potentially risking her life. If I start insisting I wear a condom, she'll guess what I've done. Oh my god! How could I have been so stupid? The answer is three pints of Stella Artois, a large gin and tonic, a tab of ecstasy, and several lines of cocaine. I'll tell her I got really drunk last night, and have a wretched hangover. That'll get me off the hook tonight. There's no way I can make love with her tonight – my penis has got friction burns.

Sunita's still at her rehearsal, and as usual the flat's clean and tidy. There's clean bedding on the futon, and the washing machine has finished a load of coloureds. That's what I love about Sunita. She's on top of domestic chores as well as being a relatively successful actress. I do my bit by removing the clean washing from the machine, and hanging it out to dry on the clotheshorse. As I hang the freshly washed duvet cover and pillowcases out, a wave of guilt breaks over me. It wasn't even a week ago that we washed the bedding, and Sunita's so good she's washed it again. She would have been loading it into the washing machine this morning, and I was sharing a bubble bath with three other people. I don't deserve her.

I check my mail. I've got a cheque for £650, for the two nights I did in Newcastle last weekend. And two items of junk mail, trying to get me to borrow money I don't need. I get my dinner jacket out of its suit bag, and hang it up. Mr Yelland the boss of the bank insisted they give me an extra fifty quid to cover the cost of cleaning it. By the time I've put all the coffee, tea, and sugar sachets from my hotel room in our kitchen, I'm feeling too week to stand any longer and I collapse on the futon. I fall asleep, grateful that I don't have to work tonight.

The phone breaks into a dream about the house in Jersey. I'm standing outside the large wooden doors where Mick showed me the photo of its tweed-jacketed owner. The female film star is with me, except she's Alison the flight attendant. She opens one of the doors very slightly, and through the crack I see there's an orgy going on. Except it isn't an orgy, it's an Oscars Ceremony. Either way, I desperately want to get inside the room, and be a part of what's happening. She won't open the door more than a tiny bit, though.

"Hi Doug, it's Gerry here. Just checking you're okay to close the show tonight."
Gerry Crook seems to think I'm on last at his venue in Soho.
"What time do you want me there?"
"Well as you know the show starts at nine. You'll be on at half ten. If you're there for ten fifteen, we'll all be happy." Gerry's soft Cork accent floats down the phone wire.
"Who else is on the bill?"
"Neil Gosling's compering, and Julian Rogers is opening, before going on to close the show at the Clap Clinic. There are a couple of guest spots in the middle. I doubt if you'll know them."
Guest spots are how we all start. You do an unpaid ten minutes. Then another one. Then another one. Eventually, if you're good and you can find a comedy club run by someone who isn't too greedy, you get promoted to being a paid act.

I didn't know I was doing this gig tonight. It's probably Melissa's fault. Like most agents, she takes bookings for her acts, and then forgets to tell them. I feel a bit too fragile to work tonight, but it'll get me out of the flat until at least midnight. Sunita's got to be up in the morning to go to her rehearsal, so there'll be less chance of her wanting to have sex with me. With or without a condom, my penis is going to need at least a day to recover.

Then of course, there's the £80 cash I'll get for the headlining spot at Gerry's little club. I drift back into a delicious sleep, and can't remember my dreams. Something's on my face. Something moist and gentle. I come round to find Sunita kissing my cheeks, eyes, and lips. I look into her perfect face. Her Dad was born in Goa, India. Her Mum came from Bradford, of white Yorkshire stock. The result is Sunita, my Anglo-Indian angel. She's got shiny black straight hair, and a smooth tanned complexion. Her nose is petite, with a slight hint of the equine about the tip. Only six inches shorter than I am, she's got the world at her feet with her fantastic looks and body, and her sharp mind.

She went to Cambridge to study law, and got so involved with the Footlights Club that she now makes a living as an actress. At the moment she's rehearsing for a stage production of Ibsen's 'Hedda Gabler'. She keeps threatening to try doing stand-up when she's got time, and I bet when she does she'll be better at it than me. When she gets time. She's been in enough demand to go from one job straight into the next for as long as I've been going out with her. I respect her, love her, and could never do anything to hurt her. Apart from having group sex with the catering staff of the Hotel Bristol.

She stands up and I marvel at how great she looks in her blue jeans and baggy black cotton jumper. Her hair matches the jumper, and her light brown skin frames a pair of lips adorned with just the right shade of red lipstick. Black boots echo the black hair and jumper.
"How was your rehearsal?"
"Not bad. We're starting Act Three tomorrow. You've got lipstick on your cheek."
I have an instant of panic, before reason tells me the lipstick is from Sunita's lips. It couldn't be anyone else's. The guilty conscience has fired its first shot.
"You don't normally wear lipstick to rehearsals."
"It's for you, treasure. Want a drink of anything?"
"Coffee, please. Gerry rang. Apparently I'm doing his gig tonight."
"Aah. I was hoping you could help me learn my lines. You look very handsome."
"I feel really rough. I got drunk last night."

She changes the subject to a dinner party we've been invited to by a mutual friend. She doesn't suspect a thing.

Chapter Nine

Gerard Street is vibrant as I push my way through the crowds of tourists and other people out to enjoy themselves. The warm early summer evening lends a holiday atmosphere to the tatty Soho streets. People sit at pavement tables outside restaurants and bars, enjoying the weather. My mood couldn't be more at odds with my surroundings. I could count the times I've taken ecstasy on the fingers of one hand. I've certainly never experienced a come down like this one. All I want is to sleep for a very long time. My nerves are shattered, and I feel on the verge of bursting into tears.

As I near the threshold of the pub whose upstairs function room houses Gerry Crook's Thursday night comedy club, I admonish myself for not telling him I can't do the gig tonight. The place is packed, and I squeeze myself up the stairs. I was asleep when he phoned – that's the problem. If I'd been awake, I would have had the presence of mind to say I can't do the gig. I normally love playing this venue. The function room holds about a hundred punters, most of who are still wearing their office clothes. In addition to the stay-in-town-after-work brigade, there's a smattering of comedy fans that couldn't afford or couldn't get into the Comedy Cave, and a handful of foreign tourists.

In the tiny dressing room I shake hands with Gerry. He runs this gig, and a couple of other small one-nighters. As comedy promoters go, he's a good bloke. He offers me a drink, and I ask for a pint of Guinness. As he goes off to get it for me, Neil Gosling the compere returns from the toilet. We shake hands and he tells me the audience are fine. No hecklers. His statement is corroborated by the roars of laughter that pour through the cracks around the dressing room door.

The second of the two guest spots is still on. Then there's a short interval, after which Neil will put me on to do twenty to twenty-five minutes to take the evening up to just before the pub closes. I'm in my regular club outfit. Blue jeans, T-shirt, and trainers. I've got just over thirty hours of beard, because the last time I shaved was in the Hotel Bristol, before my gig.

"You look knackered, mate." Says Neil.

"Yeah, well I had a heavy night last night. Got about three hours sleep." I don't include the two hours sleep I had this afternoon. The truth is the cocaine and ecstasy I had last night has only just left my system, and the comedown is getting worse by the minute. I'm feeling more nervous about this gig than I have done since I first started three years ago.

"D'you er, need a little something to pick you up?"

"No I'm fine thanks. Gerry's getting me a Guinness."

Neil laughs.

"I love your innocence, Doug. I thought you were a man of the world."

I look up from my notebook, with all my jokes notated in it. Neil is holding a small white paper packet between his thumb and forefinger.

"Got it from Arnie's doorman. It'll blow your head off."

I had no idea that Neil was into coke. He and his girlfriend have a young baby. I'd have thought he had better things to spend his money on.

"Yeah, okay. Thanks, Neil."

I take the little paper packet from him, and make to go into the toilet.

"Do it in here, Doug. Gerry won't mind. He's already had a line of this. I'll tell you what - I'll chop three lines out. One each."

I give him his little packet back. I don't think I'm co-ordinated enough to chop a line out for myself. I'm doubting that I'm fit enough to do this gig.

Gerry comes in with my pint of Guinness, and I take a slurp. That feels better. Neil rolls a twenty-pound note up and hands it to me. He's chopped the coke out on the glass of an old framed print of Lambeth Bridge that was hanging on the wall. The coke is so clean it goes up my nostrils like fresh mountain air. I hand the note to Gerry, and continue to try to focus on my material. I'm going to be on in about twenty minutes. Gerry and Neil are talking about how good the guest spots are, as they casually snort up their lines without even talking about the coke. I'm surprised to see Gerry doing it. I thought he was a clean-living Cork lad.

The first think I notice is that whereas a few minutes ago I was sitting down and found it an effort to stand up, now I can't sit down. I'm pacing every bit of floor the tiny dressing room can offer. The colours of the jaded old walls that haven't been decorated for years seem strangely vivid. A huge burst of applause in the room beyond the door indicates the second guest spot has finished his act, and Neil flings it open to get to the stage in time to take the act off and introduce the interval. I realise I've consumed most of my pint of Guinness. By god it tastes good. Gerry smiles and nods towards my glass.
"Want another one?"
"Yes please. But could you make it a pint of Stella Artois?"
"Of course." Gerry takes my glass out towards the bar. A loud hubbub gets louder as he opens the door. The audience is taking advantage of the interval to use the toilets and get more drinks. I'm about to close the door, when a girl comes through it. I close the door behind her. She's quite tall and thin, and has short brown hair. She doesn't look obviously beautiful, but she's pretty in a boyish sort of way. Her face is flushed, perspiration has caused her hair to stick to the skin of her forehead and neck, and she's vaguely out of breath. All the signs of a comic whose just come off stage.
"They loved you. My name's Doug, by the way." I proffer my hand.
"Charlotte French." She shakes my hand.
"I saw you at The Clap Clinic the other Saturday. I liked your stuff."
"I'm sorry, I didn't see you."
"I was in the audience. I haven't asked to do a guest spot at The Clap Clinic yet. I want to make sure I'm ready before Arnold sees me."

She flops into the only comfy chair in the dressing room. I like her. She's wearing jeans and a cotton sweatshirt. Very small tits. What people would describe as plain, except she oozes sex. Gerry and Neil come back in the dressing room and congratulate Charlotte on her ten minute guest spot. Gerry hands her a pint of Guinness, and me a pint of Stella.
"Okay, I'm ready to take you up on your offer now." Laughs Charlotte. Gerry removes a little zip lock polythene bag from his pocket, and starts chopping lines of coke out on the print of Lambeth Bridge. He looks up to me inquisitively.
"Doug?"

"Yes please." I answer. I'm feeling great after that first line. I'm looking forward to getting on stage. If Gerry's got the same stuff as Neil, I'm going to be entertaining the crowd by flying round the room. We all have a line, and once again, it's like breathing in pure Alpine air. By the time Neil's going on to start the final section of the show, I'm in the middle of relating a hilarious anecdote I heard about Arnold Shanks to Charlotte. We postpone it to after the gig, and all go into the function room to watch Neil.

Whilst I'm standing next to Charlotte leaning against a wall at the side of the room, I finish my pint of Stella. I offer Charlotte another drink, and she asks for another pint. Gerry notices me, and ensures I get fast track service. There's nothing worse than spending the last few minutes before going on stage trying to attract the attention of the bar staff to get a drink. I buy a pint for Gerry as well, and one for Neil ready for when he comes off stage. Not that he looks like he's ever going to come off stage. He's well into his routine about the nuns in Cork's Shandon Convent, and I'm looking at my watch and wondering if there's going to be twenty minutes left for me to do my act. It's a classic symptom of a comedian who's taken coke. He can't stop talking, and does fifteen minutes when he thinks he's done five.

I genuinely like Neil, but at the moment my thoughts for him are "Get off the fucking stage you boring bastard!"
At last he puts me on. I bound onto the stage, put my pint down on a table at the front, and take the mike off the stand. My first five lines all get huge laughs. This audience is united in its will to find every comedian hilarious. Once I've established that I've got funny jokes, I take a swig of my Stella and start to chat to the couple whose table I put my glass on. I haven't seen the rest of the show, but there's a good chance that one of the previous acts and or the compere has incorporated them, as they're right at the front and visible to most of the audience.

I quickly establish that they *have* been addressed already, and that the rest of the audience knows the bloke works for Christian Aid, and the girl works for a famous roll-on deodorant manufacturer. Straight away the picture appears in my mind. Jesus on the cross, with his armpits exposed. The thieves on the crosses either side of him complaining

about his B.O. His mother in the crowd below, deeply embarrassed. I share the vision with the audience, and they laugh deep laughter from the depths of their stomachs. I become Mary, desperate with shame:- "Oh my son, this could have been such a proud moment. But no! You embarrass me by smelling of B.O. How are your father and I ever going to live this down?" Spurred on by the audience's appreciation, especially the couple at the front, fresh pictures appear in my mind. I go off into Jesus' agent arguing with the two thieves' agents about who should headline. I become Jesus' agent
"I don't care vhat your boys stole, my Jesus is going to be huge. He should definitely be top of the hill." A round of applause and my intuition says I should move on, as I'll never top that bit of improvising. I repeat the advert slogan for the deodorant company the woman works for, and ask where they went on their last holiday. Cyprus. It just so happens that I've been to the same resort they stayed at, and so I continue ad libbing with them. They're good sports and up for a laugh, and a sequence of inspired, spontaneous humour follows. They give me good offers, and don't try to out-smart me, and the muse puts very witty lines in my mouth every time I open it. The rest of the room is totally entranced by what is obviously improvised comedy.

A bloke near the back pipes up with "I served with the RAF in Cyprus."
"Akrotiri?" I reply.
"Yes."
I've done Combined Service Entertainment shows for the RAF personnel at Akrotiri. I talk to the bloke, and get laughs by trying to trick him into giving away some classified information. I'm fired up by the effortless way I'm getting huge laughs from just working the room, and start to think what set routine I'm going to finish on. I glance at my stopwatch and see that I've done twenty-seven minutes. I'm only supposed to do twenty-five max, and I thought I've been on stage for fifteen. I carry on my extempore exchange with a group of Norwegian tourists until I get the next big laugh, and say "That's all we've got time for. My name's Doug Tucker, thank you and good night."
As I go off the audience erupts into applause, and Neil puts me on for an encore. It went so well with the couple in the front, or John and Margaret as I've found out they're called, I carry on having fun with them. Three minutes later, I wrap it up and exit to the dressing room

with shouts of "More" following me through the door. I was on stage for a total of thirty-one minutes and only did six or seven of my tried and tested one-liners. What an enjoyable gig!

The bar's closed, but Gerry's organised another drink each, and the glasses sit in a cluster on the very small table in the corner. Whilst I was on stage I finished my third pint, and drank a member of the audience's pint of lager for him, much to the glee of the audience. So I've had nearly four pints, and very quickly swallow a good proportion of my fifth pint in the dressing room. I've got a thirst on, and beer seems perfect for it. There's a knock on the dressing room door, and a head of shaggy blonde hair pops round it.
"Hi, I'm Nicky Butler, from Johnson Television. I absolutely *loved* your act."
"Come in. I didn't really do my act tonight."
Johnson Television is the independent production company that's making 'Bare in Mind', the sitcom I'm hoping to be in. Nicky Butler comes in the dressing room. Unusually for a television person, she has an apologetic air about her. She must be in her mid-thirties, and her hair is dyed blonde, with dark roots showing through. She's got it in the ruffled, flyaway style, with a wide black headband keeping it high above her puppy dog face. She's got jeans and a brown suede car coat on, despite the heat. I invite her to sit down in the one comfy chair.
"We're looking forward to seeing you at the recall. Everyone's very excited in the office, we've got studio dates for the recordings organised, and the theme tune's been written."
"I'm excited too. I don't think I met you when I came to the original audition."
"I might have been scouting for locations. I'll be producing, by the way."

It's certainly a stroke of luck that the producer herself has seen me doing a fantastic gig. I offer her a drink, hoping that my position as the final act will exempt me from the fact that the bar closed ten minutes ago.
"No thanks, I'm about to dash off. I just wanted to say hello, and congratulate you on your performance."
She gets up and goes to the door. Her manner is so awfully nice, it's hard to know how to respond. I've never seen a television producer

with such low status body language. They're usually so full of themselves they strut around like they were an officer in the Gestapo. She bumps into Neil, Gerry, and Charlotte as she goes out. Neil's coke comes out again, and I accept the offer of a third line, with the promise that I'll buy some and make it up to him.

It's eleven-thirty five when we leave the pub, and we're all bursting with energy and enthusiasm. I can hardly imagine I felt low when I arrived an hour and a half ago. I'm high on a fantastic gig, three lines of killer coke, and five pints of beer. The coke is so strong I can hardly notice the effects of the alcohol, apart from soothing warmth in my tummy, and a loosening of inhibitions.

Chapter Ten

Gerry, Neil, Charlotte and I are practically skipping along Gerard Street, and I sniff the warm evening air. I can't really smell it, as my nose is full of coke. I swallow the mucous from my nose, and a cool sensation grips my throat as more coke makes its way from my nasal cavity towards my stomach.

I remember I'm supposed to be going home to see Sunita. I put my hand in my trouser pocket and touch my knob. It isn't feeling so sore as it did earlier. I want to see Sunita, but I know she'll be about to go to sleep because she's got to be at her rehearsal in the morning. The last thing I want to do right now is go to sleep. I want action!

I stop in a phone box to ring her, and she's already in bed. She's tells me I should stay out and enjoy myself if I like, she's just come on so it wouldn't be ideal for sex. I tell her I love her and won't be out too late, and hang up. The phone box is lined with prostitute's advertising cards. Two catch my eye in particular. One with a picture of an "Eighteen year old Japanese student", and the other of a "Swedish teenage tart."
"Come on, Tucker. You're not going to a whore now."
The others are outside waiting for me. As we walk along the street we agree we want another drink.
"Maybe Doug could get a drink at one of his whores." Charlotte jests.
"I've never been to a prostitute, and never will." I'm lying. I did see one once, but never intend to again.

We start thinking of possible places for a drink, now that it's a quarter to twelve and the pubs have closed. We're in London, so there are very few places unless we start paying extortionate entrance prices. Neil suggests Arnold Shanks' club.
"The Clap Clinic? It's a bit far away, isn't it?"
The Clap Clinic is by the river in Hammersmith.

"Not when you've got a car parked just round the corner." Announces Gerry.
We pile into Gerry's Peugeot 205. Neil sits in the front, and I share the back seat with Charlotte. As soon as we're in motion, Gerry lights up a pure grass joint. He's a bit of a lad is our Gerry. I thought he was a well-organised, straight-laced comedy promoter. And here he is, driving through the West End, obviously over the drink-drive limit, smoking a neat skunk joint at the wheel. I voice my observation, and Gerry laughs, adding
"With a bag of cocaine in my pocket."

By the time we're on the Westway I've had a few hits of the joint, and my perspective on everything is even brighter than it was. The red and white lights of the other cars, the office blocks either side of the elevated section of motorway. The illuminated dashboard of Gerry's car, they're all stronger than they were. London looks magnificent as we speed past Ladbroke Grove, our conversation crackling with witticisms and references to things that only we comedians can understand. Gerry isn't a comic, strictly speaking. But he's one of the better promoters in that he's compered his own gigs and treats comedians really well. We consider him one of us.

As it's a Thursday night we park quite easily near The Clap Clinic. We clamber out of the car, which is parked next to a red Mercedes SL. Gerry points it out, and informs us it belongs to Arnold Shanks.
"I'd love one of those two seat sports cars." Says Neil.
"But the drawback is, there's no room for your friends."
"I don't think Arnold has that problem." Charlotte observes.
"You know him?" I ask.
"No, and from what I've heard about him, I don't think I want to."
"That's why he hasn't got any friends."
"He can put a lot of work your way, though." Gerry points out.
"That's why he's got a lot of acquaintances."

It's colder near the river than it was in Soho, and we're glad Charles the head bouncer is on the door. He smiles and welcomes us in. Charles was born and grew up in the North Peckham Estate. It's the largest public housing development in Europe, and notorious for drug-related violent crime. Charles has the distinction of coming from a poor black fatherless family, yet having the bearing of a king. He's just naturally a classy guy. He even speaks in a distinguished accent. Someone asked him how he could grow up in a ghetto and speak with an educated voice, and he replied that it was from watching Trevor McDonald read the news whilst he was in prison. Apparently that's the only TV prisoners are allowed to watch.

Charles is six foot four, and has his hair short. His mother came from Jamaica, and he points out that Jamaicans are warlike because they are descended from the Ebo tribe. According to Charles, before the English arrived in West Africa, the Ebo tribe ran all the security. He also points out that another reason Jamaicans are good fighters is because during the slave-trading days the troublesome slaves were transported to Jamaica, as that's where the biggest British garrison was. Charles is proud that Jamaicans are descendents of the most rebellious slaves.

No one doubts that one day Charles will be rich, but in the mean time he runs the security in Arnold's club with perfect aplomb. He also supplies comedians with the best quality marijuana, ecstasy, and cocaine, at prices only comedians can afford. Even the comics who've made it on telly and don't play the circuit anymore, pop in to Arnold's club for a social drink as a pretext to score off Charles. Arnold doesn't object, because he's Charles's biggest customer. Either that, or his supplier. Different people say different things.

The show finished an hour ago, and The Clap Clinic's had its chairs and tables cleared to make room for dancing. The bar's open until 2.00am, and a few clubbers are still arriving. We go past the half full dance floor, upstairs to the VIP bar, where comedians and their friends hang out. Beyond the VIP bar is a large dressing room complete with pool table. It's here that Arnold holds court, and comics drink and smoke dope. The party Arnold held to open the new premises of The Clap Clinic is still talked about. I wasn't there, but the story is that at the end of the evening, Arnold fucked a well-known television actress on the pool table

We get drinks from the VIP bar, and go into the dressing room, which for a Thursday night is rather empty. A couple of tonight's acts are playing pool, including Julian Rogers who was on at Gerry's club earlier. I've got £420 cash in my wallet, £100 of which Gerry paid me for tonight's gig. The guarantee was £80, but he slapped another £20 on, as it was so full. That's what makes Gerry such a popular promoter.

Neil chats to the guys playing pool, and Gerry, Charlotte, and I sit in some comfy chairs around a coffee table. The dressing room's painted in dark burgundy – pretty much the same burgundy that the big bathroom in the house in Jersey was painted. It's been really tastefully done out with a huge gilt-framed mirror on the wall near the pool table, which is full size. There are clusters of armchairs and sofas around coffee tables, and a large TV on an old sideboard, which shows a picture of what's happening on stage. Right now, the picture shows flashing lights and drunken male office workers cavorting with drunken females. For every woman, there are at least two men.

Arnold Shanks says he wants the Clap Clinic's VIP bar to be the main place where comics and celebrities hang out. Since the club opened in these new premises, it seems to be working. A lot of television people live in west London, and The Clap Clinic is convenient for them to drop by for a late drink without being bothered by members of the public. Gerry rolls another neat skunk joint, and shares it with Charlotte and me. I suggest that as I've been snorting his and Neil's coke, I should approach Charles and get some of my own to share with them. He doesn't object.

Ten minutes later, I'm chopping a line out for everyone, on the side of the pool table. Gerry joins Neil, Julian, and the other comic for a game of doubles, and I show Charlotte the balcony. She's never been up in the VIP bar or the dressing room before, and is clearly excited. The club's only been in these new premises a couple of months, and as the summer hasn't got under way yet, the balcony has yet to come into its own. French windows open onto a wooden decked balcony overlooking the River Thames. It's a dry evening, and as we stand next to each other, leaning against the railings, we look down on the roof terrace below. It's empty, but its potential to attract punters during good weather is obvious.

Arnie plans to run the club as a bar and restaurant during the daytime, and that roof terrace will be a fantastic place to eat lunch. A few swans glide over the ink black river, and another bird calls from amongst the trees overhanging the opposite bank. Charlotte and I laugh because neither of us has a clue what sort of bird it was.

"It might have been a river vole." She suggests. I catch her profile as she leans mischievously over the balustrade. She tosses her head back to swig from the bottle of Budweiser she's holding, and sniffs. The moment is perfect. I'm not trying to get off with her or anything. I'm just enjoying her company and behaving in a carefree way with her. It wouldn't be anything like this if she was a bloke. The chemistry between us is a male-female one, but it's safe. I'm so glad the other men are all playing pool together, and I've got the only woman around all to myself. I've always been more at home with feminine company.

When I scored the coke off Charles, I got some weed as well. It's a still night, so I roll a doob, and the two of us smoke it together whilst grooving on the serenity of the night time river. The unknown bird cries its cry across the water, and I repeat Charlotte's earlier suggestion. "A river vole!" We look at each other and collapse laughing. It carries on, one of those ridiculously stoned episodes when something becomes the most hilarious thing that ever happened. We laugh and laugh, our eyes fixed on each other's, as we share the wonderful stupidity of her comment.

A harsh male cheering erupts in the dressing room, and we both look towards the door because it's too much for the four guys to have made. We can't see properly, and we're both suddenly feeling cold, so we go back inside and close the door. Arnold Shanks is with an enormous bloke I've never met, and another one whose average size, also who I haven't seen before. They've just arrived, and are wearing sheepskin car coats.

"Dougie boy!" Arnold's pissed. He shakes my hand too firmly, and when I introduce him to Charlotte and say that she's a new comic, his lewdness makes us feel awkward.

"This is Tam, and this is Greg." He drawls in his thick Glaswegian accent. Arnold was born in the arse end of Edinburgh, but grew up in Glasgow, hence the accent. I shake hands with the other two Scotsmen, also pissed.

It transpires that Tam and Greg have been showing Arnold a motor yacht, moored upriver in Richmond. They've just given him the sheepskin coat, as Greg, the smaller of the two, has recently acquired fifty of them. Arnold's thinking of buying the motor yacht, because the Clap Clinic comes complete with mooring rights along its hundred feet of river frontage.
"It would be great for fucking birds on." Arnie explains.
"The desk in your office seems to be performing that function pretty well." Neil adds.
"Who told you about that?" Arnold asks proudly.
"Well it certainly wasn't Sheila Jones." Laughs Julian.
Arnold rocks backwards slightly on his feet. He's in that lascivious state of drunkenness, and Charlotte's the only woman within range.
"I'll tell you what, pet. Come and see ma office."
"If the others come too." Charlotte sensibly replies. Meanwhile Greg has put some lines out on the top of the telly, and we hoover them up before Tam, Greg, Charlotte, and I follow Arnold up the stairs to his office.

Arnold's office displays lots of wealth and no taste. Information about his past is patchy, but it involves the council estates of Greenock, and Barlinnie prison. When he moved into these premises, the comedians pitched in and bought him a present for his desk. It's a specially made sign of the type that bank managers have. Instead of saying "A. Shanks, General Manager", it says "A. Shanks, Gangland Boss." There's also one of those desk lamps with the green swivel shade that Don Corleone has in 'The Godfather'. Arnold's desk is huge and antique, and there's a framed photo of him shaking hands with a famous heavyweight-boxing champion. He goes to an antique globe drinks cabinet which clashes terribly with a hideous giant abstract oil painting behind it. He opens the cabinet to reveal several hundred pounds worth of vintage Scotch malt whiskies. He pours huge measures of obscure single malt for all of us. Charlotte doesn't drink whisky, and refuses. He insists to the point that it gets uncomfortable, and Charlotte accepts it to avoid more awkwardness.

The body language and conversation has by now made it quite clear that Greg, or Gregor as Tam addresses him, is the higher status of the two strangers. It looks very much like Tam is Gregor's minder, albeit one who's allowed to get almost as pissed as the bloke he's minding. Greg starts putting his arm round Charlotte in feigned affection. She doesn't like it, and we can all see where he's trying to take things. Maybe it's because he owns the building we're in, but Arnold definitely sees her as being under his protection.

He tells Greg to leave her alone, and Greg doesn't take too kindly to this.
"Do nae tell me who to touch and who nae to touch." He states so emphatically that the jovial atmosphere instantly evaporates.
"The lass does nae want your paws all over her." Arnold reasons. I notice Tam discreetly put his glass down on a shelf. Greg hasn't let go of Charlotte, and proceeds to grip her tightly in his arm whilst groping her tits with the hand that's holding his glass of single malt. As it sweeps over her chest it spills on her jumper.
"That's fer me to decide. I'll touch her wee titties if I fuckin' feel like it. Not that she's fuckin' got any!"
He hurls the cut glass tumbler at Arnold's head as Charlotte screams. Arnold dodges the full force of the glass, which smashes against the wall, and he's over the desk with a speed I didn't know he was capable of. Greg's still holding Charlotte, and Tam has moved in to sort Arnold out. A glint of steel betrays the presence of a knuckleduster, complete with spike, on his hand.

Tam's taller than I am, and a lot broader. He strikes Arnold with the spike, and there's a horrible cracking sound. A moment later Tam's screaming in agony. The scream is quickly stifled by Arnold's open hand whacking the huge man's chin, so his jaw snaps shut. I don't believe it! Before the spiked knuckleduster could make contact with his face, Arnold stepped out of the way, and broke the arm that was propelling it. Tam's on the floor with blood pouring out of his mouth, and Arnold's open hand now has Greg's throat. As Arnold walks forward with his arm straight, Greg let's go of Charlotte and both his hands try to break Arnold's grip on his throat. They're still trying until the instant before the back of Greg's head smacks into the wall, and he slides down it, unconscious.

67

This all happens in less than a minute. Arnold retrieves the knuckleduster from where Tam dropped it. Tam's arm is bent in the wrong direction.
"Are you alright, Pet?" Arnold asks Charlotte. She's too stunned to answer.
"Don't worry about these pieces of filth. They're just small timers I knew back in Barlinnie."
He bends over Tam and tries to turn him over in case he chokes on his own blood.
"Give us a hand, Doug. He's a big man for one to roll over."
I help him roll the huge human form over.
"Are you sure he's not dead?"
"He's nae dead, but he's just as fucking useless. I'll tell ye something ye didn't ken."
I've heard that Arnold's Glaswegian accent gets much stronger when he's drunk. It serves as a useful warning sign to his staff.
"Someone in this room's a karate black belt. Have a guess who, lassie."
Charlotte's voice is so shaky she can hardly answer.
"You?"
"Nae, not me." He kicks Tam in the side. Luckily his sheepskin car coat absorbs some of the blow.
"It's him. He's got a black belt in karate. But do ye ken why I beat 'im?"
This time it's my face that his wild eyes are piercing.
"No." is all the answer I can muster. Arnold sticks his face close to mine. His breath smells of whisky and cigar smoke.
"Because he's a nasty piece of work. But I'm nastier." He looks at Tam, and then at Greg.
"When it comes to a fight, the one who's most evil wins. And I'm more evil than these two together. Black belt or nae black belt."
He turns to Charlotte.
"So you're a budding funny girl, then Charlotte?"
Charlotte nods.
"I'll tell you what, then Charlotte. I'm going to pay you to say funny things on my stage. And whether you're on my stage, or off my stage, you'll say nothing about this. Is that understood?"
She nods again.

"By my reckoning, this big fellah's going to wake up first. You see, I hit him on the chin. There's a nerve right here. But you come round in a few minutes. That one over there got a bang to the heed. He'll be out for longer. The trouble is, I don't have much time to spare."
He looks at me as he removes his sheepskin coat.
"I was in Belfast for a while. There's a little trick I learned from the Boys. Charlotte, pet, would you be an angel and pop the kettle on?"
There's an electric kettle with some tea and coffee making equipment near the booze cabinet. Charlotte checks the water level in the kettle, and switches it on. Arnold opens a drawer in his leather-topped desk, and removes a gift box. It looks like there's a child's toy in there. It's cardboard, with a cellophane front. I think it's some sort of doll.

The kettle comes to life, and rumbles towards the boil. I'm wrong about what's in the packaging. Arnold removes a stainless steel, leather bound hip flask, complete with small stainless steel filling funnel. He tosses the hip flask on the desk, and holds the small funnel between finger and thumb.
"A corporate present from the brewery. A lot of folk think the best way to wake an unconscious person up, is to use cold water. They're wrong. Hot water is more effective. Douglas, I require our friend's trousers and pants around his knees."
"No!" Charlottes worked out what he's going to do.
"I'm afraid Yes!"
I've seen what happens if you ruffle Arnold's feathers, and disobey his command. There's a dark stain in the sleeve of Tam's sheepskin coat, and I realise its blood from his broken arm. The snapped bones have pierced his skin.
"Just out of interest, what colour belt was holding up our friend's troosers?"
There's not a lot of light to see in, but it looks black. I answer accordingly.
"Personally I don't think he should wear a black belt. It doesn't match the light brown of that sheepskin."
The kettle boils. When I get his trousers and pants down, I'm dreading being handed the funnel. Thankfully Arnold takes over. Charlotte starts to cry and moves towards the door. She's trembling, and Arnold doesn't object.

"Close the door on your way out, Pet. And if the others are still in the dressing room, tell them its closing time. Oh, and by the way – I apologise for my colleague's offensive behaviour. Perhaps some other time, we could go to the cinema together…"

Charlotte runs out of the room, failing to slam the thick, leather-padded door behind her. We hear her fall down the stairs, cry out, get up, and continue down them.
"The kettle, please, Doug."
Arnold's crazy eyes remind me of the famous picture of Jack Nicholson in 'The Shining'. My hand shakes as I hand him the kettle. I'm convinced he enjoyed inserting the funnel in Tam's anus. He holds the kettle at arms length, and moves it into position with a flourish. At the same time, he moves his feet and legs away from Tam's recumbent form."
"It's like lighting a firework. Best to stand well back."
He looks as if he's about to water a delicate sapling. He pours half a cupful of freshly boiled water into the funnel, and immediately holds the kettle away from himself and Tam. There's a horrific scream, and Tam tries to push himself off the floor. As he does so, he starts to use his broken arm. Another scream follows, before he collapses in a heap of agony. I look at Arnold, who's staring intently at Greg's slumped body. It begins to stir.
"I thought that might wake him up." Smiles Arnie.

Gregor's head tilts so his face comes into view. His throat is badly bruised. Arnold's kettle holding hand jerks and some scalding water splashes on Gregor's legs. He winces and screams. A moment later Arnold's standing over him with the kettle poised above his head.
"What was the name of that chappie you shared a cell with in Barlinnie?"
"Charlie MacCrossan."
"Yes, Charlie MacCrossan. I have nae seen Charlie for ages. Whatever happened to him?"
Gregor swallows, all the time keeping his eye on the kettle lurking above his head.
"He was found dead in the River Clyde."
"No! That's terrible."

Arnold walks back to the tea and coffee-making table, and replaces the kettle by its lead. He walks over to the window, stepping over Tam on the way. He looks out into the night.

"I'm so glad we don't get dead criminals floating in *this* river. It wouldna' be nace."

He turns and looks towards Gregor.

"There was so much unpleasantness in Glasgow, I moved to Belfast. It was even worse in Belfast, so I moved down here. I don't like unpleasantness. That's why I got into comedy. Created a nice place for folk to come and laugh. And enjoy pleasantness."

He sits in his huge seventies style black leather chair, a style that clashes totally with the classic opulence of the desk in front of it. His left hand gestures to the wet stain on the wall, caused by the tumbler of whisky that Gregor threw at him.

"I see you're into slapstick comedy, Greg. I know slapstick comedians in Belfast. But I do nae want them doon here. The slapstick they do is nae funny. Guys having their genitals removed with blowtorches – that sort of thing."

Tam moans on the floor. Arnold gestures towards him with his head.

"Perhaps it would be better for us all if you were to take your tough man and get oot of my comedy club." He stands up, removes his sheepskin coat, and throws it over Gregor's head.

"I've changed my mind aboot the coat you gave me. I've a suspicion it mate be stolen, and I don't like to break the law." He looks at me.

"That will be all for tonight, Douglas. Oh, by the way. I saw your act recently. You made me laugh. I felt really good watching you."

"Thanks Arnold."

"I could lift you up. To the top, I mean. The very top. You may go."

He winks at me, and I do my best to smile. It's hard to smile, though, at a man who's just poured boiling water into another man's anus. My principal urge is to get the hell out of Dodge, and I don't bother to say goodbye to Gregor and Tam on the way out. I figure they're not important to my career. I close the door politely behind me, and scram. The dressing room's empty. The club's all but empty. Charles greets me a warm goodnight. I'd normally wait for them to call me a taxi, but I want to get away as soon as possible.

There's no sign of Charlotte, and I flag a black cab down in the Fulham Palace Road. On the way home to Lambeth Walk, I wonder how

Arnold's dealing with Gregor and Tam. I'd have thought Tam would need to be moved by stretcher, with a badly broken arm like that. I knew Arnold was tough, but I had no idea he was so ferocious. He didn't even call on his security staff. I sit back in the taxi and watch late night London drift by. Suddenly the tiredness catches up with me. As soon as I get home I clean my teeth, crawl into bed, and snuggle next to a sleeping Sunita.

Chapter Eleven

The next thing I'm aware of is a long, complicated dream where I'm in an office. I know it's an office because it involves lots of telephones ringing. Gradually it dawns on me that I'm me and it's my telephone that keeps ringing. I stagger out of bed and find the phone, which Sunita has thoughtfully left in the lounge. The answer machine has four messages on it, and the clock on the video says it's twenty past two.
"Doug, where have you been?"
It's Melissa.
"I had a late one last night."
"Your audition for 'Bare in Mind' was at eleven fifteen."
"But that's next Friday!"
"Today *is* next Friday."
"Today is *this* Friday." I realise there's no point pursuing this, and return to the matter at hand.
"Can't I go in this afternoon?"
"The casting finished at one. The director had to leave for Heathrow. He's flying to Los Angeles."
I realise I'm desperate for the toilet.
"Can I ring you back in five minutes, Melissa?"
"Go on then."
I hang up and sit on the toilet. Fuck! I'm sure she told me it was next Friday. Even that Nicky Butler last night said she'd see me on Friday, not tomorrow. But today is Friday. Sod it!

After a shit and a cup of strong sweet tea I feel a lot better. I activate the Krups German coffee making machine that Sunita gave me for Christmas, and whilst it gurgles away I phone Melissa back. She's been ringing all morning, she tells me. There really is no chance of getting seen again. The director's making a series of three commercials in California, and they have to make a decision on 'Bare in Mind' by Monday afternoon. They're sorry they missed me, but they'll look at the tape of my original audition during the decision making process.

I've never heard Melissa so angry. We're both angry, but there's no clear target, as neither of us accepts the blame. She changes the subject. Am I aware that I'm doing Liverpool this weekend? I'd better leave soon, because the trains can take longer than they're supposed to on Friday afternoons. She hangs up on me. Fuck her! I'm not going to put up with that sort of treatment. Unless she apologises, I'm going to leave her. I look in my diary. I've got Liverpool and today's recall written in for next Friday. Someone's made a mistake, and I don't think it was me. I bet it was that stupid new assistant that Melissa's got working for her.

Whilst the bath is running, I phone the train company and find out the times of the trains to Liverpool. There are going to be engineering works on Sunday, and I'll have to use a replacement bus service for part of the journey. It's also going to cost me a fortune because I'll be travelling at peak time on a Friday. Fuck that, I'll take the car. That means I've got to leave now. I won't see Sunita before she gets back from work. I'll have to wait until I return on Sunday afternoon. That's a shame; I could do with sex. My cock seems to have recovered from the exertions of a couple of nights ago. I remember my predicament regarding the risks I took. I really must visit a VD clinic and get myself tested.

I pour some of Sunita's luxury aromatherapy bath foam into the overfilled bath. The smell of freshly brewed coffee wafting in from the kitchen reminds me that my cappuccino is ready. I treat myself to sugar, take the mug into the bathroom, and enter the bubbles for a soothing soak. Memories of last night's horrors flood into my mind. I wonder if Tam will ever regain full use of his arm... Coke! I've still got some coke. The gram I bought from Charles last night. That'll sort me out for the drive to Liverpool.

Chapter Twelve

At three fifteen I fire up my bright red 1.9 litre Peugeot 205, and lurch into Lambeth Road. A few seconds later we scoot over Lambeth Bridge, and join the stationary rush hour traffic on Millbank. I say "we" because whilst I was in the middle of shampooing my hair, Colin Homes rang and asked for a lift.

Colin's a fresh-faced twenty-two year old, who won a new act competition last Summer. He's half Irish, half Scottish, and despite only having ten minutes of decent material, he's already getting more exposure than me. He's on the bill with me in Liverpool, and I'm quite happy to drive him because he's a good laugh. Forty-five minutes later we've done two miles. It's four o'clock in the afternoon, and we've got two hundred and sixteen miles to drive to Liverpool. That means at our current speed of around three miles an hour, we'll get there in seventy-two hours, or three days time. The trouble is I'm supposed to start the show off at nine o'clock tonight, which is in five hours time. Colin points out that we need to travel at forty-three point two miles an hour without stopping, to arrive at the venue the moment the show's due to start.
"That's not practical, Colin. I'll need a pre-show poo."
Colin grins, says
"Looks like we've fucked it up." and starts to roll a joint of the same sort of skunk weed that's everywhere.
"Did you get that from Charles?"
"Yeah. He does good shit, but it's expensive."

At five in the afternoon, we're still crawling through the outskirts of London, giggling like schoolgirls as Colin rolls another killer doob. We had a tense moment earlier in Earls Court when Colin handed me a joint whilst we were in the middle of three lanes of stationary traffic. I took a toke and looked to my right – straight into the face of a uniformed police officer in a squad car. I really thought the game was

75

up, but he either didn't care or didn't notice what I was smoking. I've never raised the window so fast.

Shortly after five-fifteen we get onto the M40 and speed up to thirty miles an hour. All over London there are cars containing one, two, or more comedians grinding through the rush hour on their way to out of town gigs. And most of them will be late because they didn't set off early enough. There's something about people who have good comic timing when they're dealing with fractions of a second, but have terrible timing when it comes to how many hours to allow for the journey to the gig. The further away the gig, the worse the sense of what time to set off.

Once we've put a few miles between us and London, the traffic thins out and we speed up to ninety miles an hour. We keep this up all the way to the M42, which takes us round the bottom of Birmingham, where we pick up the M5 heading north, leaving Birmingham to our right. We've both been desperate for a piss for well over an hour, and I pull in at the Frankley services. There's still hope that we might make the gig on time, so we don't bother phoning the venue. Colin gets a couple of take away coffees, and as we accelerate onto the motorway, spills most of it over his jeans. He's not too happy about this, as they're stained with coffee and they're the only trousers he's got with him.

It all goes horribly wrong as we approach the dreaded M5/M6 interchange. We spend at least half an hour queuing at the bottleneck. At seven-twenty we finally make it onto the M6, and eight o'clock we're level with Macclesfield, and cruising along at ninety-five miles an hour. The journey is excruciating because just as we lose all hope of making it to the gig on time, the traffic thins out and we speed up. As long as there's a chance of making it, I drive as fast as the congested overtaking lane will let me. If we don't get to the gig, we don't get paid. The stupid thing is I'm only being paid one hundred and fifty pounds tonight. I'm driving so recklessly that I'm risking both of our lives.

As we approach Manchester the traffic builds up again, and we're down to fifty miles an hour, and flashing cars who don't move out of our way. If they still don't get out of the overtaking lane, we pass them on the inside. I really could do with a blue flashing light on the roof, except that would impede the tilt and slide sunroof. Not that I require the sunroof as we pass Manchester, which as usual, sits in a depressing cocoon of rain.

Colin's never played the venue before. I did it once just over a year ago. That's good, because it means I know where it is and we don't have to spend an hour driving round Liverpool looking for it. Sod's law seems to be in force again as we break free of the Manchester congestion, only to be screaming along the M62 at a quarter to nine. I've been in this dilemma before. The contract states we were supposed to arrive no later than eight-thirty for a nine o'clock start. If we stop to phone the venue and reassure them we're almost there, the time it takes to find a phone box will add another ten minutes to the journey, sabotaging all possibility of getting there for nine o'clock.

If we don't stop to ring the venue, there's a slim chance we might get there for nine, but the people who run the venue will be sitting there with a club full of people, not knowing where the comedians are, or if they're going to turn up. The other two people on the bill are arriving later, because they're doubling up with another venue in Bolton. We see a phone box on the left, and I screech to a halt, very nearly taking out a cyclist. Colin looks at me and asks for the venue's telephone number.
"I thought you had it."
"I left the contract at home. You've got yours, haven't you?"
"No."
A tense moment between us, he slams the door and I accelerate to fifty miles an hour. "How many times have I been in this situation?" I think to myself. The answer is lots of times. Horrifically late for a gig. Driving way over the speed limit in a town hundreds of miles from home. Trying to decipher a one-way system that's so complex it could have been designed by GCHQ cryptologists.

Chapter Thirteen

We eventually scream up to the back door of Stars Nightclub, somewhere in Liverpool city centre. Its five minutes past nine, and the venue manager is waiting anxiously on the pavement.
"Sorry we're late. There was a terrible accident. Blood everywhere. We were held up for hours." This excuse for being late is the one bit of material all comedians share.
"I've got three hundred punters in there. I've been doing me bleeding nut! Never mind about parking – the doormen'll look after your car. Just get on that stage as soon as you can. I'm paying for the DJ from ten-thirty onward, so the show wants coming down by twenty-five past."

We grab our bags and follow him to the musty smelling dressing room. The venue has bands playing on the nights it doesn't have comedy, and the walls are covered in graffiti, apart from the bits where the plaster's falling off due to damp. Colin disappears into the dressing room bog, and I hope he won't be long, because I'm desperate for a shit.
"Do you want a drink to take on?"
"A pint of Guinness, please."
The Venue manager goes off to get my drink. I slump onto a stinking old sofa with cushions that don't match it. Between one of the ill-fitting cushions and the arm, nestles a used condom.

I close my eyes. I've been driving virtually non-stop for five and three-quarter hours, much of it at speed. I had a line of coke before setting out, but that wore off somewhere around Stafford. I would feel exhausted, but for the adrenalin caused by the presence of three hundred northerners in the club beyond the dressing room curtain (the door has been ripped off its hinges, and a candlewick bedspread has been fastened to the door jamb with drawing pins).

I can't actually hear the audience, because they're playing loud thrash metal music over the PA, but I can sense their expectation. Colin comes out of the toilet and looks at me furtively.

"There's a line for you on top of the cistern, mate."

"Thanks", I say, and get up to go in there.

"By the way", he adds.

"The flush doesn't work, and there's no paper."

At least a pint of liquid pre-show poo is bursting to pour out of my rectum, but I snort the line first. Colin wasn't strictly right when he said there isn't any paper. Someone's thoughtfully left last week's 'New Musical Express' on the floor. I wipe my bottom with the gig guide, which includes the show I'm about to start off in a minute's time.

It's strange that on the one hand our gig is considered important enough to list in a national publication, and on the other doesn't merit a flushing toilet. I pity the other comics on the bill if they need pre-show poos (and they will), because the bog is now so full, the next person's cheeks will be touching bits of shit-smeared NME.

That line Colin gave me helps. The venue manager (I think he said his name is Jeff) has left a pint of Guinness for me, and a message with Colin to walk on stage as soon as possible. At seventeen minutes past nine, I walk on stage in front of three hundred people, most of who are in their late teens and early twenties. There's actually a loose floorboard in the stage, and on the back wall are two-foot high letters made out of expanded polystyrene spelling the word 'Stars'. It's a Friday night, and they're already pissed. Including the soundman, because he turns the stage lights up, and the microphone on, but can't seem to turn the thrash metal wall of sound off. I fill in with an exaggerated comedy dance for a few seconds. The thrash metal continues as loud as ever. It's bad enough they were playing it in the first place. Pre-show and interval music affects the mood of an audience. Quirky, tacky tunes are good. They prepare the crowd for silliness. Pumping thrash metal at high volume makes people have to shout to hear each other talk, and sets them on edge. It's aggressive and fast. No stand-up with experience would choose it before they go on.

After about thirty seconds, somebody finds the controls to the music, and switches it off. I take the mike out of its stand, and a jeer rises from three hundred throats. It sounds more like they're on the terraces of a football stadium than in a comedy club. It's my fault the show started late. It isn't my fault the music carried on longer than it was supposed to. It's made the show look shambolic, and I'm the public face of the club. The crowd isn't thinking
"It can't have been the comedian's fault the music went on too long – he was just the one stuck on stage having to deal with the result." Crowds don't think that clearly. As far as they are concerned, a mistake has been made, and it must be the fault of that bloke on stage. So they jeer at me.
"I've got my work cut out here", I think.
"Good evening, and welcome to our slick, highly efficient show."
Now they *do* sound like they're on the football terraces.
"Liverpool. Liverpool."
I deduce that the crowd has identified my accent as that of a southerner, and that the Liverpool football team has recently beaten a southern team, possibly a London side, in a match. I have to deduce this, as if it was left to me, no football would ever get played. I don't like football, and I don't hate it. I have no emotion or time whatsoever for it. I can't tell the audience this, so I mime kicking a penalty and throw my arms up in victory. They cheer and begin chanting a name I've never heard, but I guess is a member of their football team.
"Yeah I support Liverpool. I was born in Liverpool." The mob cheers.
"I've lived in Liverpool most of my life. It's just that I moved down to London three weeks ago, and I picked up the accent."
I get a laugh from most of the crowd, but some lads at the back start booing.
"Yeah, I don't blame you, lads. If I'd paid eight quid for this shit, I'd be booing." I immediately turn to the wall behind me, and yank the letter S off the beginning of the word 'Stars'. That gets a laugh.

I can't believe I'm doing this, but I hold the S by my rectum, as if it was a turd. It gets a bigger laugh.
"I've heard what you're all like. They should call this place 'Stabs' not 'Stars'. They spent a lot of money on doing it up. It's a shame they ran out just before it came to buying bog paper."

That gets a round of applause. Phew! It was close, but I've managed to unite them by focussing their aggression on the place instead of me. I subtly go into material about Liverpool. How the reason ships stopped coming to Liverpool in such numbers was because every time the crew came ashore, they'd return to the ship to find the radio had been nicked. They like that a lot. Then I make a slow transition into my usual material, and I've got them all laughing. Fifteen minutes later they're a lovely audience, who want to listen to the jokes and show everyone else they get them, by laughing heartily. I put Colin Homes on to a rousing welcome, and retreat into the dressing room.

As I relax on the filthy sofa, I contemplate the remainder of the evening. The most difficult part of my job is done. I've proved to the audience that I'm funny, and all I have to do now is take Colin off before the interval, and put the other two acts on. That shouldn't be too difficult, as there won't be time for me to do a lot. The bloke running the venue, Jeff or whatever his name is, will want to get the show over as quick as possible, so the punters will be splashing their money over the bar. As long as the other two acts arrive on time from Bolton, I'll be okay.

I'm wondering whether I should let Colin know I've got some coke, and reciprocate the line he gave me, when it occurs to me there's something I should be hearing that I'm not. Laughter. I can't hear any laughter coming through that candlewick bedspread hanging in the doorway that leads to the stage. I go over and poke my head through to see what's going on. Oh dear. Poor Colin's doing his 'excuses for not doing your homework' routine to total silence. A harsh male voice pipes up from somewhere in the throng: -
"It's a shame you didn't do your homework before coming here, mate."
The heckler gets the biggest laugh so far during Colin's act.
"What's your problem – didn't you go to school? I suppose you were playing truant stealing cars." Oh no, Colin's making a big mistake. The audience is on the heckler's side, so it's pointless to take an adversarial stance with him. He should let him have the point, play along with him, and gradually try to pull them round. Now he's lost the moral high ground as well as not being funny. I prepare myself to

go back on stage to mop up the mess. He's only done five minutes, and there's still no sign of the other two acts.

The stain in the groin area of Colin's trousers from when he spilled coffee during the journey is really shown up by the stage lighting. Someone notices it.
"At least we didn't wet our pants like you have."
The rest of the audience notices the stain, and erupts in an ecstasy of mirth. If there's one thing a comic needs to learn, it's how to die. It's like losing an erection. It happens to us all occasionally, and what matters is how we deal with the situation. If the audience doesn't want you, then get off. It's no good for anyone if you're obstinate and stay on to spite them. It's bad for the audience, it's bad for you, it's bad for the promoter, and it's bad for the person who's got to go on afterwards. Which in this case is me.

At first they enjoy the booing, but the longer Colin refuses to get off, the uglier the booing gets. Then a chant of "Off, off, off" starts up, and he still insists on talking about wanking in his Auntie's downstairs toilet whilst 'Brookside' is on telly. When the plastic beer glasses start to land on the stage, the soundman cuts the power to the microphone, and he finally gets the message it's time to do what three hundred people are telling him to do, which is fuck off.

As we pass on the stage, I mutter to him
"Never mind, mate" and pick the mike up off the stage that's sticky with stale beer. He threw away the last remnant of dignity by chucking the mike on the floor in a temper. I tap the mike to see if it's working again. Either the soundman has failed once more, or Colin broke it when he threw it down. Great! Now I'm stuck with a load of anger I didn't earn. Any venue worth its salt has a spare mike and stand on the side of the stage. I look around, but this place has hardly got a stage, let alone a backup mike.

An electronic squeaking sound indicates the mike's finally been switched back on, and I talk into it. Yep, it's working. Now I've got a dilemma. When I introduced Colin, I told them he's a fantastic comedian and a good friend. They hated him, and so if I continue to associate myself with him, the shit could spill over onto me. If I score points off him by saying something like "Sorry, I'd confused him with someone else. He was shit." I'd get a big laugh off the audience, who will identify with me, but it'll be a professional betrayal of Colin, who I'm working with all weekend. He might be inexperienced in how to die graciously, but this is a hard audience, he's a good bloke, and an okay comic. That's why he's not used to dying on his arse.

I go the middle way and announce
"Actually, Ladies and Gentlemen, he did that for a bet. Someone dared him a tenner he wouldn't be brave enough to throw the gig. So now he's got ten quid..." (I look for a suitable candidate in the front row)
"he can afford to fuck *your* mother." The bloke I point at laughs from embarrassment, and the rest of them laugh at the crap joke. I'm not proud to be doing this rubbish, but it's my job to keep the ship afloat. If anyone's going to be the target of easy laughs, I'd rather it was someone in the audience than the bloke I've got to share a car with all the way home to London.

I do another fifteen minutes, which is what Colin would have done if he hadn't died, and introduce the first interval. As I go through the candlewick bedspread curtain into the dressing room I smell the sweet aroma of a joint.
Kev Knight and Brian O'Shea have just arrived from Bolton, thank goodness. Kev Knight's the guy who wrote the article about Arnold Shanks in 'High Wire' magazine, and Brian O'Shea's a new comic fresh from Ireland who's blessed with effortless, instant success. He's nice enough, but it's hard not to be jealous of his TV exposure, and I take a secret pleasure in not telling him he's sitting virtually on top of a used condom. Colin's in the toilet, and Jeff the promoter's brought me a fresh pint of Guinness.
"The damage to the sign will come out of your wages." He says, as he hands me the drink. I smile and fake a laugh. I don't know if he's joking or not, but I treat his comment as if it *was* a joke.

I greet Kev and Brian, and mention the article about Arnold Shanks that Kev wrote in 'High Wire' magazine. Kev laughs, and says

"Anything to stay on the right side of Arnold. He's virtually keeping me in work at the moment." He glances at Brian,
"Not that Brian's going to be relying on live work for much longer."
Brian looks into his lap, coyly. Of course! He was one of the other three who got recalled for 'Bare in Mind'.
"Did you get the part?" I ask him.
He nods mildly. The lucky bastard! Brian's from Dingle, which is the western most town in Europe. He's got thick, black shaggy hair, and a soft Celtic face with a clear complexion. Girls go wild for his rugged good looks. Like many people from the west coast of Ireland, he looks slightly Spanish. This isn't surprising, as when the Spanish armada was wrecked on Ireland's western shores, a lot of shipwrecked sailors found their way into the arms of Irish women.

"Found out this afternoon." He says, bashfully. I shake his hand and congratulate him, adding
"By the way, there's a used condom between the cushion you're sitting on and the arm of the sofa." Now he's going to be in a television sitcom, I'm going to curry his favour. He sees the condom and shifts along the sofa to get away from it.
"It's a lovely dressing room you keep here, Jeff." Says Kev.
"Your lucky the spunk's in a condom, and not just fetched all over the cushion." Jeff replies.

The rest of the show passes off textbook style. I do an easy five minutes before putting Kev on, who has a few hecklers, but nothing he can't handle. Brian does five minutes over time and gets an encore. Most of the voices shouting for more are female ones. He still hasn't been on telly enough to be that recognisable. If 'Bare in Mind' does well, he's going to be a big star. He's got it all, and he doesn't have to try. As I drain my fourth pint of Guinness I console myself that even if I had made it to the recall, the part would have gone to Brian anyway. Give it another two years, and he won't be playing shitty gigs like this – he'll be selling out theatres to adoring teenage girls. For double the ticket price.

Loud rave music thunders through the candlewick bedspread curtain after the show. Brian's got a gaggle of girls all wanting to get off with him, Colin's drunk himself into a mire of self pity, and Kev's already

gone to find a telephone to talk to his wife. He's got two young kids, and doesn't really go for the comedy lifestyle.
"I'm afraid there was a shortage of hotel rooms this weekend, lads. So we've had to put you in two twin rooms. You're in the Feathers Hotel. Here are the keys."
Jeff tosses the keys onto the sofa, and gets out of the dressing room before we can challenge him. We're supposed to get our own hotel rooms, and this isn't on. It's a classic ploy of money-grabbing promoters to lie to us about not enough rooms being available, so they can save money by making us share rooms. We all look at each other, but nobody's got the energy to find Jeff amongst the throng of clubbers.

Colin decides he wants to share with Kev, who's just come back from the phone box. That's not surprising, as Kev will be going to bed straight away, and Colin isn't going to want to hang around in a club full of people who hate him. So I'm sharing with Brian, who looks like he's got the choice of all the women in Liverpool. I leave him holding court in the dressing room, and go out to move my car into the Feathers hotel car park, which is just around the corner. I'm pleasantly hungry, and wonder if the Italian takeaway near the hotel is still open.

It is, and a spaghetti Alfredo later, I'm surveying the hotel room. The fact that the Feathers hotel has two stars is the best joke of the night. Our room is on the first floor, above the kitchen. There's faded flock wallpaper, candlewick bedspreads that leave no doubt as to where the one posing as a dressing room door in the club came from, and two single beds. The windowless en suite bathroom is so small that when I sit on the toilet there's no room for my knees. Still, at least there's some paper and a lock on the door, which is more that can be said for the bogs in 'Stars'. The old sash window of the bedroom overlooks the small car park, which in Liverpool is probably a good thing, because at least I'll be able to see who's vandalising my car. The extractor fans from the kitchens are just below our window, and from the noise they're making they've got square bearings. When I look out to see my car is okay, I wish I'd parked it on the far side of the car park where it would be more visible from the room. As it is, I have to lean out of the window and look straight down to see it.

When I phone Sunita up, she's a bit off with me. I ask her what's wrong and my heart misses a beat when her next sentence begins with the phrase
"When you were in Jersey…" Normal heart rate is restored when she tells me that she had a hair cut when I was in Jersey, and I didn't notice it on my return. Now I come to think of it, it did look slightly different. I reassure her that she's the most beautiful woman in the world, and ask her what she did tonight. She saw a friend performing in a play at a pub theatre in Islington. We coo a few love words to each other, and I promise to take her to a restaurant on Sunday evening. I get into bed, turn the telly on, and smoke a couple of pipes of grass. There's an old black and white gangster film on, and as I go up on the skunk, a fistfight breaks out between James Cagney and some other gangsters.

The artificiality of the fight reminds me of the real one I witnessed last night in Arnold Shanks' office. My stomach turns over as I relive the horror. The film violence is too much for me, and I change channel. This time it's a horror film. I can't see how Arnold could have avoided calling an ambulance to deal with Tam's broken arm. I suppose the police would have been involved too. The memory of that violence makes me upset, and I'm trying to nurse myself back to a state of relaxation so I can enjoy being stoned, when there's a knock at the door. I've got all the lights switched off except for my bedside light, and the room almost passes as cosy. I open the door in my pants. A rather tipsy Brian is swaying in the doorway, with two girls sniggering in the shadows behind him.

Chapter Fourteen

They troop in, and when I see how stunningly beautiful the girls are, their magic blows my depression away. One's blonde with her hair in a ponytail, and the other's got brown hair down to just below her ears. They're wearing short A line dresses, black mascara, and bright red lipstick. I reckon they must be sixteen years old if they're a day.
"Come in and sit down," lilts Brian in that soft Kerry brogue. There's nowhere for them to sit apart from on his bed.
"This is Doug. You may recognise him as the compere. Doug, this is Maxine, and this is Melina. They're twins, aren't you girls."
They look at each other and giggle. Maxine, who's the blonde one and whose A line dress is black and silky, looks at me and smiles.
"You were dead funny tonight." Her accent leaves me in no doubt as to where she's from.
"Thanks. So you're from Liverpool."
She looks at Melina and they giggle.
"No we're not. We're from the Wirral."
The Wirral is just across the River Mersey from Liverpool. I've been there twice, both times to do gigs. To a southerner like me, the Wirral and Liverpool both count as the same, as far as accent is concerned. The only reason I'd come to either place would be for paid work, neither holds any aesthetic quality for me. Until now. As from this moment, the Wirral is sacred soil because it grew these perfect, nearly ripe fruit.

Melina's brown hair is in that Louise Brooks 1920s style. Her A line dress is scarlet, and her high heeled shoes match. Maxine's shoes are exactly the same style as her sisters, except they're black, to match the black dress. I guess they go shopping together.
"Are we disturbing your film?" asks Brian.
"No it's rubbish, I was about to turn it off." Brian turns the volume down, and goes to the meagre tea and coffee making facilities on the dressing table.

"We get dead scared by horror films, don't we Max?" Says Melina, as she lights up a Silk Cut.
"Yeah, we watched a vampire film last week, and I had to get into bed with you, didn't I?" They giggle.

Brian makes us all a cup of tea. There are only two cups, which he gives to the girls. He and I make do with the two glasses also supplied with the room. I get a pipe together, but as I hand it to Melina it occurs to me I might be supplying drugs to a minor.
"How old are you?"
They consult their watches, and hold their wrists next to each other to show them off. Both are identical.
"I'm sixteen years, twelve hours, four minutes, and thirty-three seconds. And Maxine's sixteen years, four hours, one minute, and twenty seconds."
"Do you like our watches? We got them for our birthday, didn't we Mel." They're very proud of what in this light look like regular ladies watches.
"Happy birthday." I say as I hold a lighter to relight the pipe for Melina.
"Yeah, happy birthday." Adds Brian as he playfully rubs Maxine's knee. She makes it very obvious she likes that.

Melina hands the pipe to Maxine, looks at Brian and me, flutters her eyelids, and says "Are we gonna get a birthday kiss, or what?"
Brian gives her a kiss on the lips, and she throws her arms around his neck like they were in the final scene of a romantic film. Maxine puts the pipe aside, which irks me slightly because from the amount of smoke billowing out of the bowl there's a few quid's worth of skunk going to waste. My slight annoyance melts when I see her beautiful face come towards me, her scarlet lipstick penetrating the dim light as she holds her lips open to receive mine. Her tongue darts into my mouth as her arms hold me close. We hover between playground snog and climactic kiss in 'Gone With The Wind'.
I remember Sunita, and gently pull away.
"Happy birthday, Maxine." She looks over to Brian and Melina, who's pushed Brian backwards across his bed.
"Hey Melina, don't Bogart him. You're only getting your birthday kiss."

Brian takes this as an opportunity to come up for air. Maxine joins him and Melina on his bed, and, pushing in front of her sister, kisses him. Melina disentangles herself from Brian and literally jumps on top of me. I get another dramatic kiss, and conclude these girls must spend a lot of time watching old weepy movies on telly. They kiss like 1950s film stars.

I'm surprised Melina relinquished Brian so easily, considering he's the one who headlined, and is younger and better looking than me. As I lay back under Melina's kiss, I notice she's got exactly the same kissing technique as her sister. I hear a click, and open my eyes to see that she's reached out and switched my bedside lamp off. The walls and ceiling flicker as the only source of light is from the TV high up on its wall bracket.

I don't want to be unfaithful to Sunita, I had unsafe sex with two girls a couple of nights ago, this really isn't what I should be doing. I don't even have proof that this nymph who's wriggling on top of me is sixteen. She's more like a child than a woman as she wriggles and squirms and chuckles. So far I've kept my hands fairly passive, but as I rest them on her little bottom desire floods into my viscera. Her buttocks are so tight, there's no surplus flesh to be found. And that silky dress is riding higher and higher. She blows softly into my ear
"Will you help us celebrate?"
"Your birthday. We already are, aren't we?"
"I mean that we're legal."
I laugh, and share my thought about how they both have the same kissing technique.
"Of course we have." Comes the reply.
"We practice on each other."
Her breath smells of vodka and black current. As she nuzzles her head around my neck, her hair caresses my skin, sending a tingling down my spine. I savour the smell of her hair – it's so girly it triggers an emotional response, and I can't resist when she starts tugging at the sheets.
"Let me in. Let me in, said the first little piggy."
I make some piggy squeaking sounds as I help her under the sheets. She laughs with such abandon I'm reminded of a book I read about when the first European sailors visited the Pacific Islands, and found

the young women completely free of inhibitions. She slides in with me, and doesn't stop moving down the bed. Her soft lips stroke my chest, my stomach, and my lower abdomen. I raise my hips for her to pull my pants down, and soft wetness envelopes the bulb end of my nob. Her tongue licks and flicks expertly, as her fingers caress my scrotum. From the way Brian's moaning on the other side of the room, I guess he's getting the same service.

The way she sucks and wanks me is so beautiful I feel an orgasm just around the corner, and as if she can sense this, she moves her face up to mine. As we kiss I pull her dress up, and she deposits it on the floor with a carefree flick. When she's laying back on top of me, I remove her little panties, and chuck them where I guess her dress landed. She's obviously been dancing, and her hot little body smells yummy. I put my hands beneath her shoulders and lift her up slightly, to take a look at those titties. They're bigger than I thought they'd be, considering she wasn't wearing a bra. As I suck each nipple in turn I get the delicious aroma of those armpits, and slurp away at them.

There's activity in the other bed, and something flies through the air and hits me on the left eyebrow. It falls on the pillow beside my head, and before I can investigate, Melina has scooped it up and is ripping it open with her teeth. Maxine has thrown us a condom, and Melina has it on my cock with alarming dexterity. I feel her vag, and it's wet with arousal. She's already raising herself, to sit astride me. She lowers herself onto me, and her angelic face smiles benignly as she jerks her hips backwards and forwards with a fast, firm rhythm.

I can see her twin in exactly the same position astride Brian, except the thrusting of the hips is absent. The cheap television from the Far East shows cheap actors from the Far West act out the cheaply written script in silence. A woman screams unheard as she runs away from a car, driven by a moustachioed man in a lumberjack shirt. I twitch my hips up and down to get more friction from Melina's very small pussy. As the telly shows a point of view shot of the moustachioed man driving the car over the screaming woman, I realise that I'm about to live up to the male stereotype and come after three minutes of sexual intercourse. I groan a bit and play with her nipples as she speeds up the rhythm. I can feel warm wetness on my thighs, where her buttock sweat is dripping onto me.

She moans and suddenly changes position whilst keeping her quim around my cock. She squats over me, steadying herself by pressing her right palm into the wall next to the single bed, and bobs up and down in a final flurry of rhythmic jolting. I straighten my legs and spill two days worth of semen into the condom deep inside her. From the soft sounds in her throat, and the spasms that pulse through her, I know that she comes at the same time as me. She pulls the bedding over her shoulders and settles down on top of me. I hold her close to my chest, and our breathing falls into a deep, shared, slow rhythm. She's so light I can take her weight on top of me in complete comfort. We lie there in the soft light, with my penis flaccid and snug inside her. I kiss her damp forehead and savour the smell of her hair.

On opening my eyes I see Michael Fish silently gesturing to a map of Britain that promises sunny weather all over the country. A lush scouse voice whispers in my ear "D'you always sound like a woman?"
I whisper back that I didn't realise. It dawns on me that movement and sound in the other bed never really got going. Suddenly a figure gets up and goes into the bathroom. From the youthful grace it's obviously Maxine, although there's a disappointed feel about the way she closes the door and snaps the light on. The tiny bathroom magnifies the hum of the extractor fan to almost jet engine proportions, and Melina kisses me twice on the face before extricating herself from me. She kneels beside me on the bed, and gently removes the condom from my dozing knob. She kisses it before joining her sister in the bathroom.

I lie on the bed with my hands behind my head. I know what I've just done is irresponsible, but that was heaven! The way she made love was terrific. Her faultless technique was equalled by the emotional commitment she gave. I suppose that's why she came at the same time I did. Wow. The sound of a confab between the girls competes with the noise of the extractor fan emanating from the bathroom. I can't make any words out, but there are a couple of shrieks of laughter. I'm aware that social convention requires me to say something to Brian, and remember the tea bags are still brewing in the cups and glasses.

"Do you think the tea's brewed yet?" I ask. Silence. Oh dear. I spoke quite loudly, so there's no question of Brian not hearing me. I'm mulling over what the most helpful thing I can say would be, when the door bursts open and the girls emerge. One of them gets into bed with Brian, and the other gets in with me. It's not Melina, it's Maxine, and she's just cleaned her teeth. I wonder if she brought her own toothbrush. If she didn't, I hope it's mine she used, and not Brian's.

I've got a dilemma now, because I want to enjoy this bundle of teenage beauty that's cuddling up to me, but I also need a piss. I'm about to explain my predicament, when Brian stomps into the bathroom and slams the door. They really should replace the bearings on the extractor fans in this hotel. The combined noise of the one in the bathroom and the kitchen ones on the wall outside make this more like being airside at Heathrow airport than a hotel room. Brian's certainly taking his time doing whatever he's doing in the bathroom, and I'm starting to get another erection because Maxine is nibbling my ear and stroking my thighs. I reiterate the fact that I'm now bursting for a piss, when she suggests
"Why not go in the kettle?"
"We might want to use it later."
"What about the window?"
That sounds a bit more considerate, so I go over to the window and lift the sash. Melina's in Brian's bed, which is very close to the window, and she shows a lot of interest when I go over. Maxine joins her as I project an arc of sparkling liquid through the gap. A noise below the window draws our gaze downwards, and we see a dark figure bending over the lock on the driver's door of my car. I adjust my aim, and a would-be car thief gets showered with piss. As my bladder empties the range shortens, and the piss drops straight down through the mesh guard onto the propellers of one of the extractor fans. The bloke beneath us gets splattered by a supercharged spray of piss, and I force a few more spurts down onto the fan.
He finally gets over his shock and saunters off. He doesn't even bother running.
"That'll teach him," the girls agree, and when I return to my bed, it's with both of them.
"Brian was a lot better on stage than he was on me." Maxine whispers.
"I thought you were on him."

"Were you watching us, you perv?"
"You were in my line of sight. I don't want to hurt his feelings, he's a good bloke."
"You don't want to hurt *my* feelings either. I want my birthday present."

Maxine starts kissing me, and pushes me down onto my bed. I feel a second pair of hands stroke my feet. I'm more surprised than anyone when I realise my todger has woken up and is showing an interest in the situation. Maxine cups her hands around my balls and caresses them with her long nails. She starts to suck my nipples, which doesn't do much for me. They got so badly twisted in the playground at school, any touching of them by a third party puts me ill at ease. I feel her tits, which are smaller than her sisters, and stroke her fanny. It's nice and hairy. I'm interested to know if she's blonde down there as well, and go down to investigate. It looks pretty fair to me, and despite serious reservations, I throw caution to the wind and start licking.

I'm aware that these girls got their experience from somewhere, and I don't think it all came from the same man. In addition to this worry about getting infected with something, there's the knowledge that Brian's cock was here a few minutes ago. I prepare myself for the taste of rubber, but am pleasantly surprised by salty, fresh pussy.

Maxine's head is at the bottom of my bed, and I have to bend my knees, twist my ankles, and rest my feet against the wall to make room. Melina, bless her heart, is sitting on the edge of the bed beside me, stroking and massaging my back. As I lick and suck every bit of Maxine's vagina, my hands play with her nipples and breasts. Melina's hands wander onto my buttocks, and her caresses stir my penis to a splendid stiffness. I'm lying on my front with my weight forcing it to point down towards my feet. Melina spots that if she reaches between my thighs, she can touch the underside of its tip. She strokes it with her fingertips, and pushes my thighs apart so she can also stroke the shaft.

After a few minutes of this, I'm desperate to put it inside Maxine. When they first walked in the room I found them both stunningly beautiful, but if I had to choose between them, I'd say Maxine is marginally prettier. I admit to being typical in fancying the blonde over the brunette. I also admit to wanting to 'collect the set' by having them both. Being male I'm genetically programmed to want to fertilise as many women as possible. In the absence of spending ten hours a day practicing Buddhist meditation, I haven't transcended this desire. Anyway, I left the club and came to bed on my own. They started it.

I pull my mouth away from Maxine's fanny and ask if they've got any condoms.
"Of course" comes the reply. Melina produces one within seconds, and Maxine sits up in anticipation. The telly is now showing Ridley Scott's 'Bladerunner', so there isn't much light coming from the screen. Whilst I squint at the condom in the dim light, trying to work out which way it's going to unroll, so I don't make that embarrassing mistake of putting it on the wrong way round, Maxine leans over and pops her mouth over my cock. Her tongue goes round in a non-stop circular movement. Then she sucks so hard she creates a vacuum and draws her mouth back and off it, causing a loud slurping sound. She looks up at me and grins mischievously. I put the condom on and begin to push her back onto the bed.

The girls have another idea. They push *me* back onto the bed, and Maxine straddles me and slides onto my cock in the same way her sister did earlier. As she starts to bounce up and down, my penis begins to revel in his cramped quarters. Meanwhile, Melina straddles my face, so she's facing her sister. This is probably nice for them, but it means I've got as much of her arse on my face as I have of her quim. I can smell bottom, but stick my tongue out as far as it'll go anyway. To be fair to her, she adjusts her position slightly, and the odour of bottom gives way to that of pussy.

I can taste the condom I was wearing, but I can't deny I'm enjoying myself. I open my eyes, but they're covered by Melina's hot sweaty buttocks. I can feel her juices trickling down my cheeks, and Maxine's vaginal muscles squeezing my cock. We're all sharing a nice, steady, rhythm. I feel about with my hands to find out what's going on above me. I grope the undersides of four pert little bosoms, and above them, two throats. The sisters are engaged in a long kiss! I continue groping the four little bosoms, and start to approach orgasm. I'd tell them if I could, but I'm wearing a gag of pubic hair and dribbling pink flesh. I don't even help it along with a burst of hip movement. I just lay there and allow Maxine's thrusting to bring me over the edge, and come inside her. The girls can tell this, because the thrusting activity stops, and Melina lifts her buttocks off my face. Maxine climbs off, and I ask if she's come yet.

"Nearly." She lies down on her back and I oblige with my tongue. Melina positions herself with her back to me, and her quim over her sister's mouth. I gobble away, and stick a finger inside her for good measure. A few minutes later they both exclaim with "Ahs" and "Oohs", and I lie back with both girls half beside, half on top of me. There's a cracking sound and we all lurch downwards and slightly forwards. The legs on this single bed have snapped, and the foot of the bed has crashed to the floor. As if this is the cue he was waiting for, Brian unlocks the bathroom door and comes out. He's completely uncoordinated and in the poor light he trips over the end of the bed, which has shifted a couple of feet into the path of anyone coming out of the bathroom door. He's sprawled across the floor, his shins across the twin sisters' and my feet.

The girls go into helpless paroxysms of laughter, and as Brian raises himself from the floor the bathroom light reveals a smile on his face. He looks very pale, and I wonder if he's been sick. Luckily the girls both cuddle him and smother him with feminine attention, which goes a long way in my mind to evaporating the tension arising from the fact that I've fucked both of them, and he didn't manage it with one.

A pungent, earthy aroma drifts out of the bathroom, and suddenly everything becomes clear. Why Brian couldn't perform sexually. Why he spent so long in the bathroom. And why the girls are suddenly all over him. I think they smelt it before I did, and now Brian's the man they want. Melina switches his bedside lamp on, and as he sits on his bed, they kneel and kiss his feet, pretending to be slave girls, imploring "Please. Please. Please." He smiles at me, his pupils dilated to the size of ants.

"Go and get my sponge bag." Commands Brian in that affable Irish sing song voice that'll soon be floating out of millions of television sets. The girls move so fast, they bang into each other as they try to get through the bathroom door at the same time.

As they bring him his large black leather sponge bag, he reaches into his hold all and removes a roll of Bacofoil, and large pair of orange handled Finnish-made scissors. I've never injected heroin, but I have chased the dragon several times. I know it's stupid, and I wouldn't advise anyone to do it; but I know of several people including me, who have taken smack and enjoyed it without getting addicted. I'd never seek it out, but in this situation, with Brian and two sixteen-year old angels all sitting completely naked and free of inhibition, it's a perfect way to round off the evening.

The girls tell us they aren't addicted, but they took some amphetamine sulphate in the club and are speeding. A hit of smack will level them off. Brian makes a little smoking tube out of the foil, and the girls cut out four squares of it to chase the dragon on. From the practiced way they sprinkle the brown powder into a little heap near the edge of the foil, and track the molten brown heroin with the foil smoking tube as the lighter flame melts it, I wonder how long it'll be before they *do* become hooked. This time yesterday they were still fifteen. They sparkle with youthful vitality as they have fun now, but how long before they look older than their age? I feel sad and slightly guilty as I take my turn with the skag. Brian's collapsed on his bed, and the girls rebuke me as, due to lack of experience, I fail to track the plume of smoke, and waste a lungful.

They greedily sniff the smoke I missed as it rises towards the dingy nicotine-stained ceiling.
"Did you get this in the pool?" The girls ask Brian. It's the strongest heroin I've ever smoked, and they're impressed too. Brian struggles to lift his head to speak.
"No, I got it in Dublin a few days ago." Brian's sailing close to the wind. He's on the cusp of a TV career, and he's risking being caught with heroin at Heathrow Airport. I'm distracted from such contemplation by a warm glow in my lungs, and a lightness that feels like I'm floating off the floor. In addition to my up-down bearings, my direction orientation goes too, and the room starts spinning. I lean back against Brian's bed to get some support, but it's not enough. I get to the window just as my stomach erupts.

I don't know if it's the same bloke as before, but someone who was trying to break into my car gets showered with rancid Guinness and pasta. He's still frozen in shock as I aim my second heave onto the extractor fan's propeller. He whines as a gutful of supercharged half-digested spaghetti Alfredo accelerates over him. The smell must be bad, because he wretches and throws up too. If he knew it was my car he was trying to break into, he'd probably get me back by barfing on my door handle. But he instinctively bends and aims it at the ground. I shout down to him
"The spaghetti just hit the fan."

I go through to the bathroom to wash my face and clean my teeth. Bits of debris around the top of the toilet bowl betray the fact that Brian threw up earlier. I'm feeling rather sticky and love-soiled, and take a shower. The girls come in and vomit into the bog whilst I do so. I normally hate being sick, but being sick on heroin is something else. It's almost pleasurable, like a purification.
"Can I use your toothbrush again?" asks Maxine.
"And me." Says Melina.
"Of course you can." I reply from the shower. There's the metallic sound of shower curtain rings on shower rail, and the curtain gets drawn aside.
"Can three fit in?" One of the girls asks. It's Melina. Maxine is sitting on the toilet having a wee. Melina joins me in the shower, her eyes glazed in a heroin wooze.
"I'm desperate too." She declares, and golden liquid runs down her legs. I put my hand on her fanny, and my fingers bathe in her sacred spring.

She stands beneath the cascading water, and puts her arms around me in an affectionate, younger sister-like way. Maxine comes in too, and we stand in a huddle. This hotel room might be shit, but the shower can't be faulted. It delivers copious amounts of warm water at a consistent temperature. I must admit, though, that the idea of sharing a shower or bath with a lover is better than the reality. If you're in a large hot tub, fair enough. But a glass-fibre cubicle in a third rate hotel that used to be a house is too cramped. I make my excuses and leave the girls to ablute in peace. I managed to clean my teeth and swill my mouth with mouthwash, and clean my genital area, so I'm happy to go back in the room. My bed's beyond use where the bottom two legs have collapsed, so I pull the mattress off and put it on the floor beside the bed. That pretty much takes up all the remaining floor space in the room.

Brian's laying on his side, coasting along on the smack. I've got over the nauseous phase of the heroin, and am feeling fine. I lie down on my mattress, get beneath the duvet, and my eyelids drift down over my eyes. Everything is warm and good.

I must have wafted into a slumber, because I come round to the sight of Brian sitting up in bed, propped up by lots of pillows. Maxine and Melina are draped around him like nymphets in a painting by Tadema. Melina's arm is moving up and down rhythmically near Brian's crotch. I'm glad to see they've got something good happening in the sex department, but with all the smack Brian's smoked, it's going to take a lot to induce an orgasm. I tried making love on heroin once, and it was very nice, but it took about four hours to come.
"Doug darling, we need your help." Maxine says it, but I can tell she's the voice of a conspiracy involving the three of them.
"Mmm?" My voice is throaty and deep from the opiate.
"We've been discussing Brian's sexuality. He likes to watch videos, don't you Brian?"
Brian's too shy to answer.
"The trouble is, we haven't got a video, or a video player." Continues Melina.
"What turns him on is seeing girls play with another man's cock."
"I see. I'm a bit tired at the moment. Does the cock have to be hard? Because if it does, I'm not sure I'm up to the job."
"I'm sure we could rectify that situation." The girls lick their lips and nod towards my groin area. Then I notice that one of them has a little paper packet.
"Have yous got a mirror? Fancy a line of speed?"

I really need to sleep. It's four in the morning. I've got a gig to do this evening, and I was planning to drive back to London afterwards. I don't think it would be wise to start taking amphetamine sulphate now.
"That's okay, you go ahead. I think I'll manage without." I drift for a while with my eyes closed, whilst Brian and the girls have a line of

speed. Then I feel the duvet being disturbed around my feet, and it's pulled off with a sudden jerk. Another burst of familiar girly giggling. It dawns on me that I'm about to be raped by two schoolgirls. I open my eyes and see Brian sitting on his bed masturbating, and the girls standing either side of me, still completely naked. I'm beginning to wonder if they grew up in a nudist camp.

"We're just doing what Brian wants, so don't take this personally." I must have been asleep, because six empty cans indicate they got Brian to yield his stash of Guinness. I register a twinge of disappointment at missing out on a drink. Then I realise I haven't missed out. Every drop of Guinness the girls drank is coming my way. Two streams of warm wee wee are aimed on my cock and balls. They've been saving it up, because I get at least a litre from each, and they're still going. Little splashes patter on my chest and face, but I don't bother because it's fresh, and there's a good shower close by.

Brian's masturbating furiously, and I can't deny that I'm enjoying the sensation of that lovely warm piss. It's warmer than warm. It's hot, and it's nice. I suppose the girls have got a temperature from all the drugs, and their urine is the same temperature as their bodies. By the time their golden fountains run out, my member is as hard as Brian's. If anyone had asked me if I'd like to be pissed on, I'd have refused without hesitation. But that was great. They avoided doing it on my face, and as I get to my feet the skin on the front of my body feels invigorated. My bladder's full too, so I gently move Maxine next to her sister, and empty it over two shiny pairs of tits.

Brian's wanking himself up to a crescendo that never quite happens, and breathlessly pants
"Toss him off on each others tits!"
Maybe the heroin wore off a bit during my brief sleep. Whatever, the snooze certainly recharged me, because I really get into being squeezed exceptionally hard by Melina's hand, and jerked very vigorously until I spray spunk over Maxine's throat and tits.
Brian grunts like a mental case, his face contorted with urgency. Maxine grabs his cock and keeps up the pace, yanking back and forth faster than the eye can follow. Melina positions her face in front, her mouth wide open. It must be a very, very, long time since Brian came, because he jets spurt after spurt of spunk into Melina's mouth and

onto her face. Maxine takes over, enclosing his tip with her mouth. Her throat muscles betray that she's gulping.

Brian's moaning and groaning so loud I'm worried we're going to get complaints from other guests. He collapses back across his bed gasping for breath like a man who's just been rescued from a near drowning. Melina wipes spaff off her face with the corner of Brian's duvet, and joins Maxine in stroking Brian's hair. I forget that my mattress is soaked in piss, and flop down onto it with a squelch, pulling the duvet over me.
"Oh, thank you. Thank you. That was the most fantastic experience of my life!" Pants Brian. He's so elated he's almost in tears. As I close my eyes and prepare to drift off, I feel certain that he's just had his first happy sexual experience with a third party.

A couple of minutes later, when we've all got our breath back and Melina's switched the TV and the lights off, Brian still has an emotional quiver in his voice.
"What are you two girls doing later?"
"We don't go out Saturday nights. We go and stay with our Gran."
"Yeah, we go out Fridays, and go to bed early Saturdays, don't we Mel."
"Why's that?"
"We get up early Sunday mornings. We go to mass, and teach Sunday school."
"Are you catholic?" I exclaim.
"Yeah, does it show?"
All four of us giggle. Every time it subsides, the giggling starts up again. Eventually Brian, who like me, has fallen in love with them, asks the girls
"Surely you can miss spending a Saturday evening with your Gran just once?"
"Not tonight we can't. She's doing a big birthday tea for us. Uncle Jim and Auntie Renee are coming over with presents. We can't miss our birthday, can we Mel?"
"I thought you said your sixteenth birthday was Friday."
"Did we say it was yesterday? Ooh sorry, we meant it's today."
"So you're not sixteen until later today?"
"We made a mistake, didn't we Max."

The girls giggle some more, but Brian and I remain silent. We're both pondering the same thing. Two fifteen year-olds have tricked us into sleeping with them.

I have a long, meandering dream in which I'm in a TV studio with Sunita and Brian. We're making some telly programme, and helping Brian to do it without heroin. The set is that of an Indian palace, and when we leave the studio floor and go into the dressing rooms, the entire studio building is Indian. All pointed Mogul archways, and marble floors, with brightly coloured silk hangings. Then we go on the set in the studio next door, which is built as a Roman Catholic Church. The Priest is that bloke who runs Stars Comedy Club. Jeff, or whatever his name is. Maxine and Melina are nuns, giving me some sort of blessing, which involves a ritual bracelet being placed on my left wrist. I'm lying on an altar, which is at floor level, and they move around me solemnly.

The dream returns to the hotel, and merges into oblivion. Some dreadful commercial radio station is on very loud in the kitchens immediately beneath us, and disposable pop- music, bad commercials, and fourth rate deejay thump up through the floor. The oil in the deep fat fryers smells like it hasn't been changed for ten years. The acrid stench coming from the extractor fans and up through our open window is so foul a starving man would reject breakfast in this hotel.

The reek of the deep fat fryers brings me awake more than the loud radio does. I open my eyes, wondering if the girls have managed to fit into Brian's single bed. Brian's snoring loudly on his own. There's no sign of the girls, and I look at my watch to see what time it is. Or rather, I look at my naked wrist. That's weird, I don't remember taking my watch off last night. I start to get out from under the duvet, and remember the pissing incident. It's like when I was a tiny kid and I'd wet the bed. I'm all sticky and horrible. My gaze follows my jeans, which were on the chair when I got into bed before Brian and the girls arrived. Now they're strewn across my broken bed. And my bag is upside down, its contents spilled on the floor.

I lunge for my jeans, and check the left front pocket. Mummy's knife is still there. Thank heaven for that. My heartbeat slows as I feel in the back pockets of my jeans. My wallet's gone from one of them, and my credit cards are missing from the other. No matter, as long as they left the knife. They've taken the loose change and car keys. Car keys! I lean over Brian to look out of the window. There's lots of vomit on the tarmac below, but no bright red Peugeot 205 1.9 litre hatchback. They've nicked my car!

Poor Brian. There must have been at least three grams of brown heroin in that zip lock poly bag of his. Somehow I don't think it's there now. I go into the shower and revel in the hot, steamy soft Liverpudlian water. No cash, no cards, no drugs, and no car. The little tykes certainly did well out of us. What am I going to do? Walk into the police station and say
"Excuse me, Officer. My friend and I had sex with two fifteen year-old girls in our hotel room last night. We gave them marijuana and heroin, and now they seem to have stolen our drugs and money, and driven off in my car."

I smile to myself in the knowledge that they didn't steal Mummy's knife. That fact alone redeems them as far as I'm concerned. They didn't take the knife. I don't know why, considering they took my watch. It just adds to their mystery. The heroin's still in my system, and I feel calm and whoozy. As I'm cleaning my teeth there's a thumping at the door. I open it as little as possible, as I don't think the proprietor will be pleased with the way we've trashed the room. I want to be checked out and through the front door before they find my mattress. The amount of urine in there – they'd try to put me in the Guinness Book of Records as the world's worst bedwetting case. It would be apt, as Guinness was used to achieve it.
"Check out was at eleven o'clock, mate."
"Right. What's the time now?"
"Half past twelve."
"Sorry about that. What if we pay for another night?"
"The room's booked for tonight. The cleaners finish at one o'clock, and they need to get in there."
"Okay we'll be out as soon as we can."
I try to rouse Brian. This isn't good. I haven't got any money or cards, the bed's broken, and the mattress is full of piss. If I report my car

stolen, and the police catch Maxine and Melina, Brian and I could end up in prison.

Chapter Fifteen

As I carry my bags along the fourth floor corridor of the Adelphi Hotel, I make a guess that the en suite bathroom will be on the right. It is. And what's more, room 411 has got a big telly, and a view of Lime St. I drop my bags on the floor, and flop down on the bed. I really must start behaving myself. When I've finished this bag of coke (which Maxine and Melina didn't find), I'm giving up drugs. Except for marijuana, which doesn't count. Luckily Kev Knight came to the rescue with a cash loan. He and Colin were late checking out too, and dropped by just after I finally managed to wake Brian up. Brian's gone off "shopping", which obviously means trying to score some heroin somewhere in Liverpool, where he doesn't know anybody. I'm prepared to hear the worst on that.

I've reported my cards stolen, and thanks to having a Gold card, got a replacement card there and then from a bank. We managed a quick getaway from Feathers Hotel, thanks to Kev and Colin causing a diversion in reception by falsely reporting a broken toilet in their room. I left it a few hours before contacting the police about my car. Apparently so many cars get nicked in Liverpool, the police are treating it as very low priority, so there's little danger of the girls getting implicated.

I've got a few hours to relax before the gig, and it's worth the expense to do it in Liverpool's most famous hotel. The car aside, I reckon the girls took about three hundred quid with my wallet, and about twenty quid's worth of grass. I don't have to worry if they used my cards, because being Gold, I wouldn't have to pay. I've got fully comprehensive insurance on the car, so in a way I'm not that pissed off. They were so charming and entertaining, it was sort of worth it.

And what's more – I get a free newspaper with my room at the Adelphi. I pick it up from the bed, and unfold it. The front page headline sends an icy chill through my body. 'CANAL CORPSES

IDENTIFIED.' Beneath it are mug shots of Gregor McCain and Thomas 'Tam' Mackay. My heart beats faster as I read how Gregor and Tam were found dead in the Grand Union Canal near where it meets the River Thames at Brentford, West London. Their bodies were partially decomposed. I know what that means, in the case of someone who's only been in the water for a day. They were gnashed by eels. I read how Greg and Tam had both served time for armed robbery, GBH, and theft. Gregor also had convictions for drug dealing. Police are treating the case as murder, because one of the men had a badly broken arm, and the bodies were weighted down. If it hadn't been for the fact the canal was being dredged, they would still be in the mud at the bottom. Their cause of death was drowning.

I drop the newspaper and lie there with my eyes closed. I feel sick with sorrow. They weren't nice men, but to think they were living, breathing humans in Arnie's club on Thursday night. I was in their consciousness, and now they're mutilated corpses. Their eyes, noses, and genitals will probably have been swallowed by those shiny black writhing creatures. I knew Arnold Shanks was a bit dangerous, but this! I'm not sure I want to play his gigs anymore. I wonder if Charles was involved with their murder, or was it just Arnold and his unseen consorts. Death by drowning! That must have been horrible. Especially for Tam, as he'd have been in agony from his elbow being snapped the wrong way.

I had been feeling okay, but finding out that Arnold's a murderer has made me feel quite weary. I'm not in the mood for doing a second night at 'Stars'. I want to get out of Liverpool right now, and cuddle Sunita. I look at the cheap digital watch I bought to replace the Seconda I got in duty free at Hong Kong airport, and which those naughty girls stole from my wrist. There's no point phoning Sunita now, she'll still be rehearsing. I phone home anyway, and leave a rather maudlin message on the answer machine for when she gets home, telling her I won't be home tonight as planned. I'm too tired to work out how to set the alarm on my new watch, so I phone reception and ask for an alarm call at seven forty-five this evening, and fall immediately into deep, powerful, sleep.

I'm woken up by the phone ringing.

"Telephone call for you Mr Tucker." I'm a bit surprised, because I was expecting this to be my alarm call. Colin's voice comes on the line "Where are you mate? The show's meant to be starting in five minutes!"
"What's the time?"
"It's five to nine. Jeff is doing his nut."
"I'll be there straightaway. Hang on."
I slam the phone down, swearing loudly. I hate being rushed. What happened to my alarm call? On the way through the foyer I'm so angry I stop and ask a casual young Liverpudlian receptionist why I didn't get my alarm call. Despite the fact that I'm obviously in a hurry, she takes her time to look it up on a piece of paper.
"We haven't missed your alarm call. You're down for seven forty-five tomorrow morning." Her manner couldn't be more casual.
"I asked for it at seven forty-five *this evening*!" She doesn't care, and makes little effort to disguise it. As I push my way through sauntering Saturday night Liverpudlians, I curse and notice how much my attitude to the receptionist is governed by the fact that I don't find her attractive. If I fancied her, I'd excuse her offhand manner, and dwell on the rude things I'd like to do with her.

Luckily 'Stars' is five minutes walk from the Adelphi hotel, and the audience is still coming in when, out of breath and hot from running, I drop onto the dressing room's smelly sofa. I remember the used condom between the cushion and the arm, and move a foot to my left. Colin comes in from the toilet, which smells of yesterday's shit. "There's a line on the cistern for you, mate."
"Cheers." I go in and as I snort the white powder, I'm forced to inhale the stink of the shit that's still in the toilet bowl. I almost heave. Back in the dressing room, Jeff comes in and tells us the line up is the same as last night, but with the addition of a guest spot. A girl called Charlotte French is doing an unpaid ten minutes after the first interval. I'm glad she's all right, and wonder if she's heard about Gregor and Tam being murdered.

Jeff takes our orders for drinks, and returns a couple of minutes later with a tray full of pints. I swig long at my Guinness. I feel like getting pissed tonight. I don't have to drive. The Saturday night audience is more affable than Friday night's crowd. Broadly speaking, people work

Monday to Friday, so on Friday's they're tired and get pissed quicker. They're also more likely to be aggressive because of the stress they bring from work. On Saturdays, though, they're likely to have got up later, and had a more relaxing day. Being fresher, they're easier to play to. Colin just about gets away with it, although his material's a bit contrived for the Liverpudlian sensibility. A lot of tonight's audience is older than last night's, and they can see through his formulaic content. Several of his gags get groans.

By the end of the first interval Charlotte has failed to materialise, and I do ten minutes before putting Kev Knight on. Jeff is starting to wonder what's happened to Brian. The gig in Bolton that he and Kev did last night before coming here only happens on Fridays. They were expecting Brian earlier than this. I start to wonder if he's been mugged in some heroin deal on the wrong side of town.

Kev's a decent bloke, but I don't rate him as a comic. He seems to be doing okay with the crowd, who are going with his set pieces about the personalities who figure in the world of football. I don't know what he's talking about, and find myself sipping my third pint of Guinness in the corridor near the stage door. The dressing room bog smells too vile, despite being masked by ganja smoke where Colin's celebrating the fact that he didn't repeat last night's death.

One of the bouncers comes up to me. He's got a shaved head and a thick neck, and an ancient scar over his right eyebrow. His collar doesn't quite hide the tattoos on his throat.
"We've just had a Father at the front door, looking for you." My heart stops, and I find it difficult to speak because of my constricted throat.
"Oh?"
"Yeah, he delivered your car back, and says thanks."
"Yeah? That was all, was it?"
"Yeah. You're the first act we've had who lends his car to Priests, like."
"A Priest? I thought you meant someone's father..." I'm half expecting him to throw a punch at me; I've got such a guilty conscience. His closed fist moves slowly towards me, and opens to reveal my car keys.
"Thanks." I take the keys.

"Your car's out the back. We're keeping an eye on it for you. Oh yeah, the Father asked me to give you a message. He says the twins say thank you."

"Oh right. Cheers mate."

"I didn't know you did charity work, like."

"Well you know…" I really don't know what to say.

I walk back to the dressing room, trying not to look like I've done something I could get put in prison for. How much does the Priest know? Maybe he's the one who taught the girls all they know. No, that's a ridiculous notion. I ask Jeff if I can use his phone to inform the police my car had been borrowed by a friend, and take it off the stolen list. He says, yes, I should come to his office in the second interval. He's worried that Brian still hasn't turned up.

Kev gets a loud cheer at the end of his act. The football material served him well in Liverpool. I introduce the interval and refuse the offer of a fourth pint of Guinness. Now I've got the car back, I might drive home. I hope they haven't messed it up, or I'll have to explain it to Sunita. Jeff takes me to his pokey little office, and I ring the police. As we're walking back down to the dressing room I casually ask him when Charlotte's guest spot was arranged. It was done several weeks ago, and confirmed on Tuesday. I begin to wonder if the reason she hasn't turned up is because Arnold Shanks has disposed of her for knowing too much. I just want to get this show over and return to the Adelphi and sleep.

Back in the dressing room, Brian's just arrived; and he looks so awful it would be better if he hadn't. I manage a quick word with him and he tells me he tried to buy some smack but got ripped off. He's sweating and shaking, and actually tells me he doesn't have a problem. Apparently he's feeling hung over from all the beer last night, and a bit of skag would help him through it. He asks me for a line, and I give him my wrap of coke. When he returns from the toilet I check to see how much he's left me, and there isn't enough to get a hummingbird high.

I do ten minutes to an ebullient crowd, and introduce Brian. He's at least fifteen seconds late getting to the stage, and doesn't get one laugh.

The poor sod's in such a state that each time a line falls flat, he loses confidence and fluffs the delivery of the next gag. Soon he's forgetting vital words, so the audience don't hear a complete joke. After three minutes he announces
"Sorry about this, Ladies and Gentlemen, but I had some bad news today. There's been a bereavement in my..." and he shuffles off the stage. I take the mike out of his hand and look out into a room full of stunned silence. I'm not feeling too good myself, and after finishing off his explanation for him by saying something about his mother having died of cancer, go into a routine I did earlier in the evening. As the crowd like me, someone shouts out
"You've done that already." I stand there with my mind blank for what seems like a minute, before remembering my Jesus material. Oops, I'm in a Catholic city, and they don't really go for it, so I switch into car material, and pull them back. Five minutes later, thank God, we're in full swing again, and I do half an hour to a crowd who are sympathetic to my situation. I announce next week's bill, tell them the bar's open until three, and ask them to applaud all the acts we had tonight.

In the dressing room Jeff hands out brown envelopes full of cash. There's no sign of Brian, who's fucked off. I bet he's glad the producers of 'Bare in Mind' weren't here to see *that* performance. Unfortunately Brian didn't hear my story about his mother dying of cancer, as he was throwing up in the corridor. He told Jeff his father has been killed in a car accident, a story I didn't hear because I was on stage at the time.

Being a nightclub manager, Jeff doesn't let on about this, and listens to me lie to him about us getting the news this afternoon from Ireland, and how close Brian was to his mother. It's only after we leave that Colin tells me Jeff knew that I was lying, and let me carry on doing so. All I was doing was covering for Brian, and now I've made an arse of myself to Jeff, who refused to pay Brian for tonight's show. I look in my brown envelope to see if he paid me extra for doing Brian's gig, but he hasn't. He's probably pocketed the money himself.
"He should give it to Dynorod to unblock that dressing room toilet." Observes Colin, as we get in my car. It looks like the girls spared me slashed seats, and we drive it round to the Adelphi hotel car park. I'm

not risking leaving it outside for a second night. The Adelphi's car park is underneath the actual building, with an all night attendant. I've got to pay twelve quid to put it there, but at least it'll be safe. Colin can't afford the Adelphi, so he's staying in another little hotel nearby. I'm not going to play 'Stabs' again. It's too far to come for not enough money, and the venue's crap. It's outrageous that they only provide accommodation for the one night, because we have to check out of the hotel on the Saturday morning, and then wander the streets of Liverpool all day until the club opens. If you haven't got a car, you're stuck in Liverpool for the Saturday night, because the last train leaves for London in the early evening. I'm getting more corporate gigs like the one I did in Jersey on Wednesday, and don't need to do places like 'Stars' anymore.

Chapter Sixteen

Colin's finished off his coke, but he's still got some skunk left. He offers me a smoke, and I invite him up to my room. As we come out of the lift and walk along the corridor, a scrumptious, busty woman who looks about thirty, comes along towards us. She smiles, and for a second I think I'm supposed to know her.
"Good evening, Gentlemen. Are you looking for some fun tonight?" I'm not – I was planning to phone Sunita as soon as I get into the room. I've seen a few things in my time, but I've never been solicited in the corridor of a luxury hotel. Not in Western Europe, anyway.

"No thanks, we're fine. Thanks anyway." I reply.
"Speak for yourself." Colin addresses me, and studies the prostitute, who's now standing with us outside my room. She's got a red patent handbag with a shoulder strap, a red silk collarless blouse with that crumpled-on-purpose look, and a black mini skirt. Her un-stockinged white legs look most inviting above her shiny black boots, which match her jet-black hair.
"How much?" asks Colin.
"Fifty quid for straight sex - that includes oral. Or we can discuss the price if you want anal or …"
"The fifty quid package will do fine. I'm staying in the Sunnyside Bed and Breakfast just up the road."
"Sorry, love. It's here in the Adelphi or nothing."

Colin looks appealingly into my eyes. I don't want him having sex with a whore in my sheets, and as I inhale to tell him so, she offers to do both of us for eighty.
"I'm fine, thanks. I was just going to ring my girlfriend."
"Come on, Doug. I'd do the same for you."
I've never been with a prostitute, apart from once in Amsterdam when I was nineteen. I don't ever intend to go to one again.
"You can use my bathroom, if you're quiet."

Colin looks inquisitively at the girl, who, I have to admit, looks bloody inviting. There's something about the fact that I know I can have her if I want. All I've got to do is cough up the fifty quid. Or forty, if I go into partnership with Colin. I immediately dismiss the thought from my mind. Today I made a decision. No more drugs apart from marijuana, and definitely no more being unfaithful to my wonderful Sunita.

She looks at the number on my door, and answers
"I wouldn't normally, but I'll do you a favour. This room's got a sofa. We'll use that."
I wonder how many times she's had sex in my room, to remember it's got a sofa. Has she done it in every room in the hotel?
"I'll lie in the bed, with the light off if you like." I offer, as I unlock the door.
"We'll keep the lights on if you don't mind. I've got my safety to think about." She turns to Colin,
"Have you got the cash before we go in, Sweetie?"
As Colin stumps up fifty in cash, she turns to me and says
"I should charge you at least a tenner, for letting you watch."
"And I should charge him twenty for the use of my room." I reply.

She sticks the money down her boot, and smiles
"What's your name, Lover?"
"John." Colin replies.
"And this is Keith." I start to realise Colin's used to doing this. I don't know why he's bothering with the false name. He's not going to become famous with *his* act.
I turn the wall lamps on, and the ceiling lights off.
"I'm Rita, and I'll be out in a minute. I'll have a Bacardi and Coke thanks, seeing as you're askin'."

She goes into the bathroom, and I break the seal on the mini-bar.
"Cheers, Doug. I owe you one for this, and I'll see you're all right for the drinks. Are you *sure* you don't want to come in on this with me?"
"I'm sure, thanks, Colin." I say, handing him a beer, and taking one for myself.
"The first drink's on me. The second one you pay for."
"Are you going to phone your girlfriend, then?"

"I think I'll wait until you and she have finished. It might not go down too well if there's the sound of sexual intercourse going on in the background. She might think I'm at an orgy."
"Sexual intercourse *and* oral." Colin corrects me.
"Damn. I forgot to ask how long I get for me fifty hooters. You should always ask that before you hand over the money."
"Twenty minutes, Darling." Rita's voice comes through the bathroom door. She's got bloody good hearing.
"Or should I say *Colin*."
"So the false identities have been blown, then." Colin laughs. I want to use the bathroom, but I can't because Rita is still in there doing whatever she does before servicing a client.

I turn the telly on and lie back on the bed with my beer.
"Do you mind if I have the volume up, or will it put you off?"
"It depends what you're watching."
"I was planning to catch up on the news."
"That's okay, as long as there isn't an item about a man getting his cock severed. I don't want to come prematurely and waste thirty quid."

The door opens, and out comes Rita, looking exactly the same as when she went in. Colin excuses himself and goes in, locking the door behind him. Rita comes over and sits on my bed, sipping her Bacardi and Coke. From the way she's fluttering her false eyelashes, she's pretty intent on upping her wages from fifty to eighty quid.
"Do you mind if I smoke?" She asks, producing a packet of Silk Cut. I do, but I tell her I don't. That reminds me, the reason Colin came to my room was to smoke some weed.
"Where's your stuff, Colin, I mean John?" I call towards the bathroom. Colin replies that it's in his jacket pocket, and that I should help myself. Rita nods towards the bathroom door.
"Nerves. It happens to most of 'em. They need a plop before they can do it."
"I suppose it's better that they go before, rather than during."
She gives me a furtive look as I load Colin's dope pipe with strong skunk.
"That depends. If they go during, then I'm getting a lot more than fifty quid." She realises she's not putting the right pictures in my head to lure me into spending forty quid, and continues

"Or should I say eighty?"
She winks and wiggles her bosoms. The high-necked blouse shows no cleavage, but promises something marvellous beneath. I realise I'm looking forward to seeing what's in there when they come out.
"It's a shame you're not in on this. You're a very handsome man."
I light the pipe and politeness requires me to pass it to her. I'm a bit worried about sharing it with her, in case I catch herpes. She's got the lungs of a whale, and consumes the bowlful of skunk bud in three seconds. I reload it. She shouts coarsely to Colin in the bathroom.
"Hurry up, our kid, or you'll eat into my next time slot."
"Coming..." he replies. As the skunk rush is starting to hit me, the bathroom door opens, and out comes Colin, with an erection that makes the front part of his trousers resemble a tent.

Now the bathroom's free, I have no reason not to go in and relieve my bladder. Except I'm suddenly very stoned, and I want to see Rita's clothes come off.
"Go on then." Rita smiles and nods towards the bathroom.
"Pardon?"
"You need a piss. I can tell. When you've been in this job as long as me, Love, you know everything a man's thinking and feeling. I know you better than your girlfriend does." I go in the bathroom and struggle to point my penis down towards the toilet bowl. I don't know what's wrong with me at the moment. I had three orgasms last night. Normally that would put me out of action for a couple of days. And here I am with a penis that can't wait to get back in the room with that psychic witch-whore.

"Make sure you wash those hands!" Rita calls to me. And bring us a large towel, Dearie. This is a classy place, and we should make an effort to protect the sofa fabric. As I go in and throw her the towel, I notice she's very craftily waited for me before starting to undress. She's determined to get my business. Colin's on the sofa puffing away at the skunk pipe, and Rita's starting to undo her mini skirt. It slides down her lovely legs, and liberates the bottom of her blouse, which hangs low enough to conceal her knickers and upper thighs. I'm sitting on the bed, propped up by both pillows, to afford the best possible view of sofa and TV screen. Rita's shiny black hair and scarlet blouse set each other off brilliantly. Colin hands me the pipe and returns to the sofa, as Rita crosses her hands and peels the blouse off. Her black bra is brimming with bosoms, and her G-string shows that she shaves her fanny.

When the bra comes off two huge breasts tumble out. They're full and melon shaped almost to the ends, and unmistakably the real thing. No cosmetic surgery scars on bubbly Rita. She jumps up and down to make them bounce, and almost falls over because of the high heels on her black boots. A practiced flourish of her G-string, and the boots are all that she's wearing. She bends over Colin and dangles those fantastic tits in his face, before kneeling down in front of him, undoing his jeans, and pulling them down to his ankles.
"I don't see many like this."
"Thank you," says Colin, flattered.
"I wasn't talking about your Jake, Love. I meant I don't come across many jeans with a zip-up fly. Most of them are button-fly nowadays. Not easy when your finger nails are this long." She says this whilst her left hand squeezes Colin's shaft, and the right hand removes a condom and places it between her lips. Her head lowers, and as her mouth goes down over Colin's cock, it rolls the condom over it. His throat makes contented noises, as her mouth and right hand steadily increase the rhythm. Colin's eyes are closed, and as she jerks her head up and down, Rita winks at me.

From the way Colin's moaning, her expertise has nearly brought him to a climax. I notice that her spare hand has removed some KY gel from her handbag, and applied it to her vaginal lips. Suddenly she's on her feet and straddling Colin. She gets his willy in her vagina, and is jigging up and down with a steady stroke with seamless ease, especially as she's having to balance on stiletto heeled boots. Her tits look magnificent as they bounce up and down, and her face is beautiful. As I marvel at the splendid spectacle before me, and wonder if she does yoga to be able to move her hips up and down so fast, the TV screen shows the mug shots of Gregor and Tam, followed by shots of a man with a blanket over his head being hustled into a police van. Could they have arrested Arnold Shanks? My speculation is halted by the sound of Colin having such an intense orgasm, I wonder if he's about to cry.

115

Rita removes herself from Colin and the sofa, and whooshes off to the bathroom almost in the same movement. Colin's spread out helpless on the sofa, his bagged member limp across his thigh, a white bubble dangling at the end. There's the sound of running water in the basin, followed by the toilet flushing, and Rita returns aglow with vitality. She wafts past the still panting Colin and squeezes her huge tits together before removing a fan of ten-pound notes from my hand.

She undoes my fly, I pull my jeans and pants down, and her elegant, red finger-nailed hands milk me onto those fantastic bosoms. I'll swear she has magical powers. Before she takes her leave, she gives us both a big kiss on the forehead, and we half expect her to tuck us in and switch the lights out before she closes the door. We have another pipe of skunk, and when I try to phone Sunita I get the answering machine.

Chapter Seventeen

The next morning I awake from a refreshing sleep, and have an atrocious fried breakfast in the Adelphi's restaurant. I don't even consider the tough, salty looking bacon or gristle sausages, but even if I did eat meat I'd find them disgusting. The button mushrooms have been boiled and left in a pot full of scuzzy water, and the toast is burnt on one side, and raw on the other. The only decent things about the breakfast are the corn flakes, and a gorgeous young waitress who hardly speaks English. With her black tights, short skirt, and tight white blouse, I want to take her up to my room right now. Her blonde hair is tied with a ponytail that doubles back on itself, with a black velvet frilly hair tie thing. Any fears that I won't be able to service Sunita tonight are dispelled. Despite the excesses of the last couple of nights, I'm feeling horny as hell. I phone her up and she sounds like she's looking forward to spending the evening with me as I am with her.

Colin duly arrives in reception from his budget Bed and Breakfast, and we head east along the M62 towards the M6. Despite being a Sunday, the journey takes us seven hours, because every car in Britain is squeezed onto the motorways. Without generous pipes of Colin's skunk, I think I'd have given up and checked into a pub with accommodation and got pissed. I want to get home, but sitting in traffic jams on motorways is so tedious.

I ring home to inform Sunita of our lack of progress from Newport Pagnell services (I'm going down the M1 as it's more convenient for Colin when we get to London) and she tells me Arnold Shanks has phoned. Can I phone him back as soon as possible? Presumably it wasn't him I saw being arrested last night on the telly. My heart starts to beat faster as I dial his number. His wife answers the phone, and I surprise myself by suddenly remembering her name. She's called Sue, and she's Scottish too. I've met her socially at a couple of parties, and wondered if she had any idea she was surrounded by people who knew her husband is a compulsive adulterer. In fact, many of the girls within her peripheral vision had bonked him. Sue remembers me and is really polite. Arnold is having Sunday lunch at their local pub, would I like his mobile phone number?

Another fifty pence coin later I'm talking to Arnold.
"Listen, Dougie. Are you still with that shite agent?"
"Melissa? Yes."
"Well I'm not your agent, but I've got a part for you in a TV show. Are you free tomorrow?" If it's to be on telly, I'm free any moment of the day or night.
"I've got an appointment in the afternoon, but I could cancel it." The "appointment" is to go to the drop in STD clinic in St Thomas Hospital, and get myself checked up after my recent indiscretions.
"Never mind the appointment, Doug. Just get yourself to Teddington Studios fer ten o'clock in the morning. Tell 'em Arnie sent you."
"What's the money?"
"Two hundred quid cash for the morning. I'm giving it to you because you're tall. But don't bother te get that crap agent of yours involved. She'd fuck it up, and if they like you this could be your big break."
"This isn't porn is it Arnold?"
"Fuck nay! It's a bona fide programme for the telly. It's called 'Rats Milk Cheese' and if they like it they're going to make a whole series of them. I'm doin' you a huge favour here Pal."
"Thanks, Arnold, I'll be there."
It sounds dodgy to me, but being an aspiring telly star is like being a detective on a serial murder case. You follow up *every* lead!

As I walk back to the car, I notice a scratch on the nearside wing. Those naughty girls! Ah well, it's only a lump of metal. Sunday evenings are the worst time of the week for driving in or out of London. The people who live in London and are returning for Monday morning are driving in. As are the people who live outside London, but live and work there during the week. All the people who've visited for the weekend are driving out. It's worse than Fridays. There's only one way to avoid the problem. Don't live in or visit London. It's half past seven by the time I'm standing in the hall of my flat, cuddling my beautiful Sunita.

As I hold her to me, her black hair smells of coconut oil, and her fingers reach up and caress my neck so that goose bumps of pleasure break out. She takes my hand and leads me into the kitchen, where a bottle of white wine adorns the table. It's just come out of the fridge and is wet with condensation. Sunita tosses the corkscrew to me, and gets a pair of large stem glasses out of the cupboard. The flat's warm and homely. The wonderful thing about Sunita is that she's physically beautiful, has an easygoing personality, *and* does lots of housework. Ever since she moved in with me, the flat's been tidy and spotlessly clean. In addition to all this, she's a high-achiever. We sit opposite each other at the antique beech kitchen table I bought from a shop in Clapham. The walls are bright orange, and the draining board is clear. The only things that need to be washed up are the wine glasses in our hands, and we plan to be using them for a few minutes yet.
"How was your rehearsal yesterday, Beautiful?"
"Fine. We're all getting on really well together. I've got a table booked for half eight at the Imperial Tandoori."

I take my bag from where I dropped it on the floor in the hall when I walked into Sunita's arms, through to the bedroom. The duvet looks inviting on the futon, and the blue velvet curtains are homely. I have a quick bubble bath, and go into the lounge wearing my blue cotton towelling dressing gown. Sunita's lying on the sofa watching a holiday programme on telly. She's wearing faded blue jeans and a French stripy long-sleeved T-shirt. She looks so cuddly, I can't resist kneeling next to the sofa and resting my head on her tummy. She runs her fingers through my hair, and I hum deep in my throat with contentment.

I kiss her through the cotton stripy T shirt, and as my lips move down, they come to a strip of naked flesh where the T shirt has rode up away from her jeans. I kiss the light brown skin, and rub my unshaven face on it. She squeals a bit, and I pull her T-shirt up even more. I see black silky bra, and feel cloth of boxer shorts through the end of my penis as it gets too big for the confined quarters of my Levis. As I nibble her nipples through the shiny black bra, I discreetly glance at my watch. Yep, there's enough time for rumpty tumpty before the two-minute walk to the Imperial Tandoori.

I remember about the risks I took with the girls in Jersey four nights ago, and let the thought carry on out of my head. I'm just going to have to take a chance. Anyway, my cock's never been as healthy as it has been these last few days. I just can't seem to get enough sex.

One by one Sunita surrenders her nautical stripy T-shirt, bra, jeans, and knickers. I bury my face in that exquisite wet fanny. She's shaved around the bikini line, and she must have done her legs today because they're very smooth. What a fantastic woman I live with. She comes quicker than I do, most times. A few minutes later, she's happy, and I'm round the last bend and panting towards the finishing post.
"It's not safe to come inside me at the moment, Darling."

That's easier on my conscience. I pull out and hold my cock above her stomach. She immediately starts jerking it with her hand, and I spurt on her soft brown tummy. After a minute of slurping at her chocolate nipples, I leave her supine on the lush sofa cushions and return from the bathroom with a handful of toilet paper for her to mop my spunk up. Back in the bathroom I give myself a quick shower as I got quite sweaty, and as I swill hot water under my foreskin, I decide to have a vegetable korma with aubergine bhaji side dish and pilau rice. An Indian beer will go nicely with that.

In the bedroom I'm reminded that something struck me about the futon, or to be more specific, the duvet. That's it – it's been changed since Friday. She'd put clean bedding on the futon just before I got home from Jersey on Thursday. We both slept in it on Thursday night, and now she's changed it again since I left on Friday. As I get dressed I call out to her and ask if she spilled coffee on it or something, but she doesn't hear me because she's having a quick shower.

Chapter Eighteen

When I walk onto the floor of Studio 2 at Teddington Studios, I have a strong feeling that I'm fulfilling my destiny. The set is of an oriental palace, and it looks just like the TV studio in my dream a few nights ago. I was expecting 'Rats Milk Cheese' to be a shambles, because of the way in which I was recruited. TV shows are cast by a casting director, who selects a number of artistes from a publication called 'The Spotlight', and contacts their agents. The agents then contact the artistes, who go to an audition, which is usually in a casting suite in Soho. Sometimes one has to go to a pre-casting first, in which you visit the casting director at their office and have an informal interview. If they like the way you look and talk, they invite you to the audition.

After the audition one often has to go to a recall, which is a second audition for the final few people still being considered for the part. After that, you don't hear any more unless you've got the job. If you *are* the one they've chosen, your agent gets a call, and phones you with the good news.

I got this job without an audition, less than twenty-four hours beforehand, from a gangster having a Sunday lunchtime piss up. He refused to go through my agent. I was expecting this farce to extend to every other aspect of the production. Instead, I'm sitting on a comfy sofa in a luxurious 'green room' eating smoked salmon and avocado sandwiches. There's high quality coffee in large pastel coloured fashionable mugs, expensive German chocolate biscuits, and flapjack. I've already had freshly-squeezed orange juice, and a banana from the fruit bowl. And it's free. Sunita says success comes from the direction where we least expect it. Maybe she's right.

'Rats Milk Cheese' is a proper production with a full crew, and I've got four lines to say. It's a 'broadcast pilot' for the BBC, which means that if the network bosses like the show, they'll commission a whole series. When I read the script shortly after arriving this morning, I had the feeling of "This is brilliant, I wish *I'd* thought of it." The show is a sitcom, and when the main character has a dream, it's all acted out with the proper set. Today he dreams he's in an Arabian harem, hence the silk cushions, imitation marble bath, and ornate hangings. The set must have cost a fortune, not to mention the ten beautiful harem girls. I'm playing a European envoy who's being entertained by the sultan, who is really Rufus, the character having the fantasy. Arnold has wangled the part of the other envoy for himself. Neither of us mentions the murders of Gregor and Tam. The man arrested for it was named in the newspapers, and I've never heard of him.

They've got stunt men and an actor with one arm in our scene. One of the envoys gets a bit fresh with the sultan's favourite concubine, and an argument develops. We all draw our swords, and he cuts the arm off one of the envoys. The one armed actor, who's called Tom, has an artificial arm, which has been made especially for the show. The stuntman is going to hack it off with his razor sharp sword, and a reservoir of stage blood is going to squirt out of a pressurised chamber in the arm. The stuntman will have to aim his sword at exactly the right bit of Tom's false arm. Too low, and he'll miss the pressurised blood chamber. Too high, and he'll be cutting into his stump, which is just below the elbow.

The independent company making the show for the BBC is called Grange Films, and their looking after us doesn't quite stretch to providing we envoys with our own dressing rooms. Whilst they're setting the cameras up for our scene, we do a lot of sitting around in the green room, chatting. Arnold's more amenable than I've ever known him, and we end up talking to the stuntmen, and Tom. If the show goes to a series, his character will be one of the main ones.

By late morning, we're on the studio floor doing a camera rehearsal. The director seems pretty happy with the way Arnold and I are delivering our lines, and they decide to go for a take. I'm surprised they don't rehearse the stunt before the take, and presume that was all done earlier.

One of the harem girls keeps fluffing the one line she's got to say, and the director starts to get distraught. He knows he's got to get our scene done before lunch, or we might start asking to be paid for the afternoon as well. Since Margaret Thatcher deregulated the unions and stopped 'restrictive practices', Equity rules have gone out of the window. Even so, it's hard to get actors to work for a whole day when they're only being paid until lunchtime. As it is we should be on repeat fees instead of this worldwide buyout. Finally the girl gets her line right, and we get to the shot in which we say our lines. Arnold's lack of experience shows when he forgets his line, and we have to do it again. He gets it right next time, but he's shaking with nerves.

Now there's just the shot in which the sultan cuts Tom's arm off. Arnold and I are in the frame, so they need us to do our bit of action again. I'm having a great time – I feel I belong in this TV studio, and the fact that no live audience is present makes me feel more creative, because we're playing to cameras and not a mob of drunks. What's more, the camera will capture our performance for all time, whereas a comedy club audience has forgotten your name by the time they've driven out of the car park.

The floor manager shouts "Action" and we go again. We're well into the lunch break, and everyone's hungry. We all focus on getting everything right, and we do. The argument breaks out, we draw our swords, and the stuntman lunges towards Tom. There's a flash of steel, Tom's on his knees screaming, and red liquid squirts out of his arm. Arnie and I remember to stay in character until the floor manager shouts
"Cut", but the others come out of character and drop their swords. Except for Tom, who continues screaming most convincingly. This is just as well, because the stuntman must have missed the reservoir of blood in the arm. There's blood coming out all right, but not pumping like we were told it would.

I can't believe Tom's been given such a big part, because he's wasting energy writhing around on the floor like this. Maybe he's inexperienced too. Suddenly I'm shoved from behind, and a voice shouts
"Get out of the way!" I'm about to object when I realise it's the studio's medic, and he's kneeling next to Tom, whose screaming has subsided into sobs.

I'm the last person to realise. The stuntman's hacked off the wrong arm. He's standing on his own next to a monitor, looking very white indeed. Someone's picking Tom's arm up and packing it in ice. Arnold and I walk to the green room as the sound of an ambulance siren gets rapidly louder. A few minutes ago everyone was declaring how hungry they were, but nobody's paying any attention to the buffet lunch the caterers have just put out.

I've done very little telly. A bit of walk-on for The Bill and Casualty, which was useful because it gave me experience of filming. I had the main part in a TV commercial for a bank, which earned me four and a half thousand pounds for a day's work. Then I did an unpaid student film, which provided me with valuable experience of doing lots of dialogue in close-up. The biggest thing I've done is two short stand-up spots on a show called 'The Sauce Boat'. That was really exciting – I even got recognised on a train the day after the second appearance was broadcast.

Arnold and I have located our bags and coats, and we reckon the most helpful thing we can do is get away from the place and leave them to it. Arnold's looking deeply upset, which surprises me, as he's no stranger to violence.
"That's it for me." He says, wistfully.
"I know, it's sickening, isn't it. I've never seen anything so horrible in my life."
"I de nae mean the lad getting 'is arm chopped off. Ah mean acting. I was shittin' meself. I thought it would be like posing for a still camera, but it was the scariest ordeal of my lafe."

The siren starts up again, and gets steadily quieter as Tom is rushed to hospital. The poor sod! I'd chatted to him when I first arrived. He was quite uninhibited about showing his stump. I guessed he'd lost his arm in a motorbike accident, because he had long hair and was dressed like a biker before we changed into costume. I'd asked him, and he told me that he was born like it. He was really excited, because he'd always wanted to be an actor, and this was his first break. It must have been difficult enough with one arm, and now he hasn't got any.

Arnold offers me a lift, and as we stroll across the studio car park towards his Mercedes SL, a woman's voice stops us.
"Excuse me. You're Doug Tucker, aren't you?"
"Yes."
Nancy, the assistant floor manager has followed us. She's got long straight brown hair, and jeans and a shirt. She's still wearing her talkback headphones, and looks gorgeous. I was fancying her like mad earlier.
"Simon the director would like to speak to you. If you're not rushing off."
The only thing I'd planned to do this afternoon was go to the VD clinic for a test.
"No, I'm fine." Arnold pats me on the back.
"You carry on mate. I'll see you soon, okay?" Arnold gives me the most pleasant smile I've seen him give anyone.

I stroll back across the car park towards the scenery dock with Nancy.
"That was terrible. I feel so sorry for Tom."
"It's a disaster. The production budget's nearly used up. We've got to get these scenes shot today."
"Have you been filming long?" I ask.
"This is our first day. But we've got a very tight schedule. Luckily we'd only done one quick scene with Tom before this happened."

We walk through the scenery dock onto the studio floor. A couple of stagehands are mopping Tom's blood and a pool of sick off the harem floor. Simon the director is standing in the middle of a huddle of production staff. Nancy alerts him to our presence.
"Doug. Thanks for staying. We liked the way you delivered those lines this morning. Have you met Sheila Fox? She's our producer."
I shake the hand of a woman in her forties. She's got dyed black hair, and cold eyes. She makes an attempt to smile, and looks even more bitter than before.

We're all walking towards a production office off the corridor that runs alongside the sound stage. Simon and Sheila offer me a seat on a semi-comfortable chair. I find it hard to concentrate on what Simon's saying, because of what I see on the desk. There's a cardboard model of a studio set, which was obviously made by the designer. The model

is of a church, with stained glass windows, and gold statues of saints. This is uncannily close to the dream I had on Friday night. I recover concentration in time to hear
"… is going to be in hospital for a while. We don't have time to recast. Would you like his part?"
I look at the smiling face of Simon, and the smile-that-is-a-grimace of Sheila. They're waiting for me to reply.
"Yes. I'd love to. Um…" I'm not sure what else I should be saying. I can't believe that I'm being offered a major part in a telly programme.

Sheila wafts a clipboard under my nose, and puts a pen in my hand.
"It's the same deal Tom was on. This only being a pilot, we're on a very tight budget, I'm afraid. We need you to sign before we can send you into make-up."
"Would it be possible to fax the contract to my agent?"
"We don't have time for that. If you don't want to do it, there are several other guys here who'll fit the costume. Including Terry here." She gestures to a young guy sitting at another desk. I saw him earlier. He's nearly as tall as me, wearing black jeans and a black T-shirt.
"Terry's our second choice." Adds the director. I sign both copies of the contract, and shake hands with Sheila and Simon. As Nancy leads me into make-up, Esmeralda the costume designer follows us, asking if I know my measurements. This morning I was wearing a one-size-fits-all robe. This afternoon I'll be wearing a proper costume. They've already washed Tom's blood out of it, and a wardrobe assistant is ironing it dry.

The horror of what happened to Tom is still bubbling away in the pit of my stomach, but it's rapidly being replaced by a thrilling warmth as I realise I've got myself a major acting role, and I'm due on set as soon as possible. Luckily most of this afternoon's scenes are action rather than dialogue, and as I didn't smoke lots of dope last night, it's not difficult learning the few short speeches I have.

It's all a bit unclear, but my character is called Boris, and I seem to be the main character's best friend. Either that or I'm her boyfriend, because there's a line where she refers to me as her pet. Des Jensen, an actor who's never done stand-up before, but has done quite a lot on telly, is playing the role of Rufus. He's the brother of the main character, who's called Lois. Half way through the afternoon Leah Phillips, the actress who plays Lois, the main character, arrives on set. She's famous, having been in another sitcom and a couple of British films. One of the films was a big hit in America. We're not introduced, because I'm sitting on a harem sofa whilst they light the shot. Our eyes meet briefly, but she doesn't smile at me. I don't blame her, considering the circumstances of my getting the job. Leah is shorter than I thought she'd be. She couldn't be better looking if you designed her with a computer. She's got long blonde hair, a perfect face, and (you've guessed it) big tits.

In classic sitcom tradition, the three of us live together in a house in a South West London suburb. The big comic pay off at the end of the episode is when, in his dream, Rufus finds the harem girl he's been given is Lois, his sister. I don't care if it's shit or not. I just want it to be made into a series, and to make me rich and famous. Leah's wearing black boots, blue jeans and a black leather jacket. She carries herself like a famous person whose drop-dead gorgeous. There's some indefinable "don't come near me" status around her. After a while of watching what's going on she removes her black leather jacket to reveal a baggy black jumper, which does nothing to stop the size of her bosoms becoming even more obvious. What a woman! If I was ever going to clone a human being, she'd be the one. Her, and Sunita, of course.

We finish all but one of my scenes, and I discover I've now got my own dressing room. It's even got my name on the door. It's not a star dressing room, just a small room overlooking the car park, with a single bed, an armchair, and a washbasin. There's also a TV and an open wardrobe. It's just like a small hotel room, except the bed doesn't have sheets and blankets on it. Just a bedspread, as it's a day bed. When I turn the telly on I have the option of watching what's happening down on the studio floor. I lie on the bed for a while, open the fridge, and help myself to a can of coke.

When I look at my TV I see that Lois is in her harem girl costume, and I go down to the studio floor to get a closer look. I'm standing around with a coffee in my hand, when between takes Simon the director introduces me to her. Her apparent lack of interest makes her all the more attractive. It doesn't matter how cold she tries to be, though. When we shake hands, her little hand feels hot, and it's the heat of her hand that I take away with me, not the coldness of her manner. As I go to wardrobe to change into another costume, it strikes me that because of the veil covering the lower half of her face, I didn't see whether she gave me a smile or not. I just assumed she didn't.

I'm wrapped at five, and Nancy the assistant floor manager tells me my call time for the next day is eight in the morning. What time do I want the car to pick me up? I tell her I guess at that time it could take as much as an hour and a half to drive from Lambeth Walk to Teddington.
"I'd get here quicker if I just caught a train from Waterloo."
"Okay, we'll do that, then. Your car home is waiting. See you tomorrow, and thanks for helping us out. Oh, by the way. The costume fits all right does it?" I'm not quite sure which costume she means, but as all of them did fit, I answer in the affirmative. This is fantastic! Outside is a brand new Mercedes saloon, with a driver in a white collar and dark suit. And *they're* thanking *me* for doing the job.

As the security barrier lifts to let us drive out of the studio car park, I wonder if I've just talked myself out of a good opportunity, getting driven to Teddington by Mercedes rather than having to get the train. I mentally kick myself for being so amenable. By the time the large Mercedes has made its way through the evening traffic to Lambeth Walk, it's six-thirty. I have to leave immediately to drive to Leamington Spa, where I'm performing tonight. I wish I didn't have to, because I'm not getting paid. It's a benefit for the children's home I lived at for much of my childhood. There are two messages from Melissa my agent on the answer machine. What am I going to say? I could tell her, and pay her fifteen per cent of my earnings from 'Rats Milk Cheese', or I could not pay her anything, which will almost certainly result in her dumping me. Or I could just leave her right now. I don't see why I should pay her fifteen percent of a fee she didn't get me. Which makes me wonder if Arnold Shanks is going to expect any commission, considering he got me the job.

I don't have time to ring her now anyway, so I'll just have a think about it. I grab the bits of paper with my latest jokes written down, wash my face and clean my teeth, and get into my car to head back into the rush hour. I would be feeling tired, but for the excitement of the day's events.

Chapter Nineteen

Luckily the traffic isn't too bad, and I make it to the Campion Grange Children's Home with half an hour to spare before I'm due to perform. I hate coming here. I hated it when I was a miserable little orphan, and I hate it when I return once a year to give them a free show.

As soon as I near Leamington Spa a melancholy descends over me like a prickly black blanket weighted with lead. The home is a former vicarage on the outskirts of the town. I'd like its Victorian neo gothic design, if it weren't for the memories. I turn into the driveway, and a sick foreboding settles in my viscera. The only redeeming factor is that I'm at the wheel of my own car, and I'm free to drive out again.

The number of times I've been driven through those gates and up to the front doors against my will, my vision clouded with tears, desperate for a cuddle. I spent most of my childhood unloved, with nobody. Whatever might befall me in the future, I'm secure in the certainty that I won't be as bitterly unhappy as I was during childhood. I close the door of my car, and my feet crunch across the gravel towards the building where most of that misery occurred.

I stand in the porch waiting for the front doors to open, revelling in the thought that I'm tall enough to operate the door handles. The hours I spent in the hall just the other side of these doors, wishing I was big enough to open them and run away. Then when I *was* big enough to reach the handles, I ran away in every direction possible at least once. I've hidden in orchards, next-door gardens, alleys, even in the boot of an abandoned car. And here I am, coming back to the prison on my own two fully-grown feet.

The familiar smell of the porch strikes fear into my soul. An unknown woman answers the door, and I follow her through the hall, the floor polish smell of which is almost enough to start me crying and running for my car.

"I'm Patsy. I've heard so much about you. It's very kind of you to come and help us in this way."

I follow her into Norman's office. He looks more than a year older than last time I came. I wonder if it's the same tweed jacket he wore when I lived here. It must have worn out. Maybe he bought ten of them originally, so he can keep wearing exactly the same sort of tweed jacket for twenty-five years.

He shakes my hand, and offers me a cup of tea. Patsy goes off to make it for me. I sit down facing him at his desk, as he lights his pipe. I look down at the original Victorian floor tiles. The one in the corner beneath his parrot cage is cracked. It was cracked before I came here when I was five. I used to look at it when I was called into Norman's office for our talks. It was somewhere to fix my gaze, so I could avoid looking near his face. In those days I never looked at anyone's face. How could I, when my sense of self was shattered into fragments? I closed my eyes, or I looked at the floor, or at the pictures in yachting magazines. I couldn't look at another person's face, because I had no face to offer them in return.

Norman's a thoroughly good man, and he asks me questions about my work, Sunita, and the famous comedians he enjoys on telly. He's as genuinely interested in me now as he was in the frightened little boy who was delivered to him on that cold wet Winter morning all those years ago. It wasn't his fault the new orphan was too damaged for his love to help. It wasn't anyone's fault. It was just the way the world is.

I was found in the doorway of the Leamington Spa Municipal Mortuary, late one Saturday night in January 1970. I was a few hours old, and Mummy left me there expecting me to die. She probably thought she was saving someone the trouble of taking me to the place where I was going to be stored anyway. If she'd wanted me to live, she'd have left me somewhere that wasn't closed until the Monday morning.

By pure chance, somebody else had the idea of depositing a body conveniently next to the mortuary, only in this case it was the person who was going to be dead. An alcoholic accountant, whose wife had left him, decided to kill himself on the front steps of the mortuary. In Leamington, it's down a dead end lane in a quiet part of town. He got there armed with a shotgun and a flask of whisky, and was about to end his life, when he found himself with the chance to save a new one.

He staggered back up the lane with me in his arms, a flask of whisky in his pocket, and a shotgun over his shoulder. When he got to where the lane joined a busier road, he flagged down a passing police car, and my future on this planet was assured. The accountant was charged with possession of an un-licensed firearm, but before the case came to court, he hanged himself.

My television career began and ended the next day. I was in the local news programme, shown in an incubator beside some nurses, who'd decided to call me Douglas. After I'd resided in the care of the council for a few weeks, my seventeen year-old mother came forward to claim me. It was decided to let her keep me, as she'd moved back in with her parents, who became my official guardians.

My mother was a wild child, and nobody knew who my father was. Apparently I was conceived in Felixstowe, and he was a sailor. Perhaps that's why I've been fascinated with the sea for as long as I can remember. That and the fact that I grew up in Leamington Spa, which is as far as you can get from the sea within the British Isles.

Anyway, when I was four, I walked into the bathroom to ask for my bedtime story, and found Mummy in a bath full of red water. The pruning knife she slashed her wrists with is now my most treasured possession. She was an only child, and the social services had allowed her to care for me on condition at least one of her parents was in the house with us. Mummy had been stable for over a year, and my grand parents thought it would be okay to go off for the weekend, leaving us alone in the house. I don't know what went on in Mummy's mind. Nobody did, including her. Sometimes she decided life wasn't worth living, and she got in a bath one Saturday evening, and slashed her wrists with a German pruning knife.

A few years later, I inherited the knife along with the substantial Georgian terraced house. The annoying thing is, that house would be worth a fortune now. But the idiots who worked for the council sold it shortly after my Grandparents' death, and put the money in a trust fund. Continued lousy management by council employees ensured that my inheritance dwindled to a couple of thousand pounds by the time I was eighteen. A few years ago I found out that the house had been sold below its market value, and bought by a relative of the council employee who organised its sale.

After Mummy's death my grandparents weren't deemed responsible enough to care for me, and I began several years of drifting from institution to euphemistically named institution. Whether they were labelled orphanage, care home, residential school, or hostel, they didn't provide the love and affection for which I was desperate.

The house was too big to conceal, but I managed to hide the pruning knife, with its curved blade and wooden handle. It was very easy. I buried it close to Mummy's grave. After her death my grandparents abandoned me to my fate, and I only saw them around Christmas. They both died within weeks of each other, and their ashes were buried next to my mothers. I had a good excuse to go there and check my knife was still safe. When I was old enough to have a knife, I rescued it from its dank, earthy hiding place. I'd wrapped it in oily rags, and was able to rid it of the superficial rust.

Patsy comes in with a mug of tea, and a plate of bourbon biscuits. She reminds us of the time, and that the show's due to start in a few minutes. A little black boy wanders in through the open door, wanting to see Norman's parrot. Norman introduces him to me, and he looks into my eyes with a defiant steady gaze. I don't know what to say or do. I'm more afraid of children than I am of violence. My lifestyle never puts me in contact with kids, and as soon as anyone I know has a baby, I stop seeing them. Certainly with the baby, anyway.

I know it's not rational, but if I find myself on a tube with someone who's got young kids, I have to discreetly change to another carriage. Babies, and any kid below pub age make me deeply depressed. Over thirteens aren't so bad, but young kids bring a feeling of doom over me, which nothing can cure. It's the vulnerability. No matter how doting a mother is with her baby in its buggy, she could be killed and

133

that baby would be alone and hungry. When I look at them I have to fight off a panic that years of sorrow and hurt could be waiting to slowly torture that little gurgling face. I really am genuinely afraid of that baby. If the mother were to pick it up and hold it towards me, I'd scream and run away crying.

The worst thing is when I'm watching telly and they show news footage of starving kids. I have to change channel, even if it means a few minutes of football. The younger the kid, the greater my fear. The sadness and pain are too much. I can't stand it.

I don't bother with the mug of tea or biscuits. I stand up, and try to cover my retreat by picking the plate of bourbons up and offering one to the kid. My cover is blown when he looks from the plate to my face, and asks
"Why's your hand shaking?"
I put the plate back on Norman's desk, pick my bag up, and gruffly announce
"Let's go."

We crunch across the gravel of the driveway, onto the pavement of Campion Road. The Campion Grange Children's Home is next door to the Campion Hotel, in whose function room the charity event is taking place. It's a family-run hotel, used mostly by travelling salesmen, and the increasing number of foreign tourists attracted to Leamington's well-kept Regency architecture. The local Round Table meets here, and tonight a hundred and fifty local businessmen, their wives and neighbours, are gathered for an evening of traditional food and entertainment. Leamington's premier amateur dramatic society puts on an old style music hall show, and the London comedy circuit's Doug Tucker tops the bill.

We walk across the plushly carpeted foyer towards the reception desk, and the sound of laughter fills our ears. The well-oiled crowd are enjoying a saucy song, sung by three housewives done up as Moulin Rouge can-can dancers. The double doors to the function room are like French windows, with lots of panes of glass in them. Everyone's having fun, and the event looks like as usual, it's been well organised. I would go straight to the adjoining dining room, which serves as a

communal dressing room. But I delay that, because I want to linger and talk to the receptionist.
Norman offers to get me a drink from the bar. I request Guinness, and ask the receptionist what she'd like. She replies in a thick Brummy accent that she's not allowed to drink on duty, and anyway she isn't eighteen yet. I presume she's here on work experience. I think she's rather shy, and would like me to leave her alone. She's very beautiful, though. I reckon she's about three-quarters white, and a quarter black. I want to know her. She's wearing a long-sleeved black velvet dress, and her hair is long with wet-look curls. I want to see the wardrobe where she keeps the dress, and the drawers where she keeps her underwear. I expect her bedroom furniture is cheap mass-produced chipboard, with white plastic veneer. I yearn to see her duvet cover, and her pillows, and to wake up in her bed, with her standing there in a towelling dressing gown proffering a mug of hot sweet tea.
"You're on in half an hour, Doug. We're running a bit late, I'm afraid. Would you mind announcing the raffle, as well?"
I shake hands with the bloke from the Jefferson Players, who organises this every year, and whose name I can never remember. Norman gives me my pint, and I follow the bloke towards the communal dressing room, feeling sad that I'll never know what that receptionist's bedside lamp is like, or touch its switch.

The high-ceilinged, plush dining room is buzzing with excited activity as only the dressing room of an amateur theatrical group can. The tables have been arranged around the edge of the room, to serve as dressing tables for twenty odd housewives, secretaries, computer programmers, and estate agents to live out their dreams of being stars.

I sit there with my pint of Guinness trying to conceal the fact that I'm revelling in the sight of the women's bare backs and shoulders. It's not that easy, because they're in front of mirrors, which can betray the fact that I'm looking at them. A couple of teenaged girls are changing out of their can-can gear into Edwardian dresses with bustles, and I can hardly contain my interest. With the classical décor and burgundy velvet curtains, I could almost be in a nineteenth century brothel in Paris or Dodge City. Now *there's* an idea for a porn film – cowboys and showgirls in a Western saloon.

I remove the bit of paper with my set list written on it from my pocket, and sit on a lone dining chair pretending to study it. All the time I'm watching those teenaged girls as they struggle into their Edwardian dresses. I want to lick every inch of exposed skin.

A woman in her forties who's in charge of make-up offers to do my face
"So it doesn't look shiny under the lights." I smile inwardly to myself, as the stage lighting consists of a few spotlights people buy for their front rooms in the electrical department of Debenhams. I accept her offer, though, because my need to be pampered will always be far greater than any woman's ability to pamper.

I sit in her make-up chair, and close my eyes. I love being made up, and as her soft brush applies powder to my face I relish the thought that I'll be getting this treatment on a regular basis during the next few days at Teddington Studios. The only hitch is when she accidentally knocks my half-consumed pint of Guinness over, and ruins most of her stockpile of lipsticks, eyeliner, mascara, and rouge.

I have to say that when I go on I'm absolutely brilliant. Maybe it's the excitement of the day's events at Teddington, or perhaps the joy of not being a poor little orphan boy anymore. I work the room well at the start, and local references flood effortlessly back into my head. An audience always appreciates a local reference. I suppose there's a generosity of spirit as well, because they know I'm the Campion Grange children's home's big success story, and am doing the show for free.

I do a ten-minute encore, and the crowd want me to do a second one. The bloke who runs the event is gushing at me afterwards, and I still can't remember his name. I take the bull by the horns and use a little technique I've come up with for finding out someone's name when I've forgotten it.
"Remind me how you spell your name."
"T. I. M. Tim." He replies.
"Thank you." I say. I'm wondering whether to say that I wasn't sure if he used the French way of spelling it with an "H", when we're interrupted by one of the teenaged girls wearing a bright orange silky

dress. She draws me away from Tim, and further embarrassment is avoided. I spend a glorious few minutes playing the showbiz star to the aspiring teenaged actresses, before they're plucked away by the musical director, in preparation for their final song.

An hour later, I've watched the pretty girls sing their songs, spent a few minutes chatting with Norman, and said my goodbyes. The feeling of relief when I got back through the hall and out of the front door is even greater than last time. I can imagine no misery greater than that I experienced as a child. Luckily by the time I left, all the kids were in bed, and I didn't have to face my phobia.

As soon as I'm out of Leamington, I fire up a neat grass doob, and put some Led Zeppelin on the car stereo. I haven't heard them for ages, and I think I want to hear them now because it reminds me of the time I reached adolescence, and with it the freedom of adulthood.

As I burn down the motorway, I realise I'm hungry, and stop at a service station. Mooching around the sandwiches and other ready-to-eat food, I remember the delicious food at Teddington Studios. At the moment I depend on the crap food they sell at filling stations late at night. That's one thing I wouldn't miss about doing the comedy circuit – the nasty sandwiches, and the pathetic little pasties from the cold shelf. If my TV career takes off, it'll be Teddington Studios catering for me!

I use the payphone to tell Sunita I'm on my way home. I get the answer machine. She must have gone to sleep early. She's pretty full on with those rehearsals, which is okay because as usual, I'm busy. I must find out when Sunita's play finishes, so I can take her on a holiday somewhere tropical

When the Led Zeppelin tape's over, I listen to the news. Some Scottish bloke's been charged with the murder of Tam and Gregor. I wonder if Arnold Shanks is implicated. Maybe that was why he was so nervous at the studios today. I'll give him a ring tomorrow to thank him for getting me the job on 'Rats Milk Cheese'. I'd like to find out how Charlotte French is, too. I meant to get her number off Gerry Crook, today, but events at Teddington took over.

I get home at one in the morning, to find the flat in darkness. I'm exhausted and have to be up in the morning for my first full day as a cast member of 'Rats Milk Cheese', so I decide to go straight to bed. After I've cleaned my teeth, I get undressed in the lounge so as not to disturb Sunita, and quietly slip into the bedroom without switching the light on. As I get beneath the duvet cover something strikes me as not quite right. I've got into bed like this many times, so as not to wake Sunita up, but the futon feels cold. I feel next to me, and she isn't there. All my hand touches, apart from duvet cover, is a piece of paper. I switch the bedside light on, which is a fashionable expensive one I bought for her last birthday, and read the note she's left me.

"Doug,

I'm pregnant. I'm really sorry, but I'm staying the night at Linda's because I don't know what to do.

Lots of Love,

Sunita."

That's really strange, because she usually signs her letters "All My Love". I try to phone her friend Linda, but there's no reply and no answer machine. I lay awake for a while, trying to figure it out. She's always been so understanding about my fear of babies and young children. She must be really scared of my reaction to the news.

Chapter Twenty

The next morning, as I walk past the scene dock at Teddington Studios, I bump into Nancy the Assistant Floor Manager, or AFM in tellyspeak. She smiles warmly and says "You're early, Doug." I tell her I wanted to make sure I got there on time by leaving the house at 7.30. This was just as well, because the trains were delayed out of Waterloo, and my journey took twenty minutes longer than it was supposed to. I was so sleepy when I left the flat, I forgot to bring Sunita's friend Linda's phone number with me.
"Simon's around somewhere. You're on camera at ten. I think he'd like to hear your bark before you go on the studio floor."

I give a polite little laugh, and carry on towards my dressing room, wondering what she meant when she said the director wanted to hear my bark. I'm further confused when I get in my dressing room, to find a large furry blue costume hanging on the costume rail. Before I've got a chance to phone production services to check I'm in the correct dressing room, there's a knock on the door. It's Simon the director, with a copy of the script in his hand.
"Have you read the script, Doug?"
I notice a yellow sheaf of A4 paper kept together with a metal binding, on the unit in front of the mirror.
"Um, actually, I've just arrived. My call time wasn't until…"
"Don't worry, you're not late. I just wanted to see you in your Boris costume, and check what your bark is like. I'll call someone from wardrobe to help you into it."
"That costume's mine, then?"
"Yes. Isn't it brilliant. It's made from fabric especially imported from America. Your measurements are almost exactly the same as Tom's, so it should fit perfectly."
"I'm sorry, I'm a bit confused." I say.
"I thought I was playing Boris, Rufus's brother in law."
"Oh, I see. You've only seen yesterday's script. Boris is Rufus's brother-in-law *in the dream*. Ordinarily Boris is their pet dog. It's a

great part. Look at the head you're going to wear. The eyes blink, and the jaw opens and closes. The dog is a very prominent character."
"So normally I'm in the dog costume. I was only human during the dream."
"That's right. Rufus is Lois' brother. You're her dog, and Rufus is jealous of the bond you both share. It's important that when you play Boris as a human, he retains the same movement characteristics as Boris when he's a dog."
"And how do I see?"
"You can't I'm afraid. Except when you've got your mouth open, when you can see a bit. You'll just have to learn to judge things, and move as if you can see through these eyes up here. I'd demonstrate it to you, but I put it on once and it smelled of Tom's sweat."

I'm about to walk out, when there's a knock on the door, and Simon opens it to reveal a pretty teenaged girl who'd normally have caused me to miss a heartbeat. But right now I've got things on my mind.
"Angela. This is Doug Tucker, who you'll be dressing. Doug, this is Angela, your dresser. If you could get into costume as soon as possible, we'll get you down on the floor and see what you can do. Then later we'll do some pick-ups of you as a human, during Rufus' dream. If you want a coffee, just ring production services, and they'll bring some up."

With that, Simon disappears, leaving me with the lovely Angela. She's quite small, and looks like she should be in school. Her blonde hair has pink strands in it, and her elfin face smiles with an apologetic air, revealing perfect white teeth. She's quite thin, and her white legs are adolescently scrawny. Apart from her white trainers, everything she wears is black. Short skirt, vest type thing revealing very small tits. Her shoulders and armpits look really sexy. She strikes me as having much less self-confidence than her gorgeous looks merit. Her soft voice breaks the silence.
"This is my first morning. Do you know how to put the costume on?"
"I haven't a clue. I didn't even know I was wearing it until he just told me." I gesture towards the door through which Simon just left.
"You're a bit taller than me. If you could get it down from the costume rail, we could try to get you in it."

If it wasn't for the aura of gentle calmness that glows around Angela's petite frame, I'd be marching back through reception and on the way to Teddington Station. My first morning in television, and already a devastating disappointment.

As Angela and I try to work out how I'm supposed to get into the dog's body with all the padding on, and how the head fits over my head, she tells me she's here doing unpaid work experience. She thought she was going to be assisting the wardrobe supervisor, and just got told she was Boris the dog's dresser. She's sixteen, innocent, and divine.

My paws have mechanisms very similar to bicycle break levers in them, with wire cables leading up inside the arms to the head. When I've got the costume on, I can blink the eyes by squeezing the lever in my left paw, and open my mouth by squeezing the lever in my right paw.
"You're fantastic! Have a look in the mirror." I feel Angela's hands through the foam body padding as she gently turns me towards the mirror. All I can see is the inside of the mask. Bits of loose fabric, some netting. My back teeth. I squeeze the right hand brake lever, and catch the first glimpse of my new incarnation. Instinctively I blink the eyes, and a squeal rises from Angela's throat. Encouraged, I move my head from side to side, and growl with the mouth closed. Angela lets out a short scream.
"You're scary." I'm nearly scaring myself. The Alsation head increases my height from six foot three to nearly seven feet. I look like a huge wolf, except my fur is the brightest blue. When I turn to Angela and open the mouth very slightly, I notice that as she talks to me, she's looking at my dog eyes, and not into the mouth, which is where she knows my real eyes are. The mask has already worked its power.

There's another knock at the door. I don't know who it is, but Angela must have opened it, because another feminine voice makes joyful sounds. I feel hands gripping my wrists, and when I open my mouth - or should I say Boris's mouth – I look into the face of Esmeralda, the wardrobe supervisor.
"Not bad eh? It's a perfect fit."

I ask her how Tom was going to operate the mouth, as he only had the one hand, and she replies that originally both cables were fed into the one paw.

"It wouldn't have been ideal, but the company got an EU grant for employing a disabled person. Now they've got the money, their lawyers say they have the right to use an able-bodied person to wear the costume. On the grounds that it cost £10,000. I doubt if they could find another disabled person who could do the necessary movement required for the part, and fit the costume exactly. If we tried altering its size now, we'd have to start from scratch and make a new one."

It's as if I'm being taken over by another power. Every time I get a glimpse of myself in the mirror, I automatically begin striking postures, and moving with a doggy energy.
"I hope it's not too unpleasant in the head. I fumigated it with incense to try to freshen it up for you. Tom got very sweaty during rehearsals."
I register that indeed it does smell of jasmine in here. There's also the odd twinge of stale sweat, but already my face is perspiring, and I feel the dog to be my territory. All disappointment with the fact that I'm stuck in a costume has evaporated in the excitement of this new experience. I've literally stepped into a new self.
"Let's get you down into the studio, then. I'll give you're a fur a brush when we're down there."
As Angela leads me along the corridor, I close Boris's mouth and am amazed at how easy it is to walk blind. The head and fur serve as a huge cushion, and I know that if I bump into anything, it won't be me who gets damaged. I feel strong and powerful, and despite the fact that the fur-covered head muffles sound, I hear the reactions I'm provoking in passers by, and they're all sensational.

I feel total trust in Angela as she leads me, and know I'm on the studio floor partly because she whispers that I have to step over some electric cables, and partly because I'm greeted with cheering and applause from the crew.

I go for a deep woof type bark, and it gets a definite thumbs up. I'm aware of someone cuddling me, and when I open Boris's mouth, I'm thrilled to see Leah Philips, who plays Lois, beaming away as if I've just been given to her as a present. Which in a way, I have, because Esmeralda the wardrobe supervisor attaches a dogs collar to my neck, and gives the other end of the lead to Leah. I've even got my own basket near the sofa.

Simon starts us on a script that's been rewritten since it was last printed and distributed to the cast, which is just as well because I haven't had time to read the first one they gave me. My part consists of lying in my basket, and barking and running to the front door when the doorbell rings. We do a few takes, and move on to the next scene, which involves Leah laying on the sofa, and me going over to her to be petted. After a while, she lets me get on the sofa with her, and she strokes me. It's fantastic, because despite the body padding I'm wearing beneath the costume, I can feel her hands patting and stroking me.

Everyone's thrilled with what we shoot, although it's disconcerting when Angela takes my head off for a coffee break, and Leah behaves rather coolly towards me. Maybe she's just a very good actress, and when she's petting Boris, it really is Boris and not me she loves. It's just that it's Doug Tucker who feels the stroking. When I watch the scenes back on the monitor, I'm amazed at how wonderful Boris looks. He really does look like a huge dog or wolf, and the brilliant blue fur looks even better on screen than it does in the flesh. The set has been designed with the blue dog in mind, so I compliment the colour scheme of the lounge and its three-piece suite. Even the clothes that Lois wears have been chosen with my fur in mind.

I ring home at lunchtime, but Sunita's not there. I've surprised myself at how little I've been thinking about Sunita's pregnancy, with my being focussed on playing Boris as well as possible. Watching stuff back on the monitors is really useful, and I learn much about how to improve him. Next time I'm on camera, I tilt his head to the side, and keep his face at a slight angle to the camera and it makes him even more expressive. Blinking more often than a dog normally would animates the face, and I scratch myself like a dog would. There's a euphoric atmosphere on the set when we wrap at seven in the evening, and I'm pleasantly surprised when Nancy tells me my car is waiting. The journey home in a modern Mercedes is a delight, despite the traffic being bad. The driver wears a suit and tie, and only speaks when it's necessary.

When I get home, Sunita isn't there. I have a bath, because I was hot and sweaty in that costume. Esmeralda had provided me with a pair of cotton karate trousers, and white long-sleeved cotton top to wear under the costume, and absorb the sweat. I didn't wear it though, as Angela and I were both new to our jobs, and didn't see it until I'd put the costume on. I put all my clothes in the laundry basket, and notice that Sunita has been home and gone out again. There's another note, but this one's in an envelope. I remove Mummy's German made pruning knife from the top right drawer of my desk. The wooden handle, is smooth, as are the brass pins that lie flush with the wood. The knife is over twenty years old, and opens with a reassuring clunk, as only a German-made item could. I oiled it a few weeks ago, and the newly polished blade glints in the sunlight from the window. Sunita thinks it's morbid of me to use the knife that Mummy killed herself with for my letter opener. I don't. It's one of the only objects I possess that belonged to her. I feel a bond with her every time I have it in my hand. Most of my money arrives in the form of cheques in the post, and using Mummy's knife to release the cheques from their envelopes gives me a feeling that abundance is coming from her. I was so young when she died, my most vivid memory of her is finding her cold body floating in that red water. And this blade is the one that sliced through her veins. The smooth wooden handle was touched by her hands. To use the knife as my letter opener is to connect with my beautiful mother, from whom I was so painfully separated. That's why I often take it with me when I'm working away from home.

The feeling of foreboding started when I realised Sunita had been to the flat and left again. It increased when I found the envelope with my name written in her handwriting. I surprise myself at how calm I feel as I slide the curved German steel blade beneath the envelope flap, and release Sunita's note.

Dearest Doug,

I know I'm a coward, but I can't say this to your face. I think the baby is another man's. I'm so sorry, Doug. I'll move my stuff out really soon.

You're a beautiful man and I still love you, but I never see you because you're away working all the time. I'm so sorry it had to end like this.

I'll love you always,

Sunita.

I sit down on the expensive Swedish sofa I bought last autumn. I wanted a different colour, but Sunita chose this one. I paid, of course, because her actor's wages are a fraction of mine. Now she's left me, with a sofa I don't like the colour of. Perhaps I could get it re-upholstered. The trouble is, it's so large and luxurious we had a terrible time getting it in here. It wouldn't fit in the lift, and it nearly killed the delivery men hauling it up the stairs. There's a slight scuff where we had to squeeze it through the lounge doorway after first removing the door. No, it's not worth going through all that hassle. I don't mind the expense. It's the bother I can't face. Maybe I could get a throw to cover it with.

I pour myself a gin and tonic, and lay out on the sofa. Sunita and I bought that bottle of gin in the duty free shop at Goa airport. At one year, it's the longest relationship I've ever had. Unless you count the one with Mummy, which was four years.

I suppose the father's one of those actors, or perhaps the director. I don't even phone Linda's number to see if Sunita's there. I relax with tomorrow's script, and lose myself learning my lines. Most of them consist of "Woof woof", but I'm taking this opportunity very seriously. I make sure I know every cue, so whenever there's a mistake, I'm not the one to make it.

Chapter Twenty-one

The soft leather upholstery of the BMW 700 Series sticks to my thighs. I spend so much of my time in a blue fur costume, I wear shorts whenever it's hot. I love the heat so much I asked the driver to turn the air conditioning off as soon as we left Teddington studios. I prefer the natural air conditioning called "having the window open".

We've been buried in the hideous Friday evening traffic heading for the M4 and Heathrow for over an hour, but we're not in danger of missing my plane. When you travel Business Class, you can use the fast track check-in. My seat would be First Class if they had a First Class on the flight to Nice. Instead, we're getting special treatment, and access to the First Class facilities on the ground. I look out of the open window, and as I watch Concorde climb into the sky, I lick my lips with anticipation of what the First Class lounge has to offer.

I love my life, especially the fact that I'm on my way to Nice. 'Rats Milk Cheese' won't be broadcast until the winter, but being able to say I'm working in television has upped my corporate price. I'm being paid £2,500 to perform on a motor yacht in the south of France tonight, and I'm already earning £1,000 a week playing Boris the dog. My agent Melissa wasn't too happy about my getting the part of Boris behind her back, but after a bit of discussion we agreed that she should handle the contract, in return for 5% of my earnings.

Unfortunately, the contract I signed so hurriedly the day Tom got his arm chopped off was a rip-off. If the show sells abroad or on video, I don't get anything, because it's a world-wide and video buyout. I'm on a flat £1,000 a week fee whilst we're making the show, and that's it. There's some clause saying I get a tiny bit more money if it's shown on UK terrestrial television more than seven times, but that's most unlikely. When I stop working on the show, I stop getting paid. Like all TV companies, Grange Films (who are making the show for the BBC) are pleading poverty, and not giving Equity contracts.

As the car draws to a gentle halt at departures, I feel pleased that clear blue skies will afford good views from the plane. The First Class Lounge is a delight. Calm colour schemes, ultra modern furniture, and hushed waitresses serving free drinks and sushi. I sip my gin and tonic and wonder if any of the slick moneyed ones around me are on their way to the party I'm performing at. I've done a couple of gigs on those disco boats that ply up and down the Thames, but never on a luxury motor yacht. Melissa said the client wouldn't tell her who owned the yacht. All we know is that it's his birthday party, and he saw me perform at The Clap Clinic a few weeks ago.

"Dougie my boy!" I turn round to see Arnold Shanks approaching my table. He's wearing a loud baggy Hawaiian shirt, but his beer gut still sticks out. Sebago yachting shoes, and white shorts arouse my suspicion that he might be heading to the same yacht that I am. His black dyed hair looks greasier than usual, and the gold chain around his neck is even bigger than the one he wore last time I saw him.

We shake hands, and as he sits next to me, I get a whiff of bad breath. To think that Sunita got pregnant by this man! I gesture to a waitress, in the hope that a drink will mask the smell. He orders a malt whiskey. That should do it.
"Take a look at this, Doug." He hands me a glossy colour brochure from his snakeskin-covered briefcase. It's for the 'Lady Rose', a white motor yacht one hundred and ten feet or 33.5 metres long. One photo shows her anchored in a bay, with one of her speed boats tethered to her stern. A bikini-clad figure is diving from her sun deck into the turquoise sea. Another depicts her cruising at speed off New York, with the World Trade Centre in the background. Arnold turns a page, and points out another colour photo of her saloon.
"That's where you'll be performing tonight, Doug. In the saloon, or up on deck if it's a fine night. You're on after the string quartet."
"Are you responsible for getting me this, Arnold?"
Since it came out that Arnold is probably the father of Sunita's unborn child, he's gone out of his way to ingratiate himself to me. I'm compering regularly at The Clap Clinic, and now it looks like he got me this all expenses paid gig for £2,500 on a luxury yacht.

"Awe, I would nae say that, Dougie. Mr Vermeulen thought you were very funny when he saw you at my place the other week."

Our flight is called, and we finish our drinks. I was planning to learn my lines ready for Monday's shooting whilst I wasn't looking out of the window. Now it looks like I'll have Arnold for company during the flight. I'm due at Teddington Studios at nine o'clock on Tuesday morning, and my plane back from Nice isn't due to land at Heathrow until mid-evening on Monday. I'm not required on Monday, because they're shooting scenes without Boris in. I've been working five days a week on 'Rats Milk Cheese' for three months, and doing stand-up every Friday and Saturday night, plus quite a few weeknights. It's great earning lots of money, but I was planning to make the most of this weekend aboard a luxury yacht, and learning lines wasn't part of the plan.

As I follow Arnold aboard the Boeing 737, my eyes connect with two familiar blue ones. Her blonde hair is done in a shorter style, but her name badge confirms its Alison, the flight attendant I met on the plane to Jersey.
"Good evening, Sir. Welcome aboard." She smiles at me and checks my boarding card stub. "Seat 1A. Business Class, on your right, Sir." My gaze lingers on her buxom figure for as long as possible without delaying the passengers behind me. She looked better in the red uniform than in the tacky blue British Airways outfit, but she still arouses a desperation to hold her tight, and cuddle her for a very long time. Arnold tries to sit in my window seat, but I assert my right to sit in the seat for which I hold a boarding card stub. He might be a multi-millionaire with gangland connections, but he isn't having my window seat!
"Where do you know the trolley dolly from?" He enquires.
"Alison? Oh, I met her when I was doing a corporate gig in Jersey. She worked for a different airline, then. It's funny that I'm with you now, because there was an article about you in their in flight magazine."
The gin and tonic has inspired me to be jocular, and I add:
"You're not big enough to be featured in the British Airlines rag, though. Eh Arnold?"

I'm aware of the risk of such familiarity with Arnold, and am relieved when he lets out a little laugh.

"Look again, Laddie." He replies, as he slides the copy of 'High Life' from the rack on the bulkhead in front of our Business Class seats, and tosses it into my lap. Sure enough, there's an article about maverick Arnold and his prestigious comedy club The Clap Clinic, written by Neil Gosling.

"Same company publishes both magazines. I'm in the North West Airlines one too." Says Arnold proudly.

"Think of that Doug. People flying on American domestic flights read about me!" Alison offers us pre-flight drinks, and we both choose champagne. As soon as I get an opportunity, I'm going to find out if she's staying the night in Nice. Now I'm single, I don't have to worry about my conscience, and she attracts me on a very deep level.

"How's Sunita?" I enquire, as the Ramada Hotel passes my window during our taxi to the end of the runway.

"Oh she's good. Very good, thanks Doug. I'm so glad we still get on after all that. She sends her love, by the way."

When it transpired that the source of Sunita's baby was most likely to be Arnold's sweaty scrotum I was shocked from surprise more than emotional trauma. If she'd been sleeping with a young handsome actor behind my back, I'd have been hurt. But the ridiculousness of the sophisticated Sunita getting seduced by Arnold killed my pain before it happened. If Sunita was stupid enough to be taken in by a serial adulterer, then she wasn't the girl I thought she was. Sunita and I were fairly careful about avoiding pregnancy, so the likelihood is that the baby's his. He's moved her into a flat in a riverside apartment block a little upstream from The Clap Clinic. He's told his wife, and is apparently going to move out of their marital home in Barnes, and live with Sunita. I still can't understand what she sees in him, as I'd told her about his numerous infidelities. The whole thing is unbelievable, but it had been going on for a few months before I found out. There was me thinking she was domesticated because she was so good at washing the bedding, when it was to remove Arnold's sweat and sperm. He even used my razor on one occasion. Which reminds me, I must get round to having a sexual health check. I've been so busy playing Boris by day, and doing stand-up in the evenings, I still haven't done it.

149

Windsor Castle disappears behind us as we make a series of turns to avoid the myriad planes in the crowded Friday evening sky. A few minutes later, Brighton is spread out before us, and the sight of several yachts either leaving or entering the marina prompts me to question Arnold about the owner of the 'Lady Rose'.

"Mr Vermeulen doesn't own her. He's chartered her for a week. Hopefully, he and I are going to be doing business together. He might be putting comedy shows on in Belgium and Holland, so this could lead to more work for you. When you've finished on 'Rats Milk Cheese', I mean."

"The BBC loved the pilot so much, they decided to commission another twenty-five shows. They've delayed broadcasting the pilot until they've been made. When they showed the pilot to focus groups, the reaction was overwhelming. They're convinced the show's going to be a massive hit."

"I'm really pleased for you, Doug. You deserve it. Is that Belgium down there?"

"No Arnold. That's the Sussex coast. We don't fly over Belgium on the way to Nice." Sometimes I'm amazed by other people's lack of geographical knowledge.

"Vermeulen's Flemish. He's got some hotels in Holland and Antwerp. He wants to open nightclubs in them, with entertainment. Here's your girlfriend."

Alison serves us a prawn cocktail, and champagne.

"Which novel are you reading at the moment, then?" She enquires.

"'Madame Bovary' by Gustave Flaubert. Have you read it?" I reply.

"No, but I will. I read 'Nana' by the way. Very good."

I assume she read it because I was reading it when I met her before, and feel emboldened enough to ask:

"Do you fly back to Heathrow tonight, or are you on a stopover?"

"I've got the weekend off. I fly back on Sunday evening." Her smile betrays the fact that she fancies me. As she leans over to pour my champagne, her large bosoms transcend the dreadful bitty design of the British Airways dress. I give her my brightest smile in return, and she moves on to serve some French people in the seats opposite us.

"Don't go making any commitments you may regret later, Dougie. Mr Vermeulen's renowned for the lavishness of his parties. If you know what I mean."

Arnold winks at me. I force a conspiratorial smile, realising he's unaware of the irony of what he's saying. My ex-girlfriend is alone and pregnant with his kid, and he's implying there's promiscuous sex on offer. Alison's colleague offers us a choice of guinea foul, rack of lamb, or medallions of beef. When Arnold chooses the medallions of beef, I wonder if he thinks he can wear them round his neck.

Chapter Twenty-two

At Nice airport Arnold twists his spine as he removes his enormous designer suitcase from the carousel, and has to sit down, his face contorted with pain. It's strange to see such a powerful man in such a vulnerable state.
"Oh Dougie. That's ma weekend fucked. I did ma back in years ago, and sometimes it comes back again. We'll hev tae get a porter or whatever they're called over here."

I need to get to the 'Lady Rose' as soon as possible, so I can prepare for my gig. I don't want to waste time.
"That's alright, Arnold. I'll look after your case."
I get a trolley, and load both our suitcases on to it. Arnold rallies himself, and manages to walk along behind me. I put his snakeskin covered briefcase on top of my flight bag, so he can hold both of his hands to his lower back, and shuffle along slowly as we head for customs.

An employee of Vermeulen greets us in the arrivals hall, and leads us to a white Rolls Royce Corniche.
"Arnold! Your back's better."
"Is it? So it is! Must have been a temporary glitch." He moves around painlessly. "Yep, the disc seems to have popped back into place."
I can't understand how someone could be barely able to walk one minute, and perfectly all right the next. I admire the super modern architecture of Nice airport as the Rolls Royce takes us silently in the direction of Cannes, when the penny drops.
"Arnold! You didn't. I can't believe you'd do that to me."
"I don't know what you're talking about, Doug."
"It's a coincidence that your back went just as we were going through customs. And I had your bags. Whilst you walked a safe distance behind me."
Arnold chuckles and winks at me.

"Don't worry your handsome wee head about that Dougie. We're through now, and we're going to have a party!" He taps his nose conspiratorially.
"I'll see you're alright, don't you fret. Good acting, though, eh?"

Suddenly it's all clear. I was duped into being his mule. I don't want his coke. My life is dedicated to making 'Rats Milk Cheese' a success. I was up at six this morning for the day's shooting at Teddington, and I'm due on stage at ten tonight. I thrive on this schedule, and I do it without drugs. Apart from marijuana, but that doesn't count. I don't even smoke that so much as I used to. Coke's going through the comedy circuit like a forest fire. Gerry Crook, Neil Gosling, Colin Homes – they're all doing too much of it. I adore playing Boris the dog, and I love doing stand-up, because that's what I was put on this earth to do. I had a little sleep in my dressing room during lunch, and another nap in the car on the way to Heathrow. I've never had so much energy, or felt so happy. There isn't room in my life for that crap, and I feel stupid for letting myself be tricked by a low-life like Arnold. The trouble is, I reflect to myself as we head along the coast road to Cannes. It was Arnold who got me the part in 'Rats Milk Cheese'. Most of my stand-up comedy work is for Arnold. I owe so much of my success to him.

"Do yea think that blonde bird'll come tae the party?" Arnold breaks the silence. Vermeulen's man at the steering wheel doesn't speak English, as Arnold found out when he tried to strike up a conversation.
"I hope so." I invited Alison aboard 'Lady Rose' before we disembarked the plane. She seemed interested, but it'll cost her a lot in taxi fare to come from her hotel in Nice to Cannes.
"I can't wait to see that string quartet."
"Since when did you get interested in chamber music, Arnold?"
"When I heard they're all girls, and they play in the nude. Apparently the cellist is quite something tae look at."
"Doesn't her cello obscure the view?"
"Their instruments are made of transparent Perspex. And the back of the cello's made of convex Perspex, to magnify her fanny. The violinist and viola player de nae shave their armpits. I just hope you'll do okay, Dougie. Their act will be a hard one to follow."

When we arrive, the 'Lady Rose' is moored stern to the quayside. Members of the crew take our bags aboard, and several people sit drinking around a table on the poop deck. A thin distinguished looking man stands to greet us. He's tall, in his forties, and speaks with a Dutch accent.
"Pleased to meet you, Doug. My name is Ruud Vermeulen. Welcome aboard the 'Lady Rose'".
Arnold and Vermeulen shake hands, and when I see how low status the usually cavalier Arnold's body language is, I realise our host is very powerful. It's the first time I've witnessed Arnold servile to anybody. I've seen Vermeulen somewhere before, but I can't think…that's it! Suddenly I remember the black and white framed photo on the wall of the house in Jersey. When I went back to the waiter's place with those two girls. This is the man in the tweed jacket, with the dog jumping up at _____. It's him!

I've seen pictures of gin palaces like this in magazines, but when I'm shown to my cabin the opulence overwhelms me. I have a double bed with en suite bathroom, and a colour telly with video and stereo by my bed. The colour scheme is dark red. I unpack my dinner jacket and hang it in the wardrobe. After giving my face a quick wash, I return to the poop deck with my notebook, ready to extract as much information as possible without getting shot. I want to do a good gig this evening.

Vermeulen's throwing the party to celebrate his forty-forth birthday. He tells me he lives in Brussels and Amsterdam, but wants to get a place in the south of France because he's fed up with grey skies.
"Have you been to Antwerp, Doug?" I say I haven't.
"That's where I was born. It's a most exciting city. I opened my first restaurant there, and now I own two hotels in the centre. There's a lot of money in Antwerp, because of the diamond trade. It's become a big place for fashion designers and artists, and I want to start a comedy club in the bar of one of my hotels. You made me laugh very much when I saw you at Arnold's club in London. When you have as many worries as me, you need to laugh. I liked your bit about the Schipol Airport in Amsterdam. That was really funny. Perhaps you could do this again tonight, ya?"

Of course I can. For £2,500 plus expenses, I'm very happy to do requests. As he continues, I notice the shape of Vermeulen's skull.
"Tonight is a big celebration. Not just my birthday. I bought a hotel in Amsterdam last year. Its profits are so high, I've paid off the loan early. All this, and my investments in the film and TV industry are also bringing good returns. So I am renting this yacht for a big celebration. If I like, perhaps I will buy something like her."
I'm so preoccupied with the fact that I've been in this man's house in Jersey, I fumble for a reply.
"Would you keep her in the Mediterranean, or in Holland?"
"Good question. Maybe I should buy two. One for here, and one for the North."
I ask him who's going to be in the audience, and he's cagey until I reassure him I'm interested in what language people speak, rather than what their occupations are. He hasn't introduced me to the other people at his table. They're a mix of fashion model type women, and black-haired men who turn out to be Italians. The Lady Rose is made of steel, and I notice a few tiny rust bubbles beneath her fresh white paintwork. Vermeulen tells me she was built in Holland, and that the strongest motor yachts are Dutch.
"She's been around the world twice. If I buy a motor yacht, I'll get something a bit newer, but this is nice. I first saw her in Dutch Guyana. She's a good ocean-going ship."

More guests arrive, and when I retire to my cabin to sort my act out, a wave of tiredness descends over me. I'm woken a while later by Arnold knocking on my cabin door. I didn't mean to drop off, and groggy with sleep I let my judgement slip by accepting a line of coke.

A few minutes later, I'm shaved, showered, and admiring my dinner jacket in the full-length mirror on my cabin wall. Arnold chops another line out for us, and I feel like James Bond as we emerge onto the crowded deck. Coloured lights hang from the yacht's radar mast, and the party's in full swing.

"Who are all these people!" I exclaim to Arnold. It must be like this during the Cannes film festival. Vermeulen's involved in the film industry, perhaps tonight will be my lucky break. The Lady Rose is packed with young Europeans wearing so much jewellery it's a wonder

we haven't sunk beneath the weight. It looks like an open audition for female escorts and male mafia members. Ruud Vermeulen is sitting in an armchair with a girl on his lap, and on the highest deck – I think it's called the bridge deck – is a completely naked string quartet of pretty girls playing transparent instruments. I can't work out which is lovelier – the way they look or the way they sound. I take a second glass of champagne from one of the numerous attractive waitresses, and have a rush of nerves as I realise I'm on next, and Arnold and I are about the only people here whose first language is English. I squeeze my way onto the foredeck to get away from the crowd to take a last look at the notes I've made. It's quieter here, and the lights of yachts lying at anchor are reflected in the calm dark sea. There isn't enough light to see my notebook, and I'm about to return to the party when I realise I'm not the only one here. A tuxedoed figure is leaning back against the yacht's superstructure, whilst a waitress gives him oral gratification. "Pardon, Monsieur" I apologise, as I nearly trip over the tray of champagne glasses on the deck beside where she's kneeling.
"Bella, bella, Senor." Comes the reply.

Back in the main action, the string quartet finish a tune, and the party guests go wild with appreciation. Somehow I don't think I'll be getting the same acknowledgment. I just want to get this over and done with before everyone's too pissed. I watch them start their next number. Arnold was right. The cello's made of convex Perspex, so her crotch and fanny are magnified.

In the saloon, the guests are making the most of the fact that there's no wind and plenty of light. The marble and glass table surfaces are all being used for cocaine chopping and snorting. There's even a bloke giving packets of it out, and I don't see any money changing hands. I hear French, Italian, Dutch, German, Russian, and more French being spoken. But no English.

I find Arnold standing as close as possible to the string quartet, gazing up at their naked pudenda, with a glass of champagne in one hand, and a cigar in the other. I ask him to appeal to Vermeulen to put me on as soon as possible, because everyone's getting more pissed by the second. Whilst I talk to him I'm almost knocked off my feet and I turn to see a drunken man in jeans and a brown leather jacket stagger away

from me, swearing in Dutch. He turns to look at me, and his face is sunburned, framed in shaggy blonde hair. He delivers a few more insults in Dutch, and urinates against one of the ships boats.
"Who let him on board?" I say.
"If he wasn't invited, he wouldn't be here. Take a look at the security." Arnold replies. I follow his gaze to the stern of the yacht, where several huge men with semi-automatic guns are guarding the gangplank.
"Is that allowed?" I ask.
"A lot of rich people have armed guards on their yachts. They're allowed them to protect against kidnap attempts."

Arnold finds Vermeulen, who assures me I'll be introduced when the string quartet have finished the next piece of music. He proves to be a man of his word, and I'm amazed how everyone shuts up for him to make his birthday speech. Even the naked musicians stand obeisant until he's finished speaking in a mixture of Dutch and French. I hear my name, and realise I'm on.

I start doing my act to a sea of blank faces. At first, I'm surprised why they're being so polite, because it's clear the majority of them can't understand what I'm saying. Then I realise, it's out of respect for Vermeulen that they're staying so silent. I do the bit about Amsterdam's Schipol airport, and Vermeulen's laugh is audible over the sea of upturned faces. Suddenly laughter breaks out around him. It spreads amongst some people I recognise from earlier. They speak some sort of Slavic language. I remember there was confusion over the contents of the vol-au-vents on one of the trays the waitresses were bringing round. They needed someone to translate for them, because they spoke neither French nor German. They certainly didn't speak English, and now they're laughing at my jokes. A woman with diamond earrings so huge they'd look more at home hanging from a chandelier, laughs shrilly during a set-up line. The only reason they're laughing is to please Vermeulen.

I'm booked to do twenty minutes, and I'm not sure they can keep this up that long. I look around trying to find something I can use visually to inspire some genuine laughter. There's a rigid inflatable speedboat mounted on chocks near where I'm performing. I grab a lifejacket

157

from inside, and put it on as if I was a flight attendant demonstrating the emergency procedures.

The laugh this gets is definitely genuine, and I mime there's a whistle on it, and then play the part of a shark being scared off by the whistle. Big laugh, and a round of applause. Encouraged, I milk everything I can from the flight safety demonstration. I glance over to see if Vermeulen's enjoying it as much as the rest of the crowd, but he isn't there. Maybe he's moved to another part of the audience. I keep going anyway, but get the feeling I'm not the only one who's noticed he's missing, because the laughter's not the same.

I return to the boat, to see if there are any other useful props in there. To my, and everyone else's joy, I remove a large bra. I take the lifejacket off, and mime slamming the bra onto the surface of the water and staying afloat from the air trapped in the cups. They appreciate that. Except for one person. I can't see who it is, but there's some sort of disturbance coming from amongst the back of the crowd. I ignore it, but now it's recognisable as a man's voice speaking in a slurred way. It gets louder and more frequent. Then I hear a recognisable sentence.
"A big bra for a big tit."
The faces at the front of the crowd look around anxiously, but hecklers have never been a problem for me. They're usually boring, and all the comedian has to do is let them reveal their dullness to the rest of the audience, who will tell them to shut up.
"Perhaps we could share the bra, Sir?" I reply. "There's room for another tit."

There's shocked silence, which doesn't surprise me, because hardly anyone speaks English. A drunken figure lurches into the light. It's the same man who bumped into me earlier. He's easily distinguishable because he's the only one who isn't wearing evening dress. Some people at the front recognise the man, and gasp with fear. When I look into his eyes, I understand why. He might be heavily intoxicated, but an evil vitality shines from his eyes.

"If you're a coward, Englishman, yump overboard. If you're not a coward, stay right there." The partygoers parted to let him through, and formed a clearing around where he's standing. I'm hoping Vermeulen will intervene. Or Arnold. Or a security guard. Or anybody. He doesn't seem to be staggering so much now, and having established I'm not about to dive overboard, he resumes walking towards the stage area. An Italian man steps towards him, appealing quietly in words I don't hear.

The heckler delivers what I recognise to be a win shun kung fu punch to the man's ribcage, and he's propelled backwards into the onlookers, taking a woman down with him. There's a scream, and the Italian doesn't get up again.
"Well, *you're* obviously not a coward, my friend. I'm just doing the job I'm paid for. If you don't like it, perhaps you could take it up with Mr Vermeulen. What's your name?"
"My name is Mr Vermeulen. I don't like it, and I'm not your friend. So like I said, yump off the ship, or I'll snap your elbows against their yoints." He's climbing onto the stage area, and I'm about to jump off overboard, when a loud, clear voice rings out.
"Hans." It says a lot more, but as it's Dutch I don't understand. Vermeulen has come from below decks, and leads the heckler whose name is Hans back towards the door from where he emerged. At the threshold, he turns to the crowd. Once more his voice rings effortlessly across the deck.
"Please, continue with the party. Music!"
Vermeulen gently ushers the scruffy man called Hans through the door, and 'Wake Me Up Before You Gogo' by Wham bursts from the loudspeakers. People begin talking to each other, and I realise I'm no longer the centre of attention. The sound technician strolls smiling over to me and takes the microphone.
"Hans Vermeulen. The wayward brother. He's usually in the Far East, looking after Mr Vermeulen's interests in Thailand and The Philippines. He's just arrived from Bangkok. Looks like he's been drinking for the whole flight. We try to stay out of his way."
"I can see why." I say, watching the Italian man who intervened on my behalf being led away for medical attention.
"At least you don't have to perform any more."
"Mr Vermeulen wasn't watching my act, anyway."

159

"Don't be so sure." The man discreetly indicates a CCTV camera that points towards the performing area, and begins clearing away the microphone lead and stand.

I'm buzzing from the coke, and decide champagne will mellow me out. I drift down below, aware that people can recognise me as the man who just upset Vermeulen's brother. Nobody wants eye contact. They don't want to be seen near me, let alone talking to me. Arnold is nowhere to be found, and I don't know anybody here. I wonder if Alison has turned up, and if she has, whether she's got through the security guards. On my way to the stern of the yacht, I nearly slip over in some vomit. The chief security guard speaks good English, and assures me that if a girl fitting Alison's description comes, he'll allow her onboard.

A warm, balmy breeze wafts over the boat, bringing the smell of the sea. I ought to be enjoying myself, but I have a sense of menacing danger. I wish I hadn't accepted the coke now, because I'm tired and won't sleep for a long time yet. I need more champagne. I drain my glass, and go to the saloon in search of a waitress. People are snorting cocaine everywhere I look. Even the waitress I get my drink from has white powder around her nostrils.

Equipped with another glass of champagne, I realise I haven't explored the far end of the saloon, and decide to investigate. I slowly penetrate the mass of dancers, and discover the top of a spiral staircase. There's a security man at the top, and when I try to go down it, he prevents me.
"I was the comedian. Mr Vermeulen's guest". The man still shakes his head.
"Only inner circle." There's enough debauchery going on up here, I can't imagine what must be happening at the bottom of the spiral staircase. I recognise one of the string quartet, who's now wearing a white dress. I try to make conversation. Unfortunately, I don't speak Russian, and if she speaks English, she isn't letting on. She moves on through the crowd.

I've had enough of this champagne – I fancy a beer. The kitchen is functioning as a bar, and I get myself a big glass of lager. I'm taking

my second swig, when there's a tap on my back. It's Arnold. I didn't think I'd be pleased to see him, but I'm lonely.
"Have you been down the spiral staircase?" I enquire.
"Oh aye. But that's not for the likes of you, Dougie. Only members of Mr Vermeulen's inner circle are allowed down there. Sorry about the heckler, by the way. We've all got to be careful about Mad Hans. He'll kill you as soon as look at you. Mr Vermeulen sends his apologies. Fancy another line?"

"No thanks, Arnold."
"Have you worked out what's going on with the chicks?"
"No."
"Most of them are escorts. They've been paid to provide any service you fancy."
"Including the string quartet."
"Aye."
"So what do I have to do?"
"Just ask."
"Thanks Arnold. I'll see you later."
I find the musician in the white dress sitting with her colleagues. The viola player speaks enough English for me to ascertain they're all from the Ukraine. I ask her what the one in the white dress plays. She's the cellist. I don't recognise her with her clothes on. Then I remember what Arnold said about the viola and violin player not shaving their armpits. They're all blonde, but wisps of armpit hair are visible if I look carefully enough.
"Are you staying on the boat?" I enquire.
"We all share one cabin." Replies the viola player, whose name is Vyora. I'm a bit drunk now, and having ideas of taking them to my cabin. I fancy the cellist the most. Her face has a slightly sad quality about it, and her white dress appeals to me more than the frilly affairs the others wear. Vyora tells me the cellist is called Irina.
"Please could you ask Irina if she'd like to come to my cabin?"
Vyora doesn't reply, but stands up looking suddenly alert in the direction behind me. Her three colleagues follow suit. I turn to see Ruud Vermeulen accompanied by his brother Hans. Ruud hands me a brown envelope.
"Thank you, Doug. I enjoyed your performance, and I'm sorry my brother interrupted. He's over-tired, that's all."

I take the brown envelope from him.
"It was £2,500 wasn't it? I've put a small bonus in there for your inconvenience."
"You look like a man I had a big falling out with. The sight of you aroused bad memories of him." Hans' eyes are glazed over now. I offer my hand, but if he notices it, he doesn't respond.
"Please excuse us. My duties as host require me to mingle."
Vermeulen's thin lips smile, and he leads Mad Hans off amongst the crowd. I wonder what soporific drug Hans has taken, and feel the brown envelope bulging with cash.
"Are you going to open it?" Vyora asks.
I count £3,000 in British cash. I don't have a pocket big enough to contain the wad without it causing an unsightly bulge, and invite Irina to my cabin.
She follows me meekly as though she were obeying an order. I'd like to ask her if she'd accompany me if she wasn't being paid, but I can't speak Russian.

Sitting on my bed, I can sense she doesn't want to have sex with me. She seems so sad, as she lies on her back, resigned to doing whatever I want. I look into her eyes, and smile. We're both unhappy for very different reasons, and our sadness blends into one. I lay down beside her, and we cuddle tenderly. Even the cocaine and alcohol can't make me so insensitive as to demand sex from this poor doll-like girl. She's a talented musician, and I feel that as a fellow performer, the betrayal would be even worse if I forced myself onto her delicate sensibility. My lust evaporates, and she accepts my cuddle. Despite the cocaine, we fall asleep in the spoon position, like innocent children.

Chapter Twenty-three

Two things bother me when I wake up. The first is the awareness that I went to sleep without cleaning my teeth or getting undressed. The second is that the bed is rocking slightly. I open my eyes. Irina has gone, and I'm desperate for a piss. After I've relieved myself, I look out of the porthole to see a horizon empty but for a distant sail. I'm starving, so I do my ablutions, put a clean pair of shorts and T-shirt on, and investigate the breakfast situation.

My cabin must be air conditioned, because it's a hot Mediterranean day on deck. The sun is high, and the crew worked hard whilst I was asleep, because the Lady Rose gleams freshly as she cuts through a placid sea. Most of the party guests must have left before we set sail from Cannes, because I can only see three people sunbathing. A steward greets me in the saloon, and I order a cheese and mushroom omelette with orange juice and coffee. I eat alone, watching the south of France slide by. The steward tells me we left Cannes at noon, and we're currently off St Tropez. We're heading for the Isle de Porquerolles, where Lady Rose is to drop anchor. Apparently we're meeting up with Vermeulen's friends who have their own yachts.
"You like scuba diving?" asks Franz, the steward.
"I love it. I'm a PADI advanced diver."
"Isle de Porqerolles very good scuba diving. You like much."
By the time I've finished my delicious breakfast, I still haven't recognised anyone I know. As the only people awake are some Italian men who ignore me, I return to my cabin and relax reading 'Madame Bovary' by Gustave Flaubert. Tiredness envelopes me once again, and I fall asleep with the book in my hands. It's physically demanding romping around a television set in a blue furry dog costume, and I need to catch up on sleep. I have erotic dreams featuring Alison the flight attendant and a Perspex lute.

I wake up feeling really refreshed. The sun is closer to the horizon, and I can hear classical chamber music. Inquisitive as to whether it's

being played by naked Ukrainians, I go up on deck. Arnold is sitting in the Jacuzzi with Vermeulen and two dark-haired women. The music comes from loudspeakers, and Vermeulen laughs when I ask after the naked string quartet.
"They went ashore this morning. Even I find it extravagant to hire them for *two* nights. With their clothes off, anyway."
Vermeulen introduces me to the women. One is called Mia, and doesn't speak much English. She's sitting very close to him, and watches his face, presumably searching for any warning signs of anger. The other is called Connie. Her long black hair reminds me of a magazine advert for conditioner. It hangs down in rats tails like in the 'before' photo. I always preferred the 'before' to the 'after', because I like the natural look. She speaks good English and has intelligent eyes. I wonder why she's sharing a Jacuzzi with Arnold and Vermeulen.

I accept the offer of a coffee, and ask about the Isle de Porqerolles.
"Have you heard of the French writer Andre Gide?"
"He's one of my favourite novelists." I reply honestly.
"He used to holiday on the Isle de Porqerolles."
Vermeulen is wrong. I know that Gide used to holiday on the Isle de Hyeres, another island in the same group, but I don't contradict my host. I have the £3,000 cash he gave me stashed in my suitcase, and I sense he doesn't like to be wrong.

"We'll anchor just off the island. There should be quite a few of us."
"What are your kiddie's clown skills like, Doug?" Asks Arnold.
"Non-existent. Why do you ask?"
Vermeulen's as composed as ever. I marvel that the water in the Jacuzzi has actually made him wet.
"When I celebrate my birthday, I like the poor and vulnerable to celebrate with me. Tomorrow we play host to forty-four orphans. You may need earplugs. They're a noisy lot."
He's good at reading people's faces, because I fail to conceal my shock.
"Is there a problem?"
"No. Of course not. I'm just not used to children, that's all."
My coffee cup rattles on the saucer as I replace it. I swallow involuntarily, and hot coffee burns my throat. I'm stuck on a boat that's going to be over-run with kids. I've got to get off, somehow. I can't stay on it if there are going to be children everywhere.

"How old will they be?"
"Their ages range from four to ten. Most of them are from Africa and the Far East. I run a charity that supports orphaned children. But don't worry – you won't be asked to entertain. A clown has already been engaged. Ah, here comes Fritz…"
I turn round prepared to shake hands with yet another European, and am knocked almost into the Jacuzzi by a huge Alsatian dog. He delivers a series of warm licks to my throat before a stern command in Dutch has him cowering on the deck. My heart flutters. Not from the attentions of the friendly Fritz, but from the short sharp guttural sound that came from Vermeulen's throat. It cut like an icicle into my chest, and had the same effect on Fritz, who clearly fears his master.

Another sentence in Flemish has the giant dog wagging his tail again, and he puts his paws up on the edge of the Jacuzzi. I recognise Fritz as the huge dog in the framed black and white photo I saw in Vermeulen's house in Jersey. The one who had his paws all over ____. Or at least, I recognise the collar, which is festooned with huge diamonds, glinting in the Mediterranean sun. Vermeulen pets his head, and utters some more Flemish, at which he leaps into the swirling water. Arnold and the two women barely hide their alarm as Fritz doggy paddles round in tight circles.
"Don't worry about Fritz. He likes you." Vermeulen's voice is singsong compared to its usual clipped Dutch intonation, as he reaches out to his beloved dog.
"I love dogs." I say. I'd rather a hundred Rottweilers visit the boat, than one child.
"In fact, Doug's got a certain interest in German shepherd dogs, haven't ye Doug. Especially ones with blue fur." Arnold's in a better mood today than I've ever seen him.
I explain briefly about my part as Boris in 'Rats Milk Cheese', although Fritz's sharp claws seem of more immediate concern to those in the Jacuzzi.
"Are those real diamonds on his collar?" I can't resist asking. Vermeulen smiles through thin lips.
"Oh yes. Fritz's collar is worth more than most people's house." He chuckles. "But where better to keep such expensive diamonds, than on a ferocious dog?"

165

Being seen to be on friendly terms with Vermeulen has a huge effect on the fellow guests, who behave less coldly towards me. The Saturday evening party is a more modest affair. We anchor in a bay off the Isle de Porquerolles shortly before the sun sets behind the Scots pine trees that fringe its sandy beach. Hans appears briefly, and the one time I dare to look at his face, his eyes are on me. I look briefly into two pools of viper venom, before lowering my gaze. He looks like he should be wearing a Gestapo uniform, rather than scruffy jeans and T-shirt.

A white schooner anchors close by. She's called the 'Modar', and an elderly Hungarian man with an unpronounceable name comes across in her tender. He's accompanied by several other eastern Europeans, all men in their twenties and thirties. There are about twenty of us sipping cocktails, before a lavish dinner is served. I'm seated beside Connie, one of the dark-haired women who was in the Jacuzzi. She's from Sardinia. When she's hardly touched her lobster thermidor after I've eaten mine, she reads my mind and offers me her portion. I've got a tremendous appetite today, and the food is delicious. I even finish off her pommes noisettes.

I start flagging half way through her meringue, and when the brandy and cigars come out, I get the impression our hosts want to talk business, and I'm not part of it.
"You like the Modar?" asks Connie, indicating the white schooner anchored nearby.
"Yes. I prefer sailing yachts to motor yachts. She looks like a real classic."
"She was built in Scotland in 1904."
"I suppose she's made of wood."
"Iroko planking on oak frames. Her teak decks were replaced last winter."
I look into her smooth Italian face. She's washed her hair since she was in the Jacuzzi, because it's got lovely waves in it, and smells of shampoo. It looks as nice as it did earlier, in a different way.
"You know a lot about her." I say, refusing her offer of a Sobranie Russian Black cigarette.
"I work for the company that charters the Modar and the Lady Rose. Would you like me to show you the Modar?"

"I'd love you to!" Part of my enthusiasm is because I'm still petrified about the kids coming aboard tomorrow. I've already got ideas of escaping ashore during their visit, but if I can make contacts aboard the Modar, my options may be increased.

Connie's experience at handling small boats is evident from the natural way she steps down into the tender, starts the outboard, and casts us off from the Lady Rose. She opens the throttle up, and as we speed towards the Modar, the Lady Rose looks resplendent with her coloured lights reflected in the rippled black sea.

We come alongside the Modar. A crewman takes our mooring line, and Connie gives me a guided tour of the deck and wheelhouse. The schooner is deserted but for her small crew. I've never seen so much varnished wood as she has below decks.
"I can't show you the guest cabins, for obvious reasons. Mr Vermeulen's friends aren't the sort I'd want to annoy. I don't think they'd mind if we had a drink, though."

I'm still bloated from the meal, and lean back on the cream cushions of the saloon sofa. It's big and semi-circular. Connie's skirt is short, and the backs of her knees, and her thighs look alluring as she fixes a couple of gin and tonics. She turns towards me, the drinks in her hands. There's a red scratch mark on the front of her leg just above the knee.

She walks over to me and notices me looking at it. "Fritz's claw marks. From the Jacuzzi." She smiles as she hands me a gin and tonic big enough to fill two glasses. It dawns on me that I never saw her breasts whilst she was in the Jacuzzi, because she kept beneath the water as far as her shoulders. They're quite big, and her black bra strap is visible outside her singlet. She kicks her sandals off her feet, and they skim over the varnished wooden floor. Then she flops next to me on the sofa.
Slightly shy, I gaze at her sandals, on the other side of the saloon.
"I see you like the floor. It's made from Canadian Maple."
Her face is less pretty when she smiles. But her personality shines through. I want to make her laugh and skip. Then I could see those large bosoms bounce.

"I like maple. Especially the syrup."
Her English isn't good enough for her to get my insinuation. She sighs sincerely.
"At last, I can relax. You are just a hired comedian, yes?"
"Just a hired comedian. Don't worry, I'm not in the mafia." I joke. An anxious look flickers across her face.
"I'd be very careful what you say. Some of those men would be offended if they heard you say that. But they're my clients, and my boss makes a fortune from chartering boats to them. I have to always be on my guard." She rests her head on the plush cushion, and looks coyly at me.
"But you... you are not a powerful client. I don't have to pretend that your dog's claws are not scratching me."
She lifts her skirt to reveal more scratches on her thighs.
"Ooh, do they hurt?"
She nods, eyeing me like a hurt little girl.
"Is there a first aid kit? I could put some ointment on for you."
Without saying a word she reaches for the Gucci handbag she chucked on the sofa when we first came in. She produces some Arnica lotion and tosses it into my lap.
I remove the top, and she shuffles further down the sofa.
"Lock the door." She whispers. I do so, and wash my hands in the sink next to the drinks cabinet. When I return to the sofa, she's lifted her skirt high enough to reveal a pair of white knickers. I gently apply ointment to the few scratches, and she moans exaggeratedly. I replace the top, and she gestures for me to pass her the handbag. Her delicate hand goes directly to a little zip-up compartment, and produces a packet of condoms, and a small brown glass bottle. She places them on the shelf behind the sofa, and her long fingernails caress my arms. Goose pimples rise on my skin, and she draws me down for a lingering kiss.

Kissing has never been first on my list of pleasures, but Connie takes it to a higher level. Her lower lip caresses mine, and her tongue moves slowly and gently in my mouth. As I'm on top, I become self-conscious in case some of my spit falls down into her mouth, and roll over so she's on top of me. When she wriggles her hips I realise I've got a huge erection. I haven't had an orgasm since last Sunday evening, when I gave Charlotte French a lift home from a gig Arnold runs in Luton. We were driving down the M1, when Charlotte asked me how much I wanted for petrol.

I said I didn't need any money, because she'd had to pay for a return ticket on the train. She'd missed the last train back to London, and I know she's not earning much. She replied that if I liked I could put my hand in her knickers, and so I did. She came really quickly, and gave me a hand job that lasted most of the way between junctions 5 and 4. I felt a bit embarrassed, because I took longer to come than she did. She said it didn't matter, because I had to drive the car at the same time. And that I was honoured, because she usually has sex with women. I subsequently found out that she'd had a line of coke in the dressing room.

Anyway, not having had an orgasm for a week means I'm more than ready for action, and my hands stroke the backs of Connie's thighs. When my fingertips slide beneath her knicker gusset, they find moistness, and I pull her knickers down to her knees. She finishes the job of getting them completely off, and removes her salmon pink singlet with one deft swoop of her arms. I fumble unsuccessfully with her bra strap, and she undoes it for me.

I had no idea her tits were so generous in size. They look fantastic as they sway from side to side before each nipple in turn is lowered into my mouth. I suck and suck, and gently nibble, and she groans quietly and covers my face in delicate kisses.

Then without any warning, she swings one of her legs over me, so I'm free of her weight. Her soft Sardinian hands pull my T-shirt over my head, and undo my shorts. My pants come off with them, and she squeezes my shaft.

"We've got to be careful, or I'll come too soon." I gasp. She smiles, and removes a purple condom from its packet. Deftly she puts it on me, and jerks her hand up and down a few delightful strokes, before adopting the pose to receive me in the missionary position. I have a bit of difficulty getting it into her vagina, but she quickly manoeuvres me in, and I start thrusting.

She's gasping so loudly, I start to worry about what the crew will think. It's dark outside, and anyone on deck could watch us through a gap in the saloon window curtains. I could come any second, and to break the rhythm I grab my gin and tonic and take a swig. She indicates with her eyes that she wants a swig too, and when I replace the empty glass on the shelf behind the sofa, she asks for the little brown bottle.

As I suspected, it's amyl nitrate, and after she's had a big sniff, she hands the bottle to me. I climax just as the vapour strikes my core, and spins me around. I have that experience I first had as a kid when coming round from a Nitrous Oxide general anaesthetic. The one where you have a realisation you exist, but you've no idea who or where you are. You're floating around the collective unconscious, then you become aware of being a self. You waft down into a body and you remember where it is and what you were doing. Except this time I'm not coming round from laughing gas in Outpatients. I'm a person entwined with a lovely warm woman, who's squeezing me with her thighs, and holding me close with her arms, and convulsing in a series of magnificent orgasms.

When we've both finished coming, we lay still in each other's arms, listening to our breathing gradually return to normal. We share the rest of Connie's gin and tonic, and when I withdraw my penis from inside her, the condom isn't on it. She goes to the toilet to remove it, and mop herself up. I get the dishcloth and wipe the cream-coloured textile of the sofa. I rinse the cloth out several times between wiping the wet patch. Connie's pretty fruitful in the vaginal juice department. That reminds me, I really must get round to going to the STD clinic and getting a sexual health check-up.

She returns from the toilet aglow with contentment.
"Have a shower if you like. And perhaps you could fix another drink?"
After I've mopped myself up, we discreetly sit on a different part of the sofa, to allow the wet patch to dry off. Connie looks serious, and holds both of my hands in hers.
"Doug. I'm worried about your going scuba diving tomorrow. I was in the wheelhouse of the Lady Rose earlier, and overheard them discussing the dive. It would be safer if you stayed aboard, and helped out with the children's party."

"I'll be fine, Connie. I've done a lot of diving. I'll show you my logbook – I've been to over 50 metres."

"They were talking about the dive site, and Hans asked to be your buddy."

I look at her perfectly shaped mouth. Even though she's frowning with concern, she looks more classically beautiful than when she's smiling. I can't deny that Hans asking to be my buddy is a worry. If we get separated from the rest of the group whilst underwater, Hans and I will be expected to stay together. The buddy system is a safety procedure designed to ensure no diver is allowed to go missing. At the very least, one other diver – ones buddy – is looking out for you, and available to share his air supply should you get into difficulty. That's all well and good, unless your buddy wants to kill you.

Chapter Twenty-four

By Sunday morning, a third yacht has anchored nearby. It's a fifty-foot long motor cruiser, modest in comparison to Lady Rose and Modar, both of which are over twice her length. She's our dive boat for the day, and to my enormous relief our diving party embarks for her before the kids arrive on yet another vessel. Connie comes along for the ride, and Arnold stays on the Lady Rose for the kid's party.

Four Italian men, Hans, and me, are going to dive on the wreck of a German submarine that lies in 40 metres of water. The dive boat has anchored more or less above it, and we check our equipment before going down. The visibility is excellent, and I'm surprised at how many fish we can see as we follow the shot line towards the bottom. We've got big tanks, but even so we won't be able to stay at 40 metres for very long.

When I was an unhappy child being shunted from children's home to children's home, I dreamed of becoming a professional diver. As I got older, I didn't excel in the subjects appropriate to diving. I wasn't into science and engineering, but the arts. I studied literature at Dartington College of Arts, but commercial diving companies didn't have much call for experts in the nineteenth century novel. The fascination with diving remained, and when I started earning good money as a comic, I went to the Red Sea to learn to dive.

I have no family to celebrate Christmas and Easter with. Instead I spend those times on scuba diving holidays, and celebrate in the company of fish as deep beneath the waves as possible. That's my main excitement – to dive deeper and deeper, always trying to increase my personal record. I'm lucky, because my sinuses and ears can adjust to the water pressure really quickly, so whilst most divers are still trying to equalise at 30 metres, I'm already 50 metres deep. I also have the skill of being able to slow my breathing right down, and can make a tank of air last longer than anyone I know. My personal depth record is 54.8 metres. That's 180 feet! I did that one Christmas on a diving holiday in Australia. I'm really proud of myself for doing that, because most people suffer from nitrogen narcosis at less than that depth. That's another reason why I was made for diving – nitrogen narcosis doesn't affect me at depths where other people are suffering advanced symptoms. Air contains nitrogen, which causes people to behave in a drunken way if they breathe it above a certain pressure. I saw a bloke remove his aqualung and offer the mouthpiece to a fish, and we were only 35 metres down. If I hadn't made him put it back on and coaxed him up to a safer depth, he'd have drowned. My biggest problem is finding another diver with my abilities. Usually I'm restricted to their limitations, because it's dangerous to dive alone.

It comes as no surprise that Hans, who's my buddy for the dive, gets stuck at 10 metres, and can't equalise. Noses don't like belonging to cokeheads, or scuba divers. When they belong to someone who does both, they start to complain. Which is another reason why I'm keen to avoid coke. As Hans' buddy, I'm obliged to stay with him, and consequently reduce the time I can spend at the wreck. When his facemask starts filling up with blood because his nose is bleeding, he has to abandon the dive and return to the surface. The dive leader, who's called Enzo, signals for me to join two of the other Italians. They're already way down, and I catch them up just as they're reaching the sandy bottom at a depth of 41 metres. They don't speak English, and I don't speak Italian, but we understand each other via the international sign language that divers use. We check each other's air supply, and unsurprisingly I've used less air than they have. One of them – I think his name is Fabio – has dived on the submarine before, and he leads us away from the shot line towards the wreck.

We swim over an abandoned anchor, taking care not to go too near the bottom lest our fins disturb the sand and spoil the visibility. I've seen a lot of lost anchors on various sea floors in the world. Sometimes the chain breaks, and sometimes the chain gets tangled with another vessel's anchor. It happened to a dive boat I was on in the Caribbean, and we had to cut our chain with a hacksaw.

A family of squid swim past, looking more like flying birds, because they're above us. Several shoals of fish ahead of us betray the presence of the wreck. It looms up, dark and sinister. The conning tower's still in place, but the hull's split open where one of its torpedoes exploded, and the stern is completely broken up. We don't go inside, because we only have two torches, and one of them's stopped working. It worked okay on deck because I saw it being checked, but the intense pressure at 40 metres must have broken its seal. If the second torch were to fail whilst we were inside the sub, we wouldn't be able to find our way out.

We do another safety check, reading each other's air gauges. The Italians are impressed by how little air I've used compared to them, and signal accordingly. We'll have to make some decompression stops on the way up. Some full tanks of air have been tied to the shot line at 10 metres, for our use during the ascent. This means that our time on the bottom is longer, because we don't have to save our current air supplies for the final decompression stops. Enzo and his buddy join us at the wreck, and as both their torches are working, they go inside. I don't fancy going in myself. There's always the chance of meeting a predatory fish in wrecks, and the sub strikes me as too confined. The danger is that excessive sudden movement will disturb the silt and reduce visibility. Even with the extra air tanks dangling from the shot line, there's only enough air in our tanks for a few minutes in the wreck. There isn't time to wait for the silt to settle and visibility to improve. I've heard of several deaths arising from divers not finding their way out of wrecks in time.

I signal for permission to go off on my own, and to my amazement Enzo gives it. Breaking the 'never dive alone' rule in shallow water is stupid enough, but at 40 metres we can't see the surface, and a small problem could quickly become fatal. "Italians are a law unto themselves, though." I think to myself and fin steadily to the east, because the seabed drops off in that direction. I've got notions of breaking my personal depth record. I've got to do it really quickly, though, or I'll increase my decompression times. I follow the contours of the bottom, checking my depth gauge regularly. I've got 54.8 metres to beat, and reach 50 metres in a few seconds. It's so deep in some places, I can't see the bottom, and I tell myself to relax as my depth gauge displays 56 metres. That's 183 feet. I feel so thrilled. I'm doing this for the lonely little orphan boy I once was. I used to dream of going to 200 feet, and have promised myself I'll achieve that goal one day. I'll have to do it with special equipment, though. Even I wouldn't attempt 200 feet without helium and oxygen tanks, as nitrogen narcosis would be a certainty.

The bottom's quite stony now, and I stand on a low flat rock taking a last glance at my depth gauge. 57 metres! That's 187 feet. I'm about to ascend to 40 metres, when for the first time in my scuba diving career I panic. Something huge attacks me. My first thought is that it's a shark, but I quickly realise it isn't moving. A large anchor has landed on the fin I'm wearing, trapping my right foot. The panic subsides as I realise I'm not being attacked. I quickly remove my foot from the fin, and manage to pull the fin from beneath the anchor. I put it on and start my ascent. I need to get up to 40 metres very soon, or I'm in trouble. If the yacht above had dropped its anchor any closer to me, I'd be dead. Using the anchor chain as a guide, I exhale as I rise, and get my second bout of panic. The chain stops at 49 metres, where it's tied around the feet of a man, who's writhing in agony and fear. Both his hands are pressed to his ears, where the pain of sinking from the surface to 49 metres in a few seconds is unbearable. Blood flows from his ears, his nose, and his mouth. It takes me a few seconds to register this, because the drowning man is in full clown make-up, and still wearing his red nose. The chain is much thinner than would be used for an anchor of the size he's chained to. It's wrapped around his feet and lower legs, but I can still see his ridiculously big clown shoes.

He grabs me in desperation, and I give him my mouthpiece, but it's too late. His lungs have already filled with water, and even if I had enough air to share with him, I wouldn't be able to remove the chain from around his legs. His grip on my arm goes limp. I've got to get back to the others, so I take a last look at the grotesque clown face, with its eyes blinking from the salt. He's still conscious, but to stay with him a moment longer would be to invite my own death. I go up to 35 metres, because the visibility is clear enough for me to spot the other divers when I reach the shot line, even if they're still down at 40 metres. Before I've swum very far from the clown, I see two sharks speed towards him. They've smelled his blood.

I meet up with the Italians, and we begin our first decompression stop. My heart's still thumping, I've gulped a lot of air, but there's enough in my tank to make it to the fresh ones at the next stop. A manta ray glides through the depths beneath, when another thought disturbs me. That other discarded anchor I saw had exactly the same gauge of chain as the one the clown had wrapped around his legs.

We complete the final decompression stop, and break surface. The Italians are animated with excitement from their time in the wreck. They also take me a lot more seriously now they've seen how little air I use. When I'm out of my equipment, Connie hands me a large cappuccino. The motor cruiser's Italian, and a place in the wheelhouse is devoted to a large Gaggia coffee-making machine. Its position's almost as important as the radar and other navigation instruments.

It's a hot sunny day, and Connie and I dive off the cruiser to refresh ourselves in the warm turquoise sea. I look down into the depths, and despite the warmth of the sea, I shiver at the thought of that poor man 49 metres, or 160 feet, beneath the surface. I hope the people who dropped the clown overboard didn't notice the exhaust bubbles from my aqualung.
"Look, there goes the party boat." Says Connie, treading water and nodding towards another motor yacht that's steaming from the Lady Rose, towards the French coast.
"Forty-four happy kids aboard."
"Connie, how long have you been chartering yachts to Mr Vermeulen and his friends?"
"I've been working for the company for two years. He was a valued client before I joined."
"I expect they lose quite a few anchors."
"How did you know that?"
"I didn't. I was guessing." A soft breeze blows from the Isle de Porquerolles, bringing the scent of pine trees and earth. I start swimming towards the dive boat.
"I'm hungry, shall we go back to the Lady Rose?"
"Good idea." Says Connie, and starts swimming after me.
"Do you know where he got the clown from?"
"Russia. He's not well known. Mr Vermeulen's very particular about his clowns. He likes obscure ones."
She breaks into a front crawl, racing me back to the motor cruiser. I switch to butterfly stroke, and make it to the ladder well before her. As

an isolated child, I spent a lot of time swimming up and down the local pool. That, and reading novels.

Back on deck, Enzo is frowning over the dive computer I used. Connie translates for us, and he's convinced the computer's faulty, because its maximum depth reads 57.04 metres. He doesn't believe I could have gone that deep, and I'm glad that's so. I pretend to laugh, and point away from the Lady Rose, saying that I couldn't have been so deep because it's too shallow in that direction. I don't want anyone suspecting I was near the Lady Rose during my dive. Enzo asks what depth he should enter in my diver's log book, and I say 43 metres. I'll alter it to 57.04 metres when I get home. I don't think, though, that in the 'remarks about dive' section I'll write, "Nearly killed by anchor attached to clown." I nearly share my information with Connie, but self-preservation prevails, and I decide to keep my council.

Chapter Twenty-five

We're getting a heat wave in London, and the air conditioning isn't very powerful at Teddington studios. Beneath the studio lights and a thick layer of blue fur, it's hot. Everyone keeps asking if I'm all right, but the heat doesn't bother me. Being in the suit, with the dogs head on is a bit like how I imagine it's like wearing a deep-sea diving suit. Or a spacesuit. I fantasised about being an astronaut and a deep-sea diver when I was a young kid. In a strange kind of way, playing Boris fulfils both ambitions.

Simon the director sometimes stops shooting just so I can get the head off, and cool down. I'm almost annoyed by this, because I'm happier inside the costume with the head on, than I am with the head off. Maybe I need to get back in the womb. After a couple of weeks filming, I succeed in getting them to let me stay inside the suit until I ask to come out. We're all happier, because they get more minutes of footage shot per day, and I get to stay inside my idyllic world.

Sometimes, when I'm out of shot for a while, I keep the head on, and sleep in my basket. If they need my empty basket in shot, I lie down in a corner of the studio. My thick fur and padding make the hard concrete floor as soft as the finest bed. If I keep the mouth closed, it's quite dark inside the head, making it easier to sleep. There are many scenes that involve dialogue between the other characters, with Boris in the background asleep in his basket. This is perfect for me, because for a lot of the time I really am asleep. One day, we're in the editing suite watching playback, when Simon compliments me on Boris's "changing position whilst asleep" movements. I don't know whether I should tell him that I actually was asleep at the time. This is the perfect job for me, because I'm being paid £1,000 a week to escape into comfy blue fur, and spend an hour a day sleeping. That means that I've got energy left over to do stand-up gigs during the evenings.

Arnold gives me a residency compering a new venue he books in Bournemouth. Every Thursday as soon as I'm wrapped, Angela helps me out of Boris, I leap in the shower, and run to my car. I mentally write the week's material whilst driving the 110 miles to the Bournemouth seafront, and pull up in the car park of 'The Comedy Nest' five minutes before I'm due on stage. I have fun bantering with the regular crowd, and delivering the new gags I've thought of since the previous Thursday. When the show's over, I get back in the car and tear up the M3 to London. I get to bed between two-thirty and three in the morning, and am out of bed for the next day's filming by six-thirty. I love it!

I feel sorry for poor Angela my dresser. I produce over a litre of sweat during a hot day, and much of it's absorbed into my white cotton under clothes. Angela has clean ones for me at least twice a day, but it doesn't stop sweat from seeping into the foam padding of the costume. Grange Films gets a de-humidifier to dry the costume out over night, but it's impossible to actually clean it. The foam and fur are too thick for it to be dry-cleaned. After a month of filming, the inside of Boris smells like a person who hasn't washed for months. As soon as I'm out of the costume, I remove the cotton karate trousers and long-sleeved T-shirt I wear underneath, and Angela puts them in the laundry basket. I have a shower straight away, and put a clean pair of cotton under clothes on. They've provided me with a blue towelling dressing gown to wear to the studio restaurant for lunch, and whilst wandering around the studios, sitting in script read-throughs, etc. But there's no avoiding the fact that the inside of Boris, and me as soon as I come out of him, stinks.

Angela has every reason to be repelled by the stench, but she's as sweet as my old sweat is stale. She's never late, but always waiting for me with my clean cotton under garments laid out, the blue furry suit unzipped and ready, and the Boris head wiped out with a scented cloth.

She's fresh, clean, and wears the loveliest clothes. Sometimes she dresses conventionally in blue jeans and a T-shirt, and looks fantastic. Other times she goes more like a television wardrobe person. Black leggings with a short frilly skirt, or chintz leggings with no skirt. I love everything she wears, and when I ask where she got some of the more arty creations, they're not from expensive shops on The Kings Road, but put together from jumble sales.

I wear boxer shorts beneath the white cotton karate trousers, and they're always wringing wet with sweat when I take them off. One time, we're shooting at a location on a particularly sweltering day, and my white cotton T-shirt produces over a pint of sweat when I wring it out. She never hesitates to pick them up, and is always there as soon as the First Assistant Director shouts "cut", and we have a break in filming. When she's taken my head off, she holds a flannel against my brow. Not a cold one, because that would be too much of a shock to my system. I lie or sit with my eyes closed, and feel her gently dab the sweat from my head, and I'm in heaven.

I show her extra consideration when I'm changing. Being my dresser, she's around a lot when I'm either naked or semi-naked, and I respect the fact that she's so young. As the weeks go by, though, by mutual consent we adjust the code of conduct. She initiates it one day, in my dressing room, by saying
"Don't worry, Doug. There isn't much time before you're back on camera, and I don't want you to waste your lunch break hiding yourself from me. I've seen a penis before."
"Whose?" I enquire.
"My little brother's."
I laugh, and remove my sweat-soaked boxer shorts in front of her. She gives me a towel and continues brushing the fur on Boris' paws whilst I walk to the shower in the corner of my dressing room. She doesn't realise it, but I see her reflection in the mirror, and she's ogling my bare bottom.

Sometimes, when I'm lying awake in bed, I think about Angela, and imagine licking her thin young body all over. We get on so well, and have such a fantastic working relationship, I don't want to risk spoiling it by making a pass at her. Another reason I don't cross the line with Angela, is because I'm infatuated with Leah Philips. The cast and crew are very close, and when it's someone's birthday, we meet in a restaurant and celebrate. After we've wrapped on Friday evenings, a crowd of us have a few drinks in the Crown and Anchor pub just along the riverbank from the studios. I often miss out on the Friday evening drinks, because I'm rushing off to do a gig somewhere, but as Leah's twenty-fifth birthday is on a Tuesday, I'm available for the evening celebration.

It's been another hot day, and the episode we're making concerns Lois, the character Leah plays, taking Boris the dog camping. We're using the island by Teddington Lock as a location, because it's just across the river from the studios. The episode's taking a couple of days, and Lois and I are the only regular characters in most of it. Consequently the other actors have been given two days off, and I'm getting to know Leah a lot better. Even though we've been working together for a few months, I don't really know any more about her than I did that first day we met. Until this week. We spend most of the time filming lying beside each other in the tent, waiting for the art director and the rest of the design team to reconcile their needs with those of the lighting cameraman. We kill time running and re-running our lines, because Boris speaks quite a lot in this episode. The birdsong drifts down from the unseen trees above the tent, and the afternoon mood is languid. I've got my Boris head on, and sweat drips from my face into the fabric of the inner head. Leah can't see it, and I'm glad she can't. Out of the blue she comes out with:
"You never mention your family, Doug. Don't you see much of them?"
"No."
"Why's that? Do they live far?"
"They don't live, I'm afraid. I'm an orphan."
I squeeze the lever in my right hand slightly, to ease Boris' mouth open. I can't see Lois' face, just her white legs and the lower edge of her khaki shorts.
There's a pause, in which I reflect that above the knees, even though her legs get thicker than my ideal thickness for legs, I still want to see all the way up to the top of her thighs. In fact, every atom of my being yearns to pull those shorts off. For the tenth time that day, I wonder what colour knickers she's got on, and how much pubic hair, if any, she has. Also whether it's dyed or natural.

"I'm sorry, Doug. I've been working with you all this time, and never knew."

181

"That's all right Leah. I'm happier now than I've been in my entire life. It's all turned out for the best."

"Did you never know your parents?"

"I knew my mother, until I was four."

"Please may I ask...how she died?"

I think of the beautifully engineered German knife nestling in the drawer of my desk.

"She slashed her wrists in the bath. I found her. We were alone in the house, and I couldn't get out because I was too small to open the front door."

I get a tingling up my spine when I hear Leah start to cry.

"I could reach the back door handle, but not the key, which was hanging on a hook quite high up."

I give it a pause, for dramatic effect.

"A day and a night, in case you were wondering. How long I was trapped alone in the house with her, I mean."

I feel myself grabbed suddenly, and Leah stifles her sobs in my blue furry chest. I hold her close, hoping the stench of the inside of the costume isn't reaching her nostrils. With my right paw, I softly stroke the back of her head.

"I'm drying my tears in your fur."

"Don't cry for me, Leah. I'm very strong."

She snuggles closer to me, and I'm relieved the thick foam of the costume cushions my enormous erection. I'm so close to those massive tits, and yet so far. I make a bet with myself that her fanny is half shaved, and naturally brunette.

The first assistant director's voice interrupts our cuddle.

"Okay everyone. Stand by for a take. Going from Lois' line "Boris. Don't bark at the squirrels.""

I know Leah and I are both hoping the next shot is a wide one, so the camera doesn't notice she's been crying. It wouldn't look good to make the leading lady cry on her birthday.

The director wants to make the most of the light summer evening, and we don't wrap until seven-thirty. Leah's pissed off about it, and I don't tell her the crappy contract I signed requires me to do unlimited overtime for no extra fee. At least she's getting paid double time. I don't know if it's because she feels sorry for me, or because Des Jensen, the star who plays Rufus, isn't around. But Leah is really friendly to me for the rest of the day. I get on well enough with Des Jensen, but I can't help wondering if he's jealous of me because I've got a thing going with the stand-up, and all he's got is the acting. He's a successful enough actor, but nowadays it's the stand-ups who get the glory.

Angela declines my invitation to come for a drink in the riverside beer garden of the Crown and Anchor pub. Her brother's visiting from abroad, and she has to entertain him. I'm relieved at this, because Leah and I have bonded today. The terrible truth is that her status as a famous actress wins the day no matter how magnificent a dresser Angela is. Superficial, perhaps, but that's how it works in television.
"What's it to be, Birthday Girl?" I'm getting the first round of drinks. Leah chooses a pint of strong lager, and I work my way around the crew and members of Grange Films staff taking their drinks orders. Whilst I do so, I can't help noticing that when the vision mixer tries to sit next to Leah, she tells him the seat is taken. I make my way to the bar, hoping she's keeping it for me.

When I take the tray of drinks into the beer garden, there's a cluster of people around Leah. They've recognised her from the telly, or the feature film she did. She's signing autographs and answering their predictable questions graciously. Sheila the producer freezes them out by observing that Leah's trying to have a private drink with friends, and they return to their table in another part of the beer garden. I take my seat beside Leah, and sink a third of my lager in one gulp. It's a glorious summer evening, and we've got one of the best tables in the beer garden. We're near the riverbank, and the willow trees on the bank opposite frame the swans as they swim upstream. The sun's still shining, and Leah's wearing a flowery dress. It's the first time I've seen her wear a dress other than the clothes she wears as costume in the show. She tends to wear trousers or skirts to and from the studio. Her blonde hair shines in the evening sunlight, and she's put a bit of red lipstick on. She opens one of her presents, and it's a black hair band with a plastic flower on it. She puts it in her hair, and it makes her look like an older version of Alice in Wonderland.

There's a carefree atmosphere, and we all get tipsy quite quickly. One by one, people remember it's a weeknight, and they have to be back at the studio early in the morning. By half past nine in the evening, we're down to Terry the runner, Sheila the producer, Leah, and me. Sheila's never been so friendly to me, and I know it's totally down to the fact that Leah's laughing at my jokes, and enjoying my company. As the producer, Sheila's first concern is to please her star. If Leah likes someone, that person's status is raised accordingly. Sheila knows Leah is the reason the show's been given the budget and the extra episodes. When her last series was shown, Leah got the front page of several glossy magazines. Looking at her now, with those perfect white teeth and doll like face, I can understand why. And she can act as brilliantly as she looks.

Terry makes a move, and Sheila follows shortly afterwards. It's just Leah and me, and the beer garden's filling up. A group of men at the next table make little effort to conceal the fact they're watching Leah. They've had enough drink to talk loudly about her within her earshot, and become a nuisance. It's time to leave, and the least I can do is escort her from the premises.
"I don't have to go home tonight. Where do you live?" Says Leah, as we approach the Mercedes luxury saloon that's been waiting for her since our working day finished. As the star, she can keep her car waiting for as long as she likes, whereas the likes of me have to use our car soon after being wrapped, or cancel it.
"Lambeth Walk." I answer.
"Near Waterloo."
"I know a great restaurant near there. Do you fancy it?"
I can hardly conceal my enthusiasm. We get in the back seat of her car, and she tells her driver to call at her place on the way to Waterloo. I'm intrigued to know where she lives, and it turns out to be a little Victorian terraced cottage not far from the studios.
"I spend so much time working at Teddington, it makes sense to keep my London home here." She explains, after she's reappeared from her quaint little house, outside which I was kept waiting in the car for ten minutes. I've had three pints of lager, and tell her I'm desperate for a squirt. I was hoping she'd invite me in so I could use her loo, and see the inside of her house.

"Come on Doug, you can hold yourself!" She says, playfully grasping my thigh. I almost squirm with excitement, partly because I can feel her fingernails in my thigh through the denim of my jeans, and partly from the look in her eyes. She's a real femme fatale. She emerged with a large overnight bag, the sight of which made my heart leap with hope. The most famous person I've slept with up to now is Morag McDougal, the quiz show host on BBC Scotland. But she's only regional. Leah's worldwide.

She sits by the half-opened car window, loudly chewing gum, and recounting what she's done on previous birthdays. Remembering that she voiced one of the main characters in a recent Hollywood animated film that was a box office hit, I ask her where her "non-London" home is.
"I've got a flat on the seafront in Bournemouth. And a house in France." She replies, nonchalantly.
"Whereabouts in France?" I enquire, trying not to sound too interested.
"Biarritz. Jess likes it there."
I don't ask who Jess is. Could be her boyfriend. Could be her girlfriend. Whoever it is, she isn't with Jess now, but with me.

Whilst we're waiting at a red light in Battersea, the people in the car next to us recognise her, and start waving and calling her name. She raises the window, and continues what she's talking about without pausing. It's an everyday occurrence.
I'm bursting to have a wee by the time we're near Waterloo, and I renew my request to stop. I look at every pub we pass with longing, mentally running in through the bar to the gents.

She must have a sadistic streak, because she categorically refuses my request to stop, and my alarm greatly increases when we draw up outside the restaurant to find it's closed for refurbishment. Leah lets gush some swear words even I haven't heard, and we decide to continue the short distance to my flat in Lambeth Walk.

I carry her bag for her. Luckily the lift doors open as we get to it, and three middle-aged women do a double take when they recognise Leah. I'm too desperate to hang around, and by the time the women have realised it actually was Leah Phillips getting into the lift, the doors have closed, and we're on our way up to the third floor.

"It's not a luxury flat, but it's mine and I'm proud of it." I announce as I turn the front door key and push the door open. I drop her bag in the hall, and rush to the toilet. I don't bother locking the door, because she's the only other person here and I figure she knows what I'm doing. When I hear the door open behind me, it comes as a shock. "Sorry. I didn't know you wanted to go too." I can't think what else to say. I feel a bit self-conscious now, but that doesn't inhibit the torrent of urine tumbling into the toilet bowl. I feel a pair of hands grip my buttocks, and Leah's blonde head appears to my right. I can't see her face, just the top of her head as she peers around my body to watch me piss. Her right hand reaches forward, and the palm stays in the warm yellow stream. I flinch as she's causing piss to splash on my jeans, on the edge of the toilet bowl, and even on the toilet walls.
"It's nice and warm." She coos, and her hand moves up to my cock, causing the stream to spread out even more.
"I'm glad you're doing this here, and not in the restaurant."
"Why?"
"Because I don't keep a clean pair of jeans in the restaurant."
"Take them off." She instructs. Her voice is commanding, but her fingernails stroke the underside of my cock exquisitely. I've emptied my bladder now, and she lets me step out into the hall. The toilet seat drops loudly, and she sits on the loo, her white knickers around her ankles, and has quite a long piss herself. I watch her from the hall, my eyes transfixed, wondering if they're the same pair of knickers she wore earlier under her costume shorts. I was both right and wrong about her pubic hair. It's partially shaved, but blonde.
"You're naturally blonde, then Leah?" I ask.
She's still issuing a golden stream, staring at me with complete authority, and ignoring my question.
"Take the rest of your clothes off." I oblige, dropping them right where I am in the hall.
"Go and lie down on the bed, and wait."
"Can't I go and wash …?"
"Lie down on the bed and wait!"
I go into the bedroom, but as she can't see me, I don't lie on the futon yet. I'm a bit worried about the fact that she caused piss to go all over my knob and pubic hair, so I wipe myself with tissues. She is Leah Phillips, after all. Star of TV and cinema screen.

I'd feel a lot more comfortable if I could have a quick shower, but I hear Leah go into the bathroom and close the door.

I relax on the duvet cover, and close my eyes. I've dreamed about having Leah back to my flat ever since I met her, but this isn't quite how I imagined it. Suddenly the bedroom door bursts open. I open my eyes, and there's Leah. Except she isn't wearing the floral summery dress. She's wearing a black leather mini skirt, long black boots, and a tight black PVC bodice. In her right hand, she's holding a whip. It's a whip with lots of thin strips of black leather, and she's swishing it against her thigh.

I automatically spread my arms and legs, as if I was tied to the bedposts.

"Are you sure you don't want me to go and wash?"

"Why do you ask?"

"Because you made me get wee wee on my self."

She steps closer to the futon, brandishing the whip.

"You're a dirty boy, then. Aren't you?"

"If you say so."

"If you say so, what?" She emphasises the last word with a practiced flick of the whip on my feet. It doesn't hurt. It's more of a caress.

"I don't know."

"You address me as 'Mistress Leah.'" She strokes my balls with the very end of the whip.

"If you say so, Mistress Leah." I reply.

She smiles and whispers:

"Good boy." The black bodice lifts her tits, and emphasises her cleavage. I just hope I'm going to get to see the rest of them, because they really are magnificent. My knob is twitching with desperation to be touched. I never thought I'd be into this weird stuff, but it's thrilling.

"Turn over." She commands. I turn over onto my front, and feel the whip caress my buttocks. She draws it slowly up the crease of my bum, so the strands stroke what small area of my scrotum and knob are exposed between the backs of my thighs. The first hard stroke comes down. It's not painful like a riding crop, but tantalising. The leather strands are soft, and she's treating me like a beginner. Sometimes it hurts a tiny bit, but more often I just get a rush of air as the whip swishes close to my skin. Then there's a short period of sensual stroking. I never know what's coming, or if it's going to be touching my buttocks, thighs, back, or shoulders. All I know is I love it! She launches into a sequence of whipping, and as it gets harder, it still doesn't hurt because I'm getting acclimatised to it. By the end of the flurry, the pain is delicious. Then it stops. A minute later, I'm about to ask her if she's thirsty from her exertions, when she tells me to turn over. She's helped herself to a bottle of Cointreau I've had lingering at the back of the booze cupboard for years, and she's swigging from it.

She whips me up and down the front of my body, but reduces the severity of the strokes to allow for the softness of my front. Apart from my penis, which is very hard. After she's whipped my chest and stomach, she whips my cock nice and lightly. Then she straddles me, and pours Cointreau over my mouth. I swallow some of it, and the rest dribbles over my chin and cheeks. She leans forward and licks the spilled Cointreau from my throat, before giving me a long sensuous kiss. She's even better than the Sardinian girl I had on the boat earlier this summer. Leah runs her fingers through my hair, and lifts my head so I can swig from the bottle. Then she pushes my head down onto the pillow, and stands up with one foot either side of my chest. She's a real wild child, trying to balance on the futon in high-heeled boots, the whip in one hand, and the Cointreau bottle in the other. She reminds me of a pirate, as she stands above me rocking unsteadily. I can see up her skirt, and she isn't wearing knickers. I don't know when she took them off, because she was definitely wearing them earlier. She tosses the whip onto the floor, and hands me the Cointreau bottle. I'm about to take a swig, when I suddenly hold my arm still. I don't want the bottle obscuring my view, because Leah's hands are loosening the lacing of her bodice. I groan with awe as she springs her enormous bosoms free. My mouth is still open as the first erect nipple is lowered into it. As soon as I start to suck, she pulls my head away.
"Just lick them. And the aureoles." I lick and slurp around her nipples, then she subsides onto the futon beside me, and instructs me to pour Cointreau over her tits. I do so, and lick every drop from them. Some of it's run down onto her stomach, and I lick all the way down to her vagina. I'm just getting down to some serious licking, when more Cointreau flows down from her stomach, and over her labia. I suck it from her pubic hair, and lick it from her clitoris hood. She squeezes those silky thighs around my head, and holds me tight

between them. I've never felt safer in my life. "Thank God I got round to getting myself tested." I think to myself. It was last week when the results came through. Completely free of all sexually transmitted diseases.

"Put it inside me!" I hear. I think she might have told me several times, but my ears were covered by her glorious thighs. I put it inside her. It's just as well my knob's so stiff, because her vagina is quite big. I start thrusting, and she lifts her tits together so the nipples rub against my chest as I work up and down.
"It's safe to come inside me if you want." She whispers. Her face is looking to the side, and her eyes are closed. I kiss her cheek and nibble her ear as I pump away with my hips. She opens her eyes and turns her face up towards me. We gaze into each other's eyes, and it occurs to me that I love this woman passionately. She's not playing the dominatrix now, but the soft little girl lost. Her breath comes in short gasps as I thrust and thrust. I'm not in danger of coming too soon because her vagina is so big there's not so much friction on my German helmet. My eyes are so close to hers, I'm getting a distorted image of her face. Sometimes she's got three eyes and two noses, and I have a little revelation about Picasso. This must be how he got the inspiration for those portraits of his lovers. The famous paintings that hang in the world's greatest collections are the view he had whilst fucking the subject. I make a mental note to see if I can develop the insight into a joke. Leah comes, and her tree-trunk thighs grip and hold me again. Some muscles deep inside her vagina squeeze the bulbous end of my knob, and I can feel the spunk spurting into her. We lay there panting together, my head nestled between her wonderful breasts. We fall asleep for a while, and when we wake up we drink copious amounts of water. After we've cleaned our teeth, and she's removed her make-up, her woman's intuition senses that my knob's gone hard again. I get a quick, deft hand job onto her tits, and fall asleep once more with my head buried between them. In the morning I can't remember having ever slept deeper and more powerfully. My cheek is stuck to one of her huge tits, and when I pull it away it's encrusted with my dried spunk.

Leah disappears to the toilet, and I lay there with the euphoric feeling I had the first time I spent the night with a girl. I'm amazed how early it is when I look at the alarm clock. That sleep was so wonderful, I feel as refreshed as if I'd slept for ten hours, and not six. I hear her come out of the toilet and go into the kitchen, and a few minutes later she brings two mugs of hot sweet tea. I have a quick piss, and get back under the warm duvet with her. She holds me to her bosoms, and we lay there having a lovely cuddle. I've never felt so complete in my life, and it occurs to me that Leah's four years older than Mummy was when she died.

Leah gulps her tea, sounding more like a workman than a sex symbol actress, and whilst I'm still sipping mine, her head disappears beneath the covers, and I feel her lips on my nipples. Long fingernails caress my balls. My winkle stands to attention, and is very soon enjoying his morning wash care of Leah's tongue. Her mouth is still hot from the tea, and the skill of her lips and tongue tip, combined with some quick jerking from her wrist, result in Leah swallowing her second drink of the day. She truly is a dirty girl.

When she emerges from beneath the duvet, I'm about to return her favour, when she looks me mischievously in the eye and demands coffee. When I return to the bedroom, proudly bearing two frothy sweet cappuccinos, she's turned the telly on. I get into bed beside her, and who should be on the screen but Brian O'Shea. The female breakfast TV interviewer is drooling all over him, and I must admit, Brian's looking pretty good. His shaggy black Irish hair tumbles across his earnest brow, and his clothes are a marvel of studied scruffiness. The sitcom 'Bare In Mind' has been running for two weeks now, and it's performing well in the ratings. Brian's doing the chat show rounds, no doubt because the network wants the show plugged as much as possible, as it's summer, when the viewing figures drop.

"He's gorgeous, don't you think?" Says Leah. I'm lying with both my arms around her, and my face as close as possible to her armpit. I can only see the screen from one eye, because I don't ever want to let go of Leah. I've fallen madly in love with her. I don't care if she's famous – right now I'd adore her if she was a penniless cleaning lady.

"He's all right if you like men." I reply, and nuzzle deeper into her armpit. She raises her arm so I can lick her armpit, and when I've finished, she obliges with the other one. Then I lick her nipples whilst jigging her luscious boobs. The aureoles are really wide.

"I need to phone the car company. Or the driver will be wondering why I'm not at home." I offer her the phone, but she takes one of those new mobile phones out of her bag, and dials. I continue licking her nipples while she cancels her car. I'm thrilled that she's not too embarrassed to be seen arriving at the studios in my car. She gently extricates herself from me, and goes to the bathroom. I drink my cappuccino, watching Brian talk about 'Bare in Mind', and wondering how much heroin he's taken this morning. Leah comes back in to get some pills out of her bag, and remarks casually:

"Nicky Butler's coming to work for us. She was a producer on 'Bare in Mind'".

"I've met Nicky. She's really nice."

"Yeah she's a good friend of mine. I asked Sheila to bring her on board." With that she wafts back into the bathroom, leaving me impressed that her star status allows her to choose her producers. For most people it's the other way round.

"Doug?" She calls from the toilet, where she's pissing with the door open.

"Yes?" I can hear tinkling for a while, then it stops.

"Will you come to my house some time and piss on me?"

"Okay. If you piss on me."

"It's a deal, Darling."

Chapter Twenty-six

Maybe it's because we arrive at the studios twenty minutes late, but it's not long before everyone knows Leah and I spent the night together. When I asked her if she thought word would get round, she pointed out that the car containing both of us would only be seen at the studio foyer, and everyone in the film unit would already be scattered throughout the production areas. Perhaps the women in reception started the rumour off, but whoever it was, even the carpenters and electricians know about it. I can tell because they fall silent when I walk past. More importantly, my status has shot up amongst the likes of Simon the director, and Sheila the producer. It's a win-win situation, because there's nothing I'd rather do than make love with Leah, and yet the act of doing so is a greater career move than getting six encores at The Clap Clinic. There's one huge downside, though. Poor Angela, my dresser, is heartbroken. She does her best to hide it, but I notice her hands shaking when she puts my head on, and reaches inside to adjust the cable that blinks the eyes. I feel so sorry for her, and if I could lead two parallel lives, I'd gladly oblige her. God knows I fancy her enough, and I can't fault her as a dresser or as a person. But she's only sixteen, and I'd be wrong to start a relationship with someone that young.

It's another gloriously hot day, and we finish the scenes involving Leah and Boris in the tent at the location on the other side of the river. Sheila the producer calls me "Darling", and touches my arm when she talks to me at lunch. I can barely believe that this time twenty-four hours ago Leah and I were still merely colleagues. It feels like we've been lovers for a week. I'm experienced enough not to make the mistake of giving the game away, and keep my hands off her in front of people. She's the one who 'goes public' first, by holding my hand as we walk back towards the location after lunch. Angela's getting my costume ready, and I feel really uncomfortable, because her eyes are red with crying.

"I've got terrible hey fever." She claims. I don't ask her why the hay fever didn't strike until over half way through the summer.

We rattle though our scenes, and finish ahead of schedule, which is just as well because even I am suffering from the heat inside the Boris costume. Angela's as attentive as ever, bringing me bottles of water, and mugs of hot tea. When we've done the last scene, she helps me out of the costume, and hands me my blue towelling dressing gown. It's important to wear it as soon as I come out of the costume. The hotter the weather, the more I'm soaked in sweat, and that's when a breeze could give me a chill. We've settled into a routine of me getting into costume either on the studio floor or at the location, as Boris is too bulky for long walks from the dressing room. Angela usually carries Boris, and I walk in the freedom of my dressing gown.

I get showered and take a look at tomorrow's script. Des Jensen's back on set tomorrow, and I'm surprised to see how few lines he has compared to Boris. I wonder how he's going to be taking Leah's and my fling. Before I can wonder very much, my dressing room telephone rings, and Leah's voice purrs into my freshly showered ear.
"Come up and see me, big boy." She hangs up. I make my excuses to Angela, whose busy sewing a small tear in Boris's paw, and walk along the corridor to Star dressing room One. On the varnished wooden door is a small plaque bearing the name 'Leah Philips.' I knock, and dutifully wait.
"Come in." The voice is more headmistressy now, and I enter to find Leah looking fantastic in her white towelling dressing gown, and her birthday hair band. She's sitting at her make-up mirror, holding court to Nicky Butler and an insignificant looking man. They are both seated on her sofa. The small man is introduced to me as Lawrence. I'm told he's one of the writers. He looks too young to have experienced anything to write about, but what bothers me is the sight of Leah loading sparkly white powder into a nose bullet. I've seen Arnold Shanks use one. In fact I've had a few shots from it myself, but I'm shocked to see Leah with one. Especially as she's filling it up with coke so expertly, she clearly gets plenty of practice. Last night takes on a different significance. So that's what she was doing in the bathroom. Now I understand why she showed no signs of hunger after we found the restaurant was closed, and had such a capacity for Cointreau.

193

"Sit down, Darling." I go to an overstuffed armchair by the sliding French window. There are two star dressing rooms on this floor. They both have a balcony overlooking the River Thames, and luxury three-piece suites. The en suite shower rooms are bathrooms too, and the fridges are much bigger. My dressing room is better than average, because most don't have an en suite shower room and toilet. I also get a bowl of fruit and a bowl of sweets. I notice Leah's fruit bowl is bigger and has more exotic fruit, and her sweet bowl is full of handmade Belgian chocolates and not liquorice Allsorts, like mine. No one's eating any fruit or chocolates now, though. It's nose candy they're into. Next to the white paper packet Leah's decanting the cocaine into her silver nose bullet from, is another unopened white paper packet. Next to that is a mirror flat on the dressing table, with five lines chopped out. I'm about to ask who the fifth line is for, when Sheila the producer emerges from the bathroom and sits in the chair by the coke, a silver tooting tube in her right hand.

"We've been thinking about Boris, Doug. The noises at the network have shown some preview tapes to the yanks, and they're bonkers about the show. They want to put money into a Christmas special, and they've optioned for feature film rights. They're going to screen the TV series *ahead of the British airings!*"
Sheila's face sinks to the mirror as soon as she's finished her sentence, hoovers up her line, and carries on talking with hardly a break in rhythm.
"I'm talking network in America, mind you. We're making television history, and we've yet to broadcast the first show!"
She's handed the tooter to Leah, who's putting the longest line on the mirror up her nose.
"We were wondering if you have any ideas for Boris, Doug. Seeing as you're the one inside the costume." If he'd been at my school, Lawrence would have been bullied on the first day. His body is so slight, and his voice is squeaky and I have to strain to hear what he's saying.
"I was thinking about his tail." I reply. "If I could wag his tail, I could get a lot more expression. It might be difficult to disguise my hand movement when I'm standing up, but when I'm laying in my basket or on the sofa, I could use the arm that's hidden from the camera to wag the tail."

"Fantastic!" Cries Sheila.

"Genius!" Enthuses Nicky Butler. I get the impression this isn't the first line they've done this afternoon.

Lawrence produces a small voice recorder and actually whispers into it. "Sort out tail wagging mechanism. For Boris." I'd like to know how much they're paying him, because I bet it's more than double what I'm on, and his job looks a lot easier.

"The other thing is front and end titles, Dougie." My status *has* gone up! Sheila's calling me "Dougie" now. It hadn't dawned on me that she's Scottish before, but the coke's bringing out her accent. I guess it's that posh bit of Glasgow. What's it called? That's right - Kelvinside. I did a gig at a wedding reception there once. Went down the tubes big time, but had sex with a bridesmaid in the toilet.

"We haven't shot the front titles or the end titles, and we need to get them in the can by the end of the month. The Americans want something really spectacular. They want to spend a lot of money on them, as long as they can see the money on the screen. They'll be seen every show, and they don't mind paying for something *really special*. Any ideas?"

She says this as she hands me the silver coke tooter, and I don't think she's aware of the irony.

"It's funny you should ask that." I say.

"Because I was thinking about this only yesterday." I bend down and hoover up my line. Bang! My heart accelerates, and my eyes light up. I see them in the dressing mirror. This coke puts all coke I've had so far in my life to shame. A line of this could power a nuclear submarine around the world!

"How about this?" I sniff and the coke in my nose slides down my throat. When I start speaking, I can hardly feel my throat because it's gone all cold. My voice sounds husky.

"Leah walks into the kitchen, and we see her face in close up. She does a double take. Cut to a mock up of the kitchen set, only it's a scale model. We see what caused Leah to do a double take. It's a rat, filmed in the scale model of the kitchen.

Cut to Leah milking the rat. We use the kitchen set, and a mocked-up rat for that. Then we see Leah – or I suppose I should say Lois – making cheese out of the rat's milk. She puts the rat's milk cheese on

195

the table, and goes out. Maybe there's a doorbell sound in the title music."

I notice that Lawrence is recording me on his little tape recorder, and the others are all giving me their rapt attention. I take a swig from a water bottle, and continue.
"Boris comes in the kitchen, and eats the cheese. Then he goes to the lounge and lies on the sofa. Lois comes into the lounge, and turfs Boris off the sofa. Her credit rolls across the screen, and she gets up and walks out of shot. Boris gets back on the sofa, and falls asleep again. Then Des comes in as Rufus, and turfs Boris off the sofa. His credit rolls, and he gets up and walks out of shot. Boris gets back on the sofa, and the same thing happens for all the other principal characters. The last time Boris is thrown off the sofa, he goes to his basket – where he finds the rest of the cast all asleep in a huddle. Cut to Boris waking up on the sofa – it's all a dream, inspired by eating (roll the title) 'Rat's Milk Cheese.'

I look at Leah, who looks lovelier than ever in her white dressing gown and new headband. She laughs and looks at Sheila, who's nodding with approval.

"I love it. It's surreal. It's wacky. It let's 'em know what's it's about. And it features the sitcom sofa."
"And it make sense of the title 'Rat's Milk Cheese.'" Adds Lawrence, who addresses his comment into his tape recorder as much as to the rest of us.
"And it shows the money on the screen." Adds Nicky Butler, who's clearly aiming this comment to get Sheila's approval.

I'm amazed they haven't noticed that my idea features Boris more than Leah, who's actually the star of the show. I'm sure they'll rescind their acceptance once they've realised this, but in the mean time, I'm happy to wallow in their praise.
"I'll get on to the art director to draw plans for a scale model of the kitchen, and a giant milking rat. I want big, pink teats. Lawrence – write that idea up, and I'll fax it to America to get their reaction. Dougie Poo, you're a genius. I'm going to put you in the writing team."

I'd be over the moon at what Sheila's saying, but for the fact that I've noticed a red top newspaper strewn across the floor in front of Leah's toilet. It's upside down in my vision, because whoever was last sitting down in there was reading it, and left it on the floor in front of the toilet. I can still recognise Sunita's photo, and the headline 'Pregnant Actress in Drug Arrest.' I smile politely to everyone, and go in the toilet and lock the door. Sunita was arrested by customs officers at Riyadh airport in Saudi Arabia, when they found ten grammes of cocaine in her luggage. My hands tremble as I read on. "The pregnant actress was going out to meet her boyfriend, comedy promoter Arnold Shanks. Arnold Shanks was already in Riyadh, setting up a new comedy venue for English speaking ex-pats. Pregnant Sunita Shakira could face the death penalty." Sunita never touched drugs in all the year I went out with her. I remember the trick Arnold played on me when he got me to carry his bags through French customs at Nice airport. If he set Sunita up, I'll never forgive him. I don't care who he knows in the world of organised crime.

Chapter Twenty-seven

That evening Leah invites me to her house with Sheila and Nicky Butler, but I've got a gig in Portsmouth. I tell her I've also got an upset stomach, which is partly true, because whilst I was reading the news about Sunita, I was having cocaine-inspired diarrhoea.

I drive to Portsmouth worrying about Sunita. I'm sure Arnold's responsible for the cocaine in her luggage. My gig is at HMS Dolphin, the Royal Naval submarine base. There are also a lot of personnel from HMS Vernon, the Royal Navy's Dive training establishment. They're a rowdy lot, but good-natured with it, and my knowledge of diving allows me to interact with them, and win the day. The Official Secrets Act forbids submarine crews to reveal what depth their submarines can dive to. I make a running joke of this by every so often throwing in a question to an individual in the audience like "400 metres?" Or "750 metres?" Later on I develop the gag by asking similar questions such as "7 inches?" or "6 inches?" They love this, and when I address the commanding officer with the question "Two and a half inches?" they go wild. It strikes me as pathetically predictable, but the Royal Navy personnel think it's hilarious. After the show, the Commanding Officer approaches me and thanks me for entertaining them. I've done enough military gigs to know that Commanding Officers are never offended if you take the piss out of them during the show. They see a laugh at their expense as raising their men's moral. He gets a couple of them to take me to see the submarine escape tower. Before being allowed to go in a submarine, every member of crew has to perform a practice escape by entering the bottom of the tower, which contains water. He has to float to the top, from a depth of over a hundred feet. I'm fascinated by their diving equipment, especially the oxygen re-breathing gear, and the deep submersion suits with their reinforced air hoses that allow divers to stay submerged for hours at a time.

The next day the Americans accept my idea for the front titles, despite initial reservations that a rat is a negative image with which to start a television programme. When Sheila points out that Mickey Mouse is also a rodent, and the art department comes up with a stylised, Disney-esque rat with a friendly smile on its face, they withdraw their objection. I can't believe my luck. I've climbed the greasy pole from a walk-on in the pilot, to the main part in the title sequence of the series. They tell me about the end title sequence, which the other writers thought of. It involves a dolls house replica of the stage sets, which they flood and fill with piranhas. The redeeming thing about it as far as I'm concerned, is that they have a puppet Boris sleeping on the sofa during the sequence. I say I think it's good, but privately I think the idea's weak.

Des Jensen seems friendly enough, and after we've wrapped, we all repair to the beer garden of The Crown and Anchor for a riverside evening drink. Leah looks resplendent in a black A line dress. When she laughs, it's a deep-throated one, resonating with a dirty sense of humour. There's something slightly un-hinged about her, and it pulls my heartstrings like nothing has before. I had a lucky spell during today's filming, when Boris was in shot, but sleeping in his basket. As I lay there daydreaming in full costume, I remembered my guided tour of the naval base the previous evening, and an idea for the end titles came to me.

As the evening sunshine enlivens the willow trees on the opposite bank, and glints off the windows of the cabin cruisers motoring past the beer garden, I mention my idea to Leah, Sheila, and Simon the director.
"You know the Americans want to put money into the title sequences because they're shown every time the programme's shown?" I start off.
"Absolutely." Replies Simon.
"They're adamant the front and end title sequence should be sensational. They want it talked about everywhere, by everyone."
"How about, instead of using a dolls house replica of the lounge set, we submerge the actual lounge set in a huge tank of water? I'm a qualified diver, and I could wear commercial diving equipment under

199

the Boris costume, that would take my exhaust carbon dioxide away without causing bubbles."
"What's the point of having you under water, then?" Frowns Sheila. She's not been in a good mood today, and I presume it's because she hasn't had any coke and is on the come down from when she did.
"You could fill the tank with interesting fish. Octopus, squid, …"
"Sharks. We could have sharks swimming around Boris. And conger eels. Big ones, over two metres long. And all the time you could be on the sofa, blinking your eyes. It's brilliant. I love it!"
I put my reservations about sharing a tank of water with sharks on hold, and add the last bit of my idea.
"If we had a safe area in front of the glass front of the tank, we could have lions and tigers walk in front of the sharks. It would cost a fortune, but if the Americans want to spend money on something memorable…"

The others all rave about my idea, and I assure them that I could stay under water as long as required.
"There's a large water tank at Pinewood Studios. They use it for the underwater sequences in the James Bond films." Says Simon the director.
"I'll find out how much it costs." Says Nicky Butler, who's well on board now. I'm beginning to suspect there's something going on between her and Simon, because they're often sitting next to each other.

Leah's sitting opposite me, facing the river. I'm facing the pub. I'd rather be facing the river, but Leah gets recognised less if her face isn't on view to people coming into the beer garden from the pub. I feel a hand on my knee, and it makes its way up my jeans towards my thigh. It's Leah's, but she can't reach far enough under the table to touch my groin.
"Oops, I think I dropped something." She says, and disappears under the table. I feel heat in my crotch as her mouth bites into it. Then her hands start stoking the denim above my knob. I carry on listening to Simon tell an amusing anecdote about a well-known actor he worked with who was recently knighted. Apparently he demands a prostitute in his dressing room during every recording, and one evening when his wife turned up unexpectedly, one of the production staff handed her

£500 in cash. When she asked what it was for, he had to tell her it was her husband's poker winnings. This caused a terrible scene, because the actor is a member of Gamblers Anonymous.

Leah re-emerges from under the table. We've arranged that I'm going to stay at her place tonight, and she's invited me to her house in Biarritz for the weekend. I can't wait to get her naked again, although I'm slightly apprehensive about all this pissing on each other. We make some secret signs to each other, and she's about to stand up and take me away, when a voice calls my name. I turn round to face the direction it came from, and I see a classic wooden 1930s motor yacht, gleaming with varnish and white paint. She's nosing her way towards the beer garden's mooring, and on her foredeck is Arnold. What bothers me more is who's at the controls. It's Hans Vermeulen. Sitting next to him, is Ruud Vermeulen, and three children sit dejectedly on the cabin top.

Chapter Twenty-eight

They're not so young as to give me a panic attack, but they're young enough for a black cloak of depression to descend over me. I count my blessings that they remain silently on the cabin top, looking sad.

I catch the mooring line that Arnold throws me, and tie it to the bollard.
"Hi Arnold, if you'd got here a minute later, you'd have missed us."
"Och, stay for a wee pint, Dougie. I want to show you my new toy."
I want to confront Arnold about Sunita's languishing in a Saudi gaol, but the presence of Ruud and Hans Vermeulen inhibits me. If Arnold's a snake in the grass, the Vermeulens are a minefield ahead, with a column of tanks approaching from the rear. I decide to humour them for the time being.

It transpires that Arnold knows Sheila, which doesn't surprise me, as it was him who got me involved with 'Rats Milk Cheese' in the first place. I shake hands with Ruud Vermeulen, who's impeccably dressed in a blazer and slacks, and the embodiment of courteous civility. Hans looks a lot smoother than last time I saw him, but when he shakes my hand I still feel intimidated by the look in his eyes. He looks less dishevelled than when I first met him, but in his jeans and scruffy brown leather jacket, he still has the appearance of a character in a Dutch porn film. Luckily, Leah's interested in the boat, so Arnold shows the two of us around, whilst Sheila and Simon fuss over the Vermeulen brothers in the beer garden. Arnold introduces us to the kids, who turn out to be his. They remain frozen to the coach roofing above the saloon, and as we go to the cockpit, I regain my equilibrium. They seem as keen to avoid us, as I'm keen to avoid them, and I get away with not having to confront my fear. Whilst Arnold shows me the steering position, Leah tries to draw the kids into conversation, but has to battle to get the briefest of answers, and soon gives up trying. Whilst she's doing so, Arnold winks at me, and takes his hip flask from beside the engine controls. I decline his offer of a swig, and as I watch him take his second glug, I remember the first time I saw his hip flask. It was in his office, when he removed it from its packaging, and used the filling funnel to pour boiling water into Tam's anus. I'm sure Arnold's responsible for Tam and Gregor's murders, but someone else is in custody awaiting trial. I'm not sure whether to dive off the boat and avoid him forever, or feel blessed that he treats me like an old mate. We only get a cursory look below decks, and when we join the others in the beer garden, I'm disturbed to discover that Sheila Fox the producer knows Ruud Vermeulen *as well* as Arnold. Ruud Vermeulen has bought a big chunk of Grange Films. No wonder they're clucking around him and his brother, and running to the bar to get them drinks!

The kids accept bottles of lemonade and packets of crisps, and disappear below decks. We adults sit round the beer garden table, chatting politely, and I drift off into a reverie about Sunita's imprisonment. This leads to thoughts of Tam and Gregor's bodies being eaten by eels in the canal nearby. I suddenly realise everyone's looking at me, awaiting a reply. Apparently Ruud Vermeulen said something to me, and I've no idea what it was. Wallowing in embarrassment, I say "Pardon?"

Ruud's thin grey lips smile in crisp politeness, and he repeats himself.

"I must congratulate you on finding the clown and anchor." My blood freezes and my heart stops. I look around the table at the smiling faces around me. I can't believe that Leah, Simon the director, and Sheila are all in on that poor clown's murder. I eventually stammer something

"I'm sure he deserved it. I won't tell anybody."

Everyone laughs, and it seems I'm off the hook. I have a stab of paranoia, and wonder if I've been spiked with LSD.

"I love your surreal English humour. And I love the preview tapes of the show." Announces Ruud. If Ruud's happy, everyone's happy, and we all relax after the tension that arose from my getting caught not listening to him.

"I think I might apply for a job on the show myself. If it means I can drink beer at the Crown and Anchor." We all laugh politely, and a wave of realisation comes over me. I thought Vermeulen had said he must congratulate me on finding the clown and anchor, when he was really talking about the pub whose beer garden we are sitting in – The Crown and Anchor! Phew, that was close. I look around the table

203

again. All faces are on Sheila Fox, who's regurgitating my idea for the end titles for the Vermeulen's benefit. Ruud listens enthusiastically, but when I look at Hans, our eyes meet, and his blue gaze drills into my eyes. I get a mental picture of Hans in Viking attire, and me as a Saxon farmer. He's pillaging our peaceful homestead. Raping my wife and daughter before my eyes, then killing me, burning my farm, and stealing my daughter and valuable possessions.

Suddenly I return to the moment. What did I say? "I'm sure he deserved it. I won't tell anybody." If Mad Hans twigged I was referring to the clown tied to the anchor, I could be dead soon. I make a mental note not to go sailing or scuba diving with him. And what about Arnold? He must know about the murdered clown. I don't feel he's as much a threat as Hans and Ruud, though. I know Arnold well enough to understand how his brain works. I'm sure he thinks that as long as I'm benefiting from our association, I'm not going to rock the boat. When Leah stands up and announces our departure, Arnold gives me another knowing wink. I suppose he thinks I'm not bothered about Sunita's fate, now that I'm sleeping with the famous sex symbol Leah Philips.

I snuggle up to Leah on the quilted black leather seat of her chauffeur driven BMW 700 series. She smothers me in affection, and when I ask if she's met Ruud or Hans Vermeulen before, she replies she thinks she might have seen Ruud across a crowded room at a showbiz party, but has never been introduced to him. She's never met Hans before, and finds him "creepy and frightening".

We pull up outside Leah's Victorian terraced house in Teddington, and I perk up at the idea of seeing inside it for the first time. The little front garden is full of roses, and there's ivy and some flower I don't know the name of growing around the front door. Instead of letting us in with a key, she rings the doorbell. A pretty young woman with a dental brace and an East European accent answers, and as soon as we're in the hall, my alarm bells ring. There's a plastic tractor lying on its side, and as we walk past the open door to the front room, I glimpse beanbags, a huge colourful toy box, and a kiddie's video silently showing on the TV. The house smells of the detritus of small child.

Bits of banana squashed into fabric, cheesy towels, and other odours I can't identify other than that they surround young children.

"Mummy!!" A small boy - don't ask me how old he is because I couldn't tell you if he's two or seven – runs from the kitchen into Leah's waiting arms. She's knelt down especially to receive him, and sweeps him up into a spinning hug.
"What are you doing up, you naughty boy?" She coos to him. I first see his face as he notices me over Leah's shoulder, and it transforms from smug possessiveness to sour suspicion.
"Who's that!" He demands.
"That's Doug. He's a friend of Mummy's. He's coming to Biarritz with us this weekend. Are you going to say hello?" The kid stares at me with undisguised disapproval.
"Hello."
"If you're nice to him and show him your toys, he might read you a bed time story."
My stomach churns with fear and horror. I'd rather go bungee jumping with Hans Vermeulen in charge of my rubber cord.
"Don't worry about Jess. He's always a bit shy with strangers. Go in the kitchen and help yourself to a beer, I'll just take him up to bed."
Half way up the stairs, Leah pauses, with Jess in her arms, and adds,
"There's a Jacuzzi next to the swimming pool. And it's empty. Take a look, in the conservatory." It occurs to me that this is where she plans us to have our water sports party, but I don't get as far as the conservatory. I'm already finding it hard not to bolt out of the front door.

The au pair, who's from Krakow and called Silvi, gives me a large bottle of Kingfisher Indian lager, and I sit in the only armchair in the kitchen diner. Silvi doesn't speak much English, and she explains with her hands and the word "toy" that she's got tidying up to do in the front room. I cling to the bottle of beer, and await my doom. I didn't even bother bringing my overnight bag beyond the hall. After a couple of minutes there are footsteps on the stairs, but they're not Leah's. Jess pads up to me, with a cuddly toy polar bear in his arms. He's wearing fleecy cotton pyjamas, covered in little pictures of rabbits and Bambi.

His face is sweeter now, and his blonde hair has been brushed. He smells of freshly ironed cotton and baby shampoo.

"This is George. He's my bear." Jess deposits George in my lap. When it touches me, I flinch as if it burns. I don't say anything. I just sit there and try to control my breathing.
"George wants a cuddle." Jess stands by the chair, watching my face. I know he's confused, even though I'm not looking at him. I put the beer bottle down on the floor beside me, and hold George, the cuddly polar bear. I stare at the wall opposite. There's a cork notice board, covered in post cards, and pictures drawn by Jess. I feel the first tear roll down my cheek. It falls onto my shirt as the second tear begins to roll down the other cheek. My face is quivering and contorting when Silvi comes along the hall. She starts to offer me some nuts or crisps in broken English, but doesn't finish her sentence. I hear her footsteps stop suddenly on the threshold. There's a short silence whilst she gathers her wits and decides what to do. She swiftly picks Jess up, and carries him out into the hall as the first sob convulses its way up to my throat.

There's a bit of a kafuffle on the stairs, and I feel Leah's arm around me. She gently strokes my head, and kisses me tenderly on the cheek, so my tears wet her lips.
"Doug, what's wrong?"
I try to tell her, but the words are interrupted by sobs. All I can manage is
"I'm frightened of babies and small children." I know what's going to happen, because I've experienced this scenario before. At first, the girlfriend sympathises with me, and wants to help and protect me. But she's a mother to her child before all else, and soon my inability to face the kid is experienced as a rejection. Psychologically, a rejection of her offspring is a rejection of her, and pity for me turns to resentment. End of relationship. We can hear Silvi trying to comfort little Jess upstairs. The poor kid is understandably confused and disturbed by a strange man breaking down in tears. Especially as the strange man has now hijacked his mummy's maternal affection. Leah is genuinely concerned for me, and tries to persuade me to stay the night, on the grounds that Jess sleeps right through. It's no good, there's the morning to consider, and I can't stop feeling upset as long as there's a

young child in the house. We call a taxi, and when we hug goodnight by the front door, I know this is the end.

"Okay, so Biarritz is off. But we'll work something out." Says Leah, optimistically. But the smile on her face looks forced, and her eyes have absorbed some of my sadness. In the taxi home, I feel so desolate I can't even sit up. I have to lie down on the back seat, and the driver takes some persuading that I'm not going to be ill in his cab. That reminds me I forgot to finish that bottle of Kingfisher.

Chapter Twenty-nine

The next morning, Angela's wearing a huge white ribbon in her hair. It's another sunny day, although warm rather than hot, and she's got a pair of loose cotton trousers on. They're blue and white check, with the squares really small. I compliment her on them, and say they look familiar, but not on her.
"I got them from the catering supply shop in Greek Street. They're chef's trousers." She gives me a little twirl, and I notice blue streaks in her hair. The outfit is complimented by a blue cotton singlet, which leaves her shoulders bare, and when she bends down to put my lower paws on, I get a glimpse of her left nipple. Her tits are small enough not to need a bra, even though she wears one occasionally. Today she's bra less, and those pert little breasts look more enticing than ever beneath her singlet.

When she's put my head on for the first time of the day, and I'm waiting to be called over to the set, I hear Esmeralda the wardrobe supervisor wishing Angela a happy birthday. I feel a bit guilty for not knowing, because despite my recent affair with Leah, Angela goes way beyond her official duties in looking after me. Without all her help, I couldn't play Boris so effectively on screen. The least I could do is remember her birthday and get her a card and a present.

As I plod onto the set, I realise she's got the enormous white ribbon in her hair to celebrate her birthday. Bless her. Later in the morning, the tail wagging mechanism arrives, and the designer shows how, when I've got an arm concealed from view, I can operate a small hidden lever, and wag my tail. Everyone on set greets the wagging tail with glee, and Angela shows only enthusiasm for what is more, unpaid responsibility for her. I'm lying in my basket during a bit of dialogue between Leah, Rufus, and some Jehovah's Witnesses they've invited in to discuss God. The actor playing the male Jehovah's Witness is a bit nervous, and keeps messing his lines up. During the extra time this affords me to lay in my basket, it occurs to me that Angela is now

seventeen. During a break in filming, for once Angela isn't there to mop my brow, and give me a drink of water. I ask Terry the runner to pop out to the shops and get her a birthday card, a big box of chocolates, and some WH Smith vouchers. The reason Angela isn't there to pamper me is because she's being given a very large, chocolate birthday cake by Simon the director, and the rest of the production staff. I'm feeling quite comfortable with my head on, and open Boris' mouth to get a better view of Angela as she blows the candles out, and cuts the cake. The blue streaks in her hair look fantastic. She suddenly remembers me, and looks over to see what I'm doing.
"Are you okay, Doug? I'm so sorry – I'm not looking after you." I wag my tail in my basket, and the entire crew laugh. I sit up, and beg, and she comes over and strokes my head, pretending to feed birthday cake to Boris. The crew laugh and applaud, and continue drinking coffee and eating birthday cake. Angela speaks quietly to me, asking if I'm sure I'm okay. I reply that I'm very happy, and that she should carry on enjoying her birthday. Leah gives her a cuddle, and presents her with a huge bunch of flowers, a card, and some record vouchers. I yawn inside my mask, but feel quite safe in here, cut off from the rest of the world. If only I could be Boris all the time.

As it's Friday, Leah dashes off as soon as we wrap. She's meeting Jess and Silvi at Heathrow, to fly down to Biarritz. I've got no gigs this weekend, because I was supposed to be with Leah. We put a story out that I couldn't go with her because I've got a corporate gig I can't refuse on Saturday night. So I'm free to join everybody for Angela's birthday drink at The Crown and Anchor tonight, Friday. The day got hotter, and when we come out of the air-conditioned studio, it's sweaty.

Back in my dressing room, after I've showered, Angela returns from taking Boris to the de-humidifier, so he can dry out over the weekend. I give her the birthday card and presents. She loves chocolates. Her metabolism is fast, so she can eat lots without putting on weight. She loves the WH Smith vouchers, because they can be used to buy books, which she consumes voraciously during the time I'm on camera. As soon as there's a break in filming, she's there to attend to me, but during the shooting if she came near me she'd be in shot. This gives her several hours a day to read. If she wasn't reading, she'd be hanging around, and she loves novels. Much of our conversation is about the novels we read, and we've exchanged a lot of them since we began making 'Rat's Milk Cheese'. Our biggest bone of contention is DH Lawrence. She thinks he's great, and I think he's tedious. We've had many a good-humoured disagreement about DH Lawrence.

"Do you mind if I Change out of these trousers, and put a skirt on, Doug? It's a bit hot for long trousers."
"Of course. Feel free to use the shower."
"Oh can I? That would be fantastic." I'm about to do the decent thing and vacate the dressing room for her, when there's a knock at the door. It's Esmeralda, the wardrobe supervisor, who seems to have taken over the costume designer's job too. I invite her in, and sit beside her on the sofa, taking care to face away from where Angela is removing her clothes.
"I've got a bone to pick with you, Douglas Tucker." I ask her what it is.
"Apparently you suggested we submerge Boris in a tank of water."
"I can't deny it."
"It's probably going to ruin his fur. Not to mention the eye and jaw mechanism."
"I thought they were going to do it when all the episodes are in the can."
"So nobody's told you, then. They've brought the American broadcast date forward. The water tank at Pinewood studios is booked for next week. As are two tigers, two lions, and a rhinoceros. I've got to make another Boris for Tuesday, in case this one corrodes in the salt water."
"Salt water?"
"I don't think sharks and conger eels live in fresh water, Doug."
"So they're going with the shark idea?"
"Two tiger sharks, a Great White, and a Hammerhead." Esmeralda's got a mobile phone too. It goes off, and she smiles and adds
"And a conger eel." Before she answers her phone and exits into the corridor. I can't help looking in the mirror. Angela's left the shower curtain open, and she's soaping herself. She looks up, and notices me watching her in the mirror.
"You don't have to settle for a reflection. Come and see the real thing if you like."
I can't stop myself walking over to the shower cubicle.

Chapter Thirty

"What better day to see you in your birthday suit, than on your birthday?" She turns the shower back on, to rinse the foam from her sleek seventeen year old skin. The blue streaks in her hair look darker, because her hair is wet. I lean against the dressing counter, my back to the mirror, and my arms folded. She removes the shower nozzle, and unashamedly sprays between her legs. Her pubic hair is blonde, and wispy.
"If you were a gentleman, you'd be holding a towel ready."
I get the biggest, fluffiest towel, and hold it for her.
"I can't believe you didn't know Leah's got a kid. Everyone in the company knew that."
"Word's got around, then."
"It has amongst we women. Didn't she ever mention Jess to you?"
"I think she referred to him, but I didn't ask anything out of politeness. I assumed it was a boyfriend, or a girlfriend."
"She even bought him into the studio once."
"Oh, that was him was it? I remember seeing a kid on the studio floor once, and hiding in my dressing room for the rest of the day. I don't think I was needed until later on, and he'd gone by then. Leah hardly talked to me until recently."
She switches the water off, and I give her the towel.
"Have you tried being with kids whilst you're in costume, with the head on?"
"No. It's difficult to explain, Angela. I had such a horrible childhood, seeing a kid just transports me back to the feeling of helplessness. Of having nobody in the world to turn to." I stand aside for her to come out of the shower cubicle. She dries herself, and casts the towel on the sofa. When she begins putting a pair of white cotton panties on, I wonder if it's the same pair she's been wearing all day. I hope it is, but they're laid out with the clean mini skirt. She smells fresh, of shower gel. It's the same stuff I use – it's put there by Teddington Studios. It smells much nicer on her than it does on me. She puts a clean singlet

on, and a pair of sneakers. I reckon if the singlet's clean, the knickers must be clean too.

"When I was a little kid, staff at the care centres, or school teachers, or even Foster parents, used to tell me I'd never come to anything unless I stopped being lazy. Or nobody ever became successful if they didn't get up by eight in the morning. That's the worst thing about being a kid. You don't have the experience or autonomy to know they're talking rubbish. You just believe them, and feel wretched. Now if someone tells me that, I can disagree, and go back to my own flat I've paid most of the mortgage on. If they're a real pain, I can tell them to fuck off. A seven-year old orphan doesn't question what he's told. He just stands there believing their nonsense, quaking with self-doubt."

Angela's puts some big silver hoop earrings in, and fluffs her hair in the mirror. She looks good enough to eat.
"What age does a person have to be before you're not afraid of them?"
"Pub age."
"So you're afraid of me, then."
"I meant being allowed into pubs, not old enough to buy alcohol. You're allowed in pubs. That's why I'm a stand-up comedian. I won't encounter children in pubs."
"If I'm allowed in a pub, you'd better take me to one, then."
She stands there looking up at me. I draw her to me, and we kiss for the first time. I hope it's the first of many times. She's like a mother to me, and I desperately need to be mothered. We stand there holding each other. I've got a stonking erection, but it's irrelevant. This warm bundle of love in my arms is special beyond lust or sex.
"Come on, then. Let's go and celebrate my birthday."
"I'll follow you down. I don't want to cause a scandal."
"Doug, it's all over between you and Leah. She told me so this morning." I must still look uncertain, because she adds.
"All right, if you're worried about what people think, I'll go ahead. What do you want to drink?"
"A pint of Stella please." She opens the door, her bag over her shoulder.
"And Doug?"
"Yes."
"I love you."
"I love you too."

I'm feeling really tired, and I switch the TV on to occupy a couple of minutes. It's the news, and there's a report about a kid who's gone missing. I snap the volume off, and pick up the birthday card I gave to Angela. On the back of it, the price label is still stuck on. I remove it carefully, and chuck it in the bin. After the trauma of last night, a wonderful feeling of calmness has come over me, and it's all because of Angela. I never felt comfortable during the episode with Leah, because it tore at the bond that's formed between Angela and me. I must admit, though, I'm a bit disappointed I never got to play with Leah in her Jacuzzi. She really is a magnificent lover, and those tits of hers…

I'm giving myself a little pipe of skunk before going down to The Crown and Anchor, when out of the corner of my eye I notice a couple of familiar faces on the TV screen. I lunge for the remote control, and turn the volume up in time to hear that the man held on remand for the murder of Gregor and Tam has been found dead in Wandsworth prison. Police are treating the death as suicide. The news is more shocking because the pipe of skunk is taking effect. I lie back on the sofa and contemplate my position. If it wasn't for Arnold, I wouldn't be in this television studio dressing room. Most of my stand-up income is from Arnold's gigs. At the same time, the man is quite clearly a gangland boss. I know beyond doubt that he was involved in the murders of Gregor and Tam. Now the scapegoat is dead, and will never be able to defend himself in court. Arnold's got away with murder. I resolve to extricate myself from his empire as soon as I'm famous enough. Once 'Rats Milk Cheese' hits the screens, I'm sure the success I require will be mine. I look at myself in the dressing mirror. My eyes are bloodshot, but it's still sunny enough outside to justify wearing sunglasses to hide the fact I'm stoned. Not that it matters – my bosses are on coke anyway.

Chapter Thirty-one

The next evening Angela comes round for dinner. I've been busy all day, washing the bedding from when Leah stayed, and tidying the flat. My whole life revolves around making 'Rats Milk Cheese', and doing gigs. The result is I've let the flat go. My work is also my social life, and even when I get the chance to watch TV or a video, I'm studying what I see in order to learn the craft. Working in television has inspired me to start writing some more jokes. I usually think of two good ones a week, but they arise out of improvising on stage, or come to me whilst driving. I need to discipline myself to sit at my computer and write. When 'Rats Milk Cheese' puts me in the public eye, I want to be ahead of the game, and have plenty of stand-up material I know is funny.

I've also started writing an episode of 'Rats Milk Cheese', inspired by Sheila Fox's comment about putting me in the writing team. I'm experienced enough to know you can't believe most of what a television producer says, but if I don't try, I won't know whether I can write funny dialogue or not. Being in the show has raised my hopes, and I'm feeling very ambitious. I'm laughing at a gag I've written, because it's so inappropriate, when the doorbell rings. Angela's at the threshold, smiling and holding a bottle of cheap champagne. She's dressed conservatively, by her standards. A pair of black jeans, a bright yellow sweatshirt, and lots of bangles on her right arm.

I invite her in, and show her the flat. She's perturbed by the fact that most of my plants have died, and their pots remain untended on the windowsills. If she guesses the reason is that Sunita looked after the plants, and they've died in her absence, she's got the tact not to mention it.
I show her the kitchen, and she remarks how unused it looks considering its owner has a guest for dinner.
"I thought I'd order a takeaway. Or I've got spaghetti and some jars of pasta sauce." We've already agreed we're staying in, because it would

be a novelty compared to going out. I order some Chinese takeaway to be delivered, and we open the champagne. We relax on the sofa, and soon I've got my arm round Angela, and I'm kissing the streaks of blue in her soft hair.

"Can I make a request?" She asks, as we watch some abominably bad game show.

"It depends what it is."

"They're showing 'Bare In Mind' on Saturday evenings now. It's on in five minutes, can we watch it?"

Angela's too innocent to have taken drugs of any kind, but I have a few pipes whilst we watch Brian O'Shea cavorting his way to stardom. Like hundreds of thousands of other women in Britain, Angela had never heard of Brian before 'Bare in Mind' hit the screens. Now they're all smitten with his vulnerable good looks, and rumour has it that Brian did a corporate gig for £8,000 last week.

We watch the closing credits roll, which include Nicky Butler's name.

"They've already commissioned a second series, apparently. And they've sold this series to Australia, New Zealand, France, and Germany."

I refill the champagne glasses, and we toast the success of 'Rats Milk Cheese'. I remove Angela's glass from her hand, and place it next to mine on the coffee table. We have a nice long kiss, and my hands wander down to explore her hot little body. She's so cuddly in the yellow cotton sweatshirt, but it's too warm for it in the flat, I make an executive decision and take it off for her.

She must have bought a job lot of those skimpy singlets, because she's wearing a black one under the sweatshirt. The sight of her shoulders, and the promise of those braless little tits turns me on, and I start kissing her neck. I work my way down to her shoulders, and give her armpits a lick. She's wearing some chemical deodorant that makes my tongue go all strange, so I don't hang about there. I take a swig of champagne, and move down to the gap between the bottom of her singlet and the top of her jeans, kissing her lower tummy, throwing the occasional little nip in to surprise her. Then with a quick movement, I whip her singlet up over her head and arms, and she's naked from the waist up. I growl with pleasure when I see those little titties. The

nipples are really small, and I suck and lick each one in turn, whilst unfastening the buckle on her belt.
"Doug. Doug!" She moans in my ear. "I've got something to tell you."
It transpires the shower gel that Teddington Studios provide in my dressing room shower has given her thrush. She's got Canistan cream on her fanny, and she's out of service until the thrush has cleared up. I'm surprised, because the shower gel looks quite good quality, unlike the stuff they give you in most hotels. I forgot to take my shampoo once, and used the shampoo the hotel provided. I had dandruff for a week.

The doorbell rings. The Chinese food has arrived. I look at Angela's pert bosoms, and marble white skin.
"That's okay, we'll just have a cuddle. Would you like to stay the night?"
She'd love to. That's why she's brought her toothbrush, and some clean underwear. We eat the Chinese whilst watching 'Brief Encounter' on video, and go to bed. I've turned the light off, and we've kissed goodnight, when she makes me an offer I can't refuse.
"Would you like me to satisfy you with my hand?"
"Yes Please!" I reply. She reaches through the blackness and caresses my erection. Then she pushes the duvet out of the way, and sits up beside me. I lie there in the darkness, getting an exquisite hand job and listening to the bangles on her wrist jingle faster and faster, until I squirt. She splutters, and asks if I've got any tissues. There was so much spaff in my scrotum, it spurted up her nostrils. I feel for the tissue box beside the futon, and give her a few. We fall asleep with her head resting on my chest. That was the first orgasm I've had since the other morning, when I came in Leah's mouth. I think of Angela's little vagina, nestling so close. I can't wait until she's cleared her thrush up, and she's back in action. It must be really compact – unlike Leah's, which is quite big. I connect the facts that she's had a kid, and her vagina is big. Of course, now I understand the link between those two concepts.

We're woken up at what seems like the middle of the night, but turns out to be two in the morning, by the phone ringing. I leave it to go onto the answer machine. I can't make out what the voice is saying, but I recognise it as Arnold's.

"What's he doing phoning me this late?" I wonder to myself. Angela wakes up a bit, and as her head rests on my chest, I stroke the back of her head in the darkness. She kisses my chest, and as she's awake, I start stroking her face. I whisper in the dark.

"Angela, the hair's fallen out at the back of your head." Then I stroke the back of her head, and continue.

"...and you've grown a beard on your face." I pull her hair gently, and say

"Darling, you really should trim these nostril hairs. They're very long, you know."

She giggles, and we descend into delicious sleep.

I'm having a dream where I'm looking for a toilet, and all sorts of obstacles and distractions keep preventing me from finding one. Finally I get to one, and I'm about to use it, when I wake up, in urgent need of a piss. After I've used the toilet, I wander into the lounge, turn the volume down on the answer machine so as not to disturb Angela, and listen to Arnold's message. His voice sounds unusually gentle.

"Douglas, it's Arnold. I need to speak to you urgently. Please give me a ring, mate." He leaves the number of his car phone. Everyone seems to be getting these mobile phones, now. I'll have to get one myself. It's too early to ring him now, so I slip back under the duvet next to Angela, and her leg moves so it rests on mine. She looks divine in the morning light, and I go back to sleep.

217

Chapter Thirty-two

We wake up at ten, and wander up to the River Thames, which is only six minutes walk from my flat. It's cloudy, but warm, and we have breakfast sitting outside my favourite café.
"You should get a boat." Says Angela, as she munches her omelette with goats cheese and sun dried tomatoes.
"You could use the river to get from here to Teddington."
"There's nowhere around here I could keep one. The security's too intense around the Houses of Parliament." I think of the journey up the Thames from here. It would pass The Clap Clinic, and Arnold's new classic motor yacht moored up outside. I bet the terrace restaurant is packed on a warm Sunday like today. I must return his call when we get home. He'll probably be shaking off his cocaine and alcohol hangover soon, and getting out of bed.
Angela and I talk about the novels of Virginia Woolf, and discover she thinks they're great, and I think they're okay, except for 'Orlando', which is bad. She provides stimulating conversation, for someone who's only just turned seventeen.

When we get back to my place, there are two more messages from Arnold on the answer machine. I phone him on his car phone, and he says he's close to Lambeth Walk, can he come round to see me.
"I've got company."
"It's urgent, Doug. I need to take you out for a wee drive, and ma car's only got the two seats."
"Okay." I start to give him the address, and realise that he's already been here. I explain the situation to Angela, and leave her to browse my considerable collection of novels. Standing on the balcony that runs past my front door, I expect to see Arnold's bright red Mercedes SL. When I see a black Porsche Targa swing round the corner, I know it's him. I wave from the balcony, and run down the stairs, because it's quicker than the lift.
"Changed your car?" I say, as I get in.

"No, I've still got the Mercedes SL. This was a present from Ruud Vermeulen. Look, she's only got thirty-two miles on the clock. He and I have a business arrangement. He's a bit of an Anglophile. I've got the connections in Britain, and he's got the money." Arnold shakes his head in wonder, and continues.
"And when I say he's got money, I mean he's got money. I've done all right for myself, Doug. I'm a millionaire, you know that. But Ruud Vermeulen's wealth is *awesome*."
We're driving along the river, towards Vauxhall.
"I need to talk to you, Arnold. About Sunita."
"That's what I want to talk to you about, Doug. You haven't seen today's papers, yet?"
"No."
"I'm really sorry, Doug. But Sunita committed suicide in her prison cell. If you must know, she lost her baby two days before."
Now I know why he's telling me this in the car. He's got to look at the road ahead, and I can't get too emotional strapped in a bucket seat. We stop at a red light at Vauxhall Cross, and a scruffy man, probably homeless, offers to clean Arnold's windscreen. They're a nuisance, because they often use river water.
"No thank you." Says Arnold, to the windscreen washer, who ignores him and slops his filthy cleaning rag on the windscreen.
"Hay mate. I said no thank you!" The man smiles, and continues wiping. Arnold slips the Porsche into gear, and jolts forward about a foot. His right hand reaches out and holds the man's wrist. Before he can react, Arnold's applied a martial arts lock and jerked him down to the tarmac with explosive force. The man cries out with pain. The fact that his wrist has been sprained isn't the problem. It's the fact that he's crumpled to the ground so violently, there was nowhere for his legs to go, and he's injured his back. The lights turn to green, and we collide with the man's metal bucket, which makes a horrible scraping noise as it scratches along the pristine paintwork of the Porsche.
"What a cunt." Fumes Arnold.
"Seventy fucking grand, this car cost." I look behind. The man's still lying in the road, and the person in the car behind us has got out to help him.
"Don't believe what you read in the papers, Doug. And please don't think I'm responsible for Sunita's death. I had nothing to do with that coke. I promise you. Do you believe me?"

"Do you want an honest answer, or a diplomatic one? You fooled me into taking your coke through customs at Nice. And I never saw Sunita touch drugs in the year I went out with her."
"Actually, Doug, I didn't trick you into carrying coke through customs. It was ecstasy. And if you don't think Sunita took drugs, look in the box of Sainsbury's vegetable pies at the back of your freezer. It's the bottom shelf, if I remember correctly."

We're crossing the Thames over Chelsea Bridge, the 3.5 litre engine gurgling effortlessly.
"I'll take a look when I get home." I've been meaning to go through the contents of the freezer for some time. Sunita was so good at keeping tabs on what needed to be eaten before it was in there for too long. Arnold turns left at the lights, and we head along the Northern riverbank, going upstream.
"I like you, Doug. You're a talented comedian who makes a lot of folk laugh. The world I grew up in, people didn't make people laugh. They made people scared. We admired a man who could win a fight. Laughter was a sign of weakness. I hope you realise that, Doug. I've come a long way from ma roots. I'm growing as a person."

He indicates to the left, and it dawns on me we're stopping at Cadogan Pier. The tide's in, and the moored boats are visible over the river wall.
"I'm sorry I fucked your girlfriend. But it took two of us to do the cheating. At the end of the day, Sunita was human."
We're parked on the pavement, but Arnold seems confident his Porsche won't get clamped. I close my door, and follow him to the pontoon. I recognise the classic wooden motor yacht he and the Vermeulens turned up on the other day at Teddington. He points to the stern, where freshly painted in gold lettering is the word 'Sunita'.
"Named after *her*, Doug." For a moment I think he's going to cry.
"She was a lovely girl. I'm sorry I took her away from you, and I hope you realise I'm bending over backwards to help your career. That's what's important to you, isn't it Doug. A successful career in show business."
"Yes Arnold. It is."
The wheelhouse door opens, and Hans emerges, squinting where his eyes aren't used to the light.
"Would you like to join Hans and me on Sunita?"

"Not today, thanks. I've got a guest back at the flat."
"Another time, then Doug. She served her country, you know. She helped evacuate soldiers from Dunkerque. Built on the Clyde, she was. 1924. She's been fully restored. I'm going to keep her on ma mooring at The Clap Clinic. Come aboard when you're next doing a gig there."
A taxi approaches, and Arnold flags it down.
"This will cover your fare home, Doug. And remember, don't believe what you read in the papers."
I get in the taxi, and ask him to take me to Lambeth Walk. I look at the note Arnold gave me, and it's a fifty pound one. When I give it to the taxi driver, he refuses to take it.
"Not a Bank of Scotland fifty, mate. There's a batch of forgeries going about at the moment." I give him a tenner, and resolve to pay the fifty into my bank account.
When I get home, Angela's seen the news of Sunita's death on one of the television news channels. She offers to leave me alone, but I'd like her to stay. The official story is that she took her own life by hanging herself. Saudi prisons don't have such effective precautions against suicides as we do in Britain. It strikes me as odd, because Sunita couldn't tie a knot to save her life, let alone take it. Her death is being linked to a Palestinian terrorist organisation, for who the drugs were used as currency. They're playing up the fact that she was Moslem, but again, I've met her parents, and their religion is money, not Allah. As far as I know, Sunita never saw the inside of a mosque. I resolve to question Arnold as to what story I *should* believe, if he doesn't want me to believe the official one.

Angela and I decide to get rid of Sunita's dead houseplants, and we knock them out of the pots into the bin. After Angela's gone that afternoon, I look at the back of the bottom shelf of the freezer. A box of Sainsbury's vegetable pies proves to be devoid of pies. In it there's a glass jar containing about a gramme of brown heroin, and a little paper envelope of coke. I find it very hard to believe it belonged to Sunita. I lose myself at the computer, trying to write a brilliant script for an episode of 'Rats Milk Cheese', and go to bed early. I've got to be at Pinewood Studios for eight in the morning.

Chapter Thirty-three

I've been to Pinewood Studios twice before, when I had a two-day shoot making a TV commercial for a bank, early in my career. I feel even more excited this time I arrive, because what we're going to film is destined for greater exposure than a commercial. The security guard at the main gate raises the barrier, and my driver coaxes the Mercedes saloon slowly over the speed bumps. We reach the huge sound stage built especially for the James Bond films, and I can feel the thrill in my viscera. A light rain is falling, and I'm glad for two reasons. Firstly, the countryside needs it, because it's parched from the hot summer. Secondly, however wet the day's going to be outside, I'm going to be a lot wetter in the water tank.

We park near several lorries, some of which have brought the big cats from a circus. The others were used to transport the sharks, and rhinoceros. My dressing room is even nicer than the star dressing rooms at Teddington, and as I'm early I have a hearty breakfast of eggs, toast, and vegetarian bacon. I know I shouldn't eat too much before diving, but I can't resist three of the luxury Swiss chocolates in the crystal glass bowl on my coffee table.

They're using my idea exactly, except the lions, tigers, and rhinoceros walk past me first, so the sharks and conger eel come as more of a surprise. One of the animal wranglers informs me that due to illness we only have the one lion. They've substituted a leopard. There's going to be a thick sheet of glass between the animals and me, so the morning's going to be fairly routine.

When I'm shown the fish I realise what I'm letting myself in for. The conger eel is the scariest, because he's eighteen feet long, with ferocious looking teeth.
"Was he bred in captivity?"
"No." The wrangler replies.
"*She's* called Daisy, and she was caught off The Scilly Isles. We're feeding her and the sharks all morning, so they won't be hungry when you're in the tank with them."
"Can I see jellyfish in there too?" I ask.

"Yeah, we threw ten Portuguese Men O'War in for good measure. With that fur suit, they won't be a problem. Unless one of them floats in through your mouth."

A commercial diver has been hired to supervise the practical side of things, and he's busy with Angela, working out how to fit the breathing equipment into Boris' head. Esmeralda's on edge, because the new Boris costume won't be ready for a couple of days, and if the existing one disintegrates in the water, the whole day will be a waste of money. They're not using the other actors until Wednesday, and that will be back at Teddington. As far as the water tank at Pinewood is concerned, it's just, the wild animals, the wild fish, and me.

The entire lounge set is twenty feet beneath the surface, and for continuity reasons, I have to be underwater during the shots involving the wild animals. Simon McDonagh the director and Nicky Butler definitely seem to have got it together. He's sitting in his director's chair, and she's in his lap. It takes hours to synchronise the lighting, the cameras, the diving equipment, and the wild animals, but finally, at half past ten, I'm lowered into the tank. It's freezing! They tell me they have to keep the water cold, because Daisy the conger eel is a coldwater fish, but I think the truth is that the enormous budget ran out just short of heating the many thousands of gallons of water. I'm weighted down so I don't float off the sofa, and as the cold penetrates the thin wet suit I wear to fit inside Boris, I make a bet with myself that they heat the water up for James Bond. In fact, I bet James Bond doesn't even come in the water. He probably has stuntmen for that. There had been talk of getting a professional stuntman to play Boris underwater, but I've made his movements so idiosyncratic, and it would take too long to find a diver exactly my size, and get him acquainted with the costume. They'd also have to pay him a lot more than they're paying me. Despite the vast budget, this is costing more than intended.

Once I'm on the sofa, it's fairly easy. I've got a normal facemask on inside Boris' head, and a mouthpiece in my mouth. Air is delivered to my mouth through a hose that enters Boris' costume through a specially cut slit in his fur at the back. Exhaust carbon dioxide is taken away through another one connected to it. The cables that operate the blinking eyes, jaw, and tail have all been freshly greased. What takes the time is persuading the lion to walk in front of the glass. Eventually his wrangler succeeds in coaxing him with some fresh steak from the catering truck, and by lunch Simon's got the shots he needs of all the wild animals. The rhinoceros gives the glass a little charge, which gets everyone very excited. Angela's ready with towels and my dressing gown as soon as I break surface, and I spend the lunch break lying on the sofa in my dressing room with no appetite for lunch.

I still feel cold when they lower me into the tank for the afternoon. The sharks and Daisy have all been over fed, and I'm assured I'm safe. The commercial diver has warned us that if I spend too long at twenty feet, I'll have to do a decompression stop at ten feet before coming out. When I'm back on the sofa, I notice an octopus about two feet high. His tentacles are about a metre long. I feel a bit angry they didn't warn me about him, because he's big enough to kill someone in the sea. Those tentacles could hold a diver until he ran out of air. They were hoping to give me a full-face mask with telecommunications in it. Boris' head is too small, though, so we rely on signs and a waterproof pen and clipboard for communication from me to them. They can talk to me via an earpiece.

The first shots they take are the best ones, because the fish are more inquisitive and swim closer to me. The octopus comes and sits on the sofa beside me, at the same time the leopard walks in front of the tank, and growls at the Hammerhead shark. I can hear Simon and Sheila squealing with delight. Then Daisy swims up to my head, and pukes all over my face. I can't see most of this, because I've got the mouth closed during the takes. They're giving me instructions over the talkback to look in certain directions, and wag my tail, to give the appearance of responding to the fish and wild animals. My lips are so numb from the cold, I can hardly keep the mouthpiece in my mouth, and my right ear is aching. I don't ask to come out, because I can hear so much glee over the talkback. They're getting fantastic shots, and when I get out, that's the end of filming. I'm determined to do everything in my control to make 'Rats Milk Cheese' mega-successful around the world.

Finally, the commercial diver orders them to get me out. I've been submerged over the safety guidelines for the thickness of wetsuit in this temperature. Just as I rise above the sofa, the octopus decides to wrap a tentacle around my back paw. It's great television, and we give it a minute before the commercial diver comes in and removes the octopus. It releases its ink, and the commercial diver has to kill it in case it attacks us in the darkness. Whilst I'm doing my decompression stop at ten feet, they tell me they're watching the shots of the octopus grabbing Boris' paw, and it looks like a cartoon.

I feel exhausted, very cold, and my right ear hurts deep inside, but I've never been happier in my life. The suffering only lasted an afternoon, but the stuff we've filmed could be showing in a hundred years time. Angela sits on my dressing room sofa, and I lay there with my head in her lap, coughing. She runs her fingers through my hair, and I close my eyes and fall asleep. It feels like hours, but it's only a few minutes. Simon and Sheila knock at the door, and bring a VHS tape of the rushes. They look magnificent.
"See where the conger eel vomits on your head. We can treat that with computer graphics, and make it look pink, or lots of tiny stars. Thanks, Doug. We don't need to do any more filming in the tank – we've got what we need. I think we've made television history today."

My voice is husky, and I feel like I've got the flu. Angela accompanies me in my Mercedes home. She puts me to bed with a hot chocolate that tastes strongly of whisky. She sits on the futon with my head in her lap, and reads one of my Aldous Huxley novels. The last thing she says to me before I go to sleep is that her thrush has cleared up.

Chapter Thirty-four

I wake with a start. The position of the sun as it shines through the curtains reveals that it's mid-morning. I should have been up hours ago, to get to Teddington. Then I realise, they've given me the day off. This is just as well, because that day in the water tank has given me either flu or a very severe cold. My right ear aches persistently, and I can't hear very well with it. In fact, come to think of it, I've had this hearing loss since I came out of the tank. My scuba diving friends have had this. They call it swimmer's ear. It may be that the earpiece they put in my right ear kept the water out until I got down to twenty feet. Then when the water suddenly gushed in, it hurt my ear.

Angela brings me a cup of strong sweet tea. She looks like a waif in my blue towelling dressing gown, because it's so much bigger than she is. I'd like to cuddle her, but I've been sweating so much I feel repulsive. I'm not hungry, but she's noticed the jar of drugs that Arnold told me were in the freezer. I put them in the fridge after I found them. Angela wants to throw them away, and I tell her to mind her own business. She goes into the lounge, and I get my laptop and resume my attempt at a hilarious episode of 'Rats Milk Cheese'. I need to submit it very soon if I want it to get in the first series, because soon we'll have finished filming.

I'm in deep concentration when Angela comes in with the phone. Nancy the Assistant Floor Manager is on the line.
"Doug, Simon and Sheila asked me to thank you for yesterday. They're editing the tape now, and are thrilled beyond their wildest expectations. If it goes well tomorrow, we'll have the front and end titles edited by next week. Your call time for tomorrow isn't until ten-thirty, so enjoy your lie in." It's good to hear Nancy's voice again. She's been away for a few weeks, working on a show she was previously contracted to do before she got the 'Rats Milk Cheese' job. I had vague ideas of trying to seduce her, but now I'm with Angela, I'll have to forget about that.

Angela seems to have got over being told to mind her own business over the drugs in the fridge, and brings me a mug of cappuccino. She's bright and airy, and announces she's going for a little walk. I return to the alpha state, oblivious to all but the episode of 'Rats Milk Cheese' I'm writing.

A couple of hours later, I've got as far as I can without having a break. I shave, have a bubble bath, and get dressed. Angela returns with a bag of organic compost she's bought from the Museum of Garden History, and some baby plants. Together we wash Sunita's plant pots out, and plant three baby aloe veras, and two baby papyrus plants. I can't believe my luck having Angela's love. She combines a gorgeous, young, pretty face and body, with intelligence and a nurturing personality.

I'm too poorly to go out to eat, so she cooks a delicious risotto, which we eat whilst watching a porn video of mine she's discovered. Thank goodness it's a relatively tame one. I feel rather protective of her innocence, and some of the ones she didn't find I'd consider too strong for her.
"I've never sucked a man's thingy before." She announces.
"You gave me a very good hand job the other night."
Her leg is resting on my leg, and I've got my arm around her. She puts her hand on my forehead.
"You've got a fever, Doug. You're too ill to make love tonight."
"Has anybody gone down on you before?"
"Oh yes. I've had oral sex from three blokes before."
"On the same day?"
"No." By now, I'm on my knees before the sofa, pretending to bite the fabric of her trousers. I rub her fanny with my nose, and feel the warmth through the cotton. She moans a bit, and doesn't resist when I pull her trousers down. Her cotton panties look so white against her pink thighs, and I nuzzle the cleft of her fanny through the cotton, whilst my hands have lifted the T-shirt she's wearing, and begun fondling those delightful little nipples. The T-shirt's one of mine, because she's staying longer than anticipated, and run out of certain clothes.

Growling playfully, I whip her knickers off, and start nibbling and licking around her fanny. It's small and fresh. I flick my tongue over her vulva, and into the lush, moist crevice. Then I get to work licking down over the hood of her clitoris, and ease my forefinger in for a bit of internal stroking. I'm pleasantly surprised how quickly she comes. I pluck my socks off, and quickly remove my jeans and boxer shorts. Pulling her by the ankles, I get her into a good position lying along the sofa, and gently ease myself into that tight little peach. She gasps, and I slide slowly deeper, and remain still, holding her close. She's too short for me to kiss her on the mouth, so I kiss her closed eyes. Then I start thrusting languidly, and she has her second orgasm just before I withdraw and come on her stomach and tits.

I wipe her off with my boxer shorts, and look at the videotape. Two German women are taking it in turns to fellate a large moustachioed man. There's a close up of his face as it goes into pre-orgasm contortions. Angela and I both exclaim as we recognise him. It's a younger, less play-worn Hans Vermeulen. We laugh and say his name as it cuts to his twitching knob spurting over the women's faces. I stop the tape, and the picture reverts to the programme being broadcast. It's Brian O'Shea on the Des O'Connor Show. He's recycling part of his stage act to Des, who's convulsed with laughter. I'm seeing most people I know on my telly these days. And in a few weeks, I'll be on it too.

Chapter Thirty-five

I'm up at six the following morning. I want to finish my episode of 'Rats Milk Cheese' and take it to Teddington Studios. I find it much easier to write than I thought I would. The show isn't filmed in front of a live audience, and has no laughter track. It's quirky in a David Lynch sort of way, so the gags can be more whimsical than punchy. What's difficult is the physical act of typing, because my arm aches from wagging Boris' tail in the water tank. It's easy enough in air, but twenty feet down, the resistance of the water made wagging the tail quite an effort. I'm printing the finished script and waiting for Angela to finish in the shower, when there's a ring at the doorbell.
I open the front door, and get pulled outside by two burly men in leather jackets and jeans. Two other men, in bullet proof vests and an Alsatian dog rush past me into the flat. I can hear Angela scream as they kick the bathroom door in.

"Doug Tucker?"
"Yes."
"I'm Detective Sergeant Hayle. We have a warrant to search your flat. We'd like you to answer a few questions."
"I've got to be at Teddington Studios by ten-thirty." I say, looking at the search warrant he's holding in front of my face.
"Is there anybody else on the premises?"
"My girlfriend, Angela. She works at Teddington as well."
I follow him into the hall, where Angela is wrapped in a towel, looking like a frightened pixie. Sergeant Hayle looks from her to me, and says accusingly.
"Are you sure she's of legal age. Or do we need to call the vice squad?"
"I'm seventeen. I can show you my driving licence." Says Angela. I'm impressed how assertive she is given the intimidating circumstances.
All this time, I've had one burning thought in my mind. The heroin and the coke. They're going to find the heroin and coke. And my career will be fucked up. However, after searching for an hour, the

only illegal thing they've found is about a gram of skunk weed in a film canister. They turn a blind eye to this, and compliment me on how nice it smells. They let Angela get dressed, and the Mercedes that's come to take me to Teddington takes her instead. Sergeant Hayle promises they'll give me a lift in a police car. When his men haven't found anything to suggest I'm a terrorist, he gets friendlier, and I find myself admiring his wit.

An hour after his arrival, we're sitting on my three-piece suite enjoying cappuccinos, or in the case of his colleague, a rosehip tea. The dog and his handlers have departed. Hayle asks me all about Sunita, and our year together. I haven't got anything to hide (apart from the drugs in the fridge, which they didn't find), so I tell the truth.

I used to live in a very rough neighbourhood, and experienced the sharp end of criminal behaviour. With the exception of drugs, I see myself more on the side of the police than that of criminals. It's when he asks how well I know Arnold Shanks that I feel uncomfortable. I'm stuck between a rock and a hard place. If I tell him what I know, at best Arnold will stop giving me work. At worst, he'll have me killed. If I withhold information, I'll look like I'm involved in his crooked empire. I guess that Sergeant Hayle is a detective because he's better at extracting the truth than I am at concealing it.
"Arnold Shanks owns The Clap Clinic, and books for a lot of other venues. I know him because he gives me work."
"He's planning to open 'Clap Clinics' all over Britain."
"Is he? It wouldn't surprise me. He'll make more money from owning the clubs, than just booking the acts. The big money's in the beer and food sales, not the fees for booking comics."
"Have you worked for him overseas?"
"No. He hasn't offered me the gig he books in Riyadh."
"And you haven't done any other work for him abroad?"
"No." I'm sure I look as guilty as I feel, and can't help admitting.
"Oh yes. I did a corporate gig on a yacht in France."
"How many times have you met Ruud Vermeulen since then?" Crikey. Sergeant Hayle *has* done his homework!
"Once. He was on Arnold's new motor yacht on the River Thames. They came to the beer garden of the pub next to Teddington Studios."
"The Crown and Anchor?"

"That's right." The picture of that poor dying clown comes into my mind. I can feel sweat break out on my forehead.
"Is there anything else you want to tell me? About Shanks or Vermeulen?"
"No. I don't know them very well."
"Did you know Shanks served time in prison for manslaughter?"
"I knew he'd been in prison. I had no idea what for."
"They charged him with murder, but he got off with manslaughter. I suppose you know about Ruud Vermeulen?"
"No?"
"He spent thirteen years in a Turkish prison for murder. He's a tough one, is Vermeulen."
"I can imagine you don't survive thirteen years in a Turkish prison without being tough."
"Shanks had dealings with the IRA. He and Vermeulen have got rich through criminal activity. They're putting the money into legitimate business. If those businesses absorb them, and they drift away from crime, we breathe a sigh of relief. Unfortunately, that rarely happens. Men like Shanks and Vermeulen seldom give up violence. If they don't need it for their business, they need it for their recreation. My advice is distance yourself from them. Here's my direct number. Feel free to talk in complete confidence."
"If you give me a lift to Teddington studios, I'll talk to you in the car."
I want to tell him about the murdered clown in the Mediterranean, but I don't want to be late for work at Teddington.

I tell Sergeant Hayle all about the scuba diving incident during the journey to Teddington. Hayle thinks Arnold planted the drugs on Sunita. I almost tell him she supposedly left heroin and coke in my freezer, before I realise I'd be incriminating myself for possessing them.

It's August, and the traffic is light. Hayle and I are both on the back seat of an unmarked police car. He's on my right, and I find it hard to hear what he's saying. This is made worse if there's any background noise caused by other vehicles. I really must get a doctor to look at my ear.

I intended to tell him about Arnold beating Gregor and Tam up, and my suspicion that he was involved in their murder, but we arrive at the studios before I get round to it. Maybe it's better to keep quiet about that one. Hayle shakes my hand, and I get out of the black Ford Granada.

Chapter Thirty-six

Luckily it doesn't matter that I'm half an hour late. They don't need me for a while yet. I go on the studio floor, and can't believe how much weight Leah's lost. She must have been on a severe diet. Of course! As these are the front titles to the show, how she looks today is how most people will remember her. They're pretty sure a second series is going to be commissioned, and the public will see what's filmed today, and what we filmed in the tank on Monday, every time they watch the show. It becomes apparent how Leah's been getting her exercise when I see a French bloke she's got in tow, called Laurent. She picked him up in Biarritz during the weekend, and they're having a whirlwind romance. He's wearing a vest and shorts, and he's got more body hair than a yak. The hair on his head is black, and he's wearing a gold medallion on a thick gold chain. When Nancy the Assistant Floor Manager introduces me to him, he squeezes my hand too tightly, and his eyes show little more intelligence than the plastic eyes in Boris' head.

I pop into the production office and give the episode I wrote to Terry, whose been promoted from runner to production assistant.
"I'm going to be second assistant floor manager for the next series." He says proudly.
"Is it definite they're commissioning a second series?"
"Yes, and the first series starts in America at the end of next week. Oh, I nearly forgot to tell you. Your agent phoned. She wants you to ring her as soon as possible."
I use the office phone, and amazingly I don't get the answer machine, but Melissa herself.
"Doug. You've been asked to do a ten-minute stand-up set on 'Sauce Boat'." 'Sauce Boat' is the prestige stand-up show that every comedian dreams of appearing on. It's recorded on The Marguerite, a ship that's permanently moored in Bristol docks. It's a nightclub and restaurant at night, and a bar and restaurant by day. When you've done five minutes on that show, your status goes up. Only the highly rated comics get

asked to do the ten-minute end-of-programme spot. I've done the five-minute spot twice. I feel I've arrived, now I've been invited to do the ten-minute slot. Or as I prefer to think of it – the two thousand pound slot.

"What's the fee?"

"Two thousand pounds. The same as everyone else."

"Brian O'Shea turned it down unless he got five thousand. And they're going to pay it to him."

"When 'Rats Milk Cheese' is as big a hit as 'Bare in Mind' we'll demand that sort of money. I tried to get you more, but it's the last in the series, and they're claiming the budget's used up."

"Do I get my travel expenses and hotel too?"

"First Class travel, and a superior room at the Swallow Hotel." Gosh, Melissa has excelled herself.

"Thanks Melissa. Anything else?"

"They want you to do it this Friday. Call time is three-thirty in the afternoon."

"I won't be able to get from Teddington to Bristol by then."

"I've cleared it with Sheila Fox. They're going to let you go early. You know you're headlining at The Clap Clinic tonight?"

"No."

"I must have forgotten to tell you. Julian Rogers cancelled. Charlotte French is the compere. I don't know who the first act is."

"Thanks Melissa." Efficient as always. I thank Terry and go up to my dressing room, to put my white cotton underclothes on ready for Angela's getting me in costume.

"Doug, are you all right?" She asks, when I go in. She's wearing one of my long-sleeved cotton T-shirts. It looks fantastic on her, despite being baggy, and having the sleeves turned up.

"Yeah, I'm fine." We cuddle for a full minute.

"They didn't find Sunita's drugs." I say. Angela looks at me with guilt in her eyes.

"That's because I threw them in the river."

I feel annoyed with her for meddling in my business, despite the fact that she's saved me from getting done for heroin and cocaine possession. My fingerprints were on the jar.

"I forgive you. I'd better get into costume. How's Boris' fur after a day in the water tank?"

"He's as good as new. What did the police want?"

"They just wanted to ask some routine questions about Sunita. I don't think they'll need to speak to me again."

We finally get the front title sequence in the can by eight o'clock. The show at The Clap Clinic starts at nine, and I'm not showered and out of the studio until eight-thirty. I don't have to be on stage until about ten-fifteen, but I want to watch Charlotte French compering. I hear she's developed a hell of a lot since I saw her in Luton. My driver stops the Mercedes outside The Clap Clinic at eight fifty-five, and the ever-composed Charles greets me at the entrance.

Chapter Thirty-seven

"Doug Tucker. Always a pleasure."
"Hi Charles. Don't tell me the white Porsche belongs to Arnold."
"The white Porsche belongs to Arnold. He scratched the black one."
I laugh, and pass through the foyer into the club. For a Wednesday night in August, Arnold's got a healthy sized crowd in. A bad chat-show host drinks on his own in the VIP bar, and the dressing room is deserted. I find Charlotte French, Colin Homes, and Arnold sitting on the riverside terrace. They're at a table near the water's edge, overlooking Sunita. Arnold's telling them about his motor yacht's brave service during the evacuation of Dunkerque. There's an awkward silence from the other two comics, and I guess it's because the boat's named after Sunita, and they feel embarrassed because she's dead and I used to go out with her.

"I like the new Porsche, Arnold. Did you get tired of black?"
"Aye, Doug, I did. You know me. White's more my colour. It suggests innocence."
Charlotte and Colin laugh politely. A whim of Arnolds decides whether they earn lots of money as comedians, or crap money doing day jobs. Jojo, the show manager comes out onto the terrace.
"It's filling up nicely. Shall we start at five past nine?"
"Sounds good to me." Says Arnold, gazing lasciviously at Jojo's body, which is crammed into a silky summer dress. All the women Arnold employs at The Clap Clinic are attractive. The ones who give in to his sexual advances stay. The ones who don't, leave. Jojo's been working here a week, and the comics are speculating as to how long she'll last. As Charlotte and Colin realise the show is almost upon them, I can see their rush of nerves.
"I'd better get down there." Says Charlotte, pushing her chair back to get up. Colin follows suit.
"Have a good one. I'll be down in a minute to watch the show."
Arnold and I are left alone at the table. A barman clears it, and Arnold orders a pint of Kronenburg for himself, and a pint of Guinness for

me. A disco boat passes heading upstream, and her wash causes Sunita to pull at her mooring lines. Her varnished planking and teak decks add character to the view from The Clap Clinic. For a man who's done time for manslaughter, Arnold's got great aesthetic sensibility. The Clap Clinic used to be a dilapidated warehouse, and now it's a thriving restaurant and entertainment venue, with picturesque views of the Thames. The riverside terrace and balcony are tranquil places to enjoy food and drink. There's no traffic noise, and the opposite bank is lined with mature trees. It's odd that his good taste didn't extend to the way he decorated his office.

An attractive young black waitress brings our drinks, and Arnold offers me food. I ask for the avocado, vegetarian bacon, and melted cheese ciabatta with sour cream. Whilst she writes my order in her pad, Arnold's hand strokes her bottom. She's wearing tight artificial fabric trousers, and I couldn't help noticing how nice her bum looks.
"I'm opening Clap Clinics in ten British cities next year. They'll all be next to rivers or canals. I'm planning a TV series in which I visit every club by boat. It'll be a travelogue, showing all the beautiful places the boat goes through on the way. Each programme will feature me and a comedian taking the boat through the locks, and all that stuff. Then they'll do their set at whichever Clap Clinic we reach at the end of the journey."
"Won't Sunita be too wide for the canals?"
"Sunita is only suitable for big rivers, and coastal places. We'll get a seventy-foot narrow boat for the canals. Next year I'm expanding into Holland and Belgium. Maybe Denmark and Sweden. Then we'll do the TV show using Sunita to cross the North Sea. Ruud says he'll bankroll expansion into South Africa, Australia, and New Zealand. Maybe one day nobody in the world will laugh without my say so. How did you enjoy your visit from the Special Branch?"
I aim my gaze at Sunita's wheelhouse, to cover my shock. How did Arnold know I had a visit from the police?
"Fine. I didn't realise they were Special Branch. How did you know?"
"They weren't all Special Branch. Just Andy."
"Andy?"
"Detective Sergeant Andy Hayle. I helped him get where he is."
"*You* help the Special Branch?"

"How does a copper get promoted? By solving crime. Where does he get his information? Criminals. He's just an errand boy to the guys I know. The Superintendents and Chief Superintendents of today, were beat bobbies when I was a petty thief. We've achieved success in our respective fields by helping each other up the ranks."
I try to cover my anxiety with an attempt at wit.
"I didn't know you were in the Masons, Arnold."
"I am, but it's not relevant to this. Where there's Special Branch, the SAS and MI5 aren't far off. Not to forget the Hells Angels."
I'm stuck for a reply. At last I find some words.
"I'm intrigued, but I don't want to be involved with any of them. I just want to write and perform comedy."
"That's what you're good at Doug. But so are a lot of other people. You stick to writing and performing, and I'll see to it that you join the elite. But remember, Doug. The Special Branch won't give you paid work. Just highly dangerous unpaid work, snooping where you shouldn't go. Sometimes you can't help having something to hide. Far better to have nothing to hide from me, than from them."
This conversation is making me feel uneasy.
"I'd rather not have anything to hide from anybody."
"You and the rest of us, Doug. But the entertainment business is a game of musical chairs. There aren't enough chairs to go round, and they're all dirty. You can't sit in a dirty chair without getting dirty trousers."
"And what if I take my trousers off?"
"You'll get a bigger, more comfortable chair. But it'll still be dirty. There are no clean chairs in the game. They've had to support too many arseholes."
He stands up and drains his glass.
"Let's go and watch the show. Just one thing, Doug. The man who owns the chairs is Ruud Vermeulen. Don't let Andy Hayle persuade you *he's* got any chairs. He's not even in the game. The best he can hope for is to lick his superior's stools."
As we make our way down to the cabaret room, I've got a horrible feeling Arnold knows I told Hayle about the drowning clown. We get another drink, and watch Charlotte French do fifteen minutes before introducing Colin Homes. I can't concentrate, and don't take any of her jokes in. The audience adore her, though. It's only when Colin

gets himself into a hole with a woman heckler that I remember I've got to do the second half.

The woman's celebrating her birthday, and she's so drunk she doesn't know when to shut up. By the time I get on stage, she's in a stupor, and the first ten minutes of my act goes smoothly. When she starts up again, I can't hear what she's saying, because she's stage right, and my right ear isn't hearing very well. I've got Bournemouth tomorrow night, and 'The Sauce Boat' in Bristol on Friday night. The days are busy making 'Rats Milk Cheese', so I don't know when I can get to a doctor. I definitely need to sort this ear out, though. The rest of the audience can hear the woman's heckles, and I can't. It's hard to respond with witty reposts when I'm the only one who can't hear what she's saying. If it was a man, I could go in hard. Audiences don't like comedians putting women hecklers down ruthlessly, though. They lose sympathy for the comic, even if he has been provoked. I get an encore, but at one point I nearly lose the moral high ground to the drunken woman.

In the dressing room afterwards, I share a neat grass joint with Charlotte French. Arnold's booking her at all of his gigs, and she's bought a VW Golf with her newfound wealth. She offers me a lift home to Lambeth Walk, because I didn't come in my own car. I've had a few drinks, and on the way to Lambeth Walk I ask her if she's bothered by what we witnessed in Arnold's office earlier this year.

"Witnessed what in Arnold's office?" She says. I laugh nervously.
"You know. When he beat those Glaswegian crims up."
There's a pause, and I wonder if she's said something I haven't heard, because she's on my right side, and it's a direction from which I'm getting used to not hearing things.
"I promised Arnold I wouldn't talk about it."
"I can understand that. But to me…"
"Especially to you. I feel ashamed to say this, Doug, but remember Lorna Duke?"
"No, I've never heard of her."
"Exactly. Lorna Duke and I started out in comedy at the same time. She's funnier than me, but she's given up because every time she does a great guest spot, all she gets is another guest spot in six months time.

There are too many comedians after too little work. She's so disillusioned she's training to be a teacher."

"Yuck. She *must* be fed up."

"Arnold's booking me in every club he runs."

"I can see that from your car."

"The car was a present. It's got heated seats."

"Handy in the winter."

"I won't need it for the winter. I've got a round-the-world ticket. I'll be in Australia. Or New Zealand, or Tahiti."

"Arnold?"

"He gave me twenty thousand pounds in cash. My diary's full of work when I get back."

"Did you sleep with him?" As soon as I've said it, I realise it was a mistake.

"Yes, but that wasn't part of the deal. And in case you think I've been cheating on Sunita, she was part of it. I hope you won't hate me for this, but I've been with Arnold and Sunita in your bed. If you don't believe me, you keep both volumes of The Shorter Oxford English Dictionary in the main compartment of your bedside cabinet. There are photos of your mother in the top drawer. I'm sorry, but I'm nosey. This conversation didn't take place. Arnold said those men were killers. By killing them, he's saved the people they would have hurt. Anyway – it beats being a school teacher."

"Lambeth Walk's next on the right." She turns into the road and stops the car. Her face looks yellow in the sodium street lighting.

"I've got some wicked coke, if you fancy a line."

"Another time, Charlotte. I've got to be up early in the morning." I go to kiss her cheek, and she gives me her lips.

"Another time, then. See you at the top, Doug."

"Yes. I'll see you at the top. Can I ask you one more question, Charlotte?"

"Ask."

"Are you a comedian to make money, or to make people laugh?"

"I'm a comedian to make money *so I can* make people laugh. If I don't make money, I have to do another job. I can't make people laugh if I'm being paid to teach how to work out the square root of 3.86."

"You're right. I'd forgotten what it's like to have no money. Thanks for the lift, Charlotte."

The door clunks shut as only a German car door can. When she moves off, the tyres make a brief screech on the road surface. She wants to get to the top fast. I lay awake in bed for a while, examining my motives. I've been priding myself on the fact that it's more important for me to make people laugh, than make money. If I didn't have a large cushion of money in the bank, though, it might be different. What's the point of sticking to your principles, if you have to give up comedy, and throw your life away trying to control awkward teenagers? I don't feel anger towards Charlotte for snooping in my bedside cabinet. When you're an orphan dependent on nasty adults for food and shelter, you don't have any boundaries. I don't have secrets, anyway. How can I, when I share my deepest doubts with rooms full of several hundred people?

Chapter Thirty-eight

The following day I can't hear my cues because my right ear's slightly deaf, and wearing Boris' head accentuates the problem. We have to retake a few shots because I don't hear my feed lines. I'm wrapped at two in the afternoon. Leah's dresser is off sick, and Angela is recruited to dress her. They've finished my scenes anyway, and only have a few more to do with Leah and Rufus. Simon and Sheila need to see what the special effects department have done to the title sequences before the final edit is spliced to the episodes. I'm disappointed when I hear they're not transmitting the pilot episode. It's the only one in which my face is seen, because Leah dreams Boris is a human. They say the show has evolved since the pilot, and Boris is too strong a character. If they remind the viewers it's a bloke in a suit, the mask would lose its power. I can see what they mean, I reflect, as I wander up Teddington High Street to the bank.

There's a feeling of relief and satisfaction amongst everyone at 'Rats Milk Cheese'. It's been a long shoot, and we're all tired, but thrilled at the prospect of seeing the show on telly. Especially as it goes out across America from the end of next week.

"Doug. Doug. It *is* you!" I look round to see Sue Shanks. It's a while since we last met, and the traffic noise meant I didn't hear the first few times she called my name. She looks younger and prettier than I remember. Arnold threw a pearl away when he left her.

"I hear you're a big TV star now, Doug."
"Thanks, but I wouldn't say that quite yet." One of the kids I thought was walking on his own has held Sue's hand. Another one is eyeing me gingerly from behind her shopping bag. I've already backed away involuntarily.

"Mind, Doug. Don't step backwards into the road. Didn't you hear that van? This is Steven, and this is Martine."

"Are you looking after them for somebody?"
Sue laughs in a Glaswegian accent.
"No, they're mine. Mine and Arnold's."
"I'm sorry, I thought …. my mistake. I'm a bit preoccupied. I've got to get to the bank, before I drive to Bournemouth. To do Arnold's gig on the pier."
"I understand you creative types. You were probably writing a joke in your head. Nice to see you again, Doug."
Perhaps she knows about my fear of children. I'm so distracted I walk past the bank, and have to double back on myself. If those were Arnold's children, who were the kids he said were his on the boat? In the bank queue I remember the beer garden of the Crown and Anchor, and the surprise visit from the boat that became Sunita. Those kids huddled on the cabin top didn't look like the offspring of a millionaire. I thought at the time they were a bit dark skinned to be Arnold's kids. Leah had a difficult time getting them to speak, and when Arnold and the Vermeulen brothers came ashore for a drink, the kids went down into the cabin.

My turn comes, and when I give the cashier the Bank of Scotland fifty-pound note Arnold gave me, she disappears behind the scenes. The queue behind me gets longer, and I can feel the resentment from the other customers, for causing the delay. I occupy the dead time standing at the empty window by studying the tits of the girl in the next window. They're fabulous, and I'm desperate to get them out, and lick and suck them. The cashier returns to my window. Her tits look nice, but nothing like as generous as the girl's in the window next door. Every cell of me yearns to lick her armpits. To smell and taste the rest of her body. To do so would be a deep knowing, like a computer sucking data from a removable device. Maybe this is what happens when a dog sniffs another dog's bottom. I have a need to lick and suck every woman I meet, as my ongoing search for Mummy, the great one within whom was paradise.

"I'm sorry Sir. We can't accept this fifty-pound note. It's a forgery. If you could go over to the customer services desk, the supervisor would like you to fill out a forged currency form."

Chapter Thirty-nine

I really don't feel like compering Bournemouth tonight. I haven't written any new material since last week, and I'm tired. I'd rather have an evening in with Angela. She wants to perform her first ever blowjob on me.

It hasn't rained since Monday, and there's a lot of grease on the roads. When it starts raining, the traffic slows right down, and I start to worry if I'll get to Bournemouth in time for the show. I think about Arnold, the Special Branch, and Ruud Vermeulen. If Arnold's as thick with Sergeant 'Andy' Hayle as he claims, I'm in deep shit. If Hayle tells Arnold my story about the drowning clown, and Arnold tells Vermeulen, I'm dead. I'm lost in such thoughts on the M3, when a lorry pulls out in front of me, and I nearly lose control of the car. I decide to drive less fast, and make it to Bournemouth fifteen minutes before show time.

The theatre on the end of Bournemouth pier is heaving with punters. There's a stag party in, and two hen nights. There's also a coach load of old age pensioners from Birmingham. All these in addition to the Bournemouth regulars. I sit watching the sun sink towards the horizon. The south coast is enjoying a clear sky, whilst inland is beneath a thick layer of cloud. I need a holiday. When the 'Rats Milk Cheese' shoot is over, I'll take Angela somewhere sunny by the sea. Maybe Ibiza.
"Doug, you're on. We've got a full house." Pete, the soundman has worked here as long as I have. He's a helpful person to have around.
"Someone asked me to give you this." He hands me a folded piece of paper. It's a bloke called Chris' birthday. He's got a red shirt on, and he's at the table downstage left. His mates want me to take the piss out of him. I yawn my way to the backstage area, and wait for the intro music to start. I'd like to try that bit about the women's faces in Picasso's paintings, but most of the audience are too thick or too old,

or both, to know what I'm on about. Oh for the time when I'm riding high on the success of 'Rats Milk Cheese'…

The show's quite a hard one, especially as I can't hear what the hecklers are shouting. I get to bed at two-thirty in the morning, and drag myself into the shower five hours later. I'll have to learn my lines for this morning's scenes in the car on the way to Teddington, and plan my ten minutes of material for 'The Sauce Boat' on the way from Teddington to Bristol. I feel so tired I could sleep for a year.

Angela's wearing green cotton yoga trousers, and a black cotton sweatshirt. She's added some pink streaks to the blue ones in her hair, and she looks delectable.
When I'm in Boris' costume up to the neck, and she's about to put my head on, she whispers into my ear that she's been practicing fellatio on a carrot.
"I want to make you happy, Doug. Because you make me so happy."
"Think about where you'd like a holiday in September, Angie. I want to take you there."
She says something in reply, but I don't hear because she's by my right ear, and she's lowering Boris' head onto mine.

During a coffee break, I'm relaxing on the sofa in the lounge set, when Sheila Fox comes and sits next to me.
"I'm off to the editing suite in Soho, Doug. I'll see you at the wrap party."
"I haven't received my invitation yet."
"Must have been a mistake on Terry's part. They were sent out last week. It's tomorrow night at The Clap Clinic. Apparently Arnold's got a VIP room there?"
"He certainly has. And a VIP boat. I'm not working tomorrow night, so I'll be there."
"Thank you for all your hard work, Doug." I've never known Sheila's manner so caring. She's starting to leave the set when I remember the episode I wrote.
"Oh, Sheila. Did you get a chance to read the script I gave you?"
"I thought you had some nice ideas in there. You're thinking along the right lines, but I can't use it. Must dash, Darling. See you at the party."
I don't know whether I should feel encouraged or disappointed. Soon

after we resume filming, a bulb blows in one of the lights suspended high above the set. Hot broken glass falls on the carpet, and Leah's dresser cuts her finger on a shard. She's taken off to sign the accident book and get some first aid, and I volunteer Angela to dress Leah, as I'm leaving for Bristol very soon. Nancy the Assistant Floor Manager says she'll help Terry get me out of the costume when I'm wrapped. Nicky Butler's been on the set all morning, hanging around Leah. Laurent the French gorilla seems to have disappeared, and Leah's been edgy. When Simon the director is still using me in the shot fifteen minutes after he was supposed to have released me, I mention that I have to appear in 'The Sauce Boat' in Bristol later today.
"Impossible!" says Nicky Butler.
"But I've been told I can do it. It was arranged days ago."
"You're contract is to work here until ten tonight, if I want you to. Releasing you for another TV show is discretionary. I'm in charge this afternoon, and I say you stay here."
I can't believe this is the woman who was so fawning the first time I met her. It was only a few months ago when she came into the dressing room at Gerry Crook's gig in Soho. I thought at the time she seemed rather nice for a TV producer. The dyed blond hair is the same. The clothes and jewellery are the same, but the apologetic manner is gone. The nasty sneer and the malicious eyes belong to a different Nicky Butler.
"You're a liability to this show with that act of yours. It's offensive."
"Nicky, have you got me confused with someone else? You told me you love my act."
"Not that muck about the crucifixion. A lot of people don't advertise the fact, but they are basically Christian in their beliefs. They don't want to hear you spout on about Jesus' agent, or the thieves. Stop doing it!"
"Nicky, you're referring to some ad libbing I did once, weeks before I had this part. It's not in my act."
I look at her as softly as I can. There's so little reason in her tirade, I don't feel angry. I feel sorry for her, because she's very upset about something, and it can't be me. She fires hatred at me out of her little eyes, and turns to Nancy.
"Get that dog mask on him, I can't stand the sight of his face for one second longer."

"Simon, you're the director. Am I released to go to Bristol, or what?" Simon looks at his script, he's clearly embarrassed by Nicky's outburst. This has always been a happy show, and none of us are used to such scenes.
"I'm afraid what Nicky says goes, Doug. I need you for the next scene. After that, as far as I'm concerned, you can go."

I go back in the head, and we start the next scene. It's a re-shoot of something we did a few weeks ago, but need to do again for technical reasons. Leah makes so many mistakes, it becomes obvious she's either on drugs now, or on a massive comedown from drugs she took recently. Her mistakes combined with my impaired hearing, cause us to do twenty-four takes of one shot alone. When we finally get it right, Des Jensen is so used to us stopping to do it again, he's caught by surprise and misses his cue. We're back to square one. The next time we pause and they take my head off, I ask to speak to Nicky again. She's less hostile, but still insists she can't wrap me until five. I leave a message with Melissa, who phones back a few minutes later saying she's spoken to the producers of 'The Sauce Boat', who say if I don't leave Teddington until five, I'll arrive in Bristol too late to do the show. Several comedians live in or near Bristol, and they can replace me. Nicky Butler has deliberately sabotaged my appearance on the country's most popular stand-up comedy show, and lost me the two thousand pound fee.

When five o'clock comes, I've been sitting in costume with my head off since three-thirty. Nancy helps me take the costume off.
"I can't believe Nicky spoke to you like that, Doug. 'Bare in Mind' is up for an award, and they've just heard it's going to be networked in America. The success has gone to the bitch's head."
Nancy leans close to my left ear when she says this, and I smell fresh coffee and chocolate chip cookies on her breath. She gives my hair a stroke with her hand, and presses a soft towel to my forehead. It reminds me of the times Mummy dried me when I'd just come out of the bath. I want to get out of the costume, and explore Nancy. But as soon as she's undone the fastenings, and helped me out, she has to switch her talkback on and continue her duties on the studio floor. I watch her bottom as she walks back towards the set. Her passion is

247

horse riding, and I imagine what she looks like in jodhpurs and riding boots.

I have a long shower. Angela's still busy dressing Leah, who's burst into tears twice. Word in the production office is that in France she took amphetamine sulphate to lose weight. She had such a big comedown afterwards, she's been staving it off with more sulphate and coke. Laurent's lost interest and gone back to France. I can imagine this making Nicky Butler tense, but why take it out on me? I'm too sensible to get into a shouting match with her today. I'll raise the matter with Sheila and Simon in a calm and sober situation.

My car home is late, and I have to wait in the foyer for ten minutes. When it arrives, it's a minicab. Since I began work on the show, I've always been given a BMW or Mercedes, driven by a man in a suit. This driver is smoking a cigarette at the wheel of a tatty old Vauxhall, and insists on talking to me. The attraction of being driven by a white-collar driver is that he won't talk to you unless you start a conversation. If you want to learn lines, read a book, or gaze out of the window, you can do so without having to shut him up.

This bloke's at me from the start. He wants to know what show we're doing, what part I play, what else I've done on telly. Which famous people I know. Then he starts telling me which footballers he's had in his car, whose names I've never heard, and never will. When I make the mistake of telling him I'm also a stand-up comedian, he says the inevitable
"Here's a joke you can use in your act," and tells a racist joke I heard in the school playground ten years ago, but gets the punch line wrong. I'm about to tell a white lie that I need to learn the lines to a script so I can escape his banalities, when he comes out with
"Terrible about that rozzer getting done for child abuse, isn't it." I say I don't know about it, and he tosses a copy of The Daily Mail over his shoulder. The newspaper is still in the air when I guess what I'm going to read. Detective Sergeant Andrew Hayle of the Special Branch has been suspended from duty after allegations of sexually abusing children. Not much point phoning his direct line now. How much does Arnold know about this? And the Vermeulen brothers? When I

get home I open a can of Guinness from the fridge, and fall asleep on the sofa watching The Marx Brothers.

I'm woken up by Angela letting herself in with the front door key I've given her. I feel excitement mounting within at the prospect of cuddling her, and hearing her voice. There's an unfamiliar heaviness to the sounds she makes as she approaches the lounge door and opens it. I like to have subdued lighting when I'm relaxing, especially with the telly on. I can't make out what's wrong as she stands silhouetted by the hall light in the doorway. When she comes into the room, I see the cause of her distress. Her left eye is half closed, and the area around and including the eye socket is purple. My stomach turns over, and I hold her close.
"Oh my Goodness, Angela. What happened?"
"You'll hear. Sooner or later."
"Were you mugged? Who did it?" I'm about to open my mouth to say "I'll kill him", but stop myself from uttering such a cliché.
"Your ex-lover. Lady Prima Donna Philips did it."
"Why?"
"She said I left a pin in her blouse. I didn't even touch the blouse. Then she punched me in the face."
"Did anyone else see?"
"Everyone. She did it on the studio floor."
"What did they say?"
"I'm sacked! Nicky Butler sacked me on the spot. Nobody came to help. Not one person. Not even Esmeralda, and everyone knows it was her who left the pin in the blouse."

She's sitting beside me on the sofa. She cries and cries, and I rock her gently in my arms. I feel like crying myself. A fresh sequence of sobs erupts and snot comes out of her nose onto my shirt. I cover her embarrassment by giving her my clean hanky. I close my eyes and enjoy the tenderness. After a while, I look down on her lovely blue and pink hair, and she smiles up at me.

I lean forward and take a swig of Guinness.
"I presume the blowjob's off then?"
"Not necessarily." She smiles. We cuddle again, and I offer her a drink.

"I'd like a glass of wine. Don't worry, I'll get it." While she's in the kitchen, I wonder what's going to happen about tomorrow's wrap party. I've got to go, because I'm a member of the cast, and we're doing a second series. I want to go, too. I just hope Angela's invited.

Chapter Forty

Angela and I sleep until late the next morning, and have toasted muffins and poached eggs in bed. Then we make love, and lay beside each other reading novels. She doesn't volunteer the blowjob, and I don't ask. Another subject we both avoid is tonight's wrap party. When it finally gets mentioned, she's adamant she isn't going. She says she doesn't mind me going, but I can tell she's not happy about it. I'm thinking it feels odd to be going to the Clap Clinic on a Saturday night and not performing, when Jojo the manager phones me and asks if I can headline the show. The American act who was supposed to be headlining has missed his plane, or failed to get a work permit.

I'm quite happy about that, as the party won't get going until after the show's over. This way I'll get two hundred pounds I otherwise wouldn't have earned. It's also a good excuse to go to the party, if I'm already going to be gigging at the venue. I ask Angela how much of her not going to the party is down to her black eye, and how much is due to her getting fired.
"A hundred per cent of both." She says. We cuddle a while, and she goes out to get some holiday brochures from a travel agent. We're thinking La Gomera in The Canary islands might be better than Ibiza. I go to my desk and write some ideas for jokes up on the computer. I've had a few potential jokes floating around my head, but when Angela's key sounds in the lock, I realise I've spent the last ten minutes staring out of the window thinking about Leah's tits. How could Laurent have got bored with them so quickly?

That evening I leave Angela on the sofa awash with glossy holiday brochures. We had a laugh together planning which novels we're going to take to read in the sunshine. I get a taxi to The Clap Clinic. I've got just enough money to pay the driver, because I gave some cash to Angela for a takeaway. The bar will be free during the party, and I've got two hundred pounds cash coming my way for the gig. Charles

greets me at the door, and introduces me to another suave black man called Clyde. He's been taken on as Charles's second in command.
"We've been in the same Kung Fu club for years" smiles Charles.
"I shouldn't get on with him really, because I'm from Peckham and he's from Brixton."
"Well, if you start fighting, you can always throw each other out." I say, as I pass into the bar. The show's sold out, and Jojo comes up to me with an alluring smile. She's wearing her straight black hair in a Snow White type hair band, and a turquoise cotton dress.
"The VIP room, dressing room, balcony and roof terrace are all reserved for the Grange Films wrap party, Doug. After the show's over, I'm hoping that as a member of the cast you might give me an invite."
I laugh at her modesty, and give her a wink.

The river terrace is thronged with punters enjoying a summer that's forgotten it should have ended. The breeze coming off the River Thames is warm, and the river is blue with the reflected sky. Sunita is moored alongside, and the remaining river frontage is occupied by a gleaming white new power cruiser. It's a Sunseeker, which is the Rolls Royce of the motor yacht world. She's about forty feet long, and called 'Grietje'. Beside her name her home port of Amsterdam is painted in the same seriffed writing. She's flying a Dutch flag, and I strongly suspect she belongs to the Vermeulens. There's such a jubilant atmosphere amongst the people drinking and eating in the evening sun, I slightly regret having to perform. The dressing room is thick with marijuana smoke, despite the window overlooking the river terrace being open. Neil Gosling's compering, and Julian Rogers is on first, before dashing off to headline another club in north London. Kev Knight's on second, and I've got to wait until about ten-fifteen before I can go on and close the show. I shake hands with all three, and refuse Julian's offer of a toke on the joint. Most comics smoke dope, but usually after they've been on. Julian Rogers is the exception. His memory doesn't fail him on stage despite copious amounts of strong skunk throughout the day, right up to just before he takes the stage. He can recall any of hundreds of one-liners and heckle put downs due to a special memory system he learned whilst studying for a degree in law. He's also a brilliant ad-libber, and sometimes he'll do a half hour set with only a few minutes of material. Like many comedians, he's under-rated and I think he should have his own show on telly. The curse of being a brilliant club comic is that one's skill at playing a club audience sentences one to just that – working the clubs. Other comics who are less skilled at playing a live audience are forced into writing a sitcom script, or going to more auditions, and end up doing more television work than their brilliant live colleagues. I suppose Kev Knight is a case in point. He's not so hot at stand-up, but enjoys lots of success writing for magazines and TV shows, and getting small parts in the shows he writes for.

It's a happy Saturday crowd, and Neil Gosling does a great job of getting the show started, and putting Julian on soon after. Julian's got very little time to get across London for his next gig, and the last thing he needs is a compere who does too long at the top of the show. Kev Knight's a little too cerebral for many of the crowd, but gets away with it because the stupider elements are still sober enough to listen, even if they don't get all his jokes. I've been hiding on the roof terrace for a lot of the evening, because as it advances, my anxiety about Arnold and the Vermeulens is increasing. It's during the second interval that the dressing room door opens, and Arnold pokes his head in.

"Hi Kev. Hi Neil. Doug – I want a word with you in my office, if you don't mind." I follow him up the stairs, my mouth dry and my heart pounding. Surely he's not going to smash his headline act up before he's due on stage. It wouldn't be good for business. Arnold flings the leather padded door open, and advances towards the desk. I've been imagining Ruud and Hans Vermeulen waiting for me with an array of torture implements, but Arnold's office is empty of people. On the wall above the fireplace is a large oil painting of a young girl. Arnold stands proudly beside it.
"What do you think?"
"It's lovely, Arnold. Who's it by?"
"Who's it by! Douglas – I thought you were a man of culture. It's a Jack Paliace. I paid ten grand for it."
"It's very nice. Who's the little girl?"
"His daughter. He lives near Maidenhead. I've been to his house a couple of times. Oh, this is the other reason I invited you up." He goes over to the desk, where three lines of coke are chopped out on a mirror.

"I thought I'd get you off to a flying start. We've got quite a night to enjoy."

Every time I yield to temptation and snort some of Arnold's Charlie, it's the strongest I've had, and I think it can't get any stronger. Until the next time he gives me a snort. I'm just reeling from the initial rush, when there's a knock on the door, and the new black waitress comes in.

"Your five minute call, Mr Tucker." She's wearing the Clap Clinic's uniform of tight black trousers and golden shirt. I thank Arnold for showing me his new painting, and start to leave the office. Instead of following me out, she stays. I close the door, and as I do so I see her take Arnold's solid platinum coke tooter and consume the third line. His left hand is exploring her bottom so thoroughly he's almost pushing the trouser fabric inside her anus. It looks like the price of keeping her job will be a brown mark in her knickers.

Neil Gosling starts the third and final section of the show with his 'watching telly on Sunday evenings' bit, and does well considering they're all pissed. I'm psyching myself up to go on, when he starts his hilarious 'masturbating in your grandmother's house' routine, and I'm left standing near the side of the stage feeling like a wazzock. He's just got a medium-sized laugh and positioned the mike stand centre stage ready to bring me on, when a woman's voice pipes up from the back of the room.

"You're sick, talking about old people like that."

"There's a sign outside, that says 'If easily offended, please stay away.' So my advice, Madam, is stay away."

"No, you stay away. You're not funny, and you've got no cheek bones."

This gets a laugh, because poor Neil's cheekbones are so small you can't see them. I've noticed it many times whist talking to him in various dressing rooms, but have never discussed it with anyone. He's a nice bloke and a good comic, and people are too polite to poke fun at a characteristic he had no choice in. Except for the woman who just heckled him, who I realise is a rather tipsy Sheila Fox.

Encouraged by the laugh she just got, Sheila now thinks she's the funniest person in the room.

"What were you doing at your grandmother's anyway? Asking where she hid your jokes?" Another big laugh. Then Des Jensen's voice adds:

"She hid his jokes in the same place she hid his cheekbones." Fuelled by alcohol and the pack instinct, the audience are enjoying their leader's defeat at the hands of their own peers. A man from a different part of the room shouts:

"Yeah. Less time wanking, and more time getting some jokes."

"And some cheek bones." Chimes in a woman from another corner of the room.

"Oh no, they've turned." I think to myself. My sympathy for Neil is as great as my anger towards Sheila Fox and Des Jensen. They wouldn't dare get up in front of a crowd of strangers and try to be funny, and they know it. Okay, so Neil's routine about masturbating at his grandmother's isn't the most poignant, but the audience isn't bright enough for anything much more sophisticated. I'm shocked how rude and insensitive Sheila and Des have been, especially as they didn't pay to get in. The arrogant bastards!

Neil looks like he's about to burst into tears. He rallies himself, and puts the mike into the stand. Leaning into it he announces solemnly:

"Ladies and gentlemen. Last week, my grandmother died. Soon after she was told she had cancer, she came to see me perform, and I did that routine. She said she was proud of me, and that's what matters. I don't care a flying fuck what you ignorant cunts think." The room goes silent, and Neil walks off stage to the sound of his own feet. Then he suddenly runs back on and says

"Please welcome your headliner. Doug Tucker." And runs off again. I take the stage to the sound of general muttering, and no common focus. A fat man with a bald head and goatee beard shouts

"You'd better be funny, mate. Even if you have got cheek bones." I clear my throat, and start speaking slowly and quietly into the microphone.

"I'd like to start my act by saying that Neil Gosling is a good comedian, and a personal friend. He's done lots of good jokes this evening, which you laughed at. I don't think he deserved the treatment you gave him. I'm supposed to come out here and be all friendly, and make you laugh. Quite frankly I'd rather entertain a pit full of snakes. At least they don't victimise their own species. Secondly, those of you who haven't paid have no right to heckle the acts. If you're getting the comics for free, you should be grateful, because it takes a lot of hard work to put an act together. This is a comedy club, not a prison exercise yard. Your shouting personal remarks about features the performer has no control over, was offensive."

Some people started booing earlier in my speech, but nobody joined in, and they soon lost their nerve. A few people start to applaud me at the end, and the silent majority wants in. One or two people even start to cheer. Then a voice cuts in from the rear, stage right section of the audience. I can't hear what they said, because they're on my deaf side. I quietly ask someone in the front row what the person said, and they help me out by repeating
"If easily offended, please stay away." That gets a laugh at my expense. I suppose they have got a point. If only Neil had put me on after his Sunday evening television routine instead of going on with the masturbating at his grandmother's bit, I wouldn't be dealing with this shit.
"I wish I had. I'm only here for the private party afterwards." That gets a smattering of a laugh.
"All I'm saying is if you want to perform comedy, write some material and do your own act. It's a lot harder than joining in someone else's. And if the people who heckled the compere would like to come up on stage, I'm sure we can find plenty of physical defects to laugh at." That strikes home, and gets a ripple of applause. I pull my sleeve up to reveal a small fatty lump on my upper arm.
"I saw the doctor about this lump. Apparently it's harmless, but I didn't choose to have it, so maybe you'd like to ridicule me. Or would you rather I talk about the problems I've made myself from my own stupidity?"
"Just say something funny." I recognise the voice as Des Jensen's.
"I can't. I'm a mime artist. This is you." I do a brief mime of a bloke being buggered. Why does the audience laugh at that? I don't know who I resent most. Myself for getting such a cheap laugh, or the audience for giving it to me. Either way, I've managed to get into the world of imagination, and easily link into a piece of material about haemorrhoids, which links into ointments and chemists. Soon the audience is pissing itself over my stag night material, and the earlier disruption is forgotten. Half an hour later I get off when I've finished the estate agent on drugs routine, and the audience gives me a standing

ovation. I have no choice but to do a ten-minute encore. I come off stage elated. Tonight I'm the funniest man in the world. Then I remember that line of coke Arnold gave me in his office. I want another one. I'm stumbling through the crowd as best I can, having been under lights for the last half an hour. Neil's wrapping the show up as quickly as he can, when a figure steps in front of me. I'm about to play the high status comedian and brush past him, when I realise the voice my right ear should be hearing a lot better belongs to Rudd Vermeulen. I quickly shake his hand, and feel as if I'm in a python's squeeze. His blue eyes pierce me.

"I enjoyed your performance a lot Doug. I envy your ability."

"Thank you." I can't think what to say. He looks so suave and clean, I can't imagine him in a Turkish prison.

"Is that your boat? The Grietje?"

"No that is Hans' boat. I flew in by helicopter."

"From Antwerpen?"

"No, from my new yacht, The Jager. She's moored in Shoreham Harbour. Excuse me, but I must find Hans. He was supposed to meet me at Battersea heliport in the 'Grietje'."

I greet Neil as he comes off the stage after wrapping the show up, and put my hand on his shoulder as we walk up to the dressing room.

"Well done, Mate. I can't believe two of the people who heckled you work for Grange Films. Just because they've hired the gaff for a party, doesn't give them the right to disrupt the show. I'm ashamed to know them."

"I'm ashamed I let them get the better of me. I don't think I'll hang around for the party."

"Have a good time despite those cunts. Put a brave face on."

"A brave face without cheekbones."

Nancy is guarding the way to the dressing room and VIP bar with a clipboard in her hands, and Charles is hovering discreetly nearby.

I get Neil and myself a beer, and Neil goes to roll a joint in the dressing room, whilst I look for Sheila and Des. I want to explain why I said what I did at the beginning of my act. I eventually find them talking to Arnold on the dressing room balcony. As Neil needs to change from his stage costume, it strikes me as a bit rich that Sheila and Des have invaded the one place he can get some privacy.

257

"Hi Sheila. Hi Des. I hope you understand why I said what I said on stage."

"Think no more of it, Darling. You were marvellous, by the way."

"Sheila's celebrating the final edits getting delivered to the Americans."

"They're absolutely wild about the title sequences. I've been personally congratulated by the head of the American network. He's played golf with the U.S. President you know."

Lawrence the writer is with them. He looks even more of a nonentity than when I saw him in Leah's dressing room. Which is probably why I didn't notice him at first.

"The Americans asked us for a catchphrase for the show. I came up with 'Boris the Blue Dog. He's a backward god.'"

Des puts his arm round Lawrence in a protective way.

"Isn't he a genius. First he dreams up that title sequence in the water tank, and then a brilliant hook line."

I'm wondering whether I should mention that the water tank was my idea, when I notice Ruud Vermeulen emerge from downstairs onto the river terrace below, and step aboard the 'Grietje'. Arnold spots it too, and gives me the nod to follow him. We go up to his office, and this time I know there's going to be a showdown. He sits in his company director's chair, and bids me sit down. I look across the empty desk, and it strikes me for the first time that he doesn't have a computer. He opens a drawer and removes a shiny metal object. It clunks onto the leather desktop, and I recognise the knuckleduster with which Tam attacked Arnold.

"Remember this spike was meant to go into my face, Doug?"

Chapter Forty-one

I answer in the affirmative. My voice is shaky and my mouth is dry. Arnold gets up and produces a bottle of beer from the fridge. He plonks it down in front of me.
"Would you like a glass to go with it?"
"No thanks."
"Pick the knuckleduster up, Douglas." I obey, and am surprised how heavy it is.
"You're holding a piece of evidence that could implicate me in Tam and Gregor's murder. I trust you, though Doug. I trust you to understand that if I hadn't put a stop to their violence, innocent faces would have had that spike plunged into them. Innocent female faces, which deserve to be kissed, not punctured by steel."
He pauses to light a cigar.
"I've got to get this little lecture out of the way quickly, before our Flemish friends come and join the party. Doug, Andy Hayle told you I did time for manslaughter. The truth is, I murdered him. He laughed at me, so I killed him. I hate myself for it, because he had a wife and young daughter. The first night of my prison sentence I was watching 'Fawlty Towers', and I realised what a wanker I'd been. John Cleese had millions of people laughing at him, and he's a millionaire adored around the world. And I'd killed a man for laughing at me! I vowed to myself when I got out, I'd go into comedy."
"Did you give anything to the man's wife and kid?"
"After I got out of nick I went to their flat with a bottle of vodka to apologise. Yes, I fucked his wife. But she enjoyed it. Now I'm flush I'm paying for the daughter to go to a good public school."
The beer tastes good, and drives the dryness out of my mouth. Arnold continues...
"If I could be a comedian, I'd be one. But I don't have the talent for it. Doug, you've got a wonderful gift to go out there and be funny. I watched how you changed the energy of the room tonight. That crowd wanted blood, and you transformed them into fluffy bunnies. You don't deliver spikes to the face, you deliver laughter. You're a

dolphin, not a shark. So why the fuck did you tell Andy Hayle about the clown?"

"I watched him suffer a horrific death. He was murdered. And Sunita…"

"I've already apologised to you about Sunita. She was a junkie, Doug. I'm sorry, but she was. If it hadn't been me she was sleeping with, it would have been somebody else. In fact, there were others. I promise you I wasn't responsible for her getting caught with drugs in Riyadh. As for the clown – he had it coming to him. Trust me."

"What did he do? Throw a custard pie in Ruud's face?"

He gets up and opens a window to let the cigar smoke out. Then he wanders over to gaze at his new painting.

"The clown was a Chechyen Warlord, who tried to rip the Vermeulens off. Putting him in that costume was part of the punishment. If Ruud or Hans found out you'd talked to the police about their business, you'd be dead. Hayle had to go anyway – don't think we had him dealt with on your account. You made a stupid mistake, Doug. Learn from it, and feel lucky you've got another chance. There's lot of nasty people out there." He draws on his cigar and walks to the window.

"See what that bitch did to poor Neil tonight. It's not enough to be a talented artist. You need to flush the snakes out of your cistern. Talking of which, we'd better go down and mingle. I just saw the Vermeulen's come ashore from Hans' boat. You're safe as far as they're concerned, Doug. As long as you don't go making any more stupid mistakes. Let's enjoy the party."

I suppress my disappointment that Arnold didn't chop out another line, and we go down to the VIP room, where I catch Leah's eye as she stands at the bar. She's with Esmeralda and Terry the ex-runner, now second assistant director. Leah must have had a very good sleep since yesterday, because she looks as stunning as ever. She's had her hair cut slightly shorter, and it curls forward just beneath her ears. It's held in place by a hairband. Her dress is white with a low front, and she's not wearing a bra. I return her wave, but don't know what to say to her, considering she punched my girlfriend in the face and got her sacked. I greet the vision mixer and sound engineer with an affable clink of bottles, and as mine is almost empty, the bar seems the best place to go.

Leah comes over to me, all wide-eyed and little girl lost, and gushes apologies for belting Angela.
"I've been having a really bad time, Doug. We'll get her re-instated, of course. Between you and me, I'd been doing a bit too much Charlie, and the French doctor gave me these slimming pills, which turned out to be pure speed. It's a scandal they're allowed to prescribe them. Would you like one?"
"Not just now, thanks."
"Here, have a couple for later. Do you forgive me?" She says this in a high squeaky voice, and displays her long black eyelashes by blinking several times. I put the pills in my pocket, and reply
"I forgive you, Leah. I don't know Angela well enough to know if she will." I feel her hot hands enclose mine.
"Of course you don't. You've known me for longer than you've known her."
"That's not strictly true. You didn't talk to me at the beginning." She switches the little girl voice back on again.
"That's because I was shy. Leah always love Douggy-wuggy." I might be afraid of children, but when the little girl voice is coming from Leah, it draws me in. I know she's a vixen, but the combination of her gorgeous looks, huge charisma, and sexy smell melts all resistance. She takes my other hand, and pulls me towards her lips. I'm expecting a kiss, but I get a full-blown snog. For a second I'm lost in the ecstasy of her mouth, which is surprisingly sweet for one that's had so many chemicals shoved through it. Then I remember she's one of the highest status people in the building. In show business terms, she *is* the highest status person. By kissing her in public, I'm raising my status too. Our tongues flick each other, then she breaks off and whispers in my ear.
"In my left hand, Darling." I feel a heavy metal thing pushed into my hand. Superficially my status is raised by snogging Leah at the bar, but what about morally? Everyone from Grange Films knows Angela and I are an item. My stomach's churning with self-loathing when my fingers recognise what they're holding. The cocaine bullet.
"I'll drop my cigarette lighter, and you pick it up for me. Whilst you're bending down, take a toot." I do so, and get a burst of the same coke she had that time in her dressing room at Teddington Studios.

"Here comes Des. Pass it to him." She mutters. I obey once more, and Des gives me a wink. I wonder if he begrudges what I said to him from the stage.
Arnold enters the VIP bar with Emily Johnson, the country's most glamorous female newsreader, and another bloke. My arm is nudged, and when I turn round I realise Des and Leah have been talking to me, but I didn't hear because they were on my right side.
"That's Stephen Woods." Says Des.
"Who?" I ask. It turns out he's editor of the best-selling red top newspaper.
"It's handy for us. If he's in bed with Arnold, we'll have his newspaper behind 'Rats Milk Cheese'". Says Des.
"Is there anywhere we can go to get away from everybody?" Asks Leah.
"There's the dressing room, but that's full of people. Or Arnold's office, but you have to be with Arnold to go in there, and he looks busy. Or maybe one of the boats outside…"
"Yeah. Leah want go on boat!" I know her childish talk is a flirtation technique, but it works on me so well, I might as well have a ring fitted to my nose with a rope tied to it. There's something about the way she flits from vulnerable girl to big-bosomed mother that turns my world upside down.
"Come on then." I say to her and Des. I start making my way through the throng, but when I turn round to check their progress, only Leah is behind me. Des is talking to Esmeralda.

The closer we get to the stairs, the more it occurs to me that we don't have permission to go aboard the Sunita or the Grietje. Considering I know both owners to be ruthless killers, my enthusiasm drains away with every step we take. Half way down the stairs, we spot a male American film star, and Leah knows him. She stops to chat, and at the foot of the stairs I recognise Hans Vermeulen. I see him smile for the first time, revealing jagged yellow teeth. We don't shake hands, but he asks me how I am, and I compliment him on the Grietje.
"In fact, Leah and I were wondering if we could take a look at her. Although now she seems to have found a more important friend."
"It doesn't matter. Come and take a look anyhows". It's so long since I exchanged sentences with Hans, I've forgotten his English isn't so good as his brother's.

"I'd love to." I say, realising it's a convenient way to escape Leah's devious flirting.

Hans leads me onto the non-slip glass fibre deck, and I'm thinking to myself that if I could afford such an expensive craft, I wouldn't have a plastic one, when an angelic silvery voice sings in my ears.

"Doug? I hope you're not abandoning me."

"Sorry Leah. I thought you'd got involved with a big film star."

"I wouldn't call a one-night stand getting involved. Anyway, that was last year. I've shaken him off, now Darling. He's great on screen, but a tedious bore in the flesh. And even worse to talk to."

"You've met Hans Vermeulen before, Leah. At the Crown and Anchor." I take so much care not to say "*Clown* and Anchor", it feels even more suspicious.

"Hello Hans. Nice to meet you again. Are you going to show us your boat?" Hans helps her step aboard, and we go below into the saloon. He doesn't show us the fore cabin or the owner's stateroom at the stern, but sits us down on the saloon sofas, and offers us a drink. We both take gin and tonics.

"It's Dutch gin. I've been wanting to have a talk with you, Doug. When we meet before I was in not good mind. My brother and I were having a big problem."

"No problem." I say, realising as soon as I've said it that I sound like I'm contradicting him rather than saying his reticence wasn't a problem.

"No, yes, wherry big problem. Ruud and I got cast out of group we belong in for many years. Now we have to go it alone."

"You mean you were excluded from the Dutch Chamber of Commerce?"

Leah knows the Vermeulens are major investors in 'Rats Milk Cheese', so she's putting on her concerned voice. This despite having slipped her shoes off and pulled her legs up beneath her bottom. Her braless tits are almost tumbling over the top of her white dress, and now she's showing half her thighs as well. All three of us are aware that Hans and I are preoccupied by her fantastic face and body, but are pretending to be interested in the conversation.

"Not the Chamber of Commerce. The Hells Angels." Leah dribbles her drink down her chin, and I give her my handkerchief to mop up with. As soon as her fingers touch mine during the handover, I realise I won't be able to take it home now it's got her lipstick on it.

263

"Oh my God. You're both Hells Angels?"
"Not any more. When we were younger Ruud and I was heavily into motorbikes. It was natural that we join Hells Angels. Then it all goes more respectable. Angels go into businesses, drive BMW cars and wear suits. Many times you meet Hells Angels, and not know it."
"Wow, I had no idea. Is this a secret, or can I tell people?"
"It might be better to keep it secret, as we no longer belong to them. It was a silly dispute, but as I say, enough to cause some – how do you say – consternation? At the time we first meet, I mean."
"Do you still have a motorbike?" I ask.
"I have eight. Two in Thailand, two in the Philipines. And the others are in Belgium. Actually I tell lies. One of them is in Holland."
"Have you ever bitten the head off a dog?" Leah's getting away with this sort of question only because she's pretty and a TV star. I can see that Hans doesn't like it, and try to think of a way off the subject.
"No. But I have done this, and perhaps you would like to join me?" Hans leans forward to open a drawer hidden in the electronics console above the navigation table. He removes a black jewellery box, and opens it. Plush maroon velvet lines it, and an old-fashioned syringe with metal trimmings sits in its moulded surround.
"A special party cocktail. The best. Don't worry – I have clean disposable syringes for you two. And fresh needles."
"What have you got to go in them?" Enquires Leah.
"What do you like? I have the best of anything you want."
"I had a goofball once. That's speed, smack, and coke." Leah's sitting up again now, her flirtatious exposing of her thighs forgotten.
"I can do that. And put a trace of LSD or ecstasy in as well. It goes well with the viagra."
"You inject viagra?"
"Hmm."
"Yes please!" Coos Leah.
"In the Hells Angels we call this 'The Virgin Mary's Breast milk'" Says Hans, as he mixes various powders like some nautical alchemist.
"You must be really naughty boys to get thrown out of the Hells Angels."
"Let's just say, they didn't approve of our decadent ways." Replies Hans, revealing his jagged yellow teeth in a crooked smile. Suddenly he looks up like a guard dog who's heard trespassers, and my heart jolts from the flash of menace in his eyes. Feet are tramping across the

deck. Leah kneels on the sofa and looks out of the window, revealing the tops of her thighs. Hans and I both come to the same conclusion – she isn't wearing knickers.

"It's only Stephen and Emily. I hope you've got breast milk from both of the Virgin Mary's tits. If I know those two, they're after getting loaded."

"I have enough to kill a navy." Says Hans.

"That's good, because Sheila and Nicky are right behind them."

"The more women, the merrier it is." Grins Hans to Leah, who looks away. She wants to be friendly to the show's investors, but I doubt if she fancies Hans with those dirty teeth.

We move along the sofa to make way for the new arrivals. When I started out doing five minute open spots in comedy clubs, I never thought it would lead to injecting chemical cocktails in the company of the editor of one of the country's biggest selling newspapers, the top newsreader, an international screen star, a couple of TV producers, and an ex-Hells Angel. Leah introduces me to Stephen Woods the editor, and Emily Johnson the newsreader. I'm with Leah, so Sheila Fox and Nicky Butler smile as sweetly as if I was the Pope. Leah moves along the sofa to make room for them. She's so close to me I can feel the heat of her thigh against mine. Emily Johnson sits the other side of her, and congratulates me on my performance.

"I don't know how you do it. I'd be nothing without a make-up girl and the autocue." I give her a smile, and notice she's holding Leah's hand in her crotch. Hans announces he's mixed the milk of the Virgin Mary, and asks who wants the first shot. A wave of paranoia sweeps over me, as I wonder if it's wise to inject in front of a red top editor, when he rolls his sleeve up, ties a piece of nylon rope around his arm above the elbow, and proffers his lower arm to Hans.

"Not too much, mate. I don't want to end up on my rivals' obituary page." Hans draws up a dose of the cocktail, and injects it into Stephen Woods' vein.

"Fuck!" Shouts Stephen, before sliding down the couch onto the cabin floor. He leaps up and bangs his head on the ceiling, before Emily Johnson gets him to sit down.

"I want this moment to last my whole life! Whatever's in that syringe, Man - I want the fucking recipe." Like a trained nurse, Hans chucks the syringe into a medical sharps disposal container, and prepares the next dose. Emily Johnson, Nicky Butler, and Sheila Fox all request mild doses, but Leah wants a full one. One by one, they fall back onto the couch and whoop with delight. When it's my turn, I ask for a mild dose too, but from the conspiratorial looks between Hans and Leah, I suspect I'm getting a little more. My heartbeat increases as Leah ties the nylon rope around my arm, and I flex my hand to make the veins stand out. I watch as Hans squirts a drop of the liquid out of the needle, to ensure no air enters my bloodstream. He pricks my arm with the needle, and presses the plunger. For a second I feel disappointed from the lack of effect, until a wave of warmth sweeps up from behind me.

It seems I've left the cabin and flown around the world and into another dimension. I ceased to be the individual called Doug Tucker, and suddenly I've dropped back into his body. Whatever comes to pass in this world doesn't really matter, because it's of no importance in the other dimension. When I look around me and see the others, the feeling is even stronger, because they are just like me - illusions of themselves. Suddenly the ridiculousness of life is incredibly funny. The more serious a feeling, the more funny it is, because all feelings are complete falsities. Nothing matters. Everyone grows taller, which reinforces the sense that all experience is moments of flux. Then I realise I've slipped off the sofa, which is why everything looked different. When I sit back where I was, the familiarity returns, and I become Doug Tucker a little more than I had been. I rub my hands together, and feel like I'm gliding on a warm, soft, pink mattress.

Hans gives himself a shot from the gold-trimmed syringe, and settles back into the couch with more dignity than the rest of us put together.
"Oh dear, I need Mr toilet." Shrieks Emily, and dashes to the door at the front of the cabin. We hear the sound of vomit hitting varnished teak door, and roll around in hysterics.
"Sorry about that." Says Emily, as she returns from the shower room, her lipstick smudged where she's washed her face. Meanwhile, Stephen's throwing up in the master cabin's en suite toilet at the back of the boat. My heart is pounding from the accelerators in the cocktail, and yet at the same time my eyelids are drooping, and I feel a wonderful, serene, calm. There's a pink caterpillar caressing my arm, until I look and realise its Leah's hand. All of a sudden vomit rises to my throat, and I throw up into a bucket that Hans has just placed in

the middle of the cabin floor. I hate being sick, but this is different. I look at the spew, and it mutates into elves dancing around a lake, singing and laughing gaily.

"Let's get out of here." Someone says, and we take a very long time falling over each other and collapsing with uncontrollable laughter. Everyone who was sick has cleaned themselves up as best they can considering we're all hallucinating, and I realise "out of here" doesn't mean off the boat, but into the stateroom cabin at the back of the craft. There's a huge round bed with black silk sheets on it, and we fall onto it. Hans puts 'All Right Now' by The Free on the sound system, and I lose myself in the beauty of the song. I've heard it so many times, but never comprehended how magnificent it is. I'm lost amongst mountain valleys, with pine trees and pools of black oil. Then I realise I had my eyes closed, and I move my head to see Leah sucking Emily's olive coloured breasts. I turn my head the other way, and Hans has got his jeans around his ankles. Nicky Butler's stroking his penis, which is the size of a small donkey's.

Sheila Fox and Stephen Woods are kissing and rubbing each other's waists together, and I look back towards Leah and Emily. I feel lonely and left out because I'm the only one who isn't involved in the goings on, and when I feel my crotch I realise my penis is curled up and tiny. I watch Leah flicking Emily's nipples with her tongue, and fear wells up as she becomes Regan in 'The Exorcist'. Her tongue is long and yellow, and I'm afraid Emily's going to die, until I see her pulling her own knickers off, and lifting her silky orange dress. Leah's mouth moves down to Emily's shaved vulva, and that tongue grows another few centimetres and even more pointy as it licks and flicks. The song's a different one now. I've no idea what it is, but there's a woman's voice, and all fear and anxiety drift off me like an autumn leaf. Leah's dress has ridden up over her buttocks, and I yearn to kiss them. There's a distant memory somewhere that I'm not allowed to, but I can't remember why I shouldn't, and so I lean forward and lick those white mallow bottom cheeks.

I don't know how long I lick and nuzzle her wonderful buttocks, but I become aware of a presence behind me, and I look round to see Lawrence standing in the doorway, masturbating. As soon as I see him, he ejaculates onto Stephen Woods' foot. Emily's multiple orgasm subsides, and Leah moves off her. Between them they lift Leah's white dress off. She lost a lot of weight for that end title sequence, although I preferred her with a bit more flesh. I've got big hands, and I like to have something to get hold of. Emily sucks one of her nipples, and Leah invites me to suck the other one. As I do so, Emily strokes my bottom and thighs, and my penis begins to stand up. My mouth fills with warm liquid, and I open my eyes to check I haven't got a penis in my mouth. No, it's definitely Leah's left bosom. I take my mouth away from her nipple and see that Emily's also swallowing, and has white around her mouth. I carry on drinking, confused.

"I'm lactating. Jess still breastfeeds. The Native Americans have been breastfeeding kids up to the age of seven for thousands of years." She runs her fingers through my hair, and my scalp tingles deliciously. "Drink on, my Darling Angel." I swallow the milk, as Emily's delicate fingers caress my scrotum. This is success! I've arrived.

I hear a gasping and look round to see Hans Vermeulen pumping away on top of Nicky Butler. At least they're both having a good time. Sheila Fox is fellating Stephen Woods, which is good for me as it increases the chances of 'Rats Milk Cheese' getting good press in his red top. My gaze returns to Leah's wonderful smooth stomach, and Emily's hand grips the shaft of my penis and begins a series of quick short jerks, which take me to the heights of pleasure. I look at the short wrap-around window curtain that's protecting us from unwanted eyes. It's dark blue with a planet pattern on it. There are full moons, half moons, and Saturns. I lose myself amongst them, and when I'm marvelling how realistic the curtains are, I realise my eyes are closed. When I open them, I see Emily's face more vividly than I've seen anything in my life. Her hair is growing like some lush brunette lawn, and her smudged lipstick reminds me of Robert Smith in The Cure. Leah sits up against the pillows at the head of the bed, and lights a cigarette. Emily buries her face in her muff. I lick Emily enough to realise she's oozing moisture, and slide myself into her. Her back is so lithe, and I kiss her shoulder blades and nibble the back of her neck. Her hair still seems to be growing without getting any longer. I become desperate for Emily's tits, and withdraw from her so I can pull her ankles and turn her over. She repositions her face so it's in Leah's lap, and I suck Emily's nipples and ease myself back inside her. She's a tall girl, and my face is level with hers whilst making love in this standard missionary position. I look into her eyes, and it's just like watching her read the news on telly. I saw her yesterday, reading the news of another child abduction, and I feel sad. Emily also read the news about Sunita's parents returning to Heathrow airport from Riyadh with her body. The thought of Sunita makes me feel very sad. The sadness puts more soul into the way I make love to Emily, and as she pants in time with my thrusting, we fall into rhythm with each other, and begin to approach orgasm.

I've been oblivious to the fact, but a bottle of Pastis has been handed round a couple of times, and Leah holds it to my lips so I can take a swig without interrupting the rhythm of copulation. The aniseed invasion of my mouth is magnified so it seems like my soul is being cleansed. I swallow the fortified liquid, and my insides feel a rush of warmth. Emily's panting faster, and I suddenly become aware of the pleasure in my knob. We accelerate, and Emily erupts and squeezes so I come too. I keep thrusting for a while, before collapsing onto her and burying my nose in her delicious armpit, whilst Leah caresses my back. I close my eyes, and drift off with the music. I lose sense of time, and remember I've been injected with a chemical cocktail. Its effect is so strong, I hear another layer of music, then the room starts rocking. I'm shocked at the power of the hallucinations, until I realise I'm on a boat, and it's moving with the wash of another boat. The music I heard was coming from one of the many disco boats that ply up and down the Thames.

I open my eyes again, and look around. Hans Vermeulen is copulating with a woman I don't recognise. I decide to leave them to it, and gather my trousers and pants, staggering out into the wheelhouse. I glance into the saloon, where a couple of people I don't know are rolling a joint. I have a piss in the forward bathroom, and wash my face. There's some toothpaste and some unopened new toothbrushes, so I help myself to one and give my teeth a really good clean. A swig of mouthwash later, I'm feeling reborn. When I pass back through the saloon, I recognise the couple as admin staff of Grange Films. I apologise for not remembering their names. Apparently they said hello to me as I walked through the saloon, but I didn't hear as they were on my right side. My insides churn as I realise another week has passed without seeing a doctor about my ear.

"Fancy a snifter?" Asks the man whose name I instantly forgot when he just told it to me.
"I won't say no." I say, thinking a drink would be a good idea. When I turn to accept, it's a line of coke he's offering. I snort it up, thank him, and make my way back onto the river terrace, almost slipping off the gangplank into the Thames.

The Clap Clinic is so lit up, it resembles a landlocked ocean liner. The party's in full swing, with the base line of the music rumbling my stomach, and making the tables and chairs rattle on the river terrace. That line of coke makes me feel a lot better, and I decide to make my way to the bar for a good old-fashioned pint of lager to level me off. The party's so crowded people are standing on the stairs. I pass Emily Johnson looking demure as royalty with a glass of champagne in her hand. She's re-done her make-up, and I'd never have guessed in a thousand years what she was up to a while ago. Maybe it's just a typical Saturday night for her. She's even applied an expensive perfume. As I pass she winks at me, and utters
"Nice shag, Doug". I get a beer from the VIP bar, and get ear-holed by a new comedian I was on the same bill with a few weeks ago, and whose name I can't remember. He's hungry for talk about comedy. He asks who books which venues, and actually starts reciting his act to me. I came to the bar for some normality, because I'm feeling a bit guilty about the decadence on the Grietje. A few minutes of this bloke, though, and whacking Class A drugs up, followed by celebrity group sex seems very appealing. In fact, I've got an erection right now, and this comedy bore isn't the person I want to rub it against.

I'm trying to find a gap in this bloke's monologue that's long enough for me to politely interrupt, when I feel myself being cuddled from behind. At first I think it's Leah, but the person's too small. I turn round and see Charlotte French, who's looking fantastic in a retro pinafore gingham dress. Perhaps she thought it was a fancy dress party, because the outfit is completed by having her hair in two bunches. She looks like a schoolgirl from Alabama.
"Wanna come with me, Big Boy?" She drawls in a mock Texan accent.
"Yes please." I say, desperate to escape the boring comedian. I excuse myself as graciously as I can, and Charlotte leads me by the hand towards the stairs that go up to Arnold's office. Charlotte's well in

with Arnold, because she doesn't knock on the door. I follow her in, and nearly trip over somebody lying near the leather-padded door. There's only candle light, and I realise it's two people having sex. Chill-out music is playing on the stereo, and shadowy figures lean against walls and furniture, though I can't make out who anyone is. I see psychedelic patterns in the darkness, and realise I'm still hallucinating from the injection Hans gave me. Our journey ends at Arnold's chaise langue, on which a figure reclines. Charlotte kneels in front of it, and before my eyes can adjust to recognise its occupant, a deep husky chuckle informs me it's Arnold. He turns to a sitting position, and beckons me to sit beside him.

"Welcome to my casting couch, Doug. You're just in time for the auditions." Ever since Charlotte appeared downstairs, I've been remembering that hand job she gave me when I was driving us back from the gig in Luton. I've got an erection that's as fresh as if I was just out of a Buddhist monastery, and Charlotte French looks good enough to eat. She leans towards Arnold's crotch, unzips his fly, and starts sucking.

Arnold inhales on his cigar, and without a pause in her fellating of Arnold, Charlotte unbuttons my Levis with her left hand. And I assumed she was a lesbian when I first met her! She's just starting to give me a hand job whilst continuing to suck Arnold, when I realise the regular cracking sound I've heard since I entered the room isn't coming from the sound system. Now my eyes have adjusted to the candlelight, I see the shadowy figure against the wall is a spread-eagled Simon McDonagh, the director of 'Rats Milk Cheese'. He's naked, and his wrists are chained to hooks in the wooden roof beams. A length of wood separates his ankles, which are tied to steel rings in each end. Leah, back in her white dress, is whipping his back with a cat o' nine tails. Every time she takes a swipe, her breasts wobble in a spectacular way. The copulating couple I nearly tripped over by the door turns out to be Jojo the new Clap Clinic manageress, and Stephen Woods. Charlotte starts to suck on my penis, and masturbate Arnold's. I'm watching Stephen Woods have Jojo in the doggy position, whilst running my fingers through Charlotte's hair as she sucks me, when the door opens and hits Jojo on the head. Ruud Vermeulen walks in with Nancy the gorgeous Assistant Floor Manager. They apologise to Jojo for banging her head with the door, and carefully make their way into

the room. A few moments later, Des Jensen and Lawrence the writer come in and Jojo gets her head banged with the door again.
"At least she's getting banged from both ends." I say to Arnold. Charlotte says
"I think that's a good idea." and removes both of our trousers, and positions herself in his lap so his penis is inside her. She indicates that I should stand in front of her, so she can continue sucking me. I do so, and now I'm facing a different direction I can see Nancy kneeling on Arnold's desk, whilst Ruud Vermeulen lifts her dress and alternately spanks and caresses her buttocks. "Lucky Ruud Vermeulen" I think. Meanwhile, in my peripheral vision I can see Lawrence the writer kneeling in front of Des Jensen, his head bobbing up and down.

Charlotte's bouncing away in Arnold's lap, and then she takes me out of her mouth and squeezes my penis hard whilst wanking it. All of a sudden it's too much and I spurt. Some of my sperm goes on one of her bunchies, but most of it hits Arnold in the face.
"I'm so sorry, Arnold!" I say, Picking my trousers up and reaching into an empty pocket for the hanky I gave to Leah back in Hans' boat.
"So am I, Doug. Wipe it off." A glob of my spunk hangs from Arnold's nose. He's furious, and Charlotte quickly obliges by wiping it off with the hem of her dress. She had to dismount him to do it, and when she goes to get back on him, Arnold stops her with a gesture.
"You must be a wee bit tired by now, lassie. Perhaps Doug could oblige. Just to remind me what it was like in prison." I feign laughter, but when I see his eyes, I realise he isn't joking.
"Your mouth pleasured hundreds of people in my comedy club tonight, Doug. Surely it could pleasure one more. After all, I do own the place. I've even paid the mortgage off."
"Oh come on Arnold. I'm not bisexual."
"It doesn't matter what you are, sonny. I've always liked your grace. On your knees." There's such authority in his tone, I start kneeling down instinctively, but stop half way, and stand up again.
"Please Arnold. It's not what I do." I'm wishing I had my trousers on now. I've taken a lot of shit from Arnold for the sake of my career, but I'm not sucking his cock. A sharp pain sweeps across the back of my neck, and I turn to see Leah brandishing the cat o'nine tails in one hand, and her cocaine bullet in the other.

"Has he been naughty, Arnold? I'll punish him. Just watch." She gives the cocaine bullet to Arnold, who takes a snort and hands it to Charlotte.

"Down on the floor!" She commands. Lying on the floor beneath Leah is a much better option than fellating Arnold, and I obey. Leah sits on my chest, and masturbates Arnold with her left hand. I'm thanking Leah in my mind for getting me out of the situation, when my chest feels warm. Leah's pissing on me! It's not what I'd choose, but it still beats blowing Arnold off. Charlotte French is trying to help me too, because she's taken her dress off, and is rubbing her little titties against his cheek.

I suddenly become aware that someone's farted, and I'm feeling embarrassed they might think it's me, when I feel something solid on my stomach. The stench is suddenly worse, and Leah is wiping her arse with my shirt. She's done a shit on me! Everyone's looking round to see what's caused the smell, when the door opens again. This time, Jojo's head isn't in the way, but I wish it had been. The figure in the doorway switches the lights on, and reveals itself to be Angela. Tears are already welling in her eyes as she takes in the scene. Leah's still squatting over me, and Angela's across the room in a second. I think she's about to kick me, but instead her foot swings up into Leah's face. She's sent backwards into Ruud Vermeulen, who's standing by the desk, having withdrawn from Nancy's vagina so recently, his penis is still alert. He gasps with the pain where the back of Leah's head bangs his balls, before she slides to the floor, her nose a downwards pointing fountain of blood.

I stand up unsure whether I'm going to Leah's aid, or to appeal to Angela. As I get to my feet, two large foeces roll from my stomach onto the floor.

"Not on my antique Turkish carpet!" Exclaims Arnold. He can't have noticed Leah pissing on me, then, because his Turkish carpet has already taken a wetting. Leah's slumped on her side, so I approach Angela with my arms outspread. She recoils, as revolted by my lack of morals as by the shit down the front of my shirt.

"Stick your holiday where the shit came from!" Angela screams. I had no idea such a small chest could produce a scream so shrill.

273

"If you ever come near me again, I'll kill you!" Her vehemence has us all frozen with shock. She turns and runs crying out of the door. Her outrage is so powerful, I don't go after her. Instead, I go to Leah, who's struggled to her knees, her white dress spattered with blood from her nose.

"Leah, are you alright?"

"Get off me!" She sputters. I wonder if she's had any teeth knocked out, because I can barely make out what she's saying.

"You're hired." She adds, as she staggers to her feet. I turn to see Sheila Fox standing behind me.

"I'm hired for what?" I say to her.

Simon McDonagh's voice comes from where he's still chained up.

"She didn't say you're hired, you deaf cunt." Sheila speaks next:

"She said you're fired!" As Sheila spits these words at me, there's a hatred in her eyes the Vermeulens couldn't rival.

"And I say it too. Have you got that? You're fired, you be-shitted spastic." She takes a step towards me. I'm preparing myself to block the punch she's going to throw at me, when she stops dead in her tracks, looks at her foot, and screams. Her shoeless foot has bisected the larger of the two turds on Arnold's Turkish carpet. I decide I've out-stayed my welcome, grab my trousers, and make a dash for the door. I swerve past Jojo and Stephen Woods the newspaper editor, who abandoned their intercourse and got to their feet when the shouting started. I yank the door open, and bump into Hans Vermeulen, who's just reached the top of the stairs with Nicky Butler in tow. Ruud Vermeulen barks something to him in Flemish, and everything goes dark.

Chapter Forty-two

There's a vague awareness of being marched down some stairs by Charles's new second in command. The Clap Clinic foyer is unlit, but for a lamp on Charles's table near the door. I hear myself protesting about something not being my fault, whilst Charles unlocks the front door. A push that's so strong I momentarily think I've been placed on a fairground ride, and I'm sailing through the cold night air. A wall of tarmac smacks me on the forehead, then obliges by remaining still. Sleep enfolds me, permeated by shivering and cold rain. An animal sniffs at my nose and lips. The shivering gets worse, until it's eclipsed by a throbbing pain in my head, and a raging thirst. I get up, and wander towards the Charing Cross road. Luckily a taxi stops, but when he sees the state I'm in, he won't let me in his cab. I promise him fifty pounds if he'll take me home to Lambeth Walk, but when I open my wallet, I've only got a fiver. In the chaos of the party, I forgot to get my wages for last night's gig.

It takes two hours to walk home. My front door key is in my bag, which is in the Clap Clinic dressing room. Angela doesn't answer the door when I ring the bell, and my neighbours aren't too happy when I wake them up to borrow the spare key. It's seven in the morning when I discover Angela has collected her things, and gone. I'm having a shower when it dawns on me that I don't know her phone number. I trawl my memories for a time she gave it to me. We were working together all day every day, and as she lived with her parents, she always stayed at my place. The only people I know who could give it to me are Grange Films, and I don't fancy speaking to them.

I put my soiled clothes in a bin liner, and flop into bed. Does the fact that I never got my girlfriend's address or phone number mean I'm self-centred? I check the lounge to see if she's left a note, but all she's left is the remains of a Chinese takeaway, and some torn up holiday brochures.

I go back to bed, and sleep. When I turn over in my sleep, the phone wakes me up. My left ear was pressing on the pillow, so I didn't hear it until I turned over. By the time I find it, the answer machine has taken over. I hope it's Angela or even someone from Grange Films rescinding my sacking, but it's Colin Holmes asking if I've got Gerry Crook's telephone number, because he's lost his diary. I ignore it, because my address book is in my bag, which is at the Clap Clinic. The mirror makes me feel even more despondent when I see the bruise on my face. That must be where Hans Vermeulen knocked me out. I go back to bed and try to sleep some more, but can't. I give up reading my novel after reading the same paragraph over and over again. The last time I was reading it, I was in bed with Angela, and my thoughts keep returning to her. I seek refuge in the television, only to see Leah Phillips playing a sexy young nurse. The programme is a couple of years old, and the script isn't good. I turn the telly off, go to my computer, and start writing jokes. They can sack me unfairly from a TV show, but they can't stop me doing stand-up.

The next morning Melissa my agent phones, opening the conversation with
"Doug, I've got some very bad news for you." Grange Films have terminated my contract forthwith, and Arnold Shanks has cancelled all my bookings.
"This is a disaster, Doug. You had over eight thousand pounds worth of stand-up work in the diary. Arnold Shanks books for most venues in Britain. And it's in today's papers, that a second series of 'Rats Milk Cheese' has definitely been commissioned. I don't know who they're replacing you with, but I hope you've got some money saved up."
"Yes. I've got a few quid put away."
"That's good, because you owe me £1,985.67 commission."
"But you take commission off before the money gets to me."
"I know I do. I'm talking about the cash gigs you've done this year."
"I organised them myself."
"I know, but you still give me 15%. Read paragraph three of our contract." Before I can answer, she hangs up. I'm putting a load of washing in the machine, when the doorbell rings. A motorcycle courier gives me the bag I left in the Clap Clinic dressing room. I check to see my things are in there, when I find a plain sealed

envelope. Assuming it's Saturday's wages, I open it to find a folded piece of paper. On it is written
"The day I see you again is the day you die." It's from Arnold. I open my diary, and cross out the work that was booked through him, including the gig for Ruud Vermeulen in Antwerp. There's very little left. Not enough to make a living from. A few gigs for Gerry Crook, and the odd other little independent gig, most of which I was doing more as a favour than for the money.

I go back to the kitchen and load washing powder into the machine, setting it to do a coloured load. The friendly gurgle of my Krupps cappuccino machine is salvaging my faith in life, when the phone rings. It's Gerry Crook, with an urgency that sounds alien to his soft Cork brogue.
"Doug, it's Gerry. I'm phoning to see if you can save my life, mate."
"Are you in a canal?"
"Worse. Colin Holmes has just let me down. If you go to Heathrow and get on the plane to Cork, I'll be forever in your debt."
"Just for tonight?"
"There's the rub, you see, Doug. There's a show in Cork tonight, and one in Killarney tomorrow. And Galway on Wednesday. In all, Doug, it's five days."
"Could you arrange it so my ticket home is next week?"
"No problem, Doug. I'd have to pay to change the name of the passenger – it wouldn't cost me a penny more to alter the return date."
"In that case, make the return in two weeks time, Gerry. Which terminal do I fly from?"

Chapter Forty-three

The rain drums on the roof of the telescopic thing that extends from the boarding gate to the plane door, or the jetway, as I think they're called. Considering so many things have gone wrong recently, I was lucky with the Piccadilly line, because I made it to Heathrow with time to spare. I step into the plane, and the flight attendant smiles her welcome aboard. I thought I recognised that face.
"Hello Alison."
"Good afternoon, Sir. Or should I say Doug. 19D. On the left. The seat by the window."
She looks slightly older than when I last saw her, on the flight to Nice to perform at Ruud Vermeulen's party on the yacht. Poor Alison, spending so much time at altitude has exposed her to radiation. I saw a documentary about it on telly recently. It said that flight crews age more quickly because the radiation is stronger at jet cruising height. It affects women more badly than it does men. She's still stunningly gorgeous, though. I feel an urge to rescue her from her job as a flight attendant, and look after her in a healthy place like the West of Ireland.

Curtains of rain advance across the concrete. I watch a wet man wearing ear protectors, as he prepares the plane for pushing back from the stand. I was supposed to have Angela beside me next time I flew on a plane. My tummy sinks with sadness when I think about her, and the holiday we'll never have. I miss her terribly, but I'm a comedian, and comedians do gigs. When the pilot throttles the engines up, I don't just hear the sound of jet engines, I hear the sounds they trigger off in my head. It all started after I came out of the water tank at Pinewood film studios. I've noticed the tinitus does the same with my washing machine when it's on fast spin. Also with loud music. I find it hard to distinguish which sounds are real, and which ones are the tinitus.

The plane starts moving, and I obey the request to pay attention to the emergency instructions. How can I refuse, when Alison looks so comely in that orange lifejacket? I'm sure she's put on weight. I long to snuggle up to her. I feel like a captured wolf, howling for her forest.

PART TWO

The Two Thousand and Noughties

Chapter Forty-four

It's eight hours since I left Lambeth Walk, and I'm stuck in a ten-mile tailback on the M6. To get to Stars Nightclub in time for the show I'll have to drive at sixty miles an hour for the next forty minutes. I've got this gig for two reasons. Firstly, because someone else cancelled at short notice. Secondly, because I've got a car to give the headline act a lift back to London.

At last the traffic starts to move, and hope of making it on time is rekindled. The outside lane is moving faster, so I pull out and pass the lorry I've been sitting behind for an hour. The driver looks disdainfully down at me from his cab. Perhaps he resents the fact that articulated lorries aren't allowed in the outside lane. Whereas clapped out bright red 1.9 litre Peugeot 205's are. He's probably getting paid more for driving that lorry to Liverpool than I am for the gig. We both have to do the drive, yet he doesn't have to entertain a club full of drunks when he gets there. The other time I compered Stars all those years ago, I got £150. Tonight I'm getting £100 for going on first, and they don't provide a hotel room. If I set off at noon tomorrow, I'll be lucky to be back in London before nine in the evening. Two days, and four hundred miles driving to earn £100. I could earn more as a barman, except it would be hard to do bar work with my deaf right ear.

The traffic slows to a halt again, and the feeling of wretchedness returns. Somebody's seriously injured on the motorway ahead. They need love, but they've got hatred from thousands of us trapped on the motorway behind them. If only I could get to the next junction, I could take an 'A' road in the direction of Liverpool.

By the time I get onto the M56 the manager of Stars Nightclub phones me to ask where I am.
"Just coming into Liverpool now." I lie. I'm five miles away. The show started five minutes ago, and I'm the first act. A blonde haired woman stands hitching by the side of the motorway – that could only

happen in Liverpool. I can't stop myself pulling over to get a look at her face. When she runs up to the door, I realise it's a man. Before I can drive off, the door's open, and a man with long blonde hair is sitting in the passenger seat.

"The city centre if you're travelling that way." He says. I drive on, desperately trying to expel Alison's face from my mind. I still haven't got over the pain years after she left me. That's why I stopped the car. Because I saw a blonde head of hair. I'm looking for that angel of the skies everywhere.
"I love Liverpool. So much more exciting than Buxton."
"Yeah. I'm in a hurry. I'll drop you off at Stars Nightclub."
"Fantastic man! That's where I'm going."
"Why?"
"Because they have great tunes and stuff man."
"What about the comedy show?"
"Is there a comedy show?"
"Yes. I'm supposed to be on stage there now. I'm late."
"Groovy. Can you get me in free?"
"Of course." He rummages in a polythene carrier bag, and produces a tatty VHS video of a TV programme aimed at very young kids.
"'The Teletubbies'. You can have it, man. It's my gift to you."
"Thanks, but I don't have kids."
"It's not really for children, know what I'm saying?"
"No."
"It's psychedelic. Watch it on acid or E, and you'll know what I mean. It's my favourite TV show after 'Rats Milk Cheese'."
"You don't have to give it to me, I'm going to Stars anyway."
"I *want* to give it to you, man." He puts the video in the glove compartment, and my phone rings again.
"Where the fuck are you, mate?"
"Just trying to park. I can go on as soon as I get there." I don't know why I say that, because I'm desperate for the toilet. The traffic situation in this country gets worse and worse. I allowed over eight hours for the drive from London to Liverpool. If I'd averaged twenty-five miles an hour, I'd have got to Liverpool an hour before the show. It's half an hour after the show was due to start, and I'm still driving. It's getting ridiculous. The train service is a sick joke, so comedians have to travel by road. I accelerate in a bid to get there quicker, at the

same time as I'm looking at my phone to end the call. I miss a speed camera warning sign, and two flashes of white light cause me to slow down again. I hope that speed camera wasn't loaded, because one more prosecution will cost my licence.

At last the M56 gives way to Liverpool's streets, and I see five billboard posters advertising Brian O'Shea's latest film. My passenger notices me looking at the poster whilst we're at a red light.
"I saw it yesterday, Man. What a head-rush! That Brian O'Shea's the funniest guy in the universe, Man." I smile to myself at the memory of Brian dying on stage last time I played Stars Nightclub. I had to go on and do his gig for him, and didn't get paid for my effort. I'd love to know if he's still hooked on smack. His image is so clean, superglue wouldn't stick to him. I wonder what he's doing now. Probably relaxing by one of his swimming pools. Apparently six of his homes have swimming pools.

It's lucky I stopped and gave a lift to this bloke whose name I don't know and hopefully never will, because he navigates me to Stars, saving at least ten minutes driving around looking for it. I get him in as my guest, and ask the manager, who has a spider's web tattooed on his face, if the dressing room is where it used to be.
"You're asking a lot, aren't you mate? The dressing room went years ago. I'd get to the side of the stage if I were you, the compere's about to put you on."
My rectal muscles dam up the river of diarrhoea waiting to gush from my bottom, and I join the scruffy collection of young people gathered near the stage. Gone are the chairs and three hundred people to occupy them. Stars is a rave venue now, that puts a comedy show on before the night gets going properly. About forty people stand around talking to each other, or stare at the compere, who struts around the stage shouting obscenities in a vicious Mancunian accent. The sound is so bad I don't catch most of what he says, but the drift is that the Royal Family should be slowly tortured before being lined up against the front of Buckingham Palace and shot. I suppose this must be what they call "issue-based" comedy.
"Anyway, we've got a brilliant headliner for you tonight, but before that we're gonna put our first comedian on. So clap your hands until

they're bloodier than a woman's pants during her period, and welcome Greg Tucker."
I go on to slight applause.
"Actually, it's Doug Tucker." I go into my opening routine, in which I allude to 'The Charlotte French Show'. It's a good opener because it refers to a TV show everyone's seen, and I can be visually funny when I do my impression of Charlotte giving the press conference after she was found not guilty of possessing cocaine. Everyone believes the coke was hers. But she's got very good lawyers, and public opinion was behind her. If Charlotte had gone down for ten years, there would be no new series of her show. Too many people enjoy watching it, and too many people earn too much money from making it. So Charlotte French walked away from court after having been caught with two grammes of coke in her luggage at Heathrow airport. The court case was six months ago, and since I began doing this routine, several other comics have started doing more or less the same jokes. It's inevitable, and I don't get uptight about it. The stakes are so high in this game, comedians are bound to get ripped off.

What throws me when I do my opening gags about her isn't the absence of laughter. It's a crappy room, and maybe they've seen other comics do stuff about Charlotte. After all, she is the top female comic in the country. It's the booing that I don't understand. And they're all booing with a vehemence that astounds me.
"I'm sorry, I didn't know you were all so close to her." I say, rapidly searching my memory for some material to get me out of the hole.
"We're sorry you didn't know she's red." Comes a voice from the side of the room.
"She's red?"
"*Dead!* Get a hearing aid. Then listen to the news."
"My car radio's broken. Is this true?"
The entire audience answers as one, and they've got no sympathy for the fact that I've been stuck in a car all day with a duff radio.
"Yes."
"She was killed in a car accident."
"In that case, I apologise for not realising. Moving swiftly on - it's great to be in Liverpool. Anyone a student at John Moores University?" My blonde-haired hitcher friend helps me out by shouting

"Yes."

"The only university that's sponsored by a mail order catalogue. The good thing about John Moores University is if you don't like your degree when you get it, you can exchange it for another one." That gets a small laugh, and I ask if anyone's from Manchester. The same bloke shouts that he is, and I mentally bless him.

"I love Manchester. Especially that giant Mexican Restaurant in the centre. What's it called? That's it, "The Gmex." Another okay laugh, because the crowd are all familiar with the G-mex centre. Bit by bit, I win their favour, until I'm on a roll with the industry standard three laughs a minute.

The lighting's too bright to see anyone in the audience who isn't near the front, so working the room's quite difficult, because I can't always hear the answers. My right ear's mostly deaf due to a viral infection that damaged the cochlea. I've tried two types of hearing aid, but it's like turning the volume up on a blown loudspeaker. In addition to the deafness, there's continuous tinitus. It's like having a jet engine strapped to the side of my head, twenty-four hours a day. The tinitus doesn't bother me, I've learned to ignore it. It's the difficulty in hearing that's been a broadside to my career. I haven't sunk yet, though. I can still make a crowd of people laugh.

I turn my attention to the expanded polystyrene sign on the wall at the back of the stage. It still says "tars" where I broke the "s" off the beginning of the word when I played here before. I'm amazed it's still exactly the same, and improvise a bit about how one of the letters is missing.

"There should be an s after the t, making the word "Tsars"." Someone shouts out

"What does "Tsar" mean?" and I realise I've overestimated the audience's general knowledge.

"Did you say "What does Tsar mean?" It's the Russian word for emperor, but not to worry. Here's some material about wanking." I'm getting reasonable laughs for my wanking in tents stuff. I have to think on my feet and change the object of the fantasy from Charlotte French to Leah Phillips, but it gets a big enough laugh to buy me a few seconds in which to consider what to do next. Then I remember the loose floorboard around the centre of the stage. I have a dim memory

285

of getting laughs from it the time I compered Brian O'Shea here. I go into my 'weekend in Amsterdam' routine, and during the bit about walking on frozen canals, I step on the floorboard I guess is loose. It squeaks exactly the same as it did before, and I get a round of applause because it passes so well as creaking ice. When the applause has died down, I milk it some more, and the floorboard gives way. I stop my leg disappearing up to my thigh just in time, but the sudden movement was too much for my arse muscles, and I feel a little squirt of diarrhoea go into my pants. I look at my watch and see I've done half an hour. They're still laughing at my near fall through the stage, and I replace the mike in the stand, thank the crowd, and leave to applause and one man cheering. It's probably the bloke I gave a lift to.

I make it to the toilet just in time. There's no seat or lock on the door, but it's good enough for me to relax my bowels. The leakage into my pants isn't as bad as it felt at the time. I've got away with a large brown stain.
A few minutes later, I'm celebrating the fact that I made it to the gig and it went well, with a pint of Guinness. Then I remember the news about Charlotte French. It's the interval, and I ask the nearest person to me if they've seen the news.
"Crashed her Ferrari. Killed instantly, they reckon." Announces a scouser, matter of factly.
"Where did it happen?"
"Near her villa in Italy. It's a shame. She were a right smooth bit of totty. Terrible waste of a nice bod. I feel a bit like I did when Diana died." Poor Charlotte. I haven't bumped into her for ages, but I always liked her. The TV stardom, and millions of pounds aren't worth anything to her now. She always did drive too fast, though. Someone signals something to me, and when I ask them what they want, they point to a large man on my right, whose speaking to me.
"Greg Tucker? I'm Donger Wilson, the headliner." An Australian in his early twenties with spiked hair and tattooed arms offers me his hand.
"Good to meet you, Donger. It's Doug, not Greg, by the way. Do people really call you Donger?"
"They do, Mate. It's actually the name my parents gave me. I liked your set. There aren't many of you old fashioned joke-telling comics

left." An opal pendant in the shape of a goat's skull nestles amongst the bush of chest hair.

"Thanks. I think I'm giving you a lift to London tomorrow."

"Right, Mate. I've just done two nights in the Lowry Theatre in Manchester, supporting Colin Holmes. Tomorrow night we're doing the Criterion theatre in the West End. Fancy a drink?" I ask for a pint of Guinness.

"Shame about that Charlotte French chic. Everyone's speculating who's going to get her slot. The smart money's on Leah Phillips and Des Jensen filling it with a chat show."

"Des Jensen isn't a comic. He can't say anything funny unless it's written for him in a script."

"Maybe, but look at his credentials. 'Rat's Milk Cheese II' is doing well at the box office. He could puke a foetus and the TV chiefs would buy it. Which hotel are you staying at?"

"I don't know. I didn't get here until half past nine."

"Let me know, eh. Or gimme your number." He whips his mobile out of his pocket, and I give him my number. I want to get my money and leave. I have things to do, and it doesn't involve other comedians. I checked the internet for massage parlours in Liverpool, and the only one that hasn't been shut down by the council closes in fifteen minutes. I start looking for the manager with the tattooed face. I need my cash.

None of the staff has a clue where the manager is, and in the absence of a dressing room I watch the angry Mancunian comic open the second half with a tirade against the Football Association. I haven't a clue who he's talking about, but he wants the bosses' wives and children chained up along the touch line, and the FA managers forced to play football continuously. Every time a goal is scored, the team it was scored against has to decapitate one of its wives or children. The game would continue using their head as the ball. When all the wives and children are dead, each player in turn is set on fire, to illuminate the match. The last man alive would be hung upside down from his own goal, and starving dogs released onto the pitch. I get the impression the FA have made some ruling against one of Manchester's football teams, and the compere thinks it unfair.

To their credit, the audience doesn't laugh very much, but he gets some lukewarm applause when he ends the routine with the observation that the dogs wouldn't be able to reach the upside down victim's feet. He lists which parts of the Royal Family's anatomy the man's toes should be inserted into. All this time Donger Wilson's standing next to me, waiting to go on. He must be horrified the compere's bumming the audience out with such hideously cruel fantasies. I turn to get a look at Donger's face, and catch his eye. He gestures towards the stage with his pint.

"It's great to see passion. So refreshing." I nod in agreement, and a few seconds later the compere puts Donger on. He bounds onto the stage brandishing his fists in the air like a warrior. He takes the mike from the stand and struts from one side of the stage to the other.

"G'day, I'm from Coober Pedy in Australia. It's a mining town in the outback, started by a man called Coober, and a catholic priest." Infected with his Aussie enthusiasm, the audience laughs as much to show him they got the joke as from genuine mirth.

"My name's Donger, after the church bell. My middle name's Clapper, but that's less to do with the church bell, and more to do with a disease my Mother had." I look around me at the people in the audience. My eyes meet those of a man I've never seen before, and he shares his mirth with me, laughing from deep in his stomach. Not wishing to be contrary, I smile at him.

"We don't have toilets in Australian pubs. We have internal balconies. If you want a piss, you just go up on the balcony, and piss. Don't get me wrong – we're not common. We spray it about, like." Big laugh. Every bit of Donger's body language states

"I expect you to find me the funniest man in the world." The crowd buys it without reading the small print, because there isn't any. Donger's act is big, simple, and clear.

"I was walking down a street at night, when I heard a Sheila screaming. In the shadows, there's a Bruce fucking a Sheila. I kick his head, he goes down. On the ground, I mean. Not on the Sheila. We're not sophisticated. I'm helping her to her feet, when she lands a punch on me. I say

"That's no way to thank the Bruce who's saved you from a rapist." She says

"He's not a rapist. I've got cystitis." The audience are filling the pause with a laugh when he tops it with

"So I raped the bitch." I've seen enough, and skirt around the place in search of the manager. This isn't the first venue where the person who's supposed to pay me keeps me waiting around. It's a power game. In the past I've left without the money, and got Melissa to make them send a cheque. Now, though, there's no Melissa, and my wallet's nearly empty. One of the bouncers, being slightly less indifferent than the rest of the staff, enquires on his talkback.

"He's busy in his office, Mate. He knows you're waiting. He'll be down soon, like." I've missed the massage parlour, so I make the best of being trapped in this shit hole by getting another pint of Guinness. The aggressive compere from Manchester comes to the bar too, but doesn't talk to me. I notice him give something to a bouncer, and take a roll of notes in return. Donger's electrifying the room.

"Sheilas – why do you try to kiss us after you've swallowed our spunk? The deal is: you suck our cocks, then fuck off to the kitchen. If I want a mouth full of spunk, I'll find a pouf. There's one thing I want in my mouth after I've come, and it's called beer! So get away from the telly, and *let me watch the fucking game in peace!!*" Round of applause and cheering. I go outside to check my car. It's gone. The least unhelpful bouncer says I shouldn't worry, because he knows the bloke who nicked it. When I ask why he didn't stop him, he replies

"I like my little daughter's face as it is, Mate. I don't want it re-designed with a pruning knife." I wonder why a pruning knife, because the knife Mummy killed herself with is a pruning knife, and it's in my pocket. I try to report my car being stolen to the police, but after ten minutes on hold I give up. A huge roar of clapping and cheering erupts from inside, signalling Donger Wilson's encore is over, and the rave part of the evening's about to start. I find an elated Donger being feted by the tattoo-faced manager, who's trying to persuade Donger to do their Christmas show.

I get my bag and £100 cash, and Donger gets £200 for doing ten minutes more than I did.

"So where are you staying, Dick?"

"Doug. I don't know, Donger."

I'd like to stay at the Adelphi, but it would cost more than I just got paid. To stay in a scuzzy bed and breakfast would be too soul-destroying. I've put off the decision, to avoid the reality of my predicament.

"I've got an extra bed in my room, Mate. You're welcome to it."

"You've got the pick of the girls. Are you sure you don't want some privacy?"
"I don't need to be alone to read The Bible." I laugh politely.
"I'm serious, Mate. That shit I do on stage is an act. I'm a born again believer, and proud of it."
"Born again Christians can have sex, can't they?"
"Not this one. I don't believe in sex before marriage."
"I was thinking of staying out for a while. I might disturb you."
"I'm a light sleeper. I'm in room 501. Any time you want to turn up – no worries."
"Thanks, Donger. I'll do that."
"Want me to take your bag for you?"
"Um... thanks. That's really kind of you." I get my leather jacket, because the Winter weather's started, and give him my bag.
"Don't you want your phone?"
"I won't need it tonight." Making a mental note of his room number, I turn to stalk the Liverpool streets. His loud voice stops me in my tracks.
"Doug. It's obvious you're not off to look round the Tate Gallery at this time of night. Why don't you save yourself some money and we'll have a talk?"
"About what?"
"Faith."
"Might the conversation involve Jesus?" He smiles, and shows me his forearm. It's a battleground of tattoos and shrunken veins.
"I was a Kings Cross junkie. All me mates found Jesus by going to heaven. Jesus found me before I got there. He has other plans for me." It's the coldest night of the Winter so far. I hope Jesus' plan isn't a long one.
"Jesus healed my life, and now he works through me. Behold – Donger Wilson, spiritual healer."
"You must be busy, doing that as well as your act."
"It *is* my act. I heal through laughter. But if you've got a specific thing that needs to be healed, I'll do a laying on of hands."
"Okay. I'll be up later." I walk off into the night. It's not Jesus I need. It's Mary Magdalene. I'd have received laying on of hands in the massage parlour, if that cunt with the tattooed face had coughed my wages up on time.

Chapter Forty-five

The cold, windless night tries to rain, but only hard enough to spit a few annoying droplets in my face. I wander through the city centre, my stomach knotted with desperation. Clots of drunken people in transit from nightclubs to kebab shops shout and kick litter. I don't know where the prostitutes are, but I'll find them. You could drop me blindfold in a large city where there's only one prostitute, and I'd find her before sun-up. A mixture of intuition and experience tells me they're a taxi ride away, and I start looking out for one.

A billboard poster advertises 'The Girl From the Village', Brian O'Shea's latest film. It did very well in the States, especially along the eastern seaboard, where most of America's Irish population lives. Brian's doleful face stares out from amongst his curly black hair. Behind him is the green, lush landscape of Kerry. He spends most of his time in California, but rumour has it he's bought up much of the Dingle peninsular, and given a farm to each of his brothers and sisters. His co-star stares longingly at him from a quaint stone cottage that constitutes 'the village'. She's big enough for her pretty blonde figure to attract the eye, but small enough to leave the viewer in no doubt that Brian O'Shea is the star. I heard that Leah Phillips was up for the title role, but the powers that be in Hollywood ruled her too old. She must be nearing thirty by now.

I try to flag down a passing taxi before I realise it's full of people, who make obscene gestures at me. An empty one follows behind, but doesn't stop. I look at the credits on the poster. Grange Films Proudly Presents. Directed by Simon McDonagh. Produced by Nicky Butler. Executive Producer Arnold Shanks. Screenplay by Kev Knight. I don't feel sad that I'm not up there. I need all my sadness for Alison. I'm having the usual thoughts speculating as to where she is and what she's doing. Is she still a flight attendant? If so, is she in the air now? Are those delicious boobs still alright? How many men have cupped them gently in their hands since I did? If only I were in bed with her now! The pain is rising up my gullet, ready to flow down my cheeks as tears, when an illegal minicab stops beside me. A Nigerian asks if I need his services. We do some tough negotiating over money, and a few minutes later we're cruising past the prostitutes at ten miles an hour.

I've got to have sex with a woman tonight, or I'll shrivel up and die, but these women are shagged out. I'd have to be alone on a desert island for three weeks before I could let one of these poor souls touch my knob. One of them has a face that makes her look fifty, and is very pregnant. I appeal to the driver:
"Are you sure there's nowhere else?"
"No Man. This is as good as it gets."
"Okay, drive round again." The next pass we make finds a prostitute who wasn't there the first time. A dreadlocked man is buttoning his fly as he walks away from some bushes, and the reason she's just appeared becomes apparent. She's younger than the rest, and smaller. The driver slows down so I can get a better look at her, and she comes forward, gesturing for me to open the window.

The closer she gets, the less promising she looks. Her black hair is greasy, and dotted with flakes of dandruff. Her face looks like it hasn't been washed for days, and there are crow's feet at the corners of her eyes, which are sunken in dark sockets. Narcotics have dilated the pupils, but at least I get a whiff of mint from her gum-chewing mouth. She must be so cold in that black mini skirt, and mock leopard skin short-sleeved top.

"Open the door, luv, and we can talk business." Her hand is already on the handle. In the absence of my objection she gets in and sits next to me, and the smell of unwashed clothes and stale body odour attack my desire.
"I've got me own flat nearby. It's forty for half an hour. Or you can have me here in the bushes for twenty, but to be honest it's a bit dangerous. A bloke got killed here last week."
"What do I get for the forty quid?"
"Sucking and fucking with a condom. You can do anything you want except anal – that's an extra tenner."

"Forty quid for half an hour, then. You won't ask for any more?" I've learned from experience to say this last bit. They usually do find another hidden expense, and I pay it. But it's best to let them know I'm savvy, or they'll try a bigger scam.

"Forty's it luv. That's a promise." She gives an address to the driver, and we're on our way.

"What's your name?"

"Maxine. What's yours?" Suddenly it clicks. I knew I'd heard her voice before.

"I'm John. Do you have a sister called Melina?" Her tired face drops. She's got a sore on the side of her mouth I didn't notice before. I wondered why she was keeping her face to one side.

"I did have. Mel died two years ago." For a second her lip quivers, before her face hardens to its usual expression.

"I've had you before, then luv?"

"A while back, yes. I'm sorry to hear about Melina. Was it drugs?"

"The man who stabbed her was on drugs, yes. And the row was over drugs. Is anything not about drugs? Stop here, Mate."

We stop next to a rank of boarded up shops, beneath windows that don't have a pane of glass between them. I pay the driver and Maxine asks for the forty pounds up front. I take four ten-pound notes from my wallet, which she studies as best she can to see how much money I've got. After stashing the money deep in her left knee-length boot, she leads me across the road to a terrace of houses that look like they're condemned to demolition. Most have their doors and windows sealed up with steel sheeting, but one still has a wooden, graffiti-covered front door. Its smashed windows have been repaired with polythene bags, and when Maxine pushes the front door, it opens.

"Nice flat." I say, and she silences me with an urgent

"Sshh!" The place is clearly a squat, and the hall floor and stairs are covered in junk food packaging. Hip-hop is playing in a room along the hall, and a door opens. A black man in an army surplus camouflage jacket walks aggressively towards us.

"What you wan!" He slows up when he recognises Maxine, who says something to him I don't understand, partly because she thickens her Liverpudlian accent, and partly because my deaf ear is towards her. The man gives me a hard stare, and gestures to my jacket.

"What's in your pockets?"

"Nothing. Only me hanky. I've just finished work." My answer satisfies him, and he goes brusquely back to where he came from. Maxine pushes the door of the front reception room, and it opens. There's no lock or handle, and the room is devoid of humans. A naked light bulb illuminates a floor strewn with hypodermic syringes, screwed up tin foil, cider bottles, and empty Tennants Super cans. A single bed with a sleeping bag on it is the only piece of furniture. Maxine pushes it along the wall so it blocks the door from opening into the room.

She continues her urgent "we shouldn't be here" manner, whispering to me and gesturing in the direction of the assertive man.

"You haven't given me any money." I'm confused, because I've given her £40, and she told me she had her own flat. She's brought me to a crack house, and now she's telling me I haven't paid her. She answers my confused look with:

"If he asks, you haven't given me any money."

"But I gave you £40." She waves my answer aside with her arm, as if I'm stupid, and bids me sit on the bed. I remain standing. I don't feel relaxed enough to sit down, and I don't want me or my clothes touching anything in this room, except for Maxine.

"Have you got a condom?" She asks.

"No."

"I haven't got any."

"I don't mind."

"Are you going to take your clothes off?"

"I'm okay, thanks."

"What do you want then?"

"You to take your clothes off, and wank me onto your tits." Before I've finished the sentence, she's removing her leopard skin top. I warily undo my belt, dividing my attention between the door and her as she removes her black mini skirt and knickers. She leaves the boots on. Her tits look like they've been grafted on from an old woman. Her body is covered in bruises, and there's a nasty cut above one of her elbows. She hurriedly undoes my jeans and pulls them down. I suddenly remember the little accident in my boxer shorts when I nearly fell through the broken floorboard on stage.

"Sorry about the state of my pants."

"What state's that, luv?"

"The brown stain."

"That's the cleanest pair of pants I've seen this month, luv. And I've seen a few hundred." My penis has been erect from the start, and she manipulates it with a practiced grip. She wants this over with as soon as possible, so she can get the next customer. I sigh with pleasure as her arm speeds up, and drink in her faded beauty. She isn't twenty-five yet, and she probably won't live to see thirty. Every so often I glance in the direction of the door. I've deliberately kept my trousers and pants high up my legs, ready to pull them up quickly if our crack-dealer friend bursts in. Footsteps and door slamming put a temporary halt to our activity, but whoever's in the hall walks past our door. Poor Maxine makes an effort to look seductive as she resumes her work, but she's so exhausted the veil drops, revealing a bored expression. She speeds up again, aiming my cock at her sagging little tits. My legs stiffen, and as I ejaculate she avoids a shower of semen by dodging to her right, and pointing me to her left, with split-second timing. My life force spills onto the carpet of spent needles and empty cigarette lighters. She's dressed before my breathing has recovered its regular pattern. I do my belt up, and wish I had my leather gloves. I'd feel more confident during the coming escape.

"Are you ready?" She asks.

"Yep. Is he going to ask for more money?"

"*Some* money. You haven't given me any." There's no point arguing with her, so I push the bed away from the door with my leg, pull the door open, and walk into the hall as confidently as possible. Maxine follows me, and we make it out of the front door unchallenged.

"That was lucky. He must be busy. Nice to do business with you John."

"And you, Maxine."

"You haven't got a fiver for me cab fare, have you luv?" I don't answer her straight away, because I'm too busy looking at my bright red Peugeot 206, which is parked in front of the house.

"It's called a car luv. It goes along these road things."

"I know that, Maxine. It's mine. You should recognise it, you borrowed it once." I don't know if she did recognise it, because the front door opens and the bloke in the camouflage jacket comes out with a thin, wiry, black teenager.

"What this fuckery?" The teenager is keen to prove himself to his role model.

"You lookin' at my chariot?" Before I can think of an answer, the other one says something to him. I can't make out whether it's patois or scouse, let alone what words he actually said. The result is that Maxine positions herself in front of me, and issues an impassioned plea in whatever dialect they speak. The younger bloke, who can't be older than fourteen, punches her in the face. The sound of his fist colliding with her cheek drains my strength and I want to cry. It's such a horrible sound it sums up why I'm not violent, and why I'm against war. My reactions are too slow for these street-hardened criminals. Before I've decided what to do, the older man has kicked the teenager in the groin, and when he's on the ground he kicks him again in the stomach.

"Mash you up." Is all I understand of what he hisses at the teenager as he writhes on the cracked paving stones. He pukes a river of liquid, which, as if directed by his menace, flows off the kerb around my nearside front tyre.

I automatically put my arm around Maxine, and cup her cheek with my free hand. The man tugs her away from me and throws her against the front door of the crack house.

"Get off my fucking bitch, you white shit." He punches me, but as I'm already turning to run away, the blow glances off the back of my head. The pain makes me run even faster, and after a few seconds I hear him slow down. He was smoking a cigarette, and as I don't smoke tobacco my lungs must be in a better state than his. I keep running, anticipating the sound of a gunshot and a hot bullet ricocheting around my organs, but all I hear is a woman scream. I turn round and see him kicking Maxine in the doorway of the house. I stop, and feel in my pockets. I hate myself for not bringing my phone, but I feel my car keys, and the knife Mummy killed herself with. I'm wearing training shoes, and I silently canter back to the crack house. Maxine'e screaming so loudly, I feel sure the police will be here soon. I don't know why I'm going back, apart from to protect her from the beating by the pimp or crack dealer, or whatever he is. As I get closer, my sense of self-preservation increases, especially when I see the teenaged gangster on his feet, all be it bent double, and leaning against the wing of my car. I haven't been noticed, and I mentally tell myself I'm mad as I open the blade of Mummy's knife, not knowing what I'm going to do when I reach the house.

The teenager's recovered himself enough to stand up straight now, and the man who was kicking Maxine clocks him. He turns to confront him, just as the teenager lunges at him. They lock together, and I open the driver's door of my car, and put the key in the ignition, and unlock the passenger door. Then I skirt round the struggling men, push them both over, and pull Maxine to her feet. She's survived her kicking admirably, because she gets in the driver's seat and starts the engine. The teenager is more intent on fighting his opponent than furthering his involvement with us. This keeps the big one occupied, and I get in the passenger seat just in time before Maxine screeches the tyres and we speed away. I fold the blade back into the knife, and look at Maxine's bleeding face.

"Are you alright to drive?" She doesn't answer. Just wipes some blood out of her eyes, and turns into a side road.

"I meant you to sit in the passenger seat. I was going to drive." G forces throw me towards her as she takes another turning at forty miles an hour.

"Where are you staying?"

"The Adelphi. Where are we now?"

"Toxteth. I'll drop you off in the centre."

"It's my car!"

"Not if you want me to live, it isn't. I've got to scram."

"Don't you need the hospital?"

"If I don't get out of the pool, I'll need the mortuary."

"Is there anything I can do to help?" I know what the answer will be before I've finished saying it.

"Money. And don't report the car stolen." I've only got about sixty quid in my wallet, and if I leave it too long before reporting the car stolen, the insurance won't pay. It's a moral dilemma, because I care about Maxine, but I need my cash. We trigger several speed cameras, and Maxine slows down as we approach the busier part of the city.

"You've got cash in your boot. I won't report the car stolen until tomorrow afternoon."

"I need it for longer than that. What's wrong with the radio?"

"It doesn't work. If I don't report it stolen within twelve hours of it getting nicked, the insurance is void."

"These bloody French cars are shite. Give me your knife, then."

"Sorry Maxine, I can't let the knife go." She halts the car suddenly.

"The Adelphi Hotel's down that road there. Get out quick."

"Where are you going?"

"To get drugs." As I get out of the car, I see the front of her skirt and her thighs are completely soaked in blood.

"Oh my God Maxine! Did he stab you?"

"It's just a miscarriage."

"The car's yours. Thanks for the lift." I open the glove compartment, in case something I value is in there. That 'Teletubbies' video the blonde-haired bloke gave me is in there. It doesn't look like Maxine will be needing it, so I take it. I leave her the torch, an A to Z of London, and a Madonna cassette. Since the infection in my ear, music has lost its pleasure for me. I don't just hear the music, I hear the noises it sets off in my head.

"Can I have some money for fuel?"

I give her a twenty-pound note.

"Look after yourself Maxine." I say, to a car that sped off before I could shut the door. She was lying about where the Adelphi is, and by the time I knock on the door of room 501, it's nearly three in the morning. There's no answer, so I knock some more, and go in. The lights are on, and the mini-bar door is fully open. Someone's consumed everything in it, except for the Kit Kat. The TV silently shows pictures of Charlotte French. Hosting her talk show, meeting Royalty, performing live in a theatre. Then the flower bedecked gates of a Palladian villa, thronged with television crews and journalists. A stretch of Italian road, and a shattered Ferrari Testerossa being loaded onto a lorry. A white Regency house in Notting Hill, crying fans holding candles, and a mountain of flowers. Poor Charlotte.

When I open the bathroom door it bumps against Donger's feet. He's sleeping on the floor, with his head beside the toilet. Vomit is splattered all over the seat. Out of respect for my host, I urinate in the bath. I eventually find the remote control on one of the untouched beds. I turn the TV off, get into the bed furthest from the bathroom, and escape into deep, deep sleep.

Chapter Forty-six

Donger's amazingly dapper in the morning, shrugging his mini-bar binge off with
"I stayed away from the skag, didn't I? Anyway, Jesus drank." He switches the telly on, and loses himself in one of the news channel's coverage of the fallout from Charlotte's death. There's now a sea of flowers outside her house in Notting Hill, and an array of celebrities telling the public how devastated they are by the loss of such a tremendous talent, and a lovely person.

Now my car's been 'stolen', I can't drive Donger back to London. He's very decent about it, and leaves for the train station at eleven. Check out isn't until midday, and he clears it with the hotel for me to stay in his room until then. I spend as little time in the vomit-stinking bathroom as possible, and find myself doing something I usually never allow – watching the opening credits of 'Rats Milk Cheese'. The memories flood back as those now legendary front titles roll. Even with the bathroom door shut, I can smell Donger's stale sick, which reminds me of Daisy the conger eel vomiting onto the side of my head during the filming of the end titles. If only it hadn't happened, I wouldn't have got the viral infection that made my right ear go deaf.
Leah walks into the kitchen, looking younger than she does now, and does the double take of the rat. She milks the rat, and leaves the milk to turn into cheese. I'm impressed by the skill of the editing as it cuts from the real kitchen set to the scale model. The catchy signature tune is hummed all over the world, and became a Christmas number one single. The rat's milk becomes cheese, and Leah leaves it on the kitchen table.
Then in I come in the Boris costume, and some clever editing creates the illusion that I eat the cheese. I haven't been in that costume for years, but I can still remember the view of the inside of the mask, when the mouth was closed. The metal hinges of the jaw, the netting, the green foam rubber, the smell of plastic, and my own stale sweat.

Back on the TV screen, I go over to that now famous sofa, imitations of which adorn living rooms from Vancouver to Vauxhall, from Tokyo to Tasmania, and lie down. One by one the other members of the cast come in and push me off the sofa, sit down, and walk out of shot after their name has crossed the screen in bright yellow gothic script. I remember the risotto I had for lunch just before we filmed Des Jensen rolling me off. The conversation I had with the soundman, who put the radio microphone in my head so many times. As it turned out, quite unnecessarily, as after they sacked me they used Terry's voice instead of mine. Terry who was a runner when those titles were shot, and who's now world famous for playing Boris the blue dog. Millions of people around the world think it's Terry Bilsborough on that sofa. They don't know it's me in that costume, because Grange Films run my name across the screen so quickly and in such small writing, only a few cult TV nerds know it's there.

Finally I get up off the sofa, try to get in my basket, and the rest of the cast are asleep in it. The music reaches a climax, and another episode of 'Rats Milk Cheese' beams its way into homes, hospitals, and any other place that has a TV set tuned to BBC1.

I'm about to turn it off and get my stuff ready to leave, when my phone rings. It's my good friend Neil Gosling. We've grown closer over the years. Like me, he's watched most of his peers become a highly paid celebrity. We, meanwhile, kept making audiences weep with laughter in small time pubs and clubs. Having said that, he earns several times more than I do, because he plays the venues in Arnold Shanks' comedy empire.
"Doug are you free this evening?"
"I'm afraid so."
"I've got a gig for you in Manchester, if you want it."
"That's handy. I'm in Liverpool."
"My support act has got himself a TV commercial in London tomorrow. If you can replace him tonight, you get a hundred and fifty quid. You can stay at my place." Neil's moved out of London and bought himself a flat in Manchester. He does a lot of gigs up North and in the Midlands. It wouldn't suit me to live up here, but it'll be handy to stay with him tonight. I'll see what his new place is like. He's

only just moved in. I take the details, and arrange to meet him when he's got back from which ever town he was working in last night.

The phone call over, I pick the remote control up to switch the telly off, when something stops me. Rufus, as played by Des Jensen, is doing a handstand against the door. It opens, and he falls on top of Lois, played by Leah. They roll around a bit, before disentangling themselves and standing up embarrassed. I turn the volume up, and wait for Boris to bound in barking. Leah's character adjusts her hair, and says a line I say along with her, even though I've never watched this episode, which was made after I was fired, and Terry Bilsborough took over the part of Boris. I sit on the end of the bed, and watch the rest of the episode I submitted to Sheila Fox, and which she rejected. I move closer to the screen to watch the end title sequence. There I am in the tank at Pinewood Studios. Daisy the conger eel vomits pink sparkly sick onto the side of my head, and the octopus grabs my leg. My name goes past so small and fast it's invisible, and I watch the words "written by Lawrence Smith" slide slowly past. The bastards have filmed my script, without paying me for it. The year the show was made slides past in roman numerals. The same year I got fired, so it must have been one of the first episodes of the second series. It's been sold all over the world, to TV stations, and on DVD. Someone made a lot of money from my script, and it wasn't me.

Chapter Forty-seven

"You're my second visitor. I only moved in two days ago." Says Neil Gosling, as he leads me into his trendy split-level apartment.
"I've just done two nights in Newcastle, so I haven't stayed a night here yet. That galleried bit up there is the sleeping area. There's no bedroom as such, so it's a studio flat, I suppose."
"I can see the point of buying the show flat." I say, as he shows me the tiny shower room. The place is so small it doesn't take long to show me round, and a few minutes later I'm sitting in his black leather sofa, leaning forward to load a bong on the smoked glass top of the coffee table.
"I wouldn't have chosen the brown colour scheme, but it meant I could move straight in without decorating. The window blinds, the furniture, even the telly was included. I know it's small, but the divorce cost me dear." He stands up and the top of his head bangs into the metal lampshade that hangs low over the glass coffee table.
"Fuck!" He shouts, rubbing the top of his forehead, and checking his hand for blood. I can't stop myself smiling. I've only been here five minutes, and that's the second time he's hurt his head on the edge of the lampshade. It looks very practical, having a light fitting just above the large round coffee table. There's a dimmer switch, so we can watch the wide screen TV with just enough light to illuminate our marijuana smoking equipment. As soon as I walked in and saw the leather sofa, wooden blinds, and the French windows leading onto a tiny Juliet balcony, the place said "Swanky apartment". It looks like something in a Sunday colour supplement. The flaw in the interior design is that when someone's sitting on the black leather sofa, the sharp-edged steel lampshade is out of view. When they stand up, their head collides with it, making a loud clanging sound.

Neil goes to the kitchen area, and takes a couple of beers from the fridge.

"Last week a flat in this block sold for ten thousand more than I paid for this one. And it's exactly like mine, except they didn't get furniture."
"It's a great buy, Neil. And you're so close to the city centre." Neil puts the cans on the glass-topped table, and opens the French window to show me his Juliet balcony. Manchester's Saturday night cacophony invades the living space. He wants me to appreciate the view, but as I stand up an infuriating pain flashes through my skull. The lorries and police sirens screaming along the duel carriageway outside drown the metallic clang of the lampshade, but my exclamation of pain is louder.
"It's no good. You've got to get rid of that bloody thing, Neil. It's dangerous." I squeeze next to him on the balcony. It's one o'clock in the morning, and the duel carriageway four floors below us is choked with traffic. I search for something positive to say about the noisy, grimy cityscape. Neil says something to me, but the grind of engines distorts his words, and we retreat into his minute, overpriced, corner of converted Victorian warehouse.

I can hear okay as long as there isn't background noise. Especially in an acoustically absorbent environment with soft furnishings, carpets and curtains. As soon as background noise is added, though, I can't hear what people say. If we're in a reflective acoustic environment with wooden floors, and hard furnishings, I find it much harder to hear, despite the fact that my left ear wasn't injured. The noise from outside camouflages Neil's words, and he knows it. He closes the balcony door and pushes a can of beer across the glass tabletop. I light the bong, and, coughing, hand it to him. The TV volume is turned down, probably in acknowledgement of my hearing difficulty. More news pictures of grieving fans outside Charlotte's white regency house. The story's developing though, because there's a high-ranking Italian policeman reading a statement outside an Italian Hospital, and shots of the mangled Ferrari Testarossa. Library footage of Charlotte leaving court after she was acquitted of cocaine possession, leads Neil and I to suspect she was driving under the influence of drugs. The report ends, and we return to a pristine Emily Johnson. It's unusual to see her this late at night. As the top anchorwoman in the country, she's usually reading the prime time news.
"What's she wearing round her neck?" Exclaims Neil as Emily Johnson moves on to a report about a child's torso being washed up

on a Norfolk beach. I look at the pendant Emily's wearing. It's a small cross, similar to ones worn by many, whether Christian or not. Except the horizontal part of the cross is slightly more than half way down the main upright.

"Am I more stoned than I thought, or is that an upside down cross?"

I look closer.

"I reckon it's a very subtle upside down cross."

"On a newsreader. I don't know what television's coming to."

My mouth opens to tell Neil about my sexual encounter with Emily and Leah aboard The Grietje. I feel it would be boasting, so desist.

The hydroponically grown Mancunian skunk and strong lager has dulled the pain of my spectacular death earlier on. Neil struggled with the drunken hecklers, but I went down in flames. One of Manchester's football teams (I don't even know how many they've got) beat a London team this afternoon, and the crowd were fuelled by anti-Southerner bloodlust. They hated me from the moment I went on. Telling the hecklers that which net a bunch of sweaty men kicked a ball into shouldn't decide whether or not I'm funny did nothing to endear myself. If I'd been able to hear what the hecklers were shouting, I could have outwitted them. Bad acoustics coupled with their northern accents meant I couldn't understand what they were saying, and the rest of the audience lost their patience. It didn't help that the resident compere was that aggressive Mancunian I worked with last night. He made it clear that he didn't like my act when he put me on, so I started off on the back foot.

Anyway, I'm holding most of the £150 cash I got for the ten minutes I did before getting booed off, and Neil's just started chopping a line of coke out on his smoked glass coffee table. I re-light the bong, and settle back into the soft leather sofa.

"When she comes, you'll have to turn the TV up, Doug."

"I can go out for a while, if you like"

"Don't be silly. You're my mate and I've known you for longer than her. She told me she wasn't staying tonight. Then changed her mind this afternoon."

Neil snorts his line, and hands me a twenty-pound note. He indicates the line of coke he chopped out for me.

"Snort this before she arrives. She doesn't approve of class A's."

I stand up to walk round the table, and bang my head on the stupid lampshade. He laughs a lot, because he's drunker than I've ever seen him. I'm snorting the line he put out for me, when the intercom buzzes. Neil springs to his feet, and bangs his head again. This time I laugh, because I'm also more pissed than I usually get. Neil buzzes his new girlfriend through the main entrance and hastily clears up the evidence of cocaine. A cuddly northern girl comes in, carrying an overnight bag from which she produces a bottle of Diamond White strong cider. She's just finished a six-hour shift in a call centre, and doesn't seem too pleased that I'm there. If Neil's flat had a separate bedroom, I'd be okay. I've never been one to stay where I don't feel wanted, and I decide to give Neil and his new girlfriend some space. Before Neil can protest, I've got my coat on and I'm half way to the front door.
"I fancy a drink. I'll be back a bit later."
"Okay Mate. Come back as soon as you feel like it." The new girlfriend's phone starts ringing in the bag she left at the foot of the stairs to the sleeping area. Just before I leave I see her stand up and bang her head on the steel lampshade.

'Sparkles', a twenty-four hour massage parlour, is a few streets away. I've never been there, but I've heard comedians talk about it in a dressing room somewhere. When I get there I find it boarded up. There's an emptiness inside me, an addiction to woman's touch I can't control. I feel like Mr Hyde as I stalk towards the street in the city centre where the women stand. The Dr Jeckyll part of me died when I found out Alison was seeing a flight attendant behind my back. He'd thought he was gay, until he crewed a Boeing 737 with Alison on a flight to Germany. Just before takeoff for the flight home, the plane developed a technical fault. The crew were put up in the Ramada Inn at Stuttgart airport, and Alison became the first woman he slept with. The affair continued for three months until one night she forgot to lock the keypad on the phone I bought her for Christmas. A particularly passionate encounter in the Jury Inn at Belfast International Airport caused them to roll on the phone, and inadvertently dial my number. I heard foreplay, two orgasms, and a post coital conversation about the Airline's new flexible pay system. A day later I had a broken heart, and a hilarious new bit about losing one's flight attendant girlfriend not to a pilot, but to a gay flight attendant.

The Manchester night drizzles, and I pass the remnants of a stag party, arguing about where they can get another drink. I inadvertently make eye contact with one of them, and he stops walking.
"What do you think you're looking at, spastic!" I don't bother turning round to answer, and a bottle smashes on the pavement in front of me. Charming. I'm sure people are more aggressive than they were a few years ago.

I walk past two billboard posters advertising 'The Girl From the Village'. The cold air in my nostrils makes me feel all Christmassy. This time of year always reminds me of the time 'Rats Milk Cheese' exploded onto British TV screens. It was already building momentum as a cult programme in America, but no one was prepared for the impact it made on popular culture. Grange Films very cleverly copyrighted all merchandising rights, and made as much from that as they did from the show. I failed to get compensation for the ear injury resulting from my session in the water tank at Pinewood. I would have thought they could have slipped me a few thousand as a good will gesture, but Sheila Fox and her cronies hated me. Equity refused to help me, because it wasn't an Equity contract. So here I am wandering through Manchester city centre at half past two in the morning. I helped create one of the most successful TV programmes in history, but don't reap the rewards of that success. If only I hadn't ejaculated in Arnold's face. If only I'd sucked his cock...

A shivering, fat, wreck of a woman steps out of the shadows and looks desperately into my eyes. I've found the place I was looking for. She mumbles something as I walk past, but I don't hear. The next one is even more knackered. I keep going. There's no way I could go with any of these. I'd rather have a lady boy. The drizzle has stopped, and a breeze brings the smell of the canal towards the street, which has no buildings either side of it. One side has a temporary wooden fence surrounding a building site, and the other borders an NCP car park. Out of the sodium lighting steps my salvation. She's young, pretty, and for sale.
"Are you looking for some company luv?"

"Yes."
"It's twenty pounds for sex."
"Have you got a place?"
"It's just down here. Do you want to give me the twenty?" I remove a twenty from my wallet, and give it to her. She cranes forward to see how much money there is in it, and which pocket I keep it in. We walk along the road, and already my fascination with her is flowing. Her cream PVC mac glows orange in the sodium lighting. She's wearing the obligatory knee length boots, and her jet black hair frames a heavily made up face with black eyeliner and bright red lipstick.
"How old are you?"
"Twenty. Me name's Christine. This way, luv." She starts leading me across the empty car park. I assume we're taking a short cut to where her flat is, but she stops beside the glass-fibre car park attendant's kiosk.
"Behind here, luv."
"You must be joking."
"We're alright, luv. I've been using this place for four years."
I look around. It's deserted.
"Come and see for yourself. It's quite safe."
There's a small gap between the back of the empty glass fibre kiosk, and some bushes and a small tree. Closer up the bushes turn out to be very large weeds, beyond which the car park continues. It looks like she *has* used the place for four years, and never bothered to clear up. Used condoms and heroin detritus are everywhere. A tubular steel barrier about four feet long, stands amongst the vegetation. It's waist high, like a crowd control barrier in a train station. Christine rests her hand on the top of it.
"Clients usually take me from behind against this barrier." She hoists her skirt and the back of her mac up, and pulls her knickers down to the top of her boots.
"Put this on, luv." She proffers a condom, and I take it. A black man has appeared from nowhere, and is lurking on the other side of the kiosk. Taking her from behind would mean my back would be towards the kiosk, and the black man behind me.
"There's a man there."
"He's okay, I know him. Hurry up, luv. You're wasting time."
"Does it cost the same for a blow job?" She pulls her knickers up, and starts undoing my belt.

"You should have said." As she pulls my jeans and pants down I can feel her hand trying to take my wallet out of the pocket. The black man's gone. I put my hand on my wallet, so she can tell I know what she's up to, and look around in case of attack from behind.

Neil's cocaine is strong. A generous erection sprang from my boxer shorts when she pulled them down. She takes the condom out of my fingers and puts it on my knob with the dexterity of a close up magician. She spits her chewing gum out, and starts earning her living. The condom is extra strong, and dulls the sensation of her lips and tongue. But it can't stop the warmth of her mouth from comforting my soul. I'm leaning against the crash barrier, and have to pull her hand away from my wallet again as she sucks and licks between short bursts of wanking. I look behind again, and see the black man casually strolling backwards and forwards about fifty feet away. I find Christine really attractive, but all I can see is the top of her head. I raise my head so I can see anyone approach. A huge billboard advertisement for 'The Girl From The Village' dominates the car park. I can see more of Brian O'Shea and his blonde co-star than I can of Christine.

The condom must be made for anal sex, because it's absorbing most of the sensation.
"You're taking a very long time, luv."
"I'm sorry, but the view of Manchester city centre isn't an erotic one."
"Isn't a what?"
"Erotic."
"I don't know what an erotic is, luv. And your time's up, I'm afraid."
I give her another tenner. Brian O'Shea's wanton face gazes across the car park.
"Don't worry about sucking it. Just do me with your hand." Five minutes later, I still haven't come.
"I'm sorry luv, but you really are taking a very long time."
"Here's another tenner."
"You can feel my tits if it would help things, darling."
"I don't think you'd like that, my hands are cold. I don't suppose you could do it a bit faster, could you?" She changes hand for the third time.
"Me arm's aching."

"I'm so sorry about this. That bloke over there is really putting me off." I mean the lingering street black, not Brian O'Shea.
"Honestly luv, you're quite safe here. I've used this place every night for four years."
"That's it. A bit faster. Urgh. Ah. Mmm."
I remove the condom, and drop it amongst the coke can crack pipes, sooty tin foil, syringes, and other condoms. All the time I'm anticipating the appearance of our loitering friend. As soon as I finished coming, Christine's manner has become more businesslike. She wants to get back to her soliciting patch as quickly as possible.
"I feel so sorry for the other women there."
"Don't."
"Why do you say that?"
"I'm keeping them."
"That's great. That you take care of each other."
"Not really. It's me Mam and her sister." I bid her goodnight, and she replies that she's there every night if I want her services again.
"Thanks." I stalk off in the direction of the busy road. I want to reach civilisation before I get ambushed.

A few months ago Melissa told me she couldn't represent me any more. Arnold Shanks Entertainments Ltd controls most live comedy. They don't employ me, so she could only get me gigs at smaller, independent venues. She said I'm not financially viable. She was too nice to add that Grange Films dominates television's meagre comedy output, and thanks to Sheila Fox I'm excluded from it. The last audition Melissa sent me to was for a TV commercial for a loan company. I didn't get it, but I hit it off with the casting studio receptionist. She was an American girl my age. I took her phone number, and she came to one of my gigs. She was the last girlfriend I had. On paper everything about the relationship was good. She was ready for commitment, a fantastic lover, and cared about me.

She wasn't phased by my fear of babies and children, and her family owned properties in Manhattan and upstate New York. On our second date, we had sex in her kitchen. The second time we made love was in my bed. The fourth time we made love in her bed, and I had to imagine her flatmate to keep myself interested. I managed to conceal my boredom for a month, because I wanted to be receptive to her love.

I had a gig in Ipswich, and we made a weekend of it by staying in a country hotel a few miles away. The other guests were elderly and dull, and the bar was closed by twelve. We ended up romping in the hotel grounds, pretending I was a country squire, and she was a stable girl. We play-acted an illicit encounter by the summerhouse, and I lost my erection. Even the fantasy couldn't stimulate me. Despite my knowing that here was a relationship I could grow in, I couldn't help tiring of the institutionalised sex.

A gust of wind blows an empty fried chicken box across the car park. My fingers toy with the familiar shape of Mummy's knife in my pocket. When I first got bored of sex with a girlfriend, I thought it was because we weren't suited to each other. I got bored with the next girl even sooner. And so the pattern emerged, the spiral getting tighter, until I had a one-night stand, and had to imagine she was the waitress in the wine bar I'd just picked her up in. I reach the far side of the car park, avoiding a puddle of vomit on the broken pavement. I've just risked getting arrested or mugged having sex with a junkie whore. But at no time was my penis anything but rock hard. I was so engaged with the danger of the moment, I had no need to imagine further stimulation.

A figure comes at me from the right. My deaf ear gave no warning of his approach. It's the huge black man who stood sentry during my sordid encounter in the car park. He's up close. I jump like a girl who's just seen a spider. My sharp intake of breath was like a half scream. I flinch, ready for the silvery flash of a knife. The man laughs.

Chapter Forty-eight

"What's the matter, Doug? You deaf or something?"
The upper part of his face is familiar. And that voice. It's Charles! The head of security at the Clap Clinic.
"Charles?" He smiles, as charming as he was on the door of Arnold's flagship club.
"Yeah it's me, Doug. I've been calling your name from over there, Man."
"I went deaf in my right ear. I thought you were going to kill me."
"That was my girl you just did behind the kiosk."
"I'm sorry Man. I didn't know." I prepare to be stabbed after all. Charles laughs.
"Don't worry, Bro. You paid the price. I thought it was you, I just came to say hello."
I can't believe this is the same Charles who dealt drugs to the stars. I never saw him other than pristine. He had short hair, wore the smartest designer suits. He was always so cool. The Charles in this cold, cold car park has long dread-locked hair. His beard is uneven, where it fails to grow on a deep scar running from his chin to his cheek. He's dirty, and his tatty parka is smudged with oil stains.
"So. Are you still working for Arnold?"
His expression darkens.
"Raasclaat!" He unzips his parka, and pulls a frayed jumper high above the waistband of his jeans. A pistol is tucked into his belt. Then I see what he's showing me. Even the sodium lighting can't disguise the terrible scars on his abdomen. One runs vertically from below his belt, up to his chest. The other is so bad it looks like a huge steak has been cut out of his stomach. He swivels ninety degrees, so I can see the scar continues round to his back, where a Bowie knife nestles in its leather sheath, strapped to a separate belt.

I don't want him to get any colder than he already is, and it strikes me such terrible wounds should be kept warm.
"Oh my God, Charles. It looks like you were attacked by a shark!"

"Close. Sunita's propeller. A shark was at the controls."
"And I thought I was fucked over."
"You escaped lightly, Man." Charles readjusts his clothing and weaponry, and his mobile rings. He says a few things I can't understand, and ends the call.
"You got time for a drink?"
"Yeah. I'm not in a hurry."
"Come to my office." I follow him away from the car park and around the corner of a big building covered in scaffolding. Beyond is a parade of empty shops, but for one, which houses a mini cab office. Two decrepit Nissan Bluebirds are parked outside, and Charles leads me past the reception area, populated by several surly black men, and up some stairs. He coughs a hacking cough, as our feet echo on the bare woodworm-eaten stairs. He opens the door to the room that fronts the building. An electric fire with both bars on keeps the room at tropical temperature. A poster of Montego Bay is stuck crookedly to the wall. The place is so old, the shelves look like they've been attached at an angle, but a model BMW sits comfortably next to a portable TV set, and isn't rolling off. There's a rickety wooden desk, and an old sofa with stuffing coming out. A black and white cat explains the scratch marks on the side of the sofa, the desk, and a wing armchair.
"Sit down, Doug." Charles opens a cupboard, and removes a half full gin bottle and a glass.
"This rum's from an illegal still in Jamaica." He pours a glass of the clear liquid from the gin bottle. I knock it back, and it has the same effect as some illegal poteen I drank in Bantry. Fire in the stomach, watery eyes, and a euphoric glow in the brain. I gasp and bang my glass down on an upside down tea chest that's serving as a table. He chuckles, and refills my glass.
"I've got some lemonade or cola if you want."
"Yes please. Aren't you having a glass?" Charles shakes his head as he hands me a can of coke. He gently holds his palm to his stomach.
"The propeller blades mashed my guts. One drink and I'd be dead." As if to demonstrate his closeness to death he bends double and coughs his hacking cough for a full thirty seconds. He flops into an old swivel chair behind the desk, and nearly loses balance. The cat meows and jumps into his lap, causing him to wince with pain.

"When they fished me out of the Thames, I was full of river water. I've got Weil's disease."

"Is that the one from rat's urine?"

"Yeah. I'm only alive because the River Police launch just 'appened to come along. They had to abort the execution and pretend I'd fallen overboard."

Charles takes a Pyrex crack pipe from his pocket, and loads a rock into it.

"Arnold?" Charles shakes his head and smokes the crack. Now I can see where the cough comes from. He coughs for so long, I've got a queue of questions waiting to be answered.

"When the Vermeulen brothers got their feet under the table, it was all change. They had their own security. Didn't want me dealing my stuff, competing with them. Hatred and lies took over. They convinced Shanks I was gonna kill him."

"What happened to that new guy you were with on the night of the wrap party. The one who threw me out?"

"Clyde. As far as I know, he's with them. He betrayed me big style." Charles hands me the crack pipe. I've only smoked crack once or twice. It's not something I'd make a habit of, but at three in the morning on a cold autumn night...

I cough from the crack smoke, and splutter from the rum. Charles switches the portable TV on, and I see the advert I auditioned for a few months ago, but didn't get. This is followed by a lengthy advert for 'The Girl From The Village'. It's got rave reviews in America, and we're treated to Brian O'Shea dressed as a country squire. He snogs the pretty blonde actress in an Irish meadow, in a walled garden, and a rowing boat on a lake. Finally we see them in front of an Irish country house. She gathers her dress in her hands and runs crying down a tree-lined drive. Brian shouts her name passionately, leaps on a horse, and gallops after her. Charles and I look at each other, smile, and shake our heads with incredulity.

"I wouldn't say no to Brian's career."

"You're a much better comedian than he'll ever be, Man."

"Tell that to the Hollywood casting departments."

"We all rated you, Man. All the staff at the Clap Clinic. When you were on, waitresses would invent reasons to go in the audience. It was

313

your lines we quoted in the staff room." He exhales crack smoke, and descends into another bout of coughing.
"Scum rises to the top. That dog you played. Boris the backward God. You're making people laugh all over the world every minute of the day. Don't matter they don't credit you for it. You know you done it. I know you done it. Shanks knows you done it. He don't feel good about what he done to you. None of that crowd got any soul left. They's evil, and they know it." Charles never spoke in a Jamaican accent when I knew him. A rush of paranoia momentarily convinces me it isn't Charles. That I've been set up for an execution. The advert I didn't get, and the long trailer for Brian O'Shea's film were just played on a video machine in the room next door, to taunt me with my failure. The door opens, and a younger, more aggressive black man comes in. Charles suddenly gets up from behind the desk, and fear grips my bowels. They talk in patois, and from their body language and the way Charles beckons me off the sofa, I glean that we're not in Charles' office at all. It belongs to the younger, bigger man. Charles doesn't have an office. Perhaps he shares this one with the man who just came in, but as a junior partner. Either way, we clatter down the stairs, and back into the street. Charles reaches inside his parka.
"I present you with the Charles Smith award for lifelong achievement in comedy." He hands me the bottle of rum. I accept it, and give him a little speech, in which I acknowledge his help.
"I've gotta go and look after my girls. Respect to you, Doug." We shake hands, and he quotes three of my jokes to me.
"I'm always getting laughs for your jokes."
"Charles, it's an honour to have you do them."
"I thought you were great on 'The Sauce Boat'. How come they never gave you the headline spot?"
"They were going to, but it didn't work out. Charles, can I ask you one last thing?"
"Fire away, my friend."
"When we worked at The Clap Clinic, I only ever heard you speak impeccable English. I can hardly believe you're the same man."
"I'm an orphan like you, Doug. I was brought up by a middle class white lady in Brixton. I got harassed at school for speaking like a honky. At home I got told off for speaking like a black. I didn't fit anywhere. So I joined the misfits. You're a talented man, Doug. Use it."

"I had no idea you were an orphan."
"You never asked. You weren't easy to get to know."
Charles opens his arms, and we hug. I hold him very gently, because I don't want to press those tender scars, or set his gun off. He beckons one of the minicab drivers. If Charles' status is lower than that of the man who usurped the office, it's higher than the drivers'. I get a free minicab ride back to Neil's place. I ring his bell, and look at my watch. It's ten past four in the morning. I hope they let me in. Suddenly I'm afraid I'm going to be attacked. I ring the bell again. A container lorry passes, and the panic inside me resonates with the rumble of its Diesel. A voice comes out of the entry-phone speaker.
"Yes?"
"It's Doug. Let me in!" I hear laughter from the speaker. They're laughing at me! My heart's pounding as the door buzzes. I run up the stairs, too afraid to use the lift.
Neil lets me in the flat. His girlfriend and another girl are sprawled on the leather sofa. Neil leads me into the lounge area, rubbing his head. They were laughing because he banged it on the lampshade as he got up to answer the entry-phone. He was wrong about his new girlfriend being against class A drugs. She'd denounced them because she'd been overdoing it, and wanted to give up. She thought that by telling people she was against them, she'd attract non-drug user friends.

While I was out, Neil and she discovered their mutual love of ecstasy. Alcohol got the better of their judgement, and a phone call yielded her friend Tracy with several pills in her handbag. I'm introduced to Tracy, and re-introduced to Neil's girlfriend, whose name I'd forgotten, but is Fran. They're all coasting along on E.
"Have one, Doug. We went up on ours really fast."
"No thanks, Fran. I'll have a beer, though, if you've got any left." They haven't, and I produce the rum that Charles gave me. I tell Neil about what's become of him, and my paranoia. They reassure me I've got nothing to worry about, and everyone loves me. Swept along with their love-vibe, I start to fancy Tracy. She made a remark about not having a boyfriend shortly after I came in, and I take it as a come-on. We're all drinking rum and cokes, and I contrive things so I'm sitting next to her. Neil and Fran are canoodling on the armchair, which sets the scene nicely for Tracy and me, I think. As I watch Neil entertain the girls with anecdotes about Brian O'Shea before he was famous, I

find myself wondering if Neil has actually got any cheekbones. Perhaps there aren't any in his skull. No, there must be some sort of bone in there. I make a move on Tracy, but there's nothing doing, and I retreat to the sleeping area and crash out on some cushions next to the bed.

Chapter Forty-nine

I wake up with a massive hangover. I slipped off the cushions whilst I was asleep, and was really uncomfortable on the floor, so I'm disappointed to find the bed un-slept in. Neil, Fran, and Tracy are nowhere to be seen, and I find a note on the glass table telling me they've gone out for a greasy spoon breakfast. It's a bright sunny day, but when I open the doors to the balcony, a blast of cold air takes my breath away. The noise of the duel carriageway below is even worse. I'm really hungry, but when I explore the kitchen area I find out why the others all went out. There's nothing. Not even coffee or tea. I pour myself a glass of Coke, and as an afterthought, empty the bottle of rum into it. I'm feeling weird. Like I did the day after my first LSD trip. Except then I felt vigorous and happy. Today I feel elated one moment, and crushed by anxiety the next. When I get home I'm going to sort my life out. I'm going to give up drugs, and do my accounts.

They're overdue and I'm going to have to pay a fine for late submission of my tax return. For the first time ever I've spent all the money I'd saved for tax. I'm getting fewer and fewer gigs. Several years ago I earned more in a week than I do now in three months. I drain the glass of rum and Coke. My tummy glows cozy and warm. Manchester looks drab below, but the sky looks clear and blue and exciting. That's where I want to be. I decide to treat myself, and fly back to London. Sod the money, I'll use my credit card. The views from the plane will be stunning. I'll have a few drinks on board. I'm gathering my stuff, when I notice the bowl of the bong is full of skunk. I smoke it, and go all giggly. The others will be so tired when they get back. I remember the last time Neil stayed at my place, he hid my toothpaste in the bed. He knew I was bringing a girl back, and he thought it would be funny if we couldn't clean our teeth. It really pissed me off at the time. I'll get him back.

I get his toothpaste from the bathroom, and I'm about to put the tube under the duvet, when it strikes me as a hilarious idea to squeeze the contents into the bed. Before I've had time to consider it, I've squeezed a long worm of red-streaked Signal bang into the middle of his king size black silk sheet. I'm returning the tube to the bathroom, when the thought of putting some shampoo in the bed as well makes me collapse in hysterics. I grab the shampoo and conditioner, and run up to the sleeping area. A couple of quick squirts from each bottle, and quickly down to replace them in the shower room. They could come back any moment, and I don't want the trick to be spoilt by being discovered. I run back upstairs, and make sure the duvet looks like it did before I sabotaged the bed. I can't stop laughing at my mental picture of Neil and Fran finding toothpaste and shampoo in the bed. My God, I haven't been awake half an hour, and I feel out of it. I phone British Airways. They've got a flight in two hours, or this evening. I can't wait until this evening, so I book a seat with my credit card, and order a taxi. As from tomorrow, I'm starting life afresh. I keep giggling to myself as I check to see if I've left anything behind. There's a half smoked joint in the ashtray. I don't smoke tobacco, but I make an exception and finish the joint off. I cough and wretch. It's a strong joint. I'm still laughing when I finish the note to Neil. The taxi driver phones to say he's outside. I leap up to leave, and my head hits the lampshade with such force, it bleeds.

The driver looks familiar. I've definitely seen him before. I ask him where he's from and he replies Moss Side. I take that as a veiled threat that he's violent. Then I realise how stupid I am, having such paranoid thoughts. I try to console myself by looking at the trees beside the road, but the suburban landscape depresses me. When I look back into the car, I catch the driver watching me in his rear view mirror. I definitely know him. I grab the bull by the horns.
"Where did we last meet?"
"I was in the minicab office last night. You went upstairs with Charles." Of course! How stupid of me. He's a minicab driver, and minicab drivers hang around in minicab offices. I'm berating myself for getting paranoid again, when I remember I've got a bit of coke in my pocket. The last dregs of a gram I got last week. Cocaine and airports don't go together well, so I'd better snort it before I get there. I offer to share it with the driver, and he pulls over in a lay-by. He gives me a porn magazine with a shiny cover to chop the coke out on. There's more than I thought there was, so I don't mind sharing it with

the driver. The coke stings my nose – I don't remember it as being so harsh. I go to give the porn magazine back to the driver, but he says I can keep it as payment for the line.

The baby laxative in the cocaine gives me severe diarrhoea, and I make it to the toilet in departures just in time. It's an hour before the flight, and I find the automatic check-in machine. I don't want to get caught out with a window seat above a wing, so I select 24F, the seat next to the window at the very rear of the plane. When I check my suitcase in I show my boarding card to the British Airways staff member, to double check that I've definitely got that seat. I know from experience that if any unaccompanied kids are on the flight, they'll seat them in the back row so the flight attendants can keep an eye on them. It's against airline policy to put a single man with unaccompanied children, so if there are any unaccompanied kids, I could get moved to another part of the aircraft. That would almost certainly mean an aisle or middle seat. It's still a clear sky, and I want a window seat. It's nearly as important to me as not sitting near any children or babies.

I have a craving for some Dolly Mixtures. I can't explain it, but I almost do a detour to find a shop that sells them. They'll have to wait, though. I've got to sort this seat out. When I give my suitcase to the check-in woman, I ask her if there are any unaccompanied children on the flight. Then I add
"Oh, yes. And are there any sweetshops airside?" The woman looks at me suspiciously, and says
"Why do you want to know if there are any unaccompanied children on the flight, Sir?"
I show her my boarding card, and explain about not wanting to be moved from my window seat. She deals with my suitcase, and starts making a phone call. There are three unaccompanied minors, or "unmins" as she refers to them, so I'm not allowed in the back row. She offers me a window seat just behind the wing. It's not ideal, but at least it's away from kids. She makes no mention of where I can buy sweets.

When I get on the plane, I'm next to a woman with a toddler! I'm sure this is a conspiracy. I have to put my dolly mixtures away, because the kid tries to grab them off me. He starts screaming when his mother tells him they don't belong to him. The flight is full, so I can't sit anywhere else. I keep my face pressed to the window during taxiing and take off, but I can't press my forehead to the glass, in case it starts bleeding again. I order a gin and tonic, and within a minute of the first sip, my nose starts bleeding. It gives me a good excuse to hide in the toilet. So much for good views out of the window.

The nosebleed doesn't stop until I'm in the baggage hall at Heathrow, and on the way out of arrivals, I'm stopped and searched by security. They find the Dolly Mixtures and the porn magazine. When they open it there are photos of teenaged girls. I can't tell them I only used it to snort cocaine off, but I say a taxi driver gave it to me. They tell me some of the girls might be under age. They confiscate it, log my name and address, and warn me to be careful in the future. I have a horrendous tube journey home. Every carriage seems full of screaming babies. I pick up a discarded colour supplement, and there's an interview with Brian O'Shea. 'The Girl From The Village' has broken box office records in America. He's in Britain to attend the British Premiere, and the following night he starts a forty-date stand-up comedy tour of British theatres. He truly is the golden boy.

I'm so traumatised when I get home, I collapse in front of the telly with a bottle of gin. The first commercial break has the advert for a loan company that I failed the audition for. The news has a report about Charlotte French's post mortem. Her nasal cavity was ravaged by cocaine use, and at the time of her fatal crash, her bloodstream was full of it. I have a wave of anxiety about my nose, and as if on cue, it starts bleeding again. I forgot to water my houseplants before I went up to Liverpool. The neighbours who used to look after them for me whilst I was away moved out a month ago. When I'm switching the lights off before going to bed, I notice my plants are all dead. No phone call from Neil. What's wrong with him? Didn't he enjoy the joke?

Chapter Fifty

Weeks pass, and I start to worry that Neil Gosling is annoyed with me about squeezing toothpaste, shampoo, and conditioner in his bed. Now I think about it, perhaps it was a stupid thing to do. I start getting official documents in the post, informing me speed cameras caught my car travelling over the speed limit. There are a few from Liverpool, which I've been anticipating because I was in the passenger seat at the time. Except for the first one, on the way to the gig. That's it – I'm going to lose my driving licence.

I can track Maxine's journey from the speed cameras she triggered. Lancaster, Dumfries, Glenluce, and Stranraer. It looks like she's got the ferry from Stranraer to Ireland. She was exceeding some of the speed limits by twenty, even thirty miles an hour. I'll have to report the car stolen, or I could go to prison for dangerous driving.

The weather's getting really miserable now, and the nights are drawing in. I've got so few gigs, I hardly miss the car. When I need to get somewhere, I'm reduced to using London's buses. The roads around Lambeth Walk are so congested, I could walk half way to Brixton in the time it takes the 159 to get there. I avoid getting it when the kids are on the way home from school. It's not just me that's scared of these kids – it's everybody. Some of them are so aggressive, and you can't hit them back in case they're under sixteen.

As the forty years old bus belches black Diesel smoke into the filthy Brixton air, I leap off and make my way along the Effra Road. People walk quickly, keeping their eyes on the pavement. Eye contact with a stranger is more likely to develop into trouble than the start of a beautiful friendship. I never used to orientate myself around Brixton. I went to the West End for my leisure activities. Now I'm short of money, the cheaper Brixton prices beckon. I cross the road, and approach the begrimed Victorian building that used to be a pub.

There's so much crime around here, the door's got an entry-phone.
"Who have you come to see?"
"Chantelle."
"All right." I go in, and there's a sour, fat, middle-aged black woman sitting behind a metal grill.
"Have you been before?"
"Yes." She knows I've been here before. I've come twice a week for the last fortnight. Why does she have to be so officious?
"Go up the stairs. The usual room." She buzzes me through the next door, and I'm in the building proper. My excitement manifests itself as a tingling all over my body. These visits to Chantelle are the most meaningful thing in my life. I take my shoes off, and walk into the room. Chantelle isn't here yet, but Celine her assistant is. We smile at each other, and I lie down and close my eyes, whilst she lights candles and incense on a shrine at the end of the room.

I live for what happens in here. I focus on breathing deeply, and the warmth of the room helps me drift off into a daze. I'm woken by an otherworldly female voice. It's Chantelle, starting the session with three long, vocalised sighs. I open my eyes and roll onto my side. Since I arrived, several more people, mostly women, have come in and lay down on the plush carpet. I slowly move to sit cross-legged, and Chantelle chants the opening prayer in Hindi. Celine moves gracefully around us, softly helping us to improve our posture.
"Deep, slow, breaths. Every time you breathe out, impurities are expelled from your body. As you breathe in, fresh prana fills your being." Celine's hands touch the small of my back, and I adjust my spine. Her touch is so gentle, it feels like she's blessing me. Chantelle leads us into the first sun salutation, and I try to concentrate on my posture and breathing, despite the yearning to look at the girl in front of me's bottom and luscious thighs.

These yoga classes are transforming my life. I haven't touched alcohol or drugs for two and a half weeks, and I'm feeling fantastic. It's all down to the strength I get from Chantelle and Celine. They're a lesbian couple, who spend several months of the year studying yoga in India. Chantelle's from Paris, and speaks in a divine French accent. Celine's from Birmingham, and her accent sounds really funny compared to Celine's. The way they teach yoga makes it more like a religious experience – I'm totally in their thrall. To me they're Priestesses, magically transplanted from ancient times into the present. They both have dread-locked hair, and loose cotton leggings and sweatshirts. Later in the class, they remove their sweatshirts to reveal cotton vests, and sleek black arms and shoulders. The gold necklaces and earrings they wear add to my feeling that they're from ancient Egypt or Nubia. The one and a half hour session seems timeless. It starts and ends with us lying on our backs in the corpse posture, with our eyes closed. I usually drift off into a sleep at these times, which makes the yoga session in between seem like a dream. I adore them both. They radiate calmness and divine love, and when I speak to them they smile and their eyes shine with an otherworldly light. Chantelle's laugh sends ripples of delight down my spine.

I'm trying to do the warrior pose, or asana, as the yogic term is. Chantelle puts her arms around me to encourage me to stand in a straight posture. It feels like universal energy flows from her hands into my body. She moves away and helps Celine assist an overweight white woman. I can't stop myself trying to imagine what it must be like for Chantelle and Celine when they make love. I bet they do sixty-nines and have multiple orgasms. I find it more difficult trying not to have lewd thoughts about the women in the room than I do to get into the postures. Chantelle says I'm very supple for a beginner. I wish they taught more classes, so I could come to all of them.

When the session's over, I go over to say goodbye to Chantelle and Celine, and they tell me I'm progressing really well.
"Do the asanas at home every day. You'll be amazed how powerful they are." Says Celine. Chantelle adds:
"They're not just good for your health. They change your luck as well."
"Thanks. I could do with some good luck. Will they help me to make more money?"
Chantelle's silvery laugh makes me smile, and she replies.
"If that's what you're meant to have, maybe." She reaches her forefinger towards me, and touches the centre of my forehead.
"Never mind money. Open your third eye and you'll be rich with the beauty you see."

We walk down the stairs together, and say our goodbyes. I leave them talking to the fat woman behind the grille, who transforms into a charming, gleeful creature when under their spell.

On the bus back to Lambeth Walk, I think about my third eye. Mine must be blinded by all the coke that's gone up my nose. I've still got a little scar there, where I cut my head on Neil's lampshade. I'm having a repeat of the anxious thoughts about the fact that he still hasn't phoned me, when my mobile rings. It's Neil.
"Douglas Tucker, you wanker." I don't know what to say, so I say nothing.
"Did you know toothpaste contains bleach, and bleach completely ruins expensive silk sheets and duvet covers?"
"No, I can't say I did. Sorry about that, but it was a different me to the one you're talking to now."
"Don't worry about it. You're forgiven. What have you been up to?"
"I've got hardly any work, but I've given up all mood altering substances."
"That's a shame. I was going to ask if I can stay at your place this weekend, but I'm not sure I want to now."
"Where are you playing?"
'The Clap Clinic.'
"You're welcome to stay, Neil. It'll be great to see you. I might even come off the wagon in your honour."
"I'm doing Thursday, Friday, and Saturday. Are you around Thursday afternoon?"
"I'll be leaving to do yoga at about four."
"I'll get there before then. See you Thursday."
"Looking forward to it."
When I get home, there's a message on the answering machine.
"Hi Doug, it's Gerry Crook here. Could you give me a call, please. I've got a gig for you."
Chantelle must be right. Doing yoga *is* changing my luck. I lie down on the futon, and masturbate about her and Celine.

I call Gerry Crook on his mobile. He still runs a few gigs, but hasn't booked me since I died in Dartford whilst doing the headline spot. The crowd were very volatile, and my hearing problem meant I couldn't hear what the hecklers were shouting. Gerry's had a hard job

competing against Arnold's near monopoly of the comedy market. He can't afford to risk booking an act who isn't consistent. Gone are the days of his cozy, creative little venues. Now his gigs are big beer halls, thronged with office parties, and stag and hen nights. The years of living in London have done nothing to erode his mellifluous Cork accent.
"Doug. It's like this. I need someone to support The Cretin Brothers in Coventry tomorrow night. Bobby Bum's just let me down."
"Yeah, I'd love to. I don't know the Cretin Brothers. Would they be able to give me a lift?"
"Don't you have a car?"
"Not anymore." There's a long pause.
"Sorry, Doug. Neither of The Cretin Bothers drives. I was hoping you could give *them* a lift."
"So the offer's withdrawn, then?"
"I need someone with a car. Listen, I've got to get on and find someone. I'll give you a call some time. We'll catch up."
He ends the call, and I make myself a mug of herbal tea. My doorbell rings, and when I answer it, a beautiful oriental woman is standing there. She speaks very good English.
"Hello, I'm going to be your new neighbour. My name's Trinh Tuyen."
I'm about to invite her in when a little boy, and an even smaller girl come and stand timidly either side of her.
"These are my children Sammy and Eileen. The three of us are moving in tomorrow."
Even I, with my fear of children, can't help finding these little kids rather sweet. They look like dolls. Then their charm evaporates, and a bitter fear creeps up from the pit of my stomach to my lungs.
"I'm sorry, I've got something on the hob. It might boil over. I'm Doug. Pleased to meet you. If there's anything I can do to help, don't hesitate to ask. Lovely to meet you, um…"
"Trinh Tuyen. And Sammy and Eileen. Nice to meet you too, Doug."
We shake hands, and I close the front door, feeling rather foolish. I flop down on the sofa, realising they can see in through my kitchen window as they walk past it to their flat. My cooker is in full view of the window, and there isn't a saucepan within two metres of it. I've got to sort this fear of kids out. When I could afford to see a therapist, I was too busy. Now I've got the time, I haven't the money. I've had

to increase my mortgage several times to stay afloat. Now the flat's mortgaged to the max, I'm in arrears with the re-payments, and I can't afford to pay last year's tax bill.

I turn the telly on, and Charlotte's funeral is the main item. Leah's in shot for a good twenty seconds. Des Jensen's lost weight, and doesn't look any older. I think I see a glimpse of Arnold Shanks, but it can't be him unless he's grown a beard. I've heard he's still drinking and taking more coke than ever. Why do the decadent bastards escape the consequences of their behaviour? Colin Holmes has cancelled the Aberdeen date of his tour, so he can help carry her coffin. He was never a good stand-up. He wasn't even a headliner on the comedy circuit, but then a regular part in 'East Street', the nation's favourite soap opera came his way. Now he's famous enough to sell medium sized theatres out.

I'm amazed Charlotte's funeral is considered more important than the recent baby abduction. There's a moving press conference in which the young parents – orthodox Jews from North London – break down whilst pleading for the kidnappers to return little Rebecca. Brian O'Shea pledges a million pounds for information leading to their conviction. At least he can't be accused of publicity seeking – his tour is completely sold out. After the news, 'Rats Milk Cheese' is repeated yet again, so I turn the telly off and do some yoga. I rise above my feelings of jealousy by remembering what Chantelle said. The world of television and fame is transitory, but yoga will connect me to eternal love. I'm moving from a shoulder stand to the child's pose, when I remember the speed pills Leah gave me at the 'Rats Milk Cheese' wrap party. They're still in my desk drawer. I resolve to flush them down the toilet, but think better of it. I'll give them to Neil when he comes on Thursday.

Chapter Fifty-one

The next day I've just left the lift on my way to buy some vegetarian sausages, when I hear a voice calling:
"Hi Doug." I look up to see Sam and Eileen waving from the balcony at the front of our flats. I wave back, and continue past the removal van in a quandary. Trinh Tuyen is supervising the unloading of their furniture. Her face is so bright when she says Hello to me, and she looks so loveable in her jeans and lumberjack shirt, I want to pick her up and hold her close. Her kids are really cute, but I can't suppress the horror of being left alone with them. I feel selfish and stupid, because I walk past without exchanging more than the briefest of pleasantries. The rest of the day, I can't use the kitchen, because I can be seen through the window. Trinh Tuyen is presumably single, as the removal men seem to be the only ones in her life. There's such a vacuum in *my* life, I'm already enamoured with her.

That evening I go to the massage parlour in the Westminster Bridge Road. I can't afford it, but at least it keeps me off drugs and alcohol. I'm walking back to my front door from the lift, when I bump into Trinh Tuyen. She mentions the kids are in bed, and I invite her in for a herbal tea. She has a camomile, and I have peppermint. We talk about paintings and the current exhibition at the Tate Modern. She tells me she works at a private gallery in Cork St, and she's studying part time for an MA in English and French literature. She's entranced by my huge collection of novels, and borrows 'The Collected Journals of Andre Gide.' If she didn't have kids, she'd be the perfect partner for me. She's from Vietnam. I fancy her like mad. There's something about the smooth skin behind her ears, framed by the sleek black hair, which she keeps in a little ponytail. How I yearn to lick every square inch of that light brown body. As soon as she leaves, I masturbate about her, despite having been to the massage parlour.

Neil Gosling turns up at three in the afternoon on Thursday, and almost the first thing he says is:

"Got any drugs?" I give him the speed pills that Leah gave me at the Grange Films party, and warn him how old they are.
"Is there a use by date for sulphate tablets?"
"Yep, and it's today." Says Neil, knocking one down his neck without hesitation. He sparks up a joint, and I have to open a window because I'm not used to the smell. I give him my spare key, and get the bus to Brixton for my twice-weekly fix of yoga. I'm feeling really vulnerable, so it's a relief when the fat black receptionist at the community centre smiles at me as she buzzes me up to the yoga room. There are very few of us in the class today, in fact I'm the only male. Chantelle introduces us to a bit of astanga yoga, and during the relaxation in the child's pose afterwards, I start crying. It's the first time I've cried since I stumbled into Leah's kid at her house in Teddington, before I got fired from 'Rat's Milk Cheese'. I hardly ever cry. I manage to keep it to myself, and by the time we move into a pose where my face can be seen, my tears have dried up.

I don't know what's wrong with me. I've forgotten to turn my phone off before the class, and it rings during the long relaxation at the end. Everyone's very nice about it, but I hate myself for shattering everyone's peace, and want to shoot myself in the head. After the class, I switch my phone back on. The call was from Neil, thanking me for the excellent speed, and the tip about the massage parlour. He had the best wank in his life. I feel sorry for the poor girl who serviced him, because it took an hour for him to come.
"Are you okay, Doug? You look really upset." That's all Chantelle has to say for me to break down in tears in the foyer. In front of the receptionist, Celine, and two other yoga students, one of whom I fancy. I've never been so embarrassed in my life. Chantelle comforts me, and Celine carries my bag. There's a strange heat emanating from the arm Chantelle has around me.
"Don't worry, Doug. Yoga brings a lot of stuff up from your past. It'll be good for you in the long term. We live just around the corner, come and have a cup of tea."
I'm too distraught to resist, and they usher me to their flat in the upper floor of a Victorian terraced house in Kellet Road. It smells of sandalwood, and there are Indian cushions scattered around. I'm handed a Jasmine tea in a bamboo cup, and the more they comfort me, the more I cry. Celine turns the electric light off, which wasn't very

bright anyway, shielded as it was by an Indian cotton lampshade. The plaster cornices flicker in the light of several candles, and I spend a long time in the foetal position being rocked gently by the angelic duo, sobbing so hard my torso convulses.

Afterwards we eat houmous and spinach salad, and drink wheat grass and apple juice. I tell them about my childhood, and my fear of babies and children. They give me more love in three hours than I've had in years. They say I need to heal my inner child, and doing yoga will connect me to him.

It's when I'm standing at their front door that I realise I can hear everything they're saying perfectly, despite the noise from the street. I remark about it, and Chantelle smiles and waves her palm at me. I think she means it's time to say goodbye but she intends it as an explanation of why I can hear better.
"You were too busy crying, but when we were rocking you in the foetal position, I had this hand on your ear. Don't be surprised if your hearing gets worse before it gets better. It's quite natural."

I don't get the bus back to Lambeth Walk. I wander home in a daze. Those women are a gift from heaven. The traffic is so loud in my right ear. I need to get away from the city. If only I had some money. I need to get away from Britain for a while. London makes me feel so tired. When I get home I put the 'Teletubbies' video in the machine. Maybe watching it will help me find my inner child. I fall asleep before I get as far as turning the telly on. I wake up on the sofa drunk from the depth of my sleep. It's midnight, and Neil still hasn't returned from his gig at The Clap Clinic. I stagger to the bathroom, clean my teeth, and go to bed. I've never felt like this in my life. It's like a tight knot in the middle of my chest has been untied. I lie in bed staring into the darkness, and the crying starts again. I don't feel so sad this time. I feel like a weight has been lifted off me. It was so oppressive I was choking, but now my throat is unblocked. I drift into another deep, deep sleep, until the sound of Neil coming in and banging around lifts me out of it. I hear him open my bedroom door and say my name, but I keep my head under the duvet and lie very still. He clanks around the kitchen, goes into the lounge, and turns the television on loud, but it doesn't stop me dropping back into blissful sleep.

At the end of the yoga classes Chantelle and Celine have been plugging a yoga retreat at an organic farm in Holland. I've switched off every time it's been mentioned. It's too expensive, and I need to earn money, not spend it. The information which I've been censoring from my mind re-surfaces during a vivid dream. Since I stopped taking drugs, I've been having - and remembering - the most incredible dreams. The farm is near a small town called Middleburg, on the island of Walcheren in the south west of Holland. In the dream Celine announces the retreat whilst standing on the top of an iceberg. She's wearing white, so it's hard to tell where her clothes end, and the iceberg begins. She's an angel, but she's got four wings, which rotate like the sails of a windmill. She smiles while reciting the details of the retreat. It's a very old, traditional Dutch farm, with a large barn converted into a yoga studio. Some of the accommodation is in an old windmill, and all the food is organic vegetarian. The island is famous for its quaint old villages with beautiful churches, and the yoga farm offers horse riding for a small extra fee.

In the next bit of the dream we're on the farm, and the yoga consists of a huge, graceful dance, in which the horses join in. The horses are all white, with fluttering wings. Then the snow and ice melts, and it's Summer with lush meadows, and the horse's wings turn out to be butterflies, and they take off from the horse's backs, and fly off over the water that surrounds the farm. The huge yoga dance occupies most of the dream, and all the people and horses are ecstatic with pleasure.

I wake up feeling exhilarated, like I've just been on a fairground ride. I look out of my bedroom window and see litter blowing about in the wind, and a man letting his dog shit on the footpath. I resolve to go on that yoga retreat. The money will come to me if I allow magic into my life. I knock on the lounge door, and open it. Neil's crashed out on the sofa, with the telly on. The room's dark and stale, with dope-smoking debris and empty beer cans on the floor.

I phone Chantelle and Celine, to see if there are any places left on the yoga retreat. They're thrilled I want to do it. It should be a really nice journey – I get a ferry from Dover to Ostend, where the yoga farm mini-bus will pick me and the other yoga students up. We drive over the Dutch border to Breskens on the bank of the river Schelde. From there a twenty-minute ferry ride takes us to Vlissingen, on the island of Walcheren. The farm is a few minutes drive beyond. I'm about to end the call, when I have an afterthought.

"Oh, Celine. Are there any children at the farm?"

"The people who own it have three young children, yes." She knows what I'm thinking, and adds,

"Don't worry about the children, Doug. Chantelle and I will be there to help you. In fact we were thinking about inviting you to help us with our kid's yoga class tomorrow morning."

"You teach yoga to kids?"

"Every Saturday morning in the same place you come. It appeals to a lot of middle class parents. I overheard one of them say "yoga is the new ballet.""

"Thanks, Celine. I'll have a think about it."

Neil doesn't wake up until five in the afternoon. I make him a coffee, and all he can talk about is the massage he had yesterday.

"I'm telling you, Doug. This girl was dynamite! She had the most incredible hand relief skills. She sprinkles oil on your knob and everything. I'm going back as soon as I've had breakfast. I'm going for the intercourse with fellatio option. Fancy a line of coke?"

"Please don't offer it to me, Neil. I'm leaving for Holland on Sunday. For a three day yoga retreat."

"Blimey Doug. You don't half swing from one extreme to the other."

I cook eggs, mushrooms, and vegetarian sausages whilst Neil has a shower and gets dressed. He's excited about going to the massage parlour in Westminster Bridge Road. It's only five minutes walk away, and as it's near the tube station, he can go straight to The Clap Clinic afterwards. We're sitting at the kitchen table whilst Neil smokes his post-breakfast joint and goes on yet again about the girl he's going to be massaged by, when Trinh Tuyen walks past the window, and there's a ring on the doorbell.

I open it and invite her in, but she declines. Her washing machine plug has fused, do I have any spare 13 amp fuses? I keep spare fuses in an

331

old cough sweets tin in the kitchen table drawer. I give her two, and she thanks me warmly.

"I'm sorry if I seem a bit preoccupied, but my Mother's been taken to hospital, and I have to go and visit her in Watford. It's not easy with the kids." I close the door, and go back into the kitchen. Neil's leaning back in his chair, looking rather strange.

"So do you fancy a wander by the river, Doug?"

"I thought you were off to the massage parlour." Neil exhales a lungful of marijuana smoke and shakes his head.

"I'm not going."

"Why not?"

"Because the girl I want to see isn't on duty."

"Did you just phone?"

"No. I just saw her walk past your kitchen window. That's the Chink whore I've been raving about."

"Please Neil. She's Vietnamese."

Chapter Fifty-two

When Neil goes off to do his gig at The Clap Clinic, he doesn't invite me, and I don't suggest going. I've never been there since I was ejected from the 'Rat's Milk Cheese' wrap party. I've always assumed that if I tried to go in, they wouldn't let me past the door. I'm a renegade from Arnold's ever-expanding empire. I once bumped into Charlotte, before she got her own TV show, and asked her if she could make some discreet enquiries as to my position with Arnold. I didn't hear back from her, and when I rang her she was very coy about what he'd said. In the end I managed to persuade her to tell me his response. It was "The day I see you again is the day you die." The same as what he put in the note to me, after the night when I accidentally came on his face. So no change there.

I clear the lounge up, and look at the yoga farm's website. I didn't realise rural Holland was so lovely. The site of that delightful Dutch architecture confirms my resolve to go. I book my ticket online, and watch the 'Teletubbies' video. I like the visual quality a lot. When it's over I do an hour of yoga to dissolve the yearning for a pint of Guinness and a smoke of the skunk that Neil's left on top of his suitcase. I feel so much better after doing the yoga. The feeling of calm it brings is much clearer than the relaxation derived from drugs and alcohol. That's more of a fog that dulls the senses. The deep breathing from yoga takes me to a clearer, more vivid place. The only problem is I can't get the picture of Trinh Tuyen masturbating Neil out of my head. I've put her on a pedestal as a higher being I have to strive for, and the illusion's been shattered by the fact that she's the whore whose two handed wanking technique Neil's been describing so lucidly. What bothers me even more, is the urge to go to the massage parlour whilst she's on duty, and pay her to do the same for me. I'm still infatuated with her, though. It doesn't bother me that she's a prostitute. If she was my girlfriend, I'd know she could afford to pay her way.

Neil watched some of my porn videos last night. Whilst I'm tidying them up I pop '101 Cumshots - Teen Special' in and give it a look. I must have changed recently, because all I feel is sympathy for the performers. I've left this behind. I decide to give it to Neil, and ring Chantelle and Celine. They're out, so I leave a message saying I'll be at the yoga class in the morning. Neil doesn't get back until after I've gone to bed, and from the noise he makes, he's pissed again.

I'm so scared when I see the kids and their parents at the community centre, I nearly turn on my heel and walk away. Chantelle spots me, though, and calls me over. They start the class painting cat or dog faces on the kids' faces with face paint. Most of the class is taken up with circle games, and other ways of containing their energy. I'm introduced to them whilst we're all sitting cross-legged in a circle, and I'm amazed how readily I'm accepted. One little boy attaches himself to me, with no inhibitions. I'm really worried about physical contact, because these days all you have to do is smile at a kid and the parents will think you're trying to fuck them. Celine has a discreet word in my ear, and tells me the little boy's mother died recently, and it's okay to cuddle him. The poor little urchin's desperate for affection, and when I hold him I keep him high up my chest so he's well away from my genital area. I don't want anyone thinking I'm a pervert. After a while I hand him over to Chantelle, to make it clear I'm not there for the wrong reasons. The little boy holds his arms out to me, and looks into my eyes.
"Will you be my Daddy?"
"I can't be your Daddy. Your Daddy's your Da..." Celine gives me a sign to stop, and after the class they tell me he never knew his father. He's been in a care home since his Mother died. I nearly break down and cry again.

Neil's still asleep when I get home. I feel awful not having a gig on a Saturday night, so I ring a small independent venue and ask if I can try some new material out. They say they don't have any spare stage time. Christ – I can't even give it away. I phone Gerry Crook and ask if I can do ten minutes at his gig in Soho, and he agrees to me doing five. It's embarrassing because it looks like I'm trying to get back in his favour so he'll start booking me again. Still, I don't care. I've got no ego left. I lie on my futon, daydreaming about selling the flat and going to India to learn to be a yoga teacher. I've got to find some way of earning a living, because my stand-up career seems to be over.

When Neil surfaces he announces he won't be staying at my place tonight. He's a bit coy about why not, but in the end he admits it's because Brian O'Shea dropped into the Clap Clinic last night after his show at the Oxford Apollo. He's having a party at his house in South Kensington, and invited Neil to stay the night.
"I can't turn an invitation like that down. He's in Hollywood most of the time these days. The more time I spend in his company, the more chance there is of being offered a part in his next film. Why don't you come along too?" He adds as an afterthought. I can see by his expression that he doesn't mean it. I don't blame him, either. It wouldn't be good for him socially or professionally to arrive with a pariah.
"I'd love to come, but I've got to set off for Holland in the morning."
Neil does a poor job of concealing his relief. He thanks me for my hospitality, and says his goodbyes.
"You're off early."
"I wasn't going to tell you, but I can't resist that Gook bitch at the massage parlour. I phoned and booked an appointment for an hour. By the way, Doug. I've got you back for what you did to my black silk sheets."
I look around the sofa. I can't see anything untoward, apart from an overflowing ashtray, more empty beer cans, and a mirror with remains of coke smeared on it.
"Yeah? What have you done?"
"You'll find out. But I've got you good and proper."
I give him '101 Cumshots - Teen Special', but he doesn't want it.
"'s all right, Doug. When it comes to porn, I'm more into anal. Anyway, I'm travelling light." I stand on the balcony and watch him walk out of Lambeth Walk into Lambeth Road. Poor Trinh Tuyen. Neil didn't have a shower after he got up, so she's going to have his stale body thrashing around on top of her. I saw her leave her flat earlier with the kids. I suppose she drops them off at a crèche. I tidy up after Neil, and spend several minutes looking for whatever he's done to get his revenge on me. Nothing's damp, there's no stain or bad smell. The telly works okay. Mm, I wonder what he's done. I pack my bag ready for the yoga retreat, and spend the afternoon

335

fighting the urge to go to the massage parlour for Trinh Tuyen's two-handed wanking technique.

Gerry isn't at his gig in Soho. The pub's been refurbished since I was last here, and the function room's twice the size of what it used to be. Macclesfield St has changed a lot too. There are fewer restaurants, and more bars. Every one of them has two burly bouncers on the door. They're reluctant to let me in because apparently my shoes aren't smart enough. At least I don't look like I'm going to punch anybody who makes eye contact with me, which is what most of the other men they're letting in look like. It seems the only bit of the pub that hasn't been refurbished is the dressing room. Gerry's nephew is running the show, and he introduces me to Bobby Bum. He's Canadian, and very fat.
"Hi Man. Someone told me you were Boris the Blue Dog?"
"That's right. I still appear in every show. I'm in the front and end titles, and quite a few of the generic shots that crop up in all the programmes."
"Boy you must be on a good crack for that! What are you doing playing a shit little place like this?"
I explain as briefly as possible that I don't get any repeat fees.
"That's criminal, Man. You're a living legend. 'Rats Milk Cheese' got me into comedy."
"It got me *out* of comedy."
"How come, Man? Boris the Blue Dog is the funniest thing in the show."
Luckily another act arrives, and distracts Bobby by selling him some ketamine. I've never seen Bobby Bum before, but I've seen all his material done by at least one other comic. He doesn't have an original line in his act, but that doesn't prevent the crowd from howling with laughter.

I'm on after the interval, and when I walk on something inside my head decides not to do the prepared opening line, but start talking to the audience instead. I ask a woman in the front row where she's from, and she answers
"The Isle of Wight."
"A lovely island just off the English coast. Although in my opinion, it should belong to Argentina." This gets a laugh from those who

remember the Falklands War, but sadly most of the audience don't understand what I'm referring to. Also, the PA hasn't been set up properly, and a burst of feedback killed the punch line for a lot of the audience. I can see why so many comics are covering the same base subject matter – most of the audience is ignorant, and only understands the most popular references. I think on my feet, and cut a lot of the material I was going to do. After ten minutes, I thank them for their time, and leave the stage. There's a resounding shout of `
"More. More" from the audience, and the compere puts me back on. I do another five, and leave to yet more demands for an encore despite some terrible screeching from the PA, but the compere sensibly puts the next act on.
"Doug. You said you were trying out new material, but you spent most of the time ad libbing." Says Gerry Crook's nephew, who's managing the show.
"Yeah, I decided they wouldn't understand the references in my material, so I gave them what they wanted."
"A word of advice. Don't underestimate the intelligence of the audience." With that, he goes back into the room to attend to the PA. He probably isn't twenty yet, and he's telling me how to do comedy. I'm tempted to ask how many gigs he's done, and advise him to let the comics do their job, and sort the PA out, which is his job. There isn't any point, though. I haven't got a job. I was doing it for free. I go home feeling sad. I've just proved to myself that I can still entertain an audience, it's the people who control access to that audience who I have a problem with. I go to bed early, because I plan to get to Dover well before my ferry leaves. I want to get away from London as soon as I can. I used to love living here, but now I want to be somewhere quiet. As I lay in bed, I realise what I'm thinking. London's too noisy! I didn't have one problem hearing the audience tonight, when I asked them questions on stage. I can hear better with my right ear! I'd phone Chantelle and Celine right now, but they went to Holland straight after their kid's yoga class.

I wake up early on the Sunday morning. I'm about to leave for Dover, when the door bell rings. Trinh Tuyen's standing there wearing motorcycle leathers, and holding a crash helmet.
"I'm sorry to bother you early on a Sunday morning, Doug. I've just had a call from the hospital, and my Mother's expected to die any

minute. I've got to go straight away, and the babysitter's late. Would you mind looking after Sammy and Eileen until she gets here?" I can't refuse. Trinh Tuyen ushers a bemused pair of kids into my flat, assures me the babysitter will ring my bell as soon as she arrives, and rushes off. We stand on the balcony and watch a 500cc Japanese motorbike disappear round the corner. So that motorbike I've seen parked here recently is Trinh Tuyen's. She's a mysterious woman. I turn to the kids.

"Have you had breakfast?" They both nod. They look cold.

"Would you like to come inside and watch telly?" They look shell-shocked, and I remember how I felt when I was their age. In the absence of an answer, I lead them in to the lounge, and sit them on the sofa. I put the kids channel on, and go to the kitchen to get them each a glass of apple juice. It occurs to me that I don't feel anything but affection for them. I'm cured of my fear of children! The kids channel is showing an annoying cartoon, so I ask them if they'd like to watch the 'Teletubbies' video. Their little faces light up, and I put it in the machine, and press play. The phone rings, and when I answer it, I hear Alison's voice! We haven't spoken for years, so I take the phone into the bedroom. She's phoned me on impulse. She gave up being a flight attendant and trained as a schoolteacher. She's living in Brighton, and when I ask how her boyfriend is, there's a pause.

"He decided he's gay after all. I suppose it was bound to happen, moving to Brighton."

"Do you live in the gay district, then?"

"I inherited some money and bought a seafront flat in Kemp Town. That's the gayest part. You should come down some time and see it. I'm looking out of my bedroom window now, and the sea and sky are bright blue."

"Yes, I'd like to come down and see you some time." I remember Sam and Eileen, and wander back towards the lounge. I look through the door, and see them perched on the sofa. They look entranced by the video. So it's true about those 'Teletubbies'. Children *do* love them.

"I'm really sorry about what I did to you, Doug. You were a lovely boyfriend, and you didn't deserve the treatment you got." I wander back into the bedroom.

"I forgive you, Alison." We talk for a while longer, and I proudly tell her I've got the neighbour's kids in my lounge, watching my telly. I'm about to explain how yoga has got me away from drugs, when Eileen

and Sam run into the hall. My doorbell's been rung, but I didn't hear it because the phone's pressed against my good ear. I open the door to see the girl who gave me a hand job at the massage parlour last week. The kids cuddle her legs for reassurance. They're in such a vulnerable state, they need someone they're familiar with. I tell Alison I'll ring her later, and invite the babysitter in. I remember she's called Sonia.
"Sonia's my professional name. I'm really Catherine." I shake the hand that gave me such delight last time it touched me. When I explain I've got a ferry to catch, she whisks the children away, so I can make a second attempt at my departure. The kids stopped the video, and the telly's showing the bad cartoon again, so I rewind the 'Teletubbies' and eject the tape. As I put the tape into its box, I remember there are going to be children at the yoga farm, so I pop it into my rucksack. A few minutes later I'm walking along Hercules Road on the way to Waterloo East, and feeling happier than I've felt for years. Alison wants me to visit her in Brighton! It's sunny there, and it's sunny here. I'm looking forward to the voyage on the ferry. I adjust the way my rucksack hangs on my shoulder as I cross Westminster Bridge Road and look at the massage parlour. I wonder who's on duty today.

It's not just London I'll be glad to get away from. In true British style, the train to Dover is late. Thank goodness I allowed lots of time to make the ferry. It's a bright cold day at sea, and I sit on deck dividing my attention between passing ships, and 'On The Road' by Jack Kerouac. I first read it when I was thirteen, and I'm reading it again to get into the travelling spirit. I try to ring Alison, but get her answer machine.

In the queue for Passport Control I spot a woman in her late thirties, who I walked past on the train. She's got a face that's so soulful I want to take her in my arms and cuddle her. I feel like I've known her for years. I hope she's on her way to the same yoga retreat I'm going to. Just by looking at her I know she's single. I can imagine her flat, and the things she has in her bathroom. The various womanly lotions, tweezers, and shampoos. I can see her bedside table, and the little pile of books she's reading. The alarm clock that wakes her up for work on dark Winter mornings. I feel her loneliness. The doubts and insecurities of still being single when her younger sister is married and

expecting her second child. I mentally fashion a big bubble of love and kindness, and drop it down on her. As soon as I've enveloped her in the bubble of love, she looks at me. I smile at her, and realise she's trying to draw my attention to something behind me.
"Passport, please Sir." A Belgian official is helping to reduce the queue by going along it checking passports. As he was on my right side, I didn't hear him. Chantelle was right, my ear is getting worse before it gets better. It's ability to hear seems to fluctuate.

The girl I adored in the queue is coming to the yoga retreat! Her name is Caroline, and she sits near me on the minibus. She lives in Clapham, and works in the head office of a major charity. There are five of us going to the yoga retreat from the ferry. The other male is a shaven-headed white Brixton trendy. He's got a goatee beard, and a pierced ear. I've seen him at a couple of Chantelle's classes. The flat landscape looks so well-manicured as we drive towards Holland. I love the small bricks they use in the Flemish houses, and the soft rhythm of the Dutch language our hosts speak to each other in.
"Does anybody like riding horses?" asks Dirk, the huge Dutch man who owns the farm. In the absence of a decisive answer form the other passengers, I say I haven't done it for years, but am keen to try. After the ferry ride across the river Schelde it comes out in conversation that I used to be Boris The Blue Dog in 'Rats Milk Cheese'. Caroline's face brightens.
"Oh I *love* that programme. I've got them all on DVD."
Before I can answer, Dirk the giant owner of the yoga centre exclaims from behind the steering wheel.
"Oh my God I don't believe it!" He turns round to address me. He reminds me of a young Arnold Schwarzenegger, but with a round, farmer's face.
"You're Boris the Blue Dog? Marie and I named our dog after you. And our Rabbit as well. We're crazy about 'Rats Milk Cheese'. And that title sequence at the end. Whoever thought of that is a genius."
He nearly loses control of the minibus, and turns back to face the vehicles approaching from the opposite direction. He continues, but this time watching where he's driving.
"I mean it. We call our dog Boris One, and our rabbit Boris Two. I wanted to name our son Boris Three, but Marie insisted on Franz."

"Tell me." Says Caroline, putting her hand on my forearm, and batting her eyelashes.
"Was it hot in the costume?"

Chapter Fifty-three

If the yoga in Brixton shifted a block deep inside me, three days of intensive study in rustic surroundings creates a quantum leap. I share a room in the windmill with Richard, the bald Brixton trendy. At first I didn't feel an affinity with him, but as the yoga retreat progresses, we hit it off. He was invalided out of the Metropolitan Police after taking a .22 air rifle pellet in the neck. They thought he'd be a quadriplegic, but thanks to the skill of the staff at Kings College Hospital, and a lot of will power on his part, he can move. We go to bed quite early, and during the few minutes before sleep engulfs us, swap stories about our sexual exploits. I've got more to tell than he has.

Alison doesn't return my calls, and a cold wind from Russia brings incessant rain during the first two days of the retreat. This makes the ancient Dutch farm buildings all the more cozy. We do three one and a half hour sessions of yoga each day, warmed by a roaring log fire in a huge fireplace. The food is a fusion of traditional Dutch – my favourite is croquet potatoes containing cheese – and rice and vegetables cooked South Indian style. After dinner in the evenings, we gather round the fire, and Dirk sings Dutch folk songs accompanied by his wife Marie on the zither. Chantelle plays the guitar, and sings the songs of Jacques Brel.

Caroline and I sit stroking and petting Boris One, a formidable Rhodesian Ridgeback, who's a convenient catalyst through which we can express the affection we're too shy to declare. He willingly absorbs all the fuss and love we really mean for each other. I feel like an inexperienced fourteen-year old who can't pluck up courage to ask a girl to the cinema. On the last night the kids' pet rabbit Boris Two joins us, and we all marvel how Boris One lets him nibble his nose on the huge fake fur hearthrug, in front of the two hundred-year old inglenook fireplace. Home distilled Dutch gin flows freely, but not past my newly awakened throat chakra. Boris One lies on his back with his paws in the air, and Caroline and I marvel at the size and sharpness of his teeth. After three days of petting him, I trust him enough to put my hand in his mouth. Those powerful jaws could effortlessly snap through my wrist. As we stroke him in the firelight, our hands meet in the meadow of his chest fur. Caroline's eyes look longingly into mine, and she squeezes my hand. Our silent, romantic moment is broken by Dirk announcing he's going to dye Boris One blue. He's drunk, and actually produces a bottle of blue dye. The others persuade him his fellow farmers would laugh at him whilst out shooting duck, and Caroline and I spirit Boris One outside for a late night walk.

The rain has finally stopped, and we gaze at the stars, making small talk to cover the fact that we're both too shy to make the first move.
"It's a bit incongruous that a man who runs a yoga retreat shoots duck."
"He's a farmer first. The yoga's just a way of making the farm more profitable."
This is the moment when I should take her in my arms, but I feel so nervous! I haven't had an orgasm since I masturbated about Trinh Tuyen a week ago, and I'm desperate for sex. Yet I can't pluck up courage to kiss Caroline. Boris One saves me from my indecision by bounding up to us with a bit of tree branch in his mouth. I toss the branch into the darkness, and he leaps after it. There's a loud splash. He's jumped into one of the drainage ditches, and Caroline laughs. Our eyes have adjusted to the moonless night, and we stand amazed by how fast Boris One can swim. If only I had the confidence to seize the opportunity, and kiss her. I fall back on my ability with words.
"He's such a strong swimmer, Dirk could rent him out as a tug, pulling barges along the canal." Boris One's powerful legs pull him onto the bank, and he drops the tree branch at our feet. He shakes himself dry, spraying us with ditch water. I instinctively shield her with my body, and she pulls me towards her. I taste Dutch gin as our tongues dance together. I've been feeling so much better without alcohol in my life, but the taste of it makes me want a drink right now. My hands explore her back, instinctively homing in on her bottom. After a long, languid kiss, we break off. She whispers something in my ear.
"Pardon?"
Realising her mistake, she puts her lips to my left ear.
"I thought you were never going to kiss me."

343

"I thought I was never going to kiss you either. I haven't felt this shy since I was a teenager."

"We'd better go in." We kiss once more, and some of the old confidence seeps back. I attempt a feel of the small titties I've been admiring through Lycra singlets by day, and lambs wool jumpers by evening. She deflects my hand, so I cuddle her again, pressing my desperate cock against her midriff. She wiggles against it slightly, but sadly she's not as pissed as I thought.

"Naughty." She smiles, and we hold hands as we walk back to the cozy glow coming through the French windows.

"I've got an itch." I say, the immense beast trotting at our heals.

"Where?"

"Here." I say, and playfully pull her hand and hold it against my erection.

"Douglas Tucker!" She exclaims with mock outrage.

"I want a child."

"I beg your pardon?"

"With you, Caroline. I want to have children."

"You work fast. A few minutes ago you were too shy to kiss me. Now you want me to have your baby."

"It would save the cost of a condom."

"Don't worry about that. I've got condoms." I stop us in our tracks, startling Boris One so he drops his bit of tree.

"Don't get your hopes up. They're in the drawer of my kitchen table in London." We've nearly arrived at the French windows.

"The kitchen table drawer eh? So you do it on the kitchen table." She gives my bottom a playful smack, and my eyes a mischievous look.

"Might do…"

"I hope it's a sturdy table. Or you'd better fit reinforcing struts." She feigns shock, and disappears through the gap in the French windows. Boris One tries to follow her, but can't get through with a two metres long tree branch in his jaws. I'm about to get him to drop it, when there's a snapping sound. He's bitten through a four centimetre thick piece of elder branch. I wonder if he's part dog, part crocodile, and watch him negotiate his way through the French window with the shortened stick in his mouth. After a quick look at the stars, and a savouring of the cold rustic air I follow Boris One inside and re-join the party. The decanter of homemade gin is going round again, but I opt for camomile tea.

On the Thursday morning the sky is bright blue, and I'm the only person who hasn't got a hangover. As the mini bus doesn't leave for Ostend until one in the afternoon, Marie offers to take some of us horse riding. It was supposed to cost extra, but our group has gelled so well, Dirk announces there will be no charge. There aren't enough horses for everyone, so Caroline and I volunteer to stay behind. Dirk and Marie's youngest child misses Marie and starts crying. The 'Teletubbies' video is fresh in my mind, because I saw it in my bag whilst packing. I produce it and Dirk puts it in their video machine. They've got a huge wide screen television, and we're just sitting down to watch it with their two kids, when a helicopter flies low over the fields. We rush into the farmyard to watch it, and whilst we're outside, Boris One appears with half of Boris Two dangling from his jaws. None of the kids notice, and Caroline pushes them in through the sliding French windows, before helping Dirk and me to make Boris One drop Boris Two's remains. We hide them in a stable, and Dirk gives Boris One a severe telling off before locking him in the back of the jeep.

"How am I going to tell them? They love that rabbit." We return to the kids. As we approach the French windows, instead of the sweet sound of 'Teletubbies" voices, we hear grunting. We reach the room in time to see two large penises ejaculating on a teenaged girl's face. The kids are sitting on the floor in front of the huge screen, their mouths hanging open. The little girl starts to cry, and Caroline cries out with shock and runs to the machine to stop the tape. The remote control is closer, but in her haste she runs to the source of the offence. I'm horrified, and from the way Dirk stands frozen to the spot, assume he's berating himself for leaving a porn tape where his children could find it. I'm torn between consoling him, and trying to distract his children, but all I can think of is the coincidence that he should also possess '101 Cumshots - Teen Special'.

"Doug! How could you?" Caroline confronts me with the tape she's just ejected. It's the 'Teletubbies' video. Or that's what the label says. Neil Gosling was right when he said "I've got you good and proper." No wonder he refused my offer to give him '101 Cumshots - Teen Special'. He knew it was really the 'Teletubbies' video. That was how he got his revenge on me for messing his black silk sheets up. He swapped the labels round. Thanks Neil. Bloody hilarious!

Caroline's trembling with rage, tears of anger flowing down her reddened cheeks. Her mute ferocity strikes me in the guts like an icicle, and twists her face into ugliness.

"My children. You've ruined their lives!" Dirk's voice booms from his six foot six frame. I turn to face him, but don't have time to start the case for my defence. He's launched himself at my throat, his huge Dutch face contorted with hate. His co-ordination is dulled by his hangover, and with my clear, intoxicant-free mind, I instinctively drop down so I'm squatting on my haunches. He lunges over me onto a rough wooden coffee table, landing on three bone china mugs, and a cafetiere full of hot coffee. He's still rolling onto the floor with bloodstains on the front of his chinos when I run into a closed French window, which I thought was open. There's a huge bang, and the impact knocks me out for a moment. I come to and scramble to my feet.

Dirk stands up. By the time I slip through the open part of the French window I realise he's gained so much on me he'll catch me before I'm ten feet across the farmyard. I slide the door shut, and he runs into it even faster than I did. That takes care of him long enough for me to get to the jeep. Luckily the keys are in the ignition, and Boris One is the other side of the steel barred dog grille.

Dirk has got to his feet, and shouts "Kill kill" in Dutch. Boris has been stroked, hugged, even given biscuits illegally by me for the last three days. When his master gives him the command to kill, all my caresses are forgotten. He lurches at the dog grille like a battering ram, and if he knocks it down, I'll be ripped to pieces.

"Good boy." I say, and turn the key that fires up the four-litre turbo Diesel. Dirk's got the axe from the firewood stack, and he's coming towards us like a demented Viking. I have no choice but to steal his dog and his Toyota. There's only one direction to go, and that's along the single track that serves as the farm's drive. The axe smashes through the passenger window, making Boris One bark more furiously. I accelerate, swearing aloud at Neil Gosling for doing such a stupid thing to my video tapes. Okay it was silly of me to squirt toothpaste, shampoo, and hair conditioner into his bed. But disguising hard-core porn as a video for very young children is unforgivable! He must have seen the potential for mistakes. The trouble is, he didn't, because he was stoned and pissed and probably out of it on Leah's slimming pills as well. He probably sees a 'Teletubbies' video as something students watch when they're tripping, and doesn't associate it with innocent young children.

Dirk's giving chase in the minibus, and is catching up with me, so I speed up. I scream around a corner, which is blind because of a stand of tall poplar trees and a storage barn. Chantelle, Celine, Dirk's wife Marie, and the three other yoga students are riding towards me along the track. Chantelle's horse rears up, and throws her. I swerve into the field, missing her and the other horses. Regaining control of the jeep, I look in the rear view mirror. I don't know whether it's because Dirk is so hung over his reactions are slower, or because the minibus doesn't handle as well as the jeep, but he drives straight into a horse and rider. I don't see who he hit, but the chase is over. I stop the jeep and turn back. If the minibus is too badly damaged to drive, we'll need the jeep to take the injured to hospital. Boris is still going mental in the back. Chantelle has survived being thrown from the horse, because she's run to where Dirk's wife Marie lies on the track beneath her horse.

I screech to a halt, open the door, and approach the scene of the disaster. The horse's hind leg, and Marie's head are both at grotesque angles to their respective bodies. Dirk kneels down beside Marie, closes her eyes, throws back his head and wails like a lovesick bear. The horse on top of Marie is squealing in pain, and Boris One's relentless barking is interrupted by his repeatedly head butting the rear screen. Dirk's head jolts forward, and his face turns in my direction. "You! You!" Dirk is half shouting, half whimpering as he steps towards me. The look in his eyes stops me dead in my tracks, and I realise he's going to kill me. For the second time, he chases me towards the Toyota, but I'm much closer to it than before, and as I didn't kill the engine, roar off. At least Dirk can't chase me this time, because the collision with the horse has wrecked the minibus. Boris One's barking suddenly gets loud. I look round to see he's knocked the steel grille slightly out of place, and is struggling to get to me. The track is completely straight, and the flatness of the land reveals that it's empty. In the distance, I can see a barge the size of a small ship creeping through the fields. There must be a wide canal there, so I accelerate to eighty miles an hour and hold on. A minute later I start to slow down, because the canal looks wider and deeper this close. There's a small dyke with a gentle incline leading up to the bank. I turn the corner, and follow the road running parallel with the canal. If I can get a bit further from Dirk, I can abandon the jeep with Boris One inside, and consider my options.

Suddenly Boris One smashes the dog grille off its brackets. I swerve up the dyke, which I hit at about forty miles an hour. The jeep flies through the air, the weight of the engine bringing the nose down.

Luckily we hit the water before it's down too far, and before Boris One's teeth rip my flesh. I'm wearing a seat belt, and survive the impact better than Boris One, who's thrown against the dashboard. I press the button of the electric window. Nothing happens, and I force the door open before the water pressure is too great. The hole in the passenger door window caused by the axe Dirk threw at it allows water to flood the jeep, alleviating the pressure. Boris is too busy trying to escape through the hole in the passenger door window to kill me.

I swim towards the bank, but Boris One starts barking again, his voice hoarse from the barking he's already done, and the canal water in his throat. He's chasing me, and if it weren't for the fact that he has to swim round the jeep that wallows just beneath the surface, he'd have caught me. I'm so desperate to get to the bank, my swimming strokes are ineffectual. He's going to catch me before I reach the bank, and I start to panic. There's nothing but fields either side of the canal, and no people in sight. As the furious hound closes on me, I take a deep breath, dive, and swim under water until my lungs are bursting. Luckily all the yogic breathing has increased my lung capacity. I surface, and realise I got disorientated and swam away from the bank. Boris One spots me, changes direction, and barks with renewed vigour. I'm now exhausted and out of breath and as his barking gets louder, it dawns on me that even if I could get to the bank before Boris One, it would achieve nothing. He'd find it easier to kill me on dry land, than in the water. I try to remove Mummy's knife from my jeans, but the wetness has made them too tight, and before my fingers have delved far enough into the pocket, his front paws strike me. I dive down and grab his scrotum, twisting and squeezing it as hard as I can. Then I get hold of a back leg, and try to pull him down so his head is under water. His huge body is too buoyant for me, and I swim as far away as possible from him before desperation for air forces me to surface. After several gasps, I turn to check his position, only to see him swimming towards me with renewed fury. I'm so tired I'm low in the water, unable to do more than gaze at the fangs that will tear my face off. I'm moaning from self-pity and fear, when there's a crack and Boris One's head explodes.

Chapter Fifty-four

Blood spurts out of his neck briefly, before the canal encloses it, and his body turns over to float on its side. I turn round to see the varnished wooden bows of a motor yacht loom above me, and the sound of Diesel engines being thrown into reverse. A life buoy splashes next to my head, and I grab it with my last bit of strength. I realise somebody else has taken responsibility for my life, and slip out of consciousness.

There's a blur in which I swallow cold water, and cough a lot. Water gives way to hardness, and I vomit, retch, cough more, and feel pressing on my chest. There are voices, and I assume I'm dead, because they know my name. I come round slightly, shivering violently, and get disorientated when down becomes up, and up becomes down. Warm sheets and Caroline comfort me. Then Alison offers me a hot toddy, before mutating into Tom. Tom, the actor who got his only arm hacked off by the sword. The man without whom I'd never have been offered the part of Boris. He must be dead too, because he's got both arms. I try to go back into the swirling mists of the unconscious, but Tom and the steaming mug won't go away. I come round with a start, and something bangs my head.
"Careful Mate. Mind the deck head." I lower my head back onto the softness.
"Here you are. Try this." I slurp from a mug of hot tea, which tastes and smells of brandy. It's sweet, and I gulp it down.
"There you go. I thought you'd like that." The mug falls onto the floor, because my hand is shaking, and his hand is made of plastic.
"Steady. Do you want some more?"
"Mm." I close my eyes and relax. I've got a raging thirst, and the few gulps of hot toddy were a tantalising insight into how it would feel if it was quenched. There's more clattering around, and something metallic getting dropped. A warm glow inflates my chest. I drift off again, only to be awakened by the same plastic hand holding the same mug. It's a

Cornish style blue and white striped mug, and its familiarity makes me feel secure. I sit up more cautiously, remembering the bump on my head, and swallow gulp after gulp of the bittersweet draft. There are voices, and when I open my eyes, there's a bearded face bending over me, which I immediately recognise, despite never having seen that face with a beard. The accent is Glaswegian, and it's hard to believe I haven't heard it for so many years.
"Well of all the boats in all the world he could have driven a Toyota in front of, he had to drive one in front of mine!"
"Arnold!"
"That's right, Dougie. It's your old pal Arnold. I promised the next day I saw you, would be the day I killed you. And instead, I saved your life. It looked like that doggie friend of yours was a wee bit cross. You didn't go ejaculating on *his* face too, did you?"
The image of '101 Cumshots – Teen Special' on Dirk's TV comes to my mind.
"Not exactly, no."
Arnold laughs.
"Not exactly? Oh, Doug. I'd forgotten how funny you are."
"Where's the toilet?"
"You should know, Laddie. You're on Sunita." I look around, and recognise the white painted wooden interior of Arnold's classic Dunkerque veteran. When I try to climb out of the bunk, I collapse naked onto the floor. I'm not sure whether it's because the hot toddies have made me drunk, or because I'm still weak from my ordeal. Tom does his best to help me towards the toilet with his artificial arms. Sunita is motoring along the canal, and I see a sea-going barge through the brass porthole of the toilet. The larger vessel's wash rocks Sunita, and I steady myself with one hand, holding my penis in the other. I've broken my 'no alcohol' rule. I'd feel self-rebuke, but I'm too inebriated. And anyway, I was still half-asleep when I received the brandy-tea from Tom's plastic hand. I shake the drips from my semi-erect penis, and wait for it to go flaccid by looking at the flat Dutch landscape pass by. Arnold's warm laughter floats from the saloon, and I hope he's forgiven me for coming on his face. I feel warm despite being naked, and I can't get my penis to go soft. Maybe it's because I've just woken up, and it thinks as it's the morning, its job is to be stiff. I go back into the saloon, the wooden deck warm on the souls of

my naked feet. Tom and Arnold sit around the dinette table, and a girl with yellow hair stands at the gas cooker. She looks at me, and smiles. "You might be needing those." Says Arnold, pointing to a pile of clothes on the pilot berth where I slept so deeply.
"Feel free to have a shower. There's lots of hot water." He adds. The pretty girl speaks in a Dutch accent.
"We have towels in this locker. I'm Katinka, by the way." This must have been the girl I thought was Caroline during my delirium. I go to the wooden locker Katinka gestured towards, and remove a towel more to cover my semi-erect penis than because I want a shower.
"Hello Katinka. Nice to meet you."
"Perhaps you should have a cold shower, Douglas. I see your John Thomas is as keen as ever." Arnold's eyes shine brighter and bluer than I remember them. Maybe the beard shows them off more. His scruffy white polo-necked jumper, and the brass portholes in the background make him look like a nautical Rasputin. Or Captain Haddock from 'Tintin'.
"You look like Captain Haddock out of 'Tintin', Arnold." I say as I cover my penis with the towel. Katinka wears the waistband of her jeans so low, I can see the top of her knickers, and the view does nothing to alleviate my semi-erection.
"Captain Haddock wore a blue jumper, and mine is white. You're not so far off the truth, though. We're close to Belgium, and Tintin was Belgian." I remember the ubiquitous billboard posters advertising 'The Girl From The Village'. All over the world Arnold's name is on them, crediting him as executive producer. I'd pictured him wearing a suit, sitting behind a desk in Los Angeles. Yet here he is in tatty jeans, and a jumper with frayed cuffs and a hole in one of the elbows. His beard is unkempt, and I notice for the first time that his hair is shaggy and long. He licks a king size cigarette paper, and asks Katinka to tear a bit of cardboard off the box of teabags so he can use it as roach material.
"Mind you." Says Tom. "I think Captain Haddock was English."
"Be careful, Laddie. Just because you've got no arms doesn't mean you can't be keel-hauled." Katinka pretends to yawn.
"What's that Arnold? Are you Scottish and proud of it?" She must be sleeping with him to get away with being that familiar. Of course she's sleeping with him! How could a pretty young girl like that be aboard Sunita and *not* be sleeping with him? Just in case she's overstepped the mark, I change the subject.

"You look more like a hippy than a multi-millionaire film producer."
"Make your mind up, Doug. I can't be Captain Haddock *and* a hippy." He meticulously fits the cardboard roach, and puts the completed joint in Tom's mouth.
"When you're a multi-millionaire film *and television* producer, you can look however you like." He produces a gold Calibri lighter and ignites Tom's joint. Tom thanks him.
"See how well I look after my people? I'd have that shower, if I were you. When we've had lunch, you've got work to do."
"I'm not a very experienced deckhand."
"I don't need a deckhand. I've got a part for you in my next movie. We'll be on location in a couple of hours."
I look at him, not quite knowing how to reply.
"I missed you, Doug. As you know, I've been in prison as a younger man. I know what it's like to do time. In your own way, you've done your time. You're back on board, Mate. Have your shower, and come and eat. We're all dying to know how you got to be in a dogfight in a Dutch canal." I go to the shower cabin. The highly polished brass fittings pump piping hot water in abundance, and I avail myself of some shampoo to wash my hair. Maybe Arnold's making that TV programme he told me he wanted to make. The travelogue in which he travels around in Sunita with a comedian. The soap is transparent, and smells of apple. If Arnold really *has* forgiven me and taken me back under his wing, it's too good to be true. Even if he only gave me work in his comedy clubs, I'd be affluent again. Katinka's cooking smells delicious, and I'm hungry.

Chapter Fifty-five

The towel is thick and very large. I look at the label and see it's from Harrods. The clothes that were put out for me belong to Tom, and I smile to think that the last time I put his hand-me downs on, it was the Boris the Blue Dog costume. The clothes are all clean, and almost new. I like this luxury. It suits me better than being poor.
"Fancy a beer?" Asks Tom. I unwittingly broke my no drinking rule when I accepted the tea laced with brandy, the effect of which loosens my resolve now.
"I'd love a beer, please." I say. Tom succeeds with difficulty in removing four cans of Oranjeboom from the top-loading marine fridge. Arnold has to open them for him, though. He can't do much with those plastic hands, but he manages to Pat Katinka's bottom as he passes her. So she isn't Arnold's exclusive plaything. When I'm dressed I join Arnold and Tom at the dinette table, and Katinka serves pasta Alfredo. She takes a steaming bowl of it up to the wheelhouse, and when she returns she removes her cotton apron, and joins us at the table. We clink beer cans, and I tell them about my yoga retreat in between mouthfuls of delicious hot tagliatelle. The beer goes to my head, and I make several witty comments, which get the others laughing. I'd forgotten how nice alcohol is, and how Arnold's hearty laugh can be so thrilling. Then, whilst cleaning my teeth after the meal (they've provided me with a brand new toothbrush), I remember Charles and how his stomach was ripped open by Sunita's propeller. Arnold's a man of contradictions, because he's certainly looking after Tom. Every item of clothing I borrowed has a designer label, and Arnold's continually helping him with things he can't do with his artificial arms. Maybe Charles was lying.

I'm on the point of asking Arnold about the film he's making, when his phone rings.
"Okay, I'll be there in a second." He ends the call, and I wonder how he's going to get from the boat to the person who phoned him in a second. Arnold stands up.

"Doug. Come and meet the man who saved your life." I'm hemmed in by Katinka, and have to squeeze past her to get from behind the dinette table. The smell of her hair strikes to the centre of my being, and her hands touch my bottom and back to help me past her. Speculation as to her availability mounts within my crisp new Armani boxer shorts. I follow Arnold up the companion way into the wheelhouse, realising the person at the wheel is the one who phoned him. It's Hans Vermeulen. He looks older and milder than before. Perhaps it's because he's on his native water that he appears so Dutch. He smiles, and we shake hands.

"Hi Doug. How are you feeling?"

"Much better than before, Hans. I understand you saved my life."

"Arnold's exaggerating. He shot the dog. I just pulled you from the water."

"Thank you, Hans. Are those my clothes?" There's a pile of wet clothes on the coach roof of the saloon, in front of the wheelhouse windscreen.

"They're full of dirty water."

"I was wondering if my notebook is in the pocket."

Arnold takes the wheel from Hans, and suggests I have a look. Hans goes down into the saloon. Out on deck it's very cold, and my notebook is so wet everything written in it is illegible. My phone has drowned, and I retrieve Mummy's knife from the pocket and pop it into the clean dry one of my new jeans. I was hoping to get Chantelles phone number from the notebook, but it's reduced to pulp. My wallet's got English money and Euros in it. They should hopefully dry out, although they're all heavily stained red with the dye from my leather wallet.

"You just missed Ruud, Doug. He left on his helicopter shortly before we ran into you."

"I saw it!" I contemplate the fact that it was Ruud Vermeulen's helicoptor that drew us all out of the television room. If I'd been watching the TV screen at the start of the video, I'd have seen it was '101 Cumshots – Teen Special' and not the 'Teletubbies', and stopped it. Then none of the ensuing tragedy would have happened. Strange how Ruud Vermeulen's flying past in a helicopter wrecked several lives. I always thought he had an evil power about him.

"What's your new film called, Arnold?"

"Bible Born."

"Sounds interesting." He says something else to me, but in the wheelhouse the noise of the Diesels is much louder, and I don't catch what it is. His phone rings again, and he gestures for me to take the wheel.

"Brian, how the hell are you?" He goes down into the stern cabin to conduct his conversation. I'm abandoned at the wheel of Sunita, with no training in seamanship or knowledge of the Dutch waterways. Katinka comes up to collect the pasta bowl and tea mug that Hans neglected to take down with him.

"Where's Arnold?"

"He went into the stern cabin. He's on the phone." She looks out at the empty canal and flat landscape. There's an old windmill not far from the bank. A small sailing yacht motors in the opposite direction to us, on the other side of the canal. The sun's disappeared behind a sheet of grey cloud, as flat as the landscape we're cruising past.

"We'll be reaching Veere soon."

"Veere?"

"Yah. You know it?" I shake my head, entranced by her perfectly proportioned face, and large eyes.

"Veere's a lovely port. Very old. Lots of bars. You want another beer?"

"No thanks. I'm drunk already." I love her retrousse nose.

"Coffee?"

"I'd *love* a coffee." Hans comes up the companion ladder, and takes over the helm. Katinka speaks to him in Dutch, and they exchange several rapid sentences before she laughs and goes back down into the saloon. Hans gestures towards where she was just standing.

"Greedy girl."

"Yes?" I say, not sure what he means.

"Ya. A very greedy girl."

"Are the film studios in Veere?"

"No. The film studios are near to Veere. Arnold will tell all about it. You can go if you like. It's warmer in the saloon." Hans is right, it's a bit cold in the wheelhouse. I go back into the saloon, where Tom's watching a war film on video, and Katinka's washing up in the galley. I offer to help her with the drying up, but she says the stuff will dry naturally on the draining board. I don't like the look of the film Tom's watching. There's too much shooting and screeching of car tyres. I use the loo, and as Tom's got the small TV on the dinette table, I drink my coffee on the pilot berth I woke up on. When I've finished it, I lie down and close my eyes. I wonder what Dirk and the others are doing. Poor Marie's dead. Those kids have seen hardcore porn, lost their mother, their dog, and their rabbit, all in one day. I wish there was something I could do to help. Has Dirk reported me to the police? I suppose I committed a crime by showing that video to his children. But it must be obvious I didn't mean to. If I was a pervert, I'd have found an opportunity to show it to them when no other adults were present. My bag, passport, and credit cards are all at the yoga retreat. I'll claim it was a mistake. I just have to show them the real 'Teletubbies' video with the porn label on it. Neil Gosling will have to take responsibility for his actions. Except I don't know if I could grass him up. My God, life can be complicated!

I must take responsibility for what's happened. If only I could phone Chantelle and explain! She says life is an illusion. When people do evil, it's because they're afflicted, and they do what they do as a cry for help. What happened today is in the past. From this moment on I'll create a wonderful reality of love and laughter. I'll be more spiritual. I'll do the sun salutation right now! As soon as I have the thought, I realise there isn't room on board Sunita to do yoga. I'll get Katinka to phone Dutch directory enquiries, and ask for the number of Dirk's farm. What was it called? I can't remember, I don't think it had a name. I don't know his surname, either. I close my eyes, and despite the coffee, I drift off to sleep. The vibrations of the Diesel engines accompany a beautiful dream about an angelic woman who's partly Katinka, partly Caroline, and partly Angela. Angela, the wardrobe assistant on 'Rats Milk Cheese' who dressed me so well! I wonder what became of her. I send love to her, wherever she is. I feel a gentle touch on my arm. Katinka is standing over me, smiling. She offers me a quarter of an apple with the core cut out. I haven't eaten a piece of apple like this since I was four. Mummy used to cut apples into quarters just like this, with the core cut out. She used to pretend they were little boats, so I'd want to eat them. I used to love playing with them, and she'd tell me to eat them before they got covered in germs. I've completely forgotten about this way of cutting apples into pieces since I was four. Katinka smiles as she chews a piece of apple. She offers me another bit, and I accept. I surrender my heart to her, and drift back into perfect sleep. I'm woken by Arnold coming through

from the shower cabin, naked but for a towel. He adorns his newly showered body with completely new briefs, socks, and jeans. He slips a pair of deck shoes on, and a brand new stripy Breton cotton jumper.
"Brian O'Shea sends his regards to you, Doug."
"Is that the Brian you were on the phone to?"
"Aye."
"Is Brian in 'Bible Born'?" Arnold answers me with a quizzical look.
"Have you gone deaf?"
"Yes, I have actually."
"Are you having a laugh with me, Dougy boy?"
"No Arnold. I really have gone deaf in one ear. I thought you'd have known about it."
"Oh, I *am* sorry, Doug. I didn't realise. I never said 'Bible *Born*'. 'Bible *Porn*'!"
"You want me to be in a *porn* film?"
"Don't get me wrong, I'll pay you the going rate. We're all doing it, aren't we?" Tom and Katinka nod furtively. There's a glint in Katinka's eye, as she says:
"I was looking forward to performing with you."
"You don't have to do anything you don't want to."
"Can I keep my face concealed?"
"You can wear a blue dog outfit if you like. As long as it's a biblical dog."
"What's the going rate?"
"It depends, but you won't walk away with less than a grand."
"You mean a thousand *pounds*?"
Arnold nods.
"How much further is the location?"
"We're here." It dawns on me that the Diesels aren't running any more. I get off the bunk, and look out of the porthole. All I can see is a very close up riveted black steel hull. I go up to the wheelhouse, and see we're moored alongside a huge self-propelled barge. On the other side of us is a wide expanse of water, across which is a pretty Dutch harbour town. Hans is coiling a rope on the deck, and says through the open wheelhouse door:
"Veere. We'll go ashore for a drink, later. It's a nice little haven."
"I like the sound of that." I say. Hans points to an approaching white motor yacht, bigger than Sunita, but dwarfed by the barge.

"Recognise her?" He asks. I try to find something familiar about the boat, but she's coming more or less head on, and all I can see is her sharp end.
"My old boat. The Grietje." Sure enough, as she gets closer to our stern, I recognise the motor yacht that was moored outside the Clap Clinic on the night of the 'Rats Milk Cheese' wrap party. Hans secures the coiled rope to a cleat, and moves to Sunita's afterdeck to catch a mooring line from a man on Grietje's bow. I can see her name painted on her hull, and Hans shouts something in Dutch to the man. There are some other men above us on the deck of the barge we're moored alongside. Grietje slowly eases up behind Sunita, throwing her engines into reverse so she can moor just behind us, and next to the barge. I watch the various mooring lines being thrown up to the crew of the barge, and across to Hans, and her Diesels fall silent.

The Dutch barge, the Mary, looks like many of the other small cargo ships that ply the coastal and inland waterways of Northern Europe. Shallow drafted, with a low superstructure for getting beneath bridges, she's built around a huge cargo hold. The difference between this vessel, and the other craft of her type, is that her hold has been converted into a film studio. She's a floating film and television production facility. There are even dressing cabins, a wardrobe with washing machines and tumble dryers, and a small make-up and hairdressing department. An edit suite is situated beneath the ship's bridge, and even though the galley can cater for everyone aboard, the only facilities the vessel lacks are a dining cabin big enough to seat all at one sitting, and sleeping accommodation for more than the ship's crew.
"That's not to say we can't seat everyone in the studio. But to do that we need to stop filming." Says Arnold, as he proudly shows me the sets. There's a Bedouin tent, with desert backdrop, and an Egyptian Pharaoh's throne room. Another set is being constructed by some burly East European labourers.
"What's that going to be, Arnold?"
"Mary and Joseph's house. We're doing the scene where God makes Mary with child."
"I thought she was a virgin."
"And so she will be. We're sticking faithfully to the original text. God's going to come everywhere. Gird your loins, and I'll show you

the dressing room Brian O'Shea used when we were filming 'The Girl From The Village'."

"You took this ship to Ireland?"

"Oh yes, she's paid for herself several times over. The wonderful thing is, using her to make a Hollywood blockbuster gives her credibility. People don't expect her to be used to shoot porn movies."

I follow Arnold through a watertight door into a corridor beneath the main superstructure.

"I was wondering about that. 'The Girl From The Village' is up for two Oscars. Why do you need to make porn films?"

"Doug, you've no idea how many people buy porn. It's huge. I'm a director, you know. Porn's a great way to cut my teeth before trying my hand at a feature film. Mind your head, these watertight doorways are a bit low. We have to comply with Lloyds regulations."

"Doesn't it get difficult filming in rough weather?"

"We don't even try it at sea. We only use the studio when we're in calm waters. How else could we film internal scenes in the remotest parts of western Ireland? This boat shaved millions of dollars off the budget. We even filmed external scenes on here, when the weather outside was too inclement. Do you want to see the engine room?"

Chapter Fifty-six

Nancy looks a lot more playworn than when I last saw her, which was being taken from behind by Ruud Vermeulen at the 'Rats Milk Cheese' wrap party. She still looks very attractive, though, with her long black hair, and trim body. She wears those 1950s American glasses with black frames, and looks quite sophisticated. Arnold tells me this is her last production before she retires. She climbed the greasy pole from assistant floor manager to production manager by the final series of 'Rat's Milk Cheese', and took a share in the profits of the feature film. She invested her earnings in property, and sold two houses to invest in 'The Girl From The Village', on which she was also production manager. Her percentage of the film's phenomenal box office is consolidating her multi-millionaire status. She plans to spend her retirement between her equestrian properties in Sussex and France. I'm surprised at how friendly she is.
"What happened to Sheila Fox?" I can't resist asking, because I didn't see her name in the credits of 'The Girl From The Village'. Nancy's face darkens slightly.
"Sheila died of cancer last year. It was in just about every part of her body. She was dead within a month of it being diagnosed."
"I'm sorry to hear that." I say. I'm quite sincere. I wouldn't wish cancer on anyone.
"I wasn't. Anyway, this is your dressing cabin. You're sharing it with Tom, I'm afraid. We don't have enough space on board for everyone to have their own dressing cabin."
"What part does Tom play?"
"Today, he's a disciple. Tom does a lot. He's in demand in the specialist films involving amputees. There's a big market out there amongst the stump fetishists. In tomorrow's scene, he's playing the back half of a pantomime goat. Tom earns a fortune, because he's prepared to do smaller parts. Is there anything else you need to know?"
"Do I get a fluffer?"
"I'll fluff you if you like."

"Pardon?"

"I said I'll fluff you. I always fancied you, Doug. We have so few crew on these porn shoots, we all muck in together."

"Fantastic." Nancy puts her clipboard on the Formica surface in front of the mirror, removes her body warmer, and lifts her black cotton jumper to show a bulbous pair of tits. She's kneeling in front of me and lifting my kaftan, when Tom comes in. Nancy doesn't miss a beat as she bids me hold my kaftan above my genitals.

"Hi Tom. Fancy a fluff?"

"Sure thing Nancy." Tom stands next to me, and Nancy lifts his kaftan, holding it for him until he manages to capture the folds between his stumps and his tummy. His penis is much larger than mine.

"You couldn't pop that jumper off, could you Nance? It's obscuring my view of your titties." No sooner has Tom made the request, and Nancy peels off her top, and wiggles her breasts from side to side. When her hands make contact with our penises, they're both fully erect. She strokes our scrotums, and under-shafts. It feels wonderful, but I realise I'm in danger of prematurely ejaculating, because I still haven't come since last week's wank about visiting Trinh Tuyen at the massage parlour.

"I'm so sorry, Nancy. I don't need to be fluffed after all. I just said yes because I fancy you."

"No problem, Doug. Just go on the studio floor, and join the queue for St Mary Magdalene."

I leave Nancy vigorously wanking Tom, and walk out to the Bedouin tent. I've let the hem of my kaftan fall back down to my ankles, and my penis sticks out so proudly, my kaftan rubs deliciously with every step I take. Katinka is in the Bedouin tent, laying on a pile of those eastern cushions with the tiny little mirrors stuck on them. She's dressed as St Mary Magdalene, and entertaining each disciple in turn. I'm disciple number four. I recognise the disciple before me as one of the Eastern European set builders. Thankfully, Jesus isn't here. I'm hoping he's away healing lepers, because despite my agnosticism, my Christian upbringing has conditioned me to find it too much to see the Lord with his knob out.

"I told you she's a greedy girl?" Hans is behind me, wearing a false beard.

"Oh, hi Hans. Which disciple are you?" He's dressed in an Arab djellabah robe. Even I can see that it cost a fortune. The fabric is beautifully woven, and dyed with every colour of the rainbow, and more.
"I'm Joseph. This is my coat of many colours." He says, as proud as if he was a ten year old, with a major part in the school nativity play.
"I don't think Joseph was a disciple, Hans."
"Wasn't he? My knowledge of the Bible is a bit rusty. So it was Jesus' dad who had a coat of many colours, right?"
"I think the Joseph you're playing was in the Old Testament. You're the Joseph who was overpowered by his brothers, and sold into slavery." Hans looks concerned. Then he reveals a short Arab curved sword hanging from his belt.
"Never. I have my yataghan. Sharper than a razor." He draws it from its sheath, to show me the blade.
"You like it? I paid thirty thousand dollars for it in Dubai. It's four hundred years old. Just think how many people it's killed..."
"It's beautiful, but the yataghan is an Arab weapon, and the disciples were Jews." There's an uncomfortable moment when I think Hans has taken offence.
"Jews, Arabs, they're all the same. They don't eat pig, their bread's flat, and they circlecise their cocks."

"Quiet on the studio floor, please. We're recording sound as well as vision, you know." Arnold's wearing a baseball cap, and has a camera lens hanging around his neck. He's in hog heaven, playing at being a film director. Hans carefully slides his yataghan back into its sheath, and lowers his voice to a whisper.
"Fucking Scottish. Hung up about power, because they're ruled by you English. Can you see the jewels on the scabbard? They're all real. I tell you, Doug. If anyone tries to fuck with *this* disciple, they get their head cut off." We're interrupted by the first disciple ejaculating on St Mary Magdalene's feet. I'd always imagined St Mary Magdalene as having black hair, but Katinka looks perfect with her blonde hair and scarlet robe. They stop shooting, and Hans, two Bulgarian carpenters, and I are positioned around her for a five shot. I'm glad make-up gave me a large black beard, so I won't be recognised.

To my relief, the illegal Bulgarian workmen are the only carpenters in the scene. Hans tells me Jesus doesn't appear because he's in the wilderness. During St Mary Magdalene's servicing all twelve disciples, there are cutaways to Satan tempting Jesus with various earthly delights. That scene will be shot when they've built the desert mountain set, and I don't intend to be around when they do it. My plan is to be back in London with several thousand pounds cash, and a diary full of gigs in Arnold's comedy empire. In the meantime, I can think of less pleasant ways of earning a thousand pounds than reclining on some cushions and having Katinka anoint my genitals with sweetly fragrant oil. Hans reclines on the cushions to the other side of her, and the lower status Bulgarians stand behind her, with their members at her shoulder level. It's what they call a plate spinning shot, in which she uses two hands to bring four cocks to orgasm, by keeping them all on the boil. Not surprisingly, mine is the first and most fruitful to squirt, and my performance draws compliments from the director. This is a relief, ejaculating in his presence last time caused my career to move down, not up.

I'm on camera for less than ten minutes, and as the make-up girl is too busy to remove my beard, I hang around and watch the remaining disciples receive their various sexual favours from the sacred whore. We're just the warm-up. The scene climaxes with the apostles going five up, Judas Iscariot bringing up the rear. When we're wrapped, I mention to Arnold that Joseph and his coat of many colours is from The Old Testament, and not a disciple. Despite his earlier claim to be adhering to the original, he isn't in the least bit concerned.
"In this business, Doug, it's not when you live, but who you know. Hurry up and get that costume off, we're going ashore to Veere for a drink."
"I haven't got my beard off yet."
"Just get into you jeans and jumper, and leave the beard on. It's a port. They'll take you for a sailor."

Chapter Fifty-seven

Being faster than Sunita, the Grietje is commandeered to bare Arnold, Katinka, Hans, Tom, Nancy, and me to Veere's town quay. Katinka helps Tom get ready.
"I pay her to act as my pair of hands." Says Tom. After losing his second arm shooting the 'Rat's Milk Cheese' pilot, he lived in hospitals and nursing homes, until a rival red top newspaper to Stephen Woods' started paying him attention. Before they ran an expose on how Grange Films had neglected him, Sheila Fox stepped in with an all expenses paid holiday to The Philippines, several thousand pounds, and the offer of a menial job in the company on his return. When Arnold bumped into him at their offices, he saw his potential as a porn actor, and recruited him.
"I haven't looked back since. When I was at drama school, we studied Stanislavski. He says "There are no small parts, only small actors." What he means is, it doesn't matter how brief your appearance. If you're a true actor, you play that role as if it were a leading part. I throw myself into every job I do. I'll show you my fan mail if you like. I get it from all over the world. I'm going to start my own website. So many of the people in my year at drama school are out of work, and they've got both arms. I've got no arms, and I'm VAT registered. I owe it all to Arnold. He's a great friend. Katinka darling, I need a piss."

Some of the bars and restaurants in Veere are closed for the winter, but enough are still open for our group to get merry and eat a grand meal. Whilst we're walking along the inner harbour towards the Grietje, we admire the many yachts. I start having fantasies of becoming really successful and buying one. Hans drags us into a bar for a final drink before re-boarding the Grietje. It's almost empty, and when the barmaid hears English being spoken, she obliges by switching the TV to a British channel. Even though I haven't watched 'The Girl From The Village', I've seen so many posters and magazine features about it, I recognise it on the screen. A traditional Irish rowing boat glides across a misty bay. Inside it, Brian O'Shea frolics with his scantily clad female co-star. The clip ends, and studio audience applause mixed with adolescent female screams signals the return to 'Cat's Milk Please', the new chat show hosted by Leah Phillips and Des Jensen. They've replaced 'The Charlotte French Show', and tonight they're interviewing Brian O'Shea, who is draped on a soft chair, looking dishevelled and cuddly in a corduroy suit. There's a brief close up of Des Jensen laughing at Brian's witty answer to Leah's question, before returning to a mid-shot of Leah, so the viewers can see her face and ample bosom whilst she asks Brian the next question.

"Grange Films hung on to Charlotte's slot because we could offer Leah, but Des Jensen isn't up to a chat show." Says Arnold.

"They're all saying he's an actor who needs a script. We're going to chop him when we've found a replacement. You know who I think could do that job?"

"Colin Homes?"

"You."

I almost spill my brandy down my beard.

"Do you think they'd consider *me*, Arnold?"

"Doug, with your talent to write gags on the hoof, and ad lib under pressure, you'd be perfect for that show. I'm a director and part owner of Grange Films. What I suggest tomorrow, is done by today."

As if on cue, his phone rings, and all I hear of his conversation is "Brian? How did it go?" He takes his phone outside, and I return my gaze to the TV screen on its wall bracket above the bar. Despite the dodgy picture quality, Leah's black jumper sets her red lipstick and blonde hair off perfectly. That classic look combines with a delicate balance of femme fatale and vulnerable little girl to attract as many viewers as Charlotte French did. The car and beer companies are falling over each other to spend their marketing budgets on those precious advertising slots.

"She's not a happy girl." Nancy has perched herself on the bar stool vacated by Arnold. She nods her head towards the television, and continues.

"She's lonely, I mean. Hasn't had a relationship last longer than two weeks since you knew her. Twelve thousand pounds a show, millions of men masturbating about her every night, yet she goes to bed alone and cries herself to sleep."

It's the end of the show, and as the credits roll, a wide shot reveals Des Jensen for the first time in over a minute. He's an irrelevance beside Leah on the set. Brian O'Shea shuffles in the hot seat, and security moves in to protect him from screaming teenage girls who've escaped from the studio audience in a bid to touch their living God.

"Isn't that Clyde, who used to be a bouncer at The Clap Clinic?" I ask.

"That's him. He works for Grange Films, now. There's a feature about him in 'Bonker' magazine this month. He'll probably have his own show within the year."

"I thought Brian was on tour at the moment."

"He is. They heli'd him in from his gig in Croydon to the studio, and taped the show later than usual."

Arnold comes back into the bar, and announces that he has to go to London in the morning.

"Something's come up, and I need to be there for a couple of days. Ruud'll be back tomorrow, and he'll direct whilst I'm away."

We gather to leave, and the news comes on, with the now familiar picture of the abducted baby filling the screen. The search has been widened, and there are shots of fields and woodland being scoured by lines of police and members of the public who've volunteered. The barmaid shakes her head with incredulity, and asks us how anyone could put those poor parents through such misery.

"They're looking for a body now. They say if the child is still missing after this long, it's usually been murdered." The last thing I see on the TV before I follow everyone through the glass door, is the latest press conference to be held by the police officer in charge of the case, the haggard mother, and be-skull capped father.

The drizzle that fell earlier is now being propelled by a slow wind. I tell Arnold that if I had a boat, I'd prefer a sailing boat, because the sound of the engines makes it difficult for me to hear.

"The sails flapping in the wind make as much noise as a Diesel. When you get that yacht - and you will - tell your crew that if they're going to fall over board, they should go off the port side. If they fall over on your deaf side, their cries of help will go unheard."

"Don't you hanker after a sailing yacht, Arnold?"

"Nae, Laddie." He's drunk, so his Glaswegian accent has increased ten fold.

367

"I'm a powerboat freak. I go where I want to go, not where the wind decides to blow me. Talking of being blown, I might do some more filming when we get back on board."
"It's a bit late, isn't it?"
"Not really. The technology's so good these days. You can do with a small camera and a couple of halogen lamps what it would have taken a full-size camera crew to achieve a few years ago. I wanted to do a close up money shot before leaving."
"Will my face be on camera, because this beard's itching like crazy."
"You can take the beard off. It's your John Thomas I'm interested in. From the other side of a lens, I mean. Katinka? How's your diary looking for the next hour?"
Katinka, who was engrossed in a conversation with Nancy as we walk towards the quayside, smiles and catches us up.
"I have a window. Or should I say a porthole?"

Back on board the Grietje, Hans fires the Diesels up, and steers us towards the Mary, her anchor light guiding us across the harbour. The illuminated windows in her superstructure, where the crew live, look cozy and inviting in the darkness.
Tom goes to the WC cabin, with Katinka. From the amount of time they spend in there, I assume she's wiping his bottom. I go to the other WC cabin aft of the saloon and remove my false beard. When I look at my face in the mirror, it looks unfamiliar. I'd got quite used to seeing myself with full facial hair. Back in the saloon, Arnold's lying on a berth with his eyes closed. Nancy goes to her cabin. Katinka puts the kettle on, and I hope she's washed her hands since toileting Tom. She ambles over to where I'm laying on another saloon berth, and lies next to me, until the kettle boils. My thoughts are in the studios where they record 'Cat's Milk Please'. Was Arnold serious when he mentioned the possibility of my co-hosting the show with Leah? Or was it the drink talking? Surely I'm too unknown to appear on a high-rating show like that. The kettle belts steam into the plush saloon. I'd do anything to present that show. It's where I belong.
"Coffee?" Asks Katinka.
"Yes please." I say.
"A strong one?"
"Yes please." I say again.

"Me too!" Croaks a recumbent Arnold, his eyes still closed. Katinka springs up to go and make the coffees, losing her balance for an instant as the Grietje encounters a wave. I don't know from where that girl gets her energy.

Chapter Fifty-eight

By the time we're moored alongside the Mary, there's a stirring in my system that only class A narcotics can produce. When I ask Katinka what was in the coffee, she replies
"Cocaine of course. That's what we mean by "strong coffee"".
"I gave up drugs. I meant I just wanted my coffee strong."
"Oh dear, I'd better not mention the Viagara then." Answers Katinka, with a gleam in her eye.
"Don't fret Dougie. This is film producers cocaine. Pure as Andean snow. It clears the system." Says Arnold, loading skunk into a bong.
"Mm, I must admit it's bloody nice." I say,
The wind's blowing harder than it was when we were ashore, but Arnold's adamant it's still okay to film the scene. He certainly works hard. He rouses a couple of crew, and within a few minutes we're back on the Bedouin tent set, with the lights on and two cameras ready. The shot's the same as it was before we wrapped, so Arnold doesn't have to re-light it. Katinka's done her own make-up, and I'm naked. She wears the same red garment she wore earlier. I lie back on the Indian cushions, and spread my legs to accommodate her. Before she even starts stroking my thighs, my penis is striving to look as big as possible for the cameras. I've been assured that only people who've tested negative for STDs are allowed to have unprotected sex on set. They took my word for it that I'm clean. I lie back and think of England, or rather a television studio in England, and let Katinka do what she does best. Considering she makes a very good cup of coffee, and cooks an exquisite pasta Alfredo, she has a lot to live up to. A few minutes later, I'm moaning as I come directly down the inside of her throat. I thought I'd had most experiences, but that's the first time I've had an orgasm whilst being taken deep throat.
"Thank you." I moan. Katinka gives the obligatory smile to camera, and Arnold calls:
"Cut." She rests her sweet face on my stomach,
"Is that a wrap?" I ask, rhetorically.

"Of course not. This is where you return the favour to Katinka." I know my face isn't going to be in shot, so I assume I'll be doing this with my hand.

"Reloading." Says one of the camera operators, and Katinka smiles at me before pulling her garment over her head. I haven't seen her naked close up, so I relish the sight of her white legs leading up to those lovely thighs. I look to see if she shaves her pubes, and see a small but hairy scrotum dangling beneath a vagina, and a small cock. It's no more than four inches long, and though it was limp at first sight, it's gaining strength at an alarming rate. Katinka looks like she's just won first prize in the naughtiness competition, and Arnold laughs so heartily he collapses into a fit of coughing. Katinka smiles furtively and says of her now erect little penis:

"I think he likes you." Arnold recovers enough to stand-up straight again.

"What's the matter, do you only like circumcised ones? I said I wasn't going to film your face, Dougie, but I wish I'd captured your expression just now. I'd have won awards."

"I'll do it, but only with my hand."

"Don't worry, Doug. I'm not asking you to get your botty out. I hope you've manicured your nails, though. This is a classy film I'm making."

"I won't be biting them tonight. No offence, Katinka, but this isn't really my bag. Circumcised or not." Katinka takes the position I was in on the cushions, and I do for her what others have done for me on countless occasions. Or is she a he? It's so small, it reminds me of masturbating when I was thirteen. I have to admit that I quite enjoy the experience. Especially as the gasps of pleasure are female. My technique is obviously good, although it takes my hand a minute to adjust to the unusual angle. Several minutes later, I've got Katinka's semen dribbling over my fingers, and an assistant handing me some tissues.

"You won't tell anybody will you?" I say, and Arnold laughs uncontrollably. He puts his arm around me as we walk away from the set.

"Oh Doug. You are funnier than anyone else I know!"

Back on Sunita, I drink a much-needed Islay single malt whilst Katinka explains to me that she's a genuine hermaphrodite.

"I've had no surgery or estrogen. This is the way I was made. I don't have the female organs necessary to reproduce, but I do have a vagina. Would you like to see it?"

"No, I'm okay thanks. I must say, though, I never thought I'd refuse the opportunity to see a man's vagina." Arnold's about to go to bed, when his phone rings.

"It's for you." He says, handing it to me. Nancy's voice comes from its tiny speaker.

"Hi Doug. It occurred to me that you haven't been allocated a bed yet. I've got a big double bed in my cabin. If you want to come and share with me, it would be great to have you over."

"Yes please. I'll be there right away."

"Doug, afore ye go. It'll take a long while to get a new passport if you apply for it at the British Embassy in Holland. It might be a lot simpler if you cross the channel aboard Grietje when she goes to Brighton on Sunday. They hardly ever check passports on yachts crossing the channel. Those yogic lesbian tarts might even have taken your passport back to London. If not, you can get a new one at the passport office in Victoria."

"Thanks Arnold. Have fun."

"I will, Doug. You know me well enough to be sure I always have fun."

I kiss Katinka good night, and she joins Tom in his cabin. I make my way up to the Mary and along her deck, before climbing down onto the Grietje. Nancy's wearing a long white cotton nightie, and she's brushing her hair. She leads me to her cabin, which is forward of the saloon. The double duvet is folded back, making the bed look inviting. I clean my teeth in the ensuite, the cocaine and Viagara still coursing through my veins.

When I return, Nancy is kneeling on the bed, with a mischievous smile on her lips.

"Now, where were we with the fluffing..."

I step closer to the bed, and she removes my T shirt. As she undoes my belt and fly she kisses my stomach, and licks my nipples. I step out of my jeans and boxer shorts, and clamber onto the bed. She's so cuddly in her white cotton nightie, I hold her close and nuzzle her hair. She kisses me beautifully on the mouth, and I play with her lovely soft breasts through the white cotton. When I pull her nightie over her head, it leaves her long hair in disarray, giving her a slightly mad

appearance. This turns me on all the more as I feel like I'm a psychiatrist with a mental patient. I suck and slurp at her nipples, and lick my way to her luscious, salty cleft. Remembering the first time we met, during the filming of the pilot of 'Rat's Milk Cheese' at Teddington Studios, it seems my journey has come full circle. I fancied her so much that day, when she ran across the car park to Arnold and me, and asked if I could replace Tom. At last I've got my tongue in her fanny and her thigh sweat in my hair, and all is right with the universe. She moans soulfully when she comes, and asks me to put my cock in her. I oblige, and as my pelvic thrusting gathers pace, it feels like this is the most delightful fuck I've ever had. I come inside her, and she hugs me tightly. We cuddle and breathe in unison, my penis still inside her. After a while I nuzzle her ear, and whisper
"I want to stay like this forever, Nancy, but for the fact that I need to urinate." She relaxes her grasp, and I pad across the carpet to her en suite. When I return, she's lying on her back with her bottom on a pillow and her legs leaning against the wall at the head of the bed.
"Do you know why I'm in this posture?" She asks.
"I've no idea." I reply, getting into bed beside her.
"I'm ovulating."
"That's good." I say, too hazy to assimilate the implications. I drift off to sleep, waking briefly when she turns around and lies beside me again. We fall asleep in each other's arms.

Chapter Fifty-nine

Perhaps it's because Arnold mentioned the Grietje's going there that I dream about Brighton. I have a long, lovely dream about the white Regency houses on the Kemp Town sea front. I'm in bed with Alison, in the seafront flat I've never been to. After we made love (in real life, not the dream), she used to wipe her fanny with several tissues, and walk to the bathroom with them pressed between her upper thighs. The first time she did it, I was lying with my head on the pillows recovering from my orgasm, and as she walked away from the bed, the white tissues protruding from behind her bottom looked like a rabbit's tail. I pointed her 'bunny's tail' out to her, and she looked at herself in the mirror, and wiggled her bottom, making bunny sounds. After that, every time we made love in bed, she'd make me laugh by wiggling her tissue tail and squeaking, and I'd say
'Bunny tail.' It was one of those intimate things we shared, and I missed so terribly after she left me. In the dream, Alison does the bunny tail routine, and sprouts tissue wings. She hovers above the bed, kisses my face, and flies out of the window. After she flutters away, the sound of a helicopter gets louder and louder, and I half wake up. Daylight is shining through the thin curtains covering the portholes of Nancy's cabin. I'm alone in her bed, but very warm and relaxed. The helicopter is hovering, or sitting on the Mary's deck ready to take off. The engines get even louder, before gradually getting quieter until they've completely gone. I presume the helicopter flew overhead, but as I have no directional hearing ability, I'll never know. The loudness of the engines increased the intensity of my tinitus. I'm so used to it, I drift back into a deep sleep. I wake up after a protracted dream in which I'm desperately looking for a toilet. When I eventually find it, the council has closed it down because small-penised homosexuals were using it to make pornographic films. I wake up, and have a very long piss in Nancy's en suite shower cabin. It occurs to me that the Grietje's engines are running, and we're under way. Back in Nancy's cabin, I draw the curtain, to see fields and trees moving past. I have a shower, get dressed, and open the door to the saloon. As soon as the

door is slightly open, a muzzle squeezes through, and levers it open enough for a very large furry head to push the door open. The instant I recognise the diamond encrusted collar, Fritz the Alsatian dog growls at me, setting my stomach into a knot of fear. I'd be badly bitten, were it not for a thin, icy command from within the saloon. Immediately his tail drops between his legs, and he cowers before me. I go past it into the saloon, where Ruud Vermeulen sits with a large baby in his arms.

"Forgive me if I don't shake your hand, Doug. I'm fully occupied nursing young Mox, here." Ruud Vermeulen's face looks much the same as the last time I saw him, when he was copulating with Nancy from behind at the 'Rat's Milk Cheese' wrap party. He's grown his hair, which hangs like a silver curtain just long enough to cover his ears. His nose is slightly ruddy, but his clothes are the same, smart slacks, shirt, and blazer. His shoes are polished to an immaculate shine.
"Do you remember Mia?" He nods across the cabin to a sultry looking woman in her mid-twenties. She acknowledges me without a smile, her eyes nearly as wary as the Alsatians.
"And of course, you remember Fritz. I think we were in the Jazuzzi aboard the Lady Rose when you first met both of them." Fritz the huge Alsatian returns to lie at Vermeulen's feet. I recognise Mia now, as the other woman in the Jazuzzi. She looked very young and pretty then, and though the intervening years have jaded her, she retains an air of Gypsy sensuality. When I encountered her aboard the Lady Rose, I didn't have much to do with Mia, whereas the other girl – Connie – I made amyl nitrate-fuelled love to.

Mia and I greet each other, and I stand, uncertain whether to sit down. I was prepared to meet Hans or Nancy, and now I'm swimming in the whirlpool of majesty that swirls around this formidable man.
"Please, Doug, be seated." He looks at a copy of 'Justine' by the Marquis De Sade, which lies open on the settee near him. Some Flemish rolls off his tongue, and Mia moves the book to make room for me to sit.
"Have you read "Justine"? I'm reading it in the original French, having enjoyed it as a young man in Dutch translation."
"I read it in English when I was a student. My French is nowhere near good enough to read literature. I see we're under way."

375

"Yes, a north-easterly is blowing up, and we had to leave the Veersemeer. We're moving to some less exposed waters, before we can resume filming. The Mary is steaming behind us. If my helicopter had reached the Mary fifteen minutes later, it would have been too dangerous to land. Nancy asked me to convey her apologies for not bidding you goodbye. The helicopter had to leave before the wind blew stronger, and she said you looked too tranquil to awaken."
"I suppose they flew to Rotterdam?"
"Antwerp airport. There's a convenient service from there to London. But how rude of me. You must be in need of breakfast. Mia…" He gabbles something in Dutch to Mia, who stands and asks me if I would like tea or coffee. I ask for a mug of tea, and devote myself to petting Fritz. I feel that by giving affection to Vermeulen's hound, I'm extending appropriate grace to his master.

The baby wakes up and starts to cry, and Mia abandons her tea-making duty in favour of relieving Vermeulen of the child. She calls up to the wheelhouse, whilst Vermeulen straightens his tie and blazer, to compensate the effects of holding the child. Suddenly his features assume a concerned expression.
"Oh, I'm so sorry Doug. I forgot that you're afraid of young children."
"That's in the past. I've got over all that now." I don't feel bold enough to address him as Ruud.
"Congratulations." A man comes down from the wheelhouse, and takes over Mia's tea making duty. Mia walks past me with the child, and when I glimpse its face I get a feeling of deja vu. She takes the child through to the forward part of the Grietje, where there are other cabins besides Nancy's.
"I'm glad that other things have also slipped into the past." Vermeulen continues.
"Such as your unfortunate exile from Arnold's business activities. I always took that Leah Phillips as a troublemaker. But you see when a woman has power, it goes to her heart. By the way, there's another person you should recognise." I try to remember where I saw the baby's face before, but feel confused because the only children I've seen near Vermeulen were those kids aboard Sunita, when they appeared outside the Crown and Anchor's beer garden. I'm about to admit defeat, when he indicates the man making my tea.

"Franz was aboard The Lady Rose during my birthday party." Franz turns to me, and I recognise the pockmarked face of one of the men who served our meals.
"Hello Franz. Two please." I say, in response to his holding the sugar jar up with an inquisitive expression on his face. He stirs two large spoonfuls of sugar into my mug of tea, and brings it over to me with the air of a butler. Its hot sweetness brings new life to my day.
"Would you like breakfast?"
"Yes please."
"What can I get you?"
"Eggs on toast?"
"Of course. Fried eggs?"
"Yes please."
"And ham or bacon?"
"Just the eggs please, Franz. Thank you."
Ruud says more to Franz in Dutch, and I recognise the words "oran juis", and "coffee".
"I was asking Franz for orange juice. We've just returned from the Mediterranean, and I fear succumbing to a cold. Now you're part of our inner circle, Doug, I hope you'll be interested in performing your show in our comedy clubs over here."
"I've heard there's a comedy circuit in Holland."
"I own about twenty premises which include stand-up comedy among their entertainments. It would delight me if you played them."
Mia sulks back into the saloon, without the baby. She looks very Italian with her black hair and olive complexion. Tight black jeans are tucked into Suede boots that go nearly up to her knees. The neckline of her baggy yellow sweatshirt reveals a white T-shirt underneath. The gold cross around her neck has fallen out of the neckline of both garments, and I guess this happened when she bent down to put baby Mox to sleep. I recognise that cross, but I can't remember where from. When she starts telling me about how much she loves Boris in 'Rats Milk Cheese' I get a closer look at it, and I remember where I've seen it before. Emily Johnson was wearing one exactly like it when Neil Gosling and I watched her read the news on his telly in Manchester. The horizontal line of the cross is slightly lower than half way down the vertical one, making it a subtle upside down cross. She's got earrings to match. Franz is well into cooking my breakfast, and the sound of the eggs frying interferes with my ability to hear what she's

saying. I explain my difficulty to Mia and Ruud, and they question me about how the hearing problem came about. During my story about Daisy the conger eel vomiting near my ear in the water tank at Pinewood studios, Ruud claps his hands twice. Mia quickly sits on his lap, as if she was a performing poodle obeying a circus trainer. He puts his arms around her whilst they continue to give my story rapt attention. I've nearly got to the end of explaining how background noise jams my ability to hear the sound I'm trying to listen to, when he prompts Mia to remove her baggy sweatshirt. Her black bra and its strap show through her white T-shirt. She wriggles on Vermeulen's lap, as he feels her up. I'm at a loss how to react, and continue to ramble on so I'm repeating myself. Vermeulen interrupts me.
"Who do you think should play the Virgin Mary in our nativity scene, Doug? Katinka, or Mia here?"
"Katinka's already played St Mary Magdalene, and with her black hair, Mia could better pass as Jewish."
Ruud laughs loudly at my answer, and hugs Mia tightly. I feel uncomfortable, because I don't want to fall foul of Vermeulen by giving the wrong answer.
"We're going to moor up in the Kanaal door Walcheren soon. I want to get the master shot of the nativity scene finished before dinner. You have a habit of meeting me when I'm holding a celebration, Doug. We're having a fancy dress party tonight, aren't we darling?" Mia nods bashfully, and Ruud reaches beneath her t-shirt and undoes her bra strap.
"Are you celebrating a birthday?"
"No, a new website. Arnold insists on devoting our porn operation to making DVDs, but I think he's madder than Hans. The internet's becoming the main outlet for erotic videos. I want everything we sell online to be made in-house. Or should I say, "in-ship"?"

Franz takes my breakfast over to the saloon table, and I sit down to eat it. The place where he puts my plate gives me a direct view of Ruud and Mia. The next time I look in their direction, her T-shirt has been removed. I'm unsure whether his antics are a display for my benefit, and how I'm supposed to react. I look at my eggs on toast and put more ketchup than I really want on them, as an excuse to keep my gaze averted.

"Tell me, Doug. Does Mia turn you on?" Vermeulen removes Mia's black bra to show her very large tits. Her olive skin is unblemished, and I find her incredibly sexy.
"Yes. But only if she's naked from her own choice. I never found force erotic." I've shocked myself by my direct answer, but Ruud isn't phased by it.

Franz serves us divine-smelling Dutch coffee, and withdraws to the wheelhouse.
"Did you hear that, Mia? Doug doesn't like a woman to do what she doesn't want to do." Mia nods. I can't make out whether she hates Vermeulen, or idolises him.
"Very well, my lovely. Do exactly what you want to do." All this time, Fritz has been laying close to Vermeulen's feet, watching events intently. Every so often his tail thumps nervously on the thick pile carpet. Mia stands up and goes to the stereo, where she chooses some pop music I've heard float from various radios, but couldn't identify. Then she goes to the other side of the saloon, equi-distant from Vermeulen and me, and dances seductively. She plays with her breasts, and pulls her jeans down to the tops of her boots.

Giving birth to baby Mox has done nothing to harm her figure, because her tummy's as tight as that of a teenaged model. I'm wondering how Vermeulen could have fathered such a dusky baby, when she pulls her G - string down, and I see her unshaved fanny. That's unusual these days, I reflect to myself as I chew slowly on fried eggs and undercooked white toast. I'm dreading finishing my breakfast, because I don't know what I'm supposed to do. I also don't like loud music when I'm eating. It makes me eat too fast, and get indigestion. I dare a glance over to Ruud Vermeulen, unsure what expression to wear if I catch his eye. I don't need to worry, his face is bent over a hypodermic syringe, which he's sticking into his arm. I haven't even noticed him take his blazer off, or roll the expensive linen shirtsleeve up over his pale arm. I look back to Mia, who's looking at me conspiratorially. She smiles, and wiggles her bosoms at me. Then she glances furtively in Vermeulen's direction. Suddenly she pulls her G - string and jeans up, and runs over to him. Fritz is on his feet, crying anxiously with his nose in Vermeulen's crotch. Vermeulen's semi-conscious, and vomits orange juice and coffee onto his discarded

379

blazer. It flows off it onto the soft upholstery as Mia puts his head in a safe position. She shouts up to the wheelhouse, and Franz comes down to his aid. I don't feel like eating the toast that remains on my plate. Mia turns the music off, and the saloon fills with the sound of the baby crying from beyond the door.

"I'd better look after the kid." She says to me, before rattling a load of Dutch off to Franz. Vermeulen makes a strange noise that's half gagging and half a croak, and twitches suddenly before pushing Franz away. Fritz barks from confusion, and Vermeulen orders Franz to get him a cloth.

"I'm alright." Vermeulen announces, as he stands up and removes his vomit-soiled shirt. Don't get the wrong impression, I don't usually jack up this early in the day. It's just that I've been very well behaved for a week, so I'm allowing myself to let my hair down a little." His body is thin and muscular, and a large swastika is tattooed over his heart.

"I'd offer you the needle, but your breakfast would come up quick if you did. Maybe later, eh?"

"I've stopped taking drugs." He smiles as he uses the dishcloth to wipe sick from his needle-ravaged arm.

"That's not what I heard." He hands the cloth to Franz, and I notice 'Hells Angels' tattooed across his back. He points to a windmill on the canal bank. We've slowed down, and the windmill is hardly moving past us.

"The canal narrows ahead, and we may have to wait before going further. Come up on deck and help me get the anchor ready." He barks some Dutch to Mia, who hands him baby Mox, and disappears to the forward cabin. It's whilst I watch Vermeulen bouncing the baby against his chest, the swastika next to its head that the penny drops. Of course I recognise that child. I've seen its face on telly every time the news has been on. It's the baby who was kidnapped from those orthodox Jews in London! What was her name? Rebecca. Vermeulen's nursing an abducted baby! Mia comes in with a white silk shirt and a tweed jacket for Vermeulen, and takes the child from him so he can put them on.

"Come, Doug. We probably won't need to drop anchor, but it's wise to have it ready just in case." I follow him into the wheelhouse, where Franz has joined another man I've never seen before, who's at the wheel. As soon as we leave the warmth of the wheelhouse the cold wind cuts through my thin cotton jumper. The canal's wide, and lots of barges and tugs are ahead of us.

"The Mary's behind us. Sunita's with her." I can hardly hear what Vermeulen's saying because of the noise of the engines and the wind. I follow him to the foredeck, and watch him lift the hatch of the chain locker.

"Sometimes the chain gets tangled from the motion of the boat. But it looks fine. This is a busy canal, because it leads to the River Schelde, and Antwerp." He almost loses his footing as he closes the hatch to the chain locker. He turns his face to me, and his expression is manic.

"Let's go back in. I'm not used to this bloody cold weather." I follow him back along the deck to the wheelhouse. There's a car driving along the road by the canal bank. People are walking near some trees. I want to shout to them that Rebecca, the abducted baby is on board. They're too far away, though, and I'd be dead before the incriminating words had left my mouth.

Back in the warm saloon, Mia's holding baby Mox, or should I say Rebecca. The sight of Vermeulen in that tweed jacket keeps reminding me of something, but I can't remember what. Then the memory drops into my head. The night I stayed in Vermeulens house in Jersey, after the corporate gig in the Hotel Bristol. Mick the Liverpudlian waiter showed me the framed photograph, taken on a film set. Vermeulen wore a tweed jacket, and Fritz was jumping up at ____. I haven't seen him in a tweed jacket since then. Now I've entered the black and white world of that photograph, and I understand why Mick was afraid of his absent landlord. Terror cuts through my stomach, and I almost puke. I wonder if my coffee was spiked, because I feel like I'm coming up on a bad trip.

"Are you alright, Man?" Vermeulen asks me. I say I'm cold, and he tells Mia to find me some warm clothing. I go into Nancy's cabin. Whilst I'm cleaning my teeth I wonder if Arnold and Nancy know Vermeulen's got the stolen child. My hand suddenly stops brushing my teeth, and I look at myself in the mirror. Vermeulen said he wants to shoot the nativity scene today. If Mia's going to be the Virgin Mary, then they're going to need a baby Jesus. And this is a porn video.

Chapter Sixty

I half spit, half gag the toothpaste and water from my mouth. How can I behave normally when I go back into the saloon? And why do they think *I* would get involved with child porn? Why do they think they can trust me not to tell the police? I'm shivering half from fear, half from cold, when I dry my face and go back into Nancy's cabin. Whilst I was cleaning my teeth in the en suite bathroom, someone's come in and left a clown costume on the bed. It's all clear to me now. I thought it odd that Vermeulen would concern himself with such a menial task as checking the anchor locker, when he's got two crew aboard. It can't be a coincidence that he showed me the anchor just before a clown costume appeared in my cabin. They don't care about my knowing they're using an abducted baby in a porn video, because soon I'll be chained to an anchor, feeding Dutch eels.

Back in the saloon, Ruud is on the phone. I feel sorry for the person at the other end, because he's shouting at them in Dutch. His lips are white with anger, and the baby's crying again, which makes me want to cry too. Mia and Fritz are cowed on a saloon sofa, and Mia silently asks me to hold the child, not wanting to annoy Vermeulen even more by talking loudly when he's on the phone. I don't know what he injected himself with, but he's behaving very strangely. He's dementedly pacing up and down the saloon, with uncertain balance. Mia goes through to the forward cabins, and rain starts pattering against the saloon windows. As if in a dream, I find myself obeying a decision I haven't consciously made. I take baby Rebecca up into the wheelhouse, and nod hello to Franz. Bouncing Rebecca up and down in my arms to comfort her, I surreptitiously remove Mummy's knife from my pocket, and open the blade. I point to something in the distant murk of the squall, and whilst they're distracted, I discreetly slice through a major cable that leads from the main electrical console. I make sure the cable I cut is hidden from general view behind a fire extinguisher, so they won't immediately notice it's been severed. I'm in luck, because the entire console loses power, although the engines continue to propel us forward.

Feigning surprise, I exchange glances with Franz and the other crewman, before slipping quietly out on deck whilst their attention is on the now useless steering wheel. I move swiftly to the poop, and lean into the Grietje's tender - a rigid inflatable boat that dangles from its davits over the stern. Mummy's knife cuts the outboard motor's fuel line. If they try to chase us, they'll have to use their hands to paddle, because I throw the emergency oars into the canal. Then, holding Rebecca high in my arms, I jump into the grey water. As soon as we surface, Rebecca howls with indignation at her dunking in the cold water, and I swim as best I can with one arm, whilst holding her head clear. The Grietje is motoring out of control towards the far bank, which is lucky, because all I have to do is get to the nearest bank, and find someone with a phone so we can call the police. I wish I could explain to Rebecca that screaming her head off is reducing her chances of survival, because she's giving our position away to the Grietje. I presume they'll shoot at us. I hold my breath, and dive. I've heard that babies instinctively hold their breath when submerged, because they've spent nine months under water before they're born. I hope I'm right, because Rebecca and I are under the water for about twenty seconds before I surface again. This time, she isn't crying as I swim towards the canal bank. The Grietje's drifting further away from me, and when I venture a quick look behind, Vermeulen is having a tantrum in the rigid inflatable boat. They've launched it, only to discover I've cut the fuel line.

At last I get near the bank, and, encouraged by Rebecca's spluttering noises, start looking for something I can grab to pull us out with.
"Help. Help!" I shout, in the hope someone might hear me, but the place is a no-man's land of cattle pastures and wind generators. My feet strike an underwater ledge, and I stand up. I hold Rebecca in front of me, so I can shield her from any bullets the Grietje might send our way. I wade along the canal next to the bank, amazed it's shallow enough. I fall off the ledge into deep water again, but see a steel ladder in a recess in the bank. I knew the practical Dutch canal engineers wouldn't fail me. A few seconds later, I've made it to the shore, with Rebecca still alive in my arms. There's only one thing in my mind, and

that's to get her to safety. I remember the sight of her tormented parents on the television news. I'm going to reunite them if it's the last thing I do.

There's a road going along the canal bank, but no one in sight. I could always run along the bank in the direction we came from and alert a barge crew to my needs, but Vermeulen will have phoned back to the Sunita and the Mary, both of which are following us. I don't know if Katinka, Tom, and Hans are in on the child abuse, but must assume they are. I run away from the canal across the green field. Holland is one of the most densely populated countries in the world – I can't fail to find someone soon. I seem to have found the remotest, most sparsely populated part of it, though, because there's nothing. Not even cows, just open pasture. At last I see a small shed, and run towards it. The land is so flat the shed seems closer than it is, and when I finally reach it, the place is deserted. I open the unlocked door, and find a bike. This would be good, except it's a classic Dutch bike, useless for cycling over long grass. I put Rebecca in the basket on the handlebars, and push it over the meadow. At last I find a track, and I pedal as fast as I can. The rain has stopped, but Rebecca's resumed her loud protests.

The sun emerges from behind the sheet of clouds, and as it does so, I see the track joins a road. My heart leaps, when I see a BP service station. I pedal faster, knowing I've made it to safety. When I reach the road, I see the service station is on the other side. A mini bus overtakes me, and pulls into the forecourt. So many Dutch people speak English, anyone who can get a job in a service station will be bound to speak it. All I have to do is ask them to dial the emergency number for the police, and Rebecca will be saved.

I'm so close now, I can see the people getting out of the mini bus. It must be a basketball team because they're all very tall black men, wearing identical tracksuits. The driver starts refuelling, whilst the team go into the shop. I'm so out of breath when I reach the service station forecourt, I'm panting too much to speak coherently. Two of the tall black men haven't bothered going into the shop, and they look bemused by the sight of a frantic man cycling up with a baby in the shopping basket.

A car screeches into the forecourt, and Hans Vermeulen gets out. One look at his eyes is enough to leave me in no doubt as to which side he's on. I take Rebecca in my arms, and shout to the two men "Phone. Give me your mobile phone!" They look confused, and point to a sign beside a pump, with a picture of a mobile phone with a red line through it.

"Emergency!" I say. Hans is walking towards me. Perhaps the basketball players aren't Dutch, because they don't seem to understand English. I can see that Hans is torn between his need to get Rebecca from me, and the need to behave in a way that won't attract unwanted attention from the cashiers and basketball team. Rebecca starts screaming with renewed vigour. Hans sees the opportunity to behave as if I'm causing her suffering, and makes his move. I saw how effective his Win Shun Kung Fu skills are on the Lady Rose in Cannes, and with that car waiting with its door open, he can whisk Rebecca away in a few seconds. I squeeze between the petrol pumps, and dash into the road. Someone's thrown a banana skin on the ground. It's no more than four metres from the litterbin beside the petrol pump. Maybe they intended the banana skin to go in it. In my haste to escape from Hans, I step on the banana skin, and slip over. At that moment, a lorry is driving past the service station, and I'm in front of it with Rebecca in my arms. I should have heard it, but it was approaching from my deaf side, and I saw it too late. In a final, futile attempt to save Rebecca's life, I hurl her into the sky an instant before the front nearside tyre crunches over my legs. The back wheels are double ones, they go over my hips. My legs from the ankles up are pulp. My genitals, coccyx, bowels, bladder, and lower stomach have been ground to mincemeat between the disc braked wheels and the tarmac. My head is thrown back, and the last thing I see is an upside down view of Rebecca turning in the air as she flies over the petrol pumps – into the hands of a very tall black basket ball player. If one of them had failed to catch her, any of two other pairs of hands would have done so. I don't feel pain, I'm numb but for the realisation that my going under the wheels of a lorry means the police will come. Rebecca's face has had blanket coverage in the media, so they'll recognise her. Hans' won't claim an abducted baby.

A pool of blood spreads around me. My last words are an attempt to share a joke. I try to say it to the lorry driver, who's hysterical at the sight of my pulverised body. But all that comes out of my mouth is a river of blood and breakfast. What I wanted to say was:
"It's lucky those guys play basketball, and not volleyball!"
The joke will never be heard, because I'm no longer a comedian. I'm roadkill.

PART THREE

No Time

Chapter Sixty-one

I don't hear the police sirens. I've departed my shattered shell before my death rattle is over. There's a feeling of swift, soft flight, but I'm not alone. Some feminine presence accompanies my whoosh along a curve. Then there's no up or down. I've left the nonsense of dimensions. Like time, space is a laughable lie I chose to believe. I reflect on the light until that becomes equally ridiculous. How can I see light without eyes? Darkness is light, and without light the darkness goes, so all that's left is knowledge. With no ignorance, knowledge goes, and oneness comes. The greater my separation from that moment I spent in the consciousness they called Doug, the more vividly I'm aware of the world he left.

I'm wrong about the baby. The relapse into taking drugs has clouded my perception. She's Mia's child, sired by Ruud Vermeulen. They're re-united with baby Mox in a Dutch hospital. She's declared fit, but kept overnight for tests. The twenty-four hours between the announcement of her abduction, and the press conference in which parents and baby are displayed, provokes a media frenzy. For every mawkish tear shed at the sight of the weeping mother with Mox in her arms, there's the hatred of the monster who was caught trying to kidnap her. I'm identified as the man who showed a hardcore pornographic video to Dirk's children in Holland, and Trinh Tuyen's kids in London. Chantelle and Celine believe my 'fear' of children was a paedophile ploy to trick my way into the children's yoga class.

British Airways inform the police of my questions as to whether any unaccompanied minors were on the flight from Manchester to Heathrow, and from where I could buy Dolly Mixtures. The police at Heathrow have a record of confiscating a porn magazine from me, with teenaged girls inside, and traces of cocaine on the cover. When the newspapers get hold of my identity, my fate as a hideous ogre is sealed. Stephen Woods' tabloid goes furthest in whipping up the hatred. Despite the location of my funeral being secret, its details are leaked, and a mob of vigilantes pulls what's left of me from my coffin, and rips me to shreds. As far as the press is concerned, Ruud Vermeulen is a respected executive producer of 'Rats Milk Cheese'. My stealing his baby is seen as a symptom of bitterness over my sacking. Two unsolved child murders are re-investigated for a connection to me. No proof is found, but a dead man with a knife in his pocket and no family can't answer back. Stephen Woods' tabloid throws enough at me to make sure the Vermeulen brothers et al are above suspicion. I'm remembered not for the laughter I inspired, but as a child sex killer.

It doesn't bother me in the slightest, because where I am, I know the world is an illusion. I regard my story as having the happiest ending, because I'm with my Mummy. Or at least, I think that's who she is.

THE END

About the Author

Dave Thompson's best-known role is Tinky Winky in the BBC's 'Teletubbies', which is shown all over the world.

He gained a BA in Theatre from Dartington College of Arts, before training to be a drama therapist. After practicing as a therapist in mental hospitals for three years, he became a stand-up comedian and actor. Dave has written for Harry Hill, Ben Elton, Ronnie Corbett, Bruce Forsyth, Jim Tavare, and Stewart Lee.

He played a comedian in the feature film 'Maybe Baby', written and directed by Ben Elton, and the porn star in 'I Want Candy', directed by Stephen Surgit. His third film 'Huge', was directed by Ben Miller, and released in 2011.

Dave was a commissioned writer for 'Harry Hill's TV Burp', 'The Sketch Show', and three of Boothby Graffoe's series on BBC Radio Four. He's appeared in many episodes of 'Harry Hill's TV Burp' in human or costume roles. He was in nine sitcom episodes, and many other TV shows such as 'Never Mind The Buzzcocks'.

He performs stand-up in many countries, is married with two daughters, and has homes on the South coast of England and in Budapest.